HER GRE
MISTAKE

Sarah Simpson

www.ariafiction.com

About *Her Greatest Mistake*

Eve and Gregg were the perfect couple, with the perfect marriage…which has become the perfect lie. Gone is the charming, attentive Gregg - instead Eve wakes up each morning beside a manipulative and sinister man who controls his wife's every move.

So Eve flees her immaculate marital home to keep herself, and young son Jack safe. Yet no matter how careful she has been, she knows Gregg will be relentless in his pursuit of his missing family. And that one day, when she's least expecting it, he will find them…

What was Eve's greatest mistake?

Marrying Gregg? Leaving him? Or leaving him alive…?

Katie, Amy and Ben. You were my strength to seek change. The blood flowing through my veins. My reason to be. My everything. I couldn't be more proud of you.

Anth. For making me smile when I thought I was lost. For believing in me, even when I didn't. For being my scaffold when I was swaying in the wind. For being my light in the dark.

Mom and Dad. Everything I am is because of you. Yet you've never asked me for anything.

This is for all of you, from the bottom of my heart. Sometimes words can be inadequate.

And now here is my secret, a very simple secret: It is only with the heart that one can see rightly; what is essential is invisible to the eye.

Antoine De Saint-Exupery, *The Little Prince.*

Prologue

Desperate to escape the seat belt, slicing through my neck. Vulnerability restrains me, despite my being choked by murderous primeval thoughts. Shuddering with each acceleration, gripping tighter with each perilous twist. An outlook flaunting only shades of black, unrelenting rain, mercilessly pummelling its prey.

*

What befitting, magnificent conditions for the occasion. Such power on the outside, yet so calm within. The erratic driving easing my pain, liberating my soul. Laughter rolls upward from my gut, as I see the effect it has on her. Teach the bitch a lesson. For what she has done to me. I offered her a chance. Wretchedness rises and burns. I press my foot harder to the accelerator. To control. While she looks on.

My wife the traitor.

*

Sodden falling leaves and earthly debris obscure the glass, only a subtle cloaking for what lies ahead. I hold my breath, swelling my lungs, soaking up the acrid stench of burning rubber, blistering metal. Sweaty hands slithering on cold leather. I try to plead, *please, please*, but a chalky dryness strangles each word. My gut retches with the taste of fear.

I hear the windscreen wipers at full assault. Reciting my fate, over and over.

Shallow, rapid panting thrusts my heart at its cage, pushing against the flimsiness of my incongruent T-shirt. It wasn't supposed to be this way. To you, to them, it isn't this way. I'm slipping, sliding into a helpless state. Any reasoning defeated by futility. Truth battered to the floor by lies. A cognitive crossfire feeds my mind, pilfering control, shutting down intelligence. Deep into my limbic system I plunge. Always the prisoner. Into the dark, I fall.

I realise now, someone is going to die.

Chapter One

One week after my story…

I open an eye at a time, my head being heavy, stuffed with cotton wool. Bleached, dense fluff smothers any intelligence, any rationale and all of my problem-solving capabilities. I've been here before, so many times, this feeling of being unique but not in a good way. These special feelings, mingling with my past confining me to loneliness. We've needed to become friends, get used to each other, a sad but expedient relationship. Maybe we can never be separated; our way of being is all too entwined. Even so, an extra convincing tiredness joins us today and I can't be bothered to fight it. I'm bone-weary from all the belligerence, game-playing and secrecy. Dog-tired of being isolated by the never-ending lies and imprudent perceptions. It wasn't supposed to be this way.

But then, from the outside in, it isn't this way.

I drag myself up and float across the wooden floors with a need to be close to something, finding myself in Jack's empty room. Apparently lured to the mobile sitting on his window sill, sneering without a conscience. I pick it up. I still don't know for sure

1

who was in my home the other day; the day they left something dangling in the air. I've kind of accepted this, what a peculiar response. Or is it? I understand it should be, but it doesn't change the fact; it now feels ordinary. This is in part what has muted me; my world was and is my normal, but to others, if they knew of it, it would be weird and twisted. Being a prisoner of this world for so long, I'm quite the institutionalised. Perhaps I can never live a normal life; for normal now appears alien. Whatever normal is. So, I play at life as I'm unable to live it.

I gently place Jack's deadly mobile on his chest of drawers and peel back the undisturbed duvet protecting his bed. I climb in, and curl up, wrapping the duvet tightly around me, inhaling his vulnerable scent. If someone was in our home, could this mean there is more to come? That we've come full circle? Is someone now looking for the new truth? Or is this still about the same old lies, same old unanswered questions? Or is it just me and it's all just cotton wool? Isn't it strange when everything you think you know evaporates? When truths have been held hostage by seeping lies. Then, the moment you realise, it's never been about what you know, but what you don't know. The world you perceive isn't really the world itself, but simply your story of the world, in a twinkling of fragile time.

I let my eyelids fall heavy. Some time ago, people used to refer to us as a broken home. Why? They got it so wrong. It was broken before, not afterwards. When we lived in a broken marriage; broken vows, a relationship drip-fed by abuse. But our home after we'd escaped wasn't broken. It was new, fragile, other-worldly even as we trod uncertain steps, but not broken.

You were broken, you always were. I was a fool not to notice the fine stitching at first, holding your independent components together. It was too late by the time I did. Part human, part robot, that's you. Smooth-talking hunter. I feel no comfort in believing I'm not alone with my story. Someone else out there gets cotton wool too, sees the truth as I do. Where context is everything. Hindsight is futile.

I squeeze my eyelids tightly to push away the glimpses of that night, suffocated by vulnerability, the acrid stench of burning rubber. I'm holding my breath again. Sometimes, I'm too afraid to breathe; at times I've wished I'd stop. I can still feel my hands sweating, sliding on cold leather. I have solitary moments when I ache to scream, to be heard, but my words jar and still – a chalky dryness strangles me. The tang of bile repulses me. It's been a while but I can still taste the sourness of fear. I think I always will. I think we both will. Our past being the backbone of all we know.

Sedentary remains, rotting flesh hidden under floorboards but too pungent to ignore.

I watched you that night, how calm you were. Your uncertainty forcing your foot harder to the pedal proffered you some mislaid control, didn't it? I mean, knowing the effect it was having on me. Your steady upturned lips, fighting back your laughter. Inwardly flying high. Though it was never just about that night, more about the lives you stole. It didn't happen overnight, but by stealth. Day by day. Year on year.

I tug at the duvet to cover my asphyxiated mind. It wasn't meant to be this way; I'd intended we'd be free by now. But at the very last minute you stole that too, didn't you? Now, I fear it's all too late; for me it is anyway.

Three years ago, I thought I could finally change things. I was wrong.

Chapter Two

Cornwall 2016

A little over three years ago we escaped to Cornwall. We simply packed our belongings, discarding the contaminated, and closed the weighted door firmly behind us. I bequeathed our dirty possessions to appreciative good causes. Soiled by life; lies and debauchery. It was all far too easy to do. Sometimes, the most difficult deeds are also the easiest to embrace. We both yearned for new beginnings. To cast away from the dark waters that nearly consumed us. Jack was just ten, but had witnessed and heard things to choke his conscience for the rest of his life. Like a polluted smog.

My son Jack; how unfair he was born into this. He's fourteen now; it's been almost ten years since he was in your grip. The white-collar psychopath, clever, manipulating and sinister. My ex-husband. Jack's father. You embezzled years from us both. You took me in, chewed me up and tried to swallow the mangled remains. Until I hit you where it hurt the most, and you spat me out. Before vanishing. So many years, looking over our shoulders, waiting, wondering. You didn't return.

Are you dead? I truly hope so. And so does Jack; he told me so. I hope you died a slow and painful death. I suspect I'm not the only one who lives in hope.

It wasn't always this way. *I only want to look after you,* you told me. I believed you, believed you loved me. Chosen and special. Only now, I understand there was always something not quite right about you. Initially, I found you to be sweet and protective. Unaware it, I, was all part of your game, mistaking your rule for care, your lies for truths. I was nothing more than a tool; you needed a wife. In actuality, you were not capable of loving anyone but yourself. Eventually, Jack became your tool too, to keep me even further under your jurisdiction. Imprisoning me for further years.

Deluded, I stood.

By the time I opened my eyes, it was too late.

We followed the conventional path of dating, to marriage. The trodden path of Hansel and Gretel, with no obvious way back. You laid the way, I stupidly followed. Though the birds didn't eat the crumb trail; I cleared it myself. Blinded by the charm, flattered by the engineered care and hoodwinked by my virtue. *You're mine now,* you'd tell me softly, *and I will take care of everything.*

You have everything, you're so lucky, friends would say from their observation point. Friends, whom I later betrayed; let go of. Because I was nothing more than a prisoner in a figurative cell, with no key. I couldn't accept visitors; I was too ashamed, too lost. The worst I have to live with is knowing it was me who locked myself in. Now, it makes me shiver, my skin crawl. How could I have been so pathetically stupid? I truly hate hindsight.

We were married in less than a year. Fraudulent vows disguised by context. The perfect couple, weren't we? Two professionals in their twenties, everything ahead of us. Wasted dreams and fruitless hopes fell at the mercy of power. Greed. Ego. It only took a year to tread the path to my cell. Then, soon after, the arrival of Jack opened my heart but firmly locked the door. Trapped. *If you could only learn to behave yourself, Eve, you wouldn't need to be punished,* you'd kindly advise me. *You know, you only have yourself to blame, if only you would do as you're told. Be less pig-headed. Argumentative.* I still wonder – how can an apparently intelligent person find herself as ensnared as I did? This still bites at my scars. But things aren't always what they seem: we don't always tell the truth; we don't always see the truth. Even when we're honest, the truth deceives.

Easier to lie. Often to ourselves, but especially to others.

Everything turned black; this was the last time we saw you. That night in the car, etched into my mind.

Not the only scar but one of the deepest. The screeching brakes, the cracking of my skull, then you were gone. I can't remember anything after the impact; until the bright fluorescent lights, only subdued by the high-pitched bleeping. The harsh smell of disinfectant. Fear smacked me across the face and woke me: *where is Jack?* To this day, I'm not sure how much Jack has buried away in his subconscious I don't think he realises either. Time will tell.

Time isn't always a healer; it can be an incubator too.

You disappeared after this. Though you made one final visit to our house. Sometime between the disinfectant and us returning, or at least someone did. The house was ransacked. I knew what the perpetrator was looking for. They never would have found it; it was submerged deep in the dirt. A little like me: deep in the dirt. I didn't call the police; it was too soon. Why would I hand over my most valuable weapon? You were not the only one with something to hide.

For some years after, Jack and I tried hard to rebuild, but our existence in Warwickshire was soiled. It was no longer the happy place I grew up in, deep in family traditions and teenage escapades. Home-made picnics under the sweeping willows gracing the river Avon. Yearly thespian visits to the

Royal Shakespeare Theatre. Then, frivolous, drunken nights queuing outside the nightclub on the river, having sampled alcoholic pleasures from a pub on the riverbank. All became smothered memories. Instead, palpitations would grab me, simply driving familiar lanes, or strolling through the town. Needlessly pumping adrenaline. As if you were still with me. Maybe you were? Watching and waiting. Either way, we were unable to escape the superficial grasps you left behind. We needed a fresh start, but could that ever really be? When lies and dark secrets churned like pea soup. I continued to lie, hoping to convince me and Jack everything would be okay. Deep down I knew it wasn't over. Psychopaths never give in, never forget. In your eyes, I owe you, don't I?

If you were still alive, you would find us. Barefaced. Unashamed. Bastard.

Chapter Three

Before

I observed you getting ready most mornings; the 06.00 rise through to the 07.10 departure paralleled a military operation. Hindsight nags me: how did I not see the signs? Everything planned, nothing happened in your world. When I think back, even simple bathroom procedures exposed fanatical behaviours. Me, an expert on the human mind?

You stood, a white fluffy towel wrapped around your waist.

Steam filling the air. 'What the...?' You interrogated your aftershave balm. 'Bloody cleaner, for Christ's sake, why do I have to be landed with the thickest cleaner? Leave my goddam things where they belong, woman. Have you ever wondered why she's just a sodding cleaner? Jesus, how hard can it possibly be?'

You always hate the cleaners, I thought. In your eyes, she meddled with your day, challenged your authority.

Your eyes met mine through the mirror. 'Are you listening to me, Eve?'

'Of course,' I told you. 'I was just…' wondering if Jack was awake, I was going to say.

'If I wanted my shaving balm there, I would have bloody put it there, wouldn't I? How many times before she gets it?' You caressed the lavish ointment into smooth skin. 'You'd think even she has the intelligence to work it out. How am I supposed to get ready when my stuff is all over? Simple-minded idiot.'

You grabbed at my face wash and launched it from your perfect shelf into my basket on the floor. 'That's not even mine. Eve, perhaps if you were not so bloody chaotic with your things, she might have got it right.' Past tense, the cleaner was in trouble.

I liked my chaotic basket. I wanted a home, not a clinic. I wanted a husband, not a computer. Your personal vindictiveness towards others made me blush. But then, you didn't often reveal it in person; you were far too shrewd. Everything occurred behind the scenes. Meddling cleaners came and went. So did the gardeners, window cleaners and anyone else who interfered. Frequently replaced, discarded as easily as a once-used dish cloth.

'Having strangers in the house… It's not right. I don't trust any of them. Perhaps, if you were at home a little more often, we—'

'I work too, Gregg!'

'Hmm. So you say.'

'I think you're being a little harsh, to be honest, if—'

'For pity's sake, why do you always have to try and understand people? Drives me insane.' You moved towards your dressing area, running frustrated hands through your hair. 'Get shot of her before I return this evening.'

'But she hasn't really done anything wrong. And she really needs the money. You need to give her a chance; it's only been a couple of weeks! I'm sure—'

'Wrong. I'm not required to do anything. I'm not required to give anyone a chance. She should have thought about needing the money a little more, shouldn't she? Not my problem. Call a different agency, then get rid. Stop making excuses. I sometimes wonder whose side you're on. Jesus. Stupid woman!'

Me or her? I wondered. What must it be like to be so without conscience, never giving a second thought of repercussions for people? How much lighter and freer must you feel? Freedom or isolation? But then I'd learned: you could never feel isolated, could you? Not with so much ego filling the void. You never lost sleep over such issues, as I would. But then, as you often bragged, *'Sleep is for the weak. I can survive on a few hours if necessary!'* To be fair, you often did. Were you part robot? A cog for a brain, a casket for a heart?

You were senior partner material in a respected firm of solicitors. You worked ridiculously long hours, demanding the obligatory networking and entertaining at extortionate costs to the clients. There were other things too, though I wasn't supposed to know about those. And I didn't initially, leaving my conscience so much lighter then too. But as time bellyached on, I heard things I shouldn't have. Clumsy speak of clandestine meetings. I heard murmurs; I wished I hadn't. These changed us for good. I say us, but there never really was an us, was there?

'Eve? Where are you this morning? You look vacant.'

I bit my tongue. 'I'm listening.' How you relished being the centre of attention, exhibiting a burly confidence, fine-tuned into mists of abundant charm. But to me you were becoming a monster, banqueting on compliments and far-reaching praise. This was your fuel, was it not? In so many ways I saw a walking contradiction, a complete enigma, but in others, a straight and concrete operator. You led without followers being aware. A consistent crowd of disciples and hangers-on. Callous motives lay behind those eyes. Nobody else seemed to notice.

You removed your trousers from the overused press. 'You think too much,' you said.

I ignored you. 'Did you sort things with Andy yesterday?' I asked.

You fished out your belt from the wardrobe. 'Huh. Of course. I just told him – we're working late tonight.' Flashing a smile at yourself in the full-length mirror.

'He wasn't amused – *"I can't, I've family matters, Gregg."* So I replied, "Okay, fine. But you really should have mentioned your lack of commitment before." *"But, Gregg, I've worked late for the last two months. It's my daughter's birthday,"* you mimicked your colleague as you fastened your tie, still smiling.

'I told him, "As long as we're both reading from the same sheet, realise where your priorities lie. Of course, join your family. Please do, pass on my very best wishes."' You smirked, reaching for your jacket. 'Sometimes, I can't resist pulling rank. He'll learn.'

I bit hard on my lower lip. I wondered at your ability to interchange or amputate your emotions. In the next breath you would send flowers to a senior partner's wife. A thoughtful anniversary gift. You'd wine and dine and charm your disciples. Deliver compassion, empathy and concerned expressions. Learn of their weaknesses and plot their demise. I take little solace in knowing you deluded even the most astute. Ruthless, spellbinding. You, the sculptor. You didn't fall at the feet of empathy. You picked it up and stored it. A human emotional jukebox. Selecting and demonstrating appropriate emotions to achieve the required outcome.

'Don't worry, he'll learn. Or lose his job, whichever comes first,' you said.

Bile threatened my throat. How many people had fallen at your feet? How well you were camouflaged in your professional suit.

'Don't wait up.' You smirked over your shoulder. 'Oh, and say hi to Jack from his daddy. Tell him I'm going to make us rich.' You smiled. 'Very rich.'

A sixth sense forewarned me there was still far worse to come.

Chapter Four

Cornwall 2016

The dashboard clock ticks to 08.02 on a typical autumnal Cornish morning. A low sun hangs between turning leaves. A morning warranting a mindful appreciation. But I'm switching in and out of autopilot as my world attempts to submerge my floating body. I see the beautiful horizon; I don't feel it. My mind is a stew of rapid bubbling thoughts and images, desperately trying to push back each mutinous ingredient.

Just because I'm a psychologist, people assume I'm so together; if only they knew the half of it. Had some appreciation of my inner turmoil. I've even noticed recently, I've been afraid of time alone. Too much interfering noise, thumping at my rationale. Ever since the phone call. Not so much a phone call as a silence. A drawn-out silence, with someone listening intently at the other end. The number was withheld but I understood the message. I ended the call – my instincts told me to – gathering a small amount of feigned control.

I see my knuckles pale, so I reduce the grip on the steering wheel. Shaking off the shiver running down my spine. Nothing too strange about receiving withheld calls, wrong numbers. But this wasn't one of those; this was a message. Glancing at the dashboard clock, I see I've seven minutes before you call again. You've called every day since that first call, at 08.10 sharp.

There's something else pushing the adrenaline button, a horrible nagging feeling. Jack missed his school bus this morning, so I was chasing him around the house like a sergeant major, his ability to interpret the notion of moving quickly being non-existent. I've been rerunning through the events since, over and over, but I can't quite remember.

I waved the Geography book in front of Jack's face, having spent the previous ten minutes hunting for it. 'For God's sake, Jack! Why didn't you look for this last night instead of messing about on that stupid game? We're going to be late. I'm going to be late for clinic. Again!'

He was sitting on the sofa, squashing the back down on his shoes, rather than undo them, to slide his feet in easily. 'Because… I didn't think about it last night, did I?' He rolled his eyes.

'Exactly! You didn't think about it!'

'Yeah. Exactly, how could I have looked for it, then, if I didn't even think about it?'

'Again, this conversation is going nowhere. This attitude of "only think about it when I have to" has to change. Jack. Are you even listening to me?'

He frowned. 'What?'

'Just hurry up. I'll see you in the car.' I reached for my mobile and keys, then opened the front door. 'One day it would be nice to leave the house without my blood pressure reaching for the sky.'

'Yeah, sure, Mum. Sounds cool.' He continued lifting cushions and throwing them back down again. 'Before you go, have you seen my—?'

'No, I haven't.'

So, I was running late, in such a fluster. For the life of me, I can't remember – did I lock the kitchen door? Did Jack do it? I'd let our cat, Humphrey, out before we left, but did I lock the door after him? I keep trying to retrace my steps in my mind. But all I come back with is brick walls and fuzz. With a twisted stomach, I continue to wind my way home to St Agnes, my home village, postcard pretty. It's 08.09. Until the phone calls, we'd almost managed to stuff our heavy baggage deep down in the dark limbic system. Now, stress hormones are gradually creeping back through the back door. My sleep cycle has bowed to their intrusion. Hence why I keep forgetting things, doubting myself. I'm anxious but haven't the time to be. Is Jack aware? My little absorbent sponge, soaking up my emotions, internalising them as his?

I jump at the trill of my mobile, breaking hard, I squeeze my car into the bramble and stop. I snatch at the device, to answer your call. I don't speak. Each intake of air hurts; something is crushing my chest. I hold the phone at a distance on loudspeaker, not wishing to be close to you, in any way. Silence. I see you smirk, loving your perceived power. You don't see it, do you? Despite my fear, I will not bow down to you again. I've too much to lose. At 08.11, I hang-up. Why do I play your games? Because it's the only way I will ever be rid of you. However much it pains me, playing your game is the only way. Sometimes, I scare myself, no longer recognising who I've needed to become. It revolts me to think I've needed to behave anything like you, in order to survive.

I head back off, being roughly only five minutes from home, switching on the radio. Anything to shroud the images of you. The curse of the imagination, I tell my clients, re-establishing old neural pathways. The greater the imagination, the greater the fear. How often I see people's lives destroyed by this and worrying, the perverse comfort blanket. Somewhere along the twisted life line it's believed worrying keeps us safe. Always on-guard, balanced on the lookout post, with a gunshot startle response. Last night it meant I slept with my car keys and mobile laid ready in position on my bedside table. Just in case.

From my objective position in clinic I ask anxious clients, *'What evidence do you have for this worry? Actual facts, not subjective reasoning?'* Mostly, they have none, but my worries are fed from past battered memory templates. Preparing me for fight or flight. With the smell of impending danger. A whiff of insanity. A scent of you. I do have the evidence. We relocated to Cornwall to escape. But even then, how do you ever escape something implanted in your mind? I turn off the radio, or the Pied Piper of emotions, as I prefer to call it. Each track to be vetted as a potential co-conspirator, sneakily partnering up with emotions in a microsecond. Does perspective change with music? Or does music change perspective?

Then there are the shadows too, the feeling of being watched, opaque dark shapes playing with my eyes. Not long before that first phone call, they seemed to appear. When I leave work, when I'm at home, something in the air, something dark, lingering. Biding time. I can't go to the police; experience tells me I'd be wasting my time. Not long after our divorce proceedings began, you were there, waiting, and watching. I know you were; I could feel you. Following us home from the park, waiting for me to leave for work, just outside the window –

whilst I read Jack his bedtime story. You were there. No crime without evidence though.

Just a feeling of being watched. That's it? they said.

How stupid would they make me feel again?

Miss Sands, what exactly do we have to go on? they'd say. *Other than an empty phone call, and what else was it you mentioned? Oh, yes, shadows in the dark?*

History repeating. I was married to a psychopath. Years of hell. Near-death experiences. The things I thieved, how about those?

It's 2016. There's been no contact for ten years. That's a very long time ago. We'll need something more concrete to implicate your... ex-husband? they'd demand.

Something else: there's been a definite shift in Jack's carefree demeanor; I'm sure he senses you too, your presence. Hunted, wounded animals, aren't we? Or, even worse than sensing your proximity, maybe Jack knows something he hasn't wanted to share with me? He's really only a child but even so he tries to protect me, from you, from the memories. He's been a little secretive with his mobile, now I think of it. But he's just being a teenager, normal. Isn't he?

I will not go back to my cell of old but how can I deny I remain locked in your world? Too many lies; too many secrets. The world we created together.

Both of us declaring to be the casualty. But now I hold the key to freedom, there doesn't appear to be a door, never mind a keyhole.

You have the door; I have the key.

Waiting and watching.

You're getting closer again, aren't you?

Chapter Five

Nothing can be obvious; discreetly does it.

No one will realise I was ever here.

How bloody crazy; why leave the door unlocked? Especially you.

A foolish mistake or, in your defence, an overwhelmed mind? Both.

Dangerous. Good job I'm here.

Still, can't help getting a thrill, being places I shouldn't be, operating behind the scenes. Takes me back to the good old days. To be fair, I could only observe for so long; I needed to gain access to what lay inside. For your sake and mine.

My mind has become an expert camera.

Record an image and store.

Move important object to become an untrue image.

Return to reflect the true image.

Time; I must be aware of time.

I'll secure the back door before I leave, then exit via the front.

Come on, you should know, Eve, the truth is dangerous in the wrong hands.

Chapter Six

Cornwall 2016

I creep nervously into my own home; listening. Silence. Keys clasped tightly in my hand. No obvious signs of an intruder, no kicked-down doors or shattered crockery strewn across the floor. My heart pounds in my ears like a damp drum as I slink through the kitchen towards the back door. Startled, as a dark shadow thuds at the window. I jump and drop my keys. The minute sound of my keys hitting hard floor fills the room. 'Christ, Humphrey, why did you do that?' He waits in total nonchalance at the foot of the door outside. I rattle the handle, and breathe again. Thank God, I did lock the door.

But still there is something alien dangling in the air. If I didn't know better, if the door had been unlocked, I'd swear someone has been in my home.

I pull open the door to an appreciative ball of fluff; he wraps himself around my legs. Purring. I pick him up and snuggle my face into indulgent fur, allowing my heartbeat to return to baseline. 'You're coming upstairs with me, mister, keep me company whilst I get ready for work. Frightening me like that, how could you? Haven't you realised you're living with a neurotic woman?'

I survey the sitting room as I creep through, before gingerly taking the stairs, still half-expecting someone to jump out. 'What's wrong with me, Humph, eh? Why can't you talk to me? Did you see anyone?' I sneak along the landing towards my bedroom, stopping to check Jack's room first, all the usual potential hiding places. The wardrobe, under the bed. Nothing but used crockery – Jack and his blinking late-night cereal cravings. Still with Humphrey purring in my arms, I move on to my room.

I place him on my bed, where he immediately stretches out to fill the abstract shape of sun rays. 'So tell me, Humph, to pull myself together. No one's been in the house. The door was locked and there's no other way in.' Big round eyes glare back at me before he begins his grooming process. 'No useful words of wisdom, eh? Anything will do? Or have you been silenced? Coerced to the dark side?' He gives me the look of disdain only cats can do. 'I get it, you're just refusing to humour me. Wise move.'

I convince myself it's safe for the moment. I need to get a move on for work. An invigorating shower of soft florals, all the time with a watchful eye on the door. Only panicking when the shampoo temporarily obscures my vision, rinsing it through as quickly as if my life depends on it. Not long later, I leave the house, double-checking the locks. Not bad, a transformation from home-comfort clothes to a tailored azure dress. Softly applied make-up, coral lips. Elegant shoes with a sharp distinguishing echo. Finally, my files, mobile and diary. All in less than thirty minutes. Trepidation has its perverse benefits.

Ready for another borrowed day.

Choosing where to open my clinic was easy. I peered through sash windows before a toadying agent opened the door to the pretty, terraced, Cornish sandstone and slate building. Proudly nestled between its charming unassuming neighbours. Two mottled slate steps lead the way to the solid wood door of 39b Lemon Street. Warm, humble and crammed with character. Inside, a large reception window films passing life, sweeping down to the heart of Truro. 'Sometimes, things just feel right,' I'd agreed with the toady agent.

Knowing Ruan, my fresh-faced, uncomplicated-by-life assistant, will always be there to open up first is a blessing. Despite his ungodly early morning jaunt to catch the sunrise waves. He's then usually followed by Bea, the physiotherapist who sublets a room. Today, when I push through the door, characteristically late, the sunlight fills the reception area, elbowing through the leaded window. The cream slatted blinds are pulled back tight to allow shimmering beams to create a warming ambience. Thoughtful shadows grace the archetypal dense walls. Not all shadows are dark, I remind myself.

'Hey,' Ruan greets me, sauntering away from my room. He nods towards a rigid-looking man sitting in Reception between us, who's eyeballing the window. Gazing anywhere other than at me.

'Morning, Ruan. Here, grab these, will you?' I pass him the loose bundle of files trying to leap from my arms.

'For your room or filing?'

'My desk, please. Any chance of a—?'

'Coffee? Yep, already on it.' He smiles, feigning to stagger with my files.

'You're an absolute star, have I told you? I couldn't ever be without you.' I indicate towards my client. Ruan shakes his head. No, I didn't think he'd accept a coffee.

My room leads directly from Reception, where old fosters new, modern, light and airy but still entirely intimate. The colours are cool yet warm, shades of white, pale blues and citrus-fruit seasonings. Natural oak shelving engulfs the walls; heavy with journals and books, some receding to my undergraduate and training days. Two hardbacks take precedence on the top shelf. One of these, an extremely worn leather-bound *Complete Works of William Shakespeare*. The other being *The Meaning of Dreaming*, my early allure to the workings of the human mind. Little did I know then the importance of dreaming, the power of REM sleep. As I sat cross-legged on the floor devouring its contents, I trustingly believed all dreams became true. Now, I understand, it's only the nightmares.

I reach for the timeworn literature bible; inside the cover, an old-fashioned script reads:

Mervyn Oliver 18th April, 1909

My grandfather. I grew up in Stratford-upon-Avon. It still riles me that I was never a fan of Shakespeare; his works were, though, significant to someone who was significant to me.

I jump with the awareness of movement behind me. 'Coffee time!' Ruan swirls my china mug under my nose before placing it on the desk. 'Hot and strong, just for you.'

'Thank God for small mercies. Has he been here long?' I nod towards the Reception.

'Only pacing the pavement, waiting for me to open up,' he whispers. 'He's not exactly forthcoming with conversation. Think you might have your work cut out with him.'

'Hmm.'

'Eve, do you mind me asking you something?' He steps closer to me.

I look up to see his creased brow. 'Sounds ominous. Do I have a choice?' Ruan shrugs. 'Go on, then, hit me with it.'

'Is everything okay? It's just, me and Bea were saying, we think you've been kind of distracted, just lately.'

'So you've been talking about me?' I tease.

'Well, yeah.'

'I see. Distracted?' Why am I questioning him? I know I have.

'A little bit distant, not your usual, not...' he holds out his hands, and I smile as he delivers a boyish grin, trying to select an inoffensive word '... you know, just not you.'

'Not me?' I turn away to sip coffee, avoiding eye contact. 'Interesting. Can you elaborate?'

'No. Stop doing that throwing-the-question-back-at-me thing.'

'Sorry.' I turn to smile at him. 'I've not meant to be different. Just a little tired, I guess, not been sleeping brilliantly this last couple of weeks.' This isn't a lie.

'But nothing's worrying you, is it? To stop you from sleeping?'

'No, Ruan, really, I'm fine. I'd tell you both, if I wasn't.' This is a lie. I can't tell you, Ruan. I wouldn't even know where or how to begin. I don't want to lie to you. But I can't tell you the truth either. Please don't press.

'Okay, cool. What's that you're looking at?' He points at my book.

'It belonged to my grandfather.' I shut it and turn to place it back on the shelf. I can't help wondering, what do you think of all this, Mervyn? Shocked, sad, scared for me? How did I get to this? How did my life go so wrong? I still don't get it either. How could I have been such a complete fool? 'He was a silent type of man, a huge reader, a wealth of knowledge.'

'For sure, that's pretty smart.' Ruan grins and leaves me to it at the sound of the front door opening.

I'm not long behind, to collect my client from Reception. Instantly recognisable from the few notes I have. Each condition parades under a distinctive cloak, hanging over people as obvious as the clothes they're wearing. He is now perched opposite a harassed-looking mum waiting with her son; her mind being in many other places at the same time. Her son, staring at his mobile, immersed in whatever lies behind the screen. Bea must be running late again; she talks too much, can't seem to help herself.

I glance back to my man; his feet lightly touching the floor so he can run should he need to. He's studying them, anything to avoid any eye contact with the woman or her son. He clearly doesn't want to be here and who could blame him? If I'd stalled another few minutes, I may now be looking at an empty seat. Talking of empty, this is how he's feeling: empty, heavy and helpless. Depression etched on his forehead. I get it. He lifts his head to me uneasily as I step forward with my hand held out. I smile at him; he can't feel it. Burdened eyes stare back with a particular darkness. I get the feeling I'm his last hope.

I introduce myself as he stands to face me. But his words bump together, jarring in his throat, joining a long traffic jam of unheard utterings; he nods, instead. I sense the weight of him behind me as we head for my room, despite his slight covering on wide shoulders. Sometimes people ooze desolation, debilitated by despondent and hopeless thought processes. People of all guises, backgrounds and ages, men, women and children. Mental health problems are always without prejudice.

I softly close the door behind us and gesture for him to take a seat in one of our tub chairs, snuggly enveloping the body securely at both sides. His eyes dart from my desk, laden with files – I'm not the most organised – to the floor. I smile at him. I've work to do too; he needs to relax before we begin.

'It's lovely to meet you.' I smile again, hoping to meet those eyes. 'Though I'm guessing you'd rather not have to meet me at all.' A half-smile regards me, no words. What an odd thing for me to say: it's lovely that you've hit rock bottom, so are forced to come to me. But wouldn't it be rude not to suggest it? He regards me as if I'm some form of mind-reading witch. I'm used to it.

We talk for some time, around symptoms and the considerable changes to his everyday life. Gradually, his eyes begin to meet mine, then he asks me if he will always feel the way he does, encounter dark thoughts. I fight with my thoughts, as I remember promising myself fifteen years ago my state of mind was merely a short-term turmoil. I'd come through the other side, even laugh back on it. Perhaps I should be sitting in the opposite chair.

'Were you born feeling this way, thinking these thoughts? Have you always felt and thought in this way?' I challenge his rationale; mine is useless.

'No, of course not,' he says. 'Only in the last year, or so.'

'Exactly. These thoughts belong to depression, not you. Depression is a black cloud hovering. It's not inside you, it's not who you are, it just seems so. At the moment, your perception of you, of life in general and how you interpret it, is not the truth. A symptom. Like pain is a symptom of a broken leg, blood is a symptom of a cut.' The difference between me and this client is – I can't shake the psychopath off my trail. You are the black cloud. The similarity is if I allow you to be part of me, to creep inside my mind again, then you win.

'You must remember: this is not your real world. Our emotions can distort how we think. We can become inflexible, thinking in black-or-white, all-or-nothing terms. But life has many grey areas. We can also become extremely negative, forgetting to count or even see any positives. Catastrophising and personalising, disqualifying what is working, still and despite. We forget about all the resources we have to help us. Is this ringing any bells?' I see the bells are resonating for us both. This is all very well and good, but often easier said than done. He untenses his legs, allowing them to fall into a more comfortable position.

'Yes, but how do I get back to how I used to be?' he asks. I've asked myself this so many times. The simple answer is – I will never return to a carefree and light-hearted body. I can't ever untread the steps I've taken; I've trained myself to think as a psychopath. As the words roll off my tongue, practised advice, a genuine wish to help my client, the irony hammers at my head. Never make judgment at surface level. No one knows what lurks beneath the muddy obscured depths. The ones who do not reveal, who do not speak, tell lies to cloak and bamboozle, are often the ones nearest the edge. What I hold in my mind is mine; what you think you know is probably wrong. I will never sit in the chair opposite.

Fifty minutes later, I show him out of my room. Ruan is busy on the phone, so I close my door behind me. You are my depression, aren't you? Attempting to conquer. Hungry to isolate. Pilfering my confidence. Chewing away at my energy. Were you in my home, this morning? The kitchen door was locked after all, but I'm not wrong: something alien was definitely lurking in the atmosphere.

Chapter Seven

Before

I notice eyes; they speak to me. I always observe the eyes. Your eyes didn't see the truth. Didn't express the truth. They told lies. Lies I was too young and naive to see through. I wanted to believe; my beliefs let me down. I gathered information to fit the perspective I sought to hold. A downward spiral, eventually taking my self-belief with it. Then it was too late. Immersed and pulled under the tidal waves and layers of life. Swimming to drowning. A seamless transition. Then, as I struggled against the current, I cut the very lifelines that might have kept me afloat. You watched me do it, one by one, friends and family; holding tightly to isolation. Cast away from the shore without an anchor. How did I not realise it was all part of your game?

We began so ordinarily.

An evening enjoyed in a plush dining establishment determined the first stage of entrapment. So speedily it happened. After I secured a work experience secondment in a brain rehabilitation hospital. Not long graduated, working towards my doctorate. So much to be happy for. This time highlighted the preciousness of life; unbeknown to me, I was about to lose the freedom to live it. Do you remember how you were so thoughtful, so interested in my work, my clinical cases? And you were, just not for genuine reasons. I was merely one of your textbooks; you bookmarked my chapters as useful or not.

We were introduced through respective managers, by caustic chance. An organised charity meal, mixed tables peppered with professional heads. Following that evening, my manager attempted to warn me; his friend being the senior partner at some eminent solicitors in Birmingham. Apparently you were renowned for being a sharp operator. It didn't trouble me; I knew better. Being a psychologist, I understood people, no worries. Why was I born pig-headed? Sharp doesn't come close though, does it? You asked me to join you the following week for a fine dining experience in Brindleyplace, Birmingham.

Why would I not accept?

An eatery I longed to visit, but my student debt persuaded me otherwise. A French chef stolen from a legendary bistro, assured to delight the palate. The surroundings were chic, with colourings and textures of planet Earth. Atmospheric dimmed lighting to complement diners of all shapes, ages and demeanours. Candlelight danced to the sound of the centrepiece waterfall. Extravagant yet gracious. I couldn't wait.

You were early, I was late.

You hooked me from this first date. You stood to greet me, leapt to pull back my chair ahead of our waiter. In the pretence of a gentleman. I was charmed.

The dawn of the deception.

Didn't we chat so easily with your sharp sense of humour, such an acute attention to detail, to me? An analytical brain, taking observant notes. You used it to flatter and empathise. Nothing slipped past you, such diverse conversation, so effortless. Considered and articulate. Watching, studying all the time.

'May I say, your work sounds so incredibly fulfilling, Eve, so meaningful. You must gain an enormous amount of satisfaction. Unbelievably fascinating, isn't it, the human mind? I've always been captivated by what makes us tick. Nothing in your league obviously; popular psychology mostly.'

'Hmm, there's a lot of it about, that's for sure. Not everyone thinks as you do though, trust me; some people avoid me like the plague, thinking I'm some form of witch. I either break up the conversation entirely or I'm expected to know each and every intimate detail within two minutes of meeting someone. Special powers, I don't have.'

You smiled warmly. 'They assume you can read minds, am I right? So tell me, what am I thinking right now?' You chuckled.

I laughed. 'Exactly, yes, seriously, people do actually believe I can, and say those things.'

You swirled your wine with purpose. 'How amusing. If only you could, Eve. How incredibly useful that would be. Though I would be an extremely worried man. Tell me more – what's it really about?'

'Well, it's often rewarding, though it's also incredibly sad at times too.' You raised your eyebrows as if surprised. 'I mean, my cases don't always hold a happy ending. Take last week, a man in his thirties was admitted, following a car accident. Out with his family for the day, his wife was driving, she asked him to pass her something from the footwell. He took his belt off for a few seconds, to reach for it, just as the car left the road, collided with a tree. Two young girls, he has, now he's in a coma. His prospects are poor. Given the region of the brain damage, he'll never be the same again, if he wakes. Very probably never recognise his children again. Sometimes it's crueller still for the families. You're not really allocated time for the families, but I often give them my break time. Honestly, if you could see the damage it does, you'd do the same. Or we'll meet up after my official shift has finished in the café at the hospital. They often feel so completely helpless. It's all so truly heart-wrenching.'

You rubbed your smoothly shaven chin, took a cool swig from your enormous wine glass. 'Hmm. But at the end of the day – you can't win them all.'

'Win?'

'Your cases – some you will be required to let go of, I'm sure, in order to focus on those you can win, help, I mean.'

'Oh, I see, yes, I guess, it's a sorrowful fact – life isn't always simple, is it? Not if you're human.'

You smile, deep in thought. 'No, but it's the challenges that make life fun. Or in your case more, more worthwhile.' Your eyes so intense.

'Uh-huh, I suppose that's one way to look at it. We do have debriefing sessions, but can you ever accept, come to terms with, such appalling sadness?'

You shrugged.

'But you're right, focusing on what I can do, rather than what I can't do, is the only way.'

'Exactly. No point in dwelling. I'm sure you do all you can, Eve. Detachment is probably key.' You refilled our glasses, to our hovering waiter's dismay. I mouthed thank you to him.

'At the end of the day, I'm lucky to have this opportunity. Working at the hospital, it's not easy landing a placement. They turn away graduates weekly. It's so tough to secure the experience required to progress. So, I feel relatively fortunate too.'

'No such thing as luck, Eve, believe me. You made it happen. You're obviously extremely talented, so are justly rewarded. Take the credit you clearly deserve.' You raise your glass to me. 'Enjoy it. Nothing happens in life by chance. We create our own luck.'

Such confidence, if only I could have a share. 'Thank you.' I reluctantly pocketed it. Compliments don't always sit comfortably with me. 'What about you? Where do you hope to go with your job?'

You sat back. 'Job? It's hardly a job, Eve.' You ran a manicured hand through thick styled hair, a flicker in your eye. 'It's a vocation. As yours is. But in answer to your question, to the top, the very top.' Your eyes scanned the room. 'I have allowed myself five years to achieve senior partnership. If for some reason I'm not obliged by then, I'll go elsewhere. I attract enough offers. I'll not be waiting around like the rest of the duds. I mean, I do sympathise with them, of course, but, as I said, you need to make things happen in this world. There's no hope involved either. Just belief.'

'It must be so reassuring, flattering, to be head-hunted, wanted by others. You're evidently very good at what you do. So ambitious and determined, I note.'

'Why waste time? To be honest, Eve, between the two of us…' you leant into me '… it will not be too difficult. The company homes far too much dead wood. It's being stifled, lacking in enterprise. Too many jobsworths. You must appreciate where I'm coming from, what with working within the NHS. The entire partnership would benefit from a good shake-up, you must agree.'

'Oh, I'm not sure I have the right to say. We're NHS but we're such a specialist unit. Though the amount of paperwork is ridiculous, that I can agree. If we spent less time on compulsory filling out tick forms, assessing targets and debriefing meetings, we'd get to meet more patient targets, for sure. Do you believe you're the one to take your company forward, then?'

'Absolutely. Why not?' You gestured to the waiter to replace the emptied bottle. 'Let's have a toast to our future.' You raised your glass to clink against mine. 'And, of course, Eve, our new-found partnership.' You winked a lying eye.

Sold on your self-assured calmness. Your refreshing direct dialogue yet sensitive tongue, eloquent in expressing all the correct words. I had never met anyone quite like you. It was so rare to meet such a competitive nature, fuelled by a robust self-esteem, yet so empathic and telekinetic. A one-off.

The following morning, a striking arrangement of blossoms, shades of white, stippled with greens, smothered my modest desk. A card surreptitiously tucked beside a silky petal informed me:

It was a delight, Eve. Forgive the haste – I believe you are all I have been looking for.

I need look no more. You are perfect!

A car will collect you at 20.00 tonight, come dressed for the occasion.

Exquisite. X

Caught in a whirlwind. Hindsight judges me now. It informs me the romantic hidden deep inside misled me. Unbelievably foolish. It doesn't stop, the questioning of my stupidity; if it were a stick, I'd be forever black and blue. It all so quickly became sour.

Sometimes I feel nothing but self-hatred.

We were married in less than twelve months. No obvious telltale signs until then. When the big day arrived, I admit, I was struck numb. I mistook it for nerves; I was told it was, but I now comprehend it was more than that.

'What is it, Eve?' Sam, my childhood friend, angled her head at me. 'You look so worried. Come on, this is your day to shine. It's what you wanted. Isn't it?'

'I feel a little sick.'

'Of course, you do, silly. It's called nerves. You look so beautiful, by the way. Scrub up okay really, don't you?' She winked at me. 'Oh, come on, smile! Everyone gets last-minute nerves. It's a huge moment in your life – it doesn't get much bigger than this.' I watch her in the mirror tweaking my veil.

'I don't feel nervous, though, just numb. Not real, kind of strange, removed.'

'That is nerves.' She smiled less convincingly. I was making her nervous too; she wasn't her usual fizzy self. 'You should know. Affects us all differently, doesn't it? Some people freak out and some freeze, I guess. You tell me.'

I knew what she meant but it wasn't that.

'It's just…' I began, thinking back to the previous night.

'What? What is it?' A worried look spread over her face.

I decided not to say anything. I wasn't stupid. Sam didn't need any ammunition; she hated you, it couldn't be any more obvious.

'Nothing, you're right, as always. Must be nerves. Shall we join the others downstairs, have ourselves a glass of champagne, if they haven't already guzzled it all?'

'Sure. I'm sorry, Eve.' Turning and reaching for the bedroom door, she looked back at me; for the first time I could recall, she was obviously struggling to find the words she needed. My incongruent mood must have put her on edge. 'I really am sorry.'

'Oh, Sam, for what? None of this is your doing. Don't you dare apologise. I couldn't love and appreciate you more than I do. I know it's a bit sloppy, but, seriously, what would I do without you?'

I'm sure I saw her eyes sparkle with tears. 'I'm still sorry,' she said.

'For what?'

'For you feeling like you say.' She shrugged, her curled tresses falling over her silvery-silk-covered shoulder. 'Today. I wanted you to be happy. I didn't ever want it to be like this for you.' She blew me a heartfelt kiss before leaving the room.

I forced back the threatening tears.

I couldn't tell Sam; she'd probably think me silly. But I couldn't get your text out of my mind. So unusually insensitive, uncaring. Not Gregg-like. I'd tried to call you on several occasions. Left a couple of voicemails you didn't return. Around 23.00, you texted me.

Stop calling my mobile. I'm busy. Don't appreciate being checked on. Get some sleep. I need you to look your best tomorrow.

Then, as an afterthought, a following text with a single *X*. I didn't reply. I called Sam, but it diverted to voicemail. The feeling in my stomach was new. The cold text played on my mind. Made me question other events. Late nights. Unanswered calls. Cancelled arrangements. Guarded phone calls. But it was too late, so much already invested. So many people I cared about, caught up and expecting. I was probably overreacting, an out-of-character text, nothing more. Stop overthinking things, I chastised myself. But the feeling stirred deep within my gut.

The day happened. Uneventful, lots of expense, beautiful floral displays and delectable food. Witty speeches and much jubilant conversation. Normal. But no matter how hard I tried, I couldn't feel relaxed, happy. I dutifully beamed but inside I was peculiarly anaesthetised. The day took place within a glass dome; I kept wishing someone would shake it up, change the scene. No amount of self-talking could lift the unsettling tizzy beneath my ribcage. It was a relief when it was all over. When the residual onlookers dwindled away, I gathered my discarded bouquet of white lilies. I hate white lilies; they remind me of death. But they're a favourite of yours; you insisted I chose them.

I retreated for the night. Exhausted by the façade. Angry with myself. Heartbroken, I had missed my big day. What was wrong with me? Everyone else was happy.

*

Two months later

Just another tool in your box, wasn't I? You are perfect, resonates through my mind. You forgot to add, 'for my purpose'. A befitting piece of equipment for senior partnership conditions. Eventually, I would learn your intentions more often than not became your reality. But you had so many other admirable traits. Sucker. I always saw more good than bad. On reflection, the signs were unmistakable, except if you're not looking, you don't see. Once you look, it's obvious. What comes next is judgment. An arrogant human response – we think we know what we would do in the circumstance. But we truly never do.

The first flick of the switch. A deliberate shift in the relationship.

You glared at me across the opulent Georgian hotel room. The word exasperation penned across your face. A new word I hadn't seen before, or had I simply not noticed? With folded arms, you tipped back against the door. What was your problem? A thick vapour of glacial air filled the room. You observed me awkwardly applying antiseptic spray-on plaster to my heel.

'Not sure why I'm bothering with this. Talk about inadequate. Still, hopefully it will suffice,' I attempted to engage you. 'You wouldn't think something so silly could be so painful. So much yucky fluid. Eew. Did you see the state of my sock yesterday? Had to throw it. Rank.' All falling on deaf ears.

You sighed. 'I did *say* to wear your boots in. But you don't ever listen, can't be told,' you snapped. 'It's your own fault. What did you expect, for Christ's sake, with new boots? Sometimes, Eve, your lack of thought is flabbergasting. There's not a chance we're backing out of today. You do realise the importance of this weekend? Talk about picking your times. Our first corporate weekend. Christ!' You flicked your mobile to check the time. 'We need to leave. Now. You're making us late.'

You did advise me to wear my boots in; I should have. Best intentions and all that. The shadow of a ten-year-old crawled over me. I shifted my seat on the bed in a befitting manner. Why did my intentions not come to fruition? Badly organised, you advised me often. I preferred too carefree; it's less harsh.

'You did, but I forgot. No, actually, I ran out of time. Taking on the extra work case didn't help, probably. Do you have any proper plasters?' I smiled, despite not feeling very happy with your 'I told you so' comments.

You sniggered. 'A new case. If that's what you call it. You shouldn't have bothered; it's not as if it offers you any gains. Waste of your and now our time.' Ouch, how could you? You knew how sad this particular case was.

'It's not such a big deal, you know. It's just a blister. A blinking, big fat one, yes, but that's all it is.' Talk about blowing things out of proportion. 'And I do appreciate how important this weekend is for you. I won't let you down. I just need to sort this, then I'll be with you.'

'Do you, though? Do you appreciate how influential some of these guys are?' You gestured at the door. 'Not sure you do. I'm not sure you even care, considering your behaviour.' You strode towards your side of the wardrobe. Everything perfectly hung, unlike my jumbled side.

'Yes, I do, that's not fair,' I say. 'But it's supposed to be fun too. Isn't it? I didn't realise it was a resilience test. It's not like I've broken my leg. I'll be good to go once I've expertly patched this up.'

You snatched at the pristine chocolate leather washbag. Of course, you'd have plasters. Always prepared. Strange place to keep a washbag. Then, I remembered how cross you were as someone had *soaked* the bottom of the bag. '*Probably the cleaner'*, you'd said. *Brain-dead,* apparently. You launched the unopened packet of plasters. To me or at me? I didn't look up.

'Thank you,' I offered.

As I fumbled to open the new box, your eyes burned through me. A child watched to ensure they appreciate their wrong. A rush of emotion sidled over me. Tired from the all-embracing previous day's walking. Forced conversation. Washed down by an exceptionally drunken night. With a few hours of tossing and turning and too many spectre-like visits to the bathroom. God, I wished you'd just leave.

How would Sam respond? She'd probably hurl her boot at you, tell you to go on your sodding walk, without her. I daren't tell her; this would go with the other new filed-away confidential experiences. Their dislike for each other was exasperating. Fed up of being the arbitrator, I increasingly neglected to tell her things. She was incapable of seeing your good points; you refused to see hers. It was easier to keep you apart. My teachers used to inform me I'd make an excellent political negotiator. I hadn't realised it would end up being between my husband and best friend.

Propping up the door frame, fully attired for the hike, itching to leave the room, you blatantly snorted at your watch at least twice. 'I hate being late. I've fired people for less.'

'Gregg, for goodness' sake, go down without me, please. Mr Punctuality.'

'I'm sorry?' Your eyebrows rose.

'I'll see you all in Reception, okay. I won't be too long.' Anything to stop the breathing down my neck. 'Carry on ahead. Please.'

'If you're not down in ten, I'll leave without you!' You shut the door firmly behind you. If it hadn't been a fire door, it would have slammed. Thank God. Why so intolerant today?

The day dragged on from bad to worse, the inadequate plaster overwhelmed by a raw, weeping heel. I couldn't continue. My stomach knotted; how would I tell you? As I hobbled along, I rehearsed chosen words to soften the blow. Jesus, Eve, get on with it. Eventually, I told you. You uttered the words of a compassionate partner, but your eyes conveyed something else. I would have retreated alone but the kindness of your group forced you to join me. The air throbbed with resentment.

'No, Gregg, you go back with poor Eve, of course you should. We'll catch you later for pre-dinner drinks in the bar. No problem at all.' Why did they have to be so damn considerate?

You walked and I limped back in silence. The pain was excruciating. Silent tears popped. You were aware of my tears; we both pretended otherwise. Back in the centre of Keswick, I asked to rest, grab a coffee.

'Are you for real? You've completely wrecked my day. My chances. Embarrassed me. How the hell's a coffee going to help? I'm going back to the hotel. Try and work out how to limit the damage. If at all possible. You do whatever you bloody like, sure you will anyway. Just give me some space.'

You paced ahead without looking back. Had I missed something? A shadow of gloom hung, yet I still tried to make excuses. Searched for reasons. I didn't want to see what my heart was aching to show me. Your puffed-up figure strode into the distance. My hobble interspersed with anger. Humiliation. Then sadness. The rise of my secrecy. The lies, the covering, the deceit. Why? Because I was ashamed. By the time I reached the hotel you were nowhere to be seen. I assumed you were back in our room. I loitered; did I go up to find you, or not, maybe down to a medicinal drink in the bar instead? The latter would have won, if the need to remove my tacky boot wasn't so overbearing.

After several minutes of vigorous door-knocking, nothing. No response. I limped back down to Reception, thankful for the authentic albeit slightly rickety lift. Charming, if not in pain.

I checked the bar area.

The thought of a subterranean, warm soapy bath hailed me. Locked out of the room like a naughty teenager, I requested a spare key from Reception. I was duly informed you had made a further reservation for me in a separate room, in the newer part of the hotel. My belongings were in the process of being relocated. A self-conscious blush tiptoed up my neck. I swiftly tried to recover my pride, which was running for the door. The haughty, smug receptionist eyed me.

'Yes, of course, that's what I meant. I need the key to my new room, please. Not the old room. You can't beat your own space, can you?' I lied.

A telepathic moment transferred between us. It informed me she knew I was lying; I had been well and truly dumped by the charming man I'd arrived with only yesterday. Apparently as man and wife too. I thanked her for her service and passed back a telepathic not so polite message. I considered leaving until I remembered I didn't have the car keys, or the house keys. I didn't even have my purse, or change of clothes.

I reached my new, more like staff quarters room. Plonked onto the not so sumptuous single person's bed and began to ease off what looked like a boot recovered from a murder scene. My thoughts returned to you. I sieved through the events of the previous evening, with no plausible justification for your behaviour today. You were a little uptight. But no one seemed to notice. The pressure of being a climber at a corporate event. Calculating each manoeuvre, each upward step. '*Watch what you say, Eve*', you'd advised me. I hadn't realised I was so stupid. '*No, just think about what you give away*', you'd corrected. '*Don't discuss any of my comings and goings. Put on your best performance for me*', you had asked, taking my hand.

Performance? We are who we are, surely? It wasn't my fault my glass was continually refilled, and then they played the best dance music. You didn't want to dance, but I had a great time.

I fell in a heap on the bed, with an overwhelming urge to close my eyes.

I slept for some time; it was dark when I awoke. Rudely stirred by a familiar buzzing sound from my jacket, strewn across the floor in a manner you would disapprove of. I shuddered at the thought of you being witness to the rooms Sam and I had shared on our travels. Now, disorientated, it took a few moments to recall where I was, or why I was there.

My mobile. I stretched to drag my jacket from the floor by its hood. Sickness crept over me with recalls of our horrible day. A new message from you popped up.

Bet you're bored out your pants! Soon be over. Give me a call about plans for next weekend. Really looking forward to it. xxx

Odd? What the hell? Was that text even meant for me? I wasn't bored, I was fed up and in agony. What did you mean about the weekend? You knew I was going away.

You texted me again.

Hope you got the message – from your 'friend' Joe. You'll not be able to find it. I deleted it last night, while you frolicked on the dance floor! Did I not mention – I despise betrayal.

Shit!

Great! So that was what this had been about. You looked over my messages, put two and two together, came up with ten. But you knew about my friend Joe. Talk about a mind-bender.

'A few too many males in your contact list for my liking,' you casually joked. It wasn't jest, though, was it? I thought it was endearing; you were obviously jealous but didn't know how to show it.

Why did I feel so guilty? I hadn't done anything, not really. I felt indignant. Why were you sneaking through my messages anyway? Didn't you trust me? I always considered those who distrusted were the ones to be wary of. Hung without a trial. Angry, guilty or nervous. A train whizzing through the station of all three, no time to stop at either.

Shaky hands flicked to my contacts list. Joe was no more; you'd deleted him. I'd told you I was away the next weekend; I was going with Sam to London. I'd left out the details, sidestepped the issue of Joe coming with us, but only because I knew you wouldn't like it. Chewing it over, it did look a little bad. But it was innocent. Yet I felt like a dirty cheat.

You texted me again.

I don't expect to see you at dinner tonight. You have a migraine. What happens next? I haven't decided.

*

I didn't go to London. I tried to call Joe; he didn't respond. You informed me you'd had *'a little chat with Joe'*. And that I needed to decide if it was to be you or Joe? Then Joe wouldn't be in contact again.

A lesson learned, Eve.

I questioned us, for the first time.

'Come on, Eve! Do you want to be responsible for hurting your parents? Surely not after they've invested so much into our marriage. Especially now they've announced they'll be moving abroad soon. Can you imagine the position you would put them in? Unthinkable. Just be a little more aware of your actions, that's all. In time I'll forgive your betrayal. We'll be good together. It's early days.'

My parents were in the beginnings of planning to relocate to pastures new, now I was apparently so settled. How convenient for you. You used anyone I cared for as a weapon, didn't you?

Chapter Eight

Cornwall 2016

He negotiates the stairs; ensuring he doesn't step on the bottom one. Treading through the small tiled inner hall; he raises an elbow to switch on the light. At the front door, he knocks once, twice, before opening it onto the unfamiliar street to check no one has parked too closely to his beloved car. The cones he placed at either end are still in position. Personal space is so important. He closes the door, sighing. Yet another transitory rental property, it will have to suffice. It certainly isn't the worst he's endured, and it won't need to be for too long.

He turns on his heel in pursuit of coffee, regarding each foot treading the way to the kitchen. His heart rate ups at the sight of a loose lace dragging along the contaminated floor. Sweat threatens his brow, flaunting thoughts of germs, hammering at the sole, creeping up the leather, seeking weakness in the stitching. Resist, bloody resist, come on, he urges. He can't. And diverts to the cleaning box, still stacked with the others in the dining area. Eight boxes in total. His whole life in eight boxes; it was ten, a few months ago. It would have been seven this time, had he not spread the contents to ensure the even number. With hands now in rubber he removes the soiled lace, from shoe to the bin. This had better not be an omen for today. He unravels a new untainted lace; he has an unlimited supply. A practised hand feeds it through holes without the need to touch.

He looks around his unfamiliar surroundings. It was dark and he was tired when he arrived last night. There is a small but adequate kitchen, reasonably clean to the naked eye. Picking up his kettle – it always travels separately with his suitcase – he removes the lid, peers in, replaces the lid. Yep, still empty. He obeys his orders from above, tipping the spout over the sink regardless. No old water. Measuring sufficient water for two cups, no more. He replaces the lid, returns the kettle to its base, spout facing at forty-five degrees from the switch.

Breathe. Relax. Something about alien dwellings. Dirty buggers everywhere. I am doing the right thing in coming here, aren't I? He considers. I've waited years, but still? No, don't bottle it now.

The moment he passed the Cornwall border last night, hurtling down the A30, he thought he might be sick. He'd known it wouldn't be easy, with it being so many years since his last visit. Time builds barriers. In another life, he'd have loved it here. But Cornwall's too diseased now. He quickly spins, nearly missing his moment. Successfully lifting the kettle just before it hits the point of rapid boil. Close. One, two, and a pinch of strong instant coffee hits the base of his mug. No milk unfortunately, it rolled out of the box into the rear footwell last night, where it still lies. A job for gloves later on. He stirs the black liquid four times in a clockwise direction.

Seasoned hands rub his sore head. Whisky seemed like a good idea at the time. A hangover in the morning, he considered, no big deal. Live for the moment, I'll be fine in the morning, he justified.

I never am, though, so why did I do it? Today of all days, he needs his head. Have a word with yourself next time, will you? he reprimands. A glance at the kitchen clock informs him he has precisely thirty-two minutes before he has to leave. Needing to be at the appointment, waiting ten minutes before he's to be seen. Otherwise, he won't be able to go ahead with it. The scorching coffee sears its way down his throat onto an edgy stomach. It will be the shorter bathroom sequence this morning. Being late is not an option.

Fifty-three minutes later, he counts his way up the few steps to the front door of the small building, apologetically standing between the grander Edwardian neighbours. This is it, the beginning of some form of closure, finally.

With a deep breath in, he absorbs the air of the tired reception area; musty and old but kind of comforting.

'Mr Austin?' a middle-aged lady with a nose piercing and numerous jangly bangles enquires.

'Yep, that's me.' He squints at the insufficient ticking clock. 'I'm a little early.'

'That's fine, love, no problem. Please take a seat. Susie will come and get you in a minute.' She indicates to the hard, school-resembling chairs positioned along the wall.

He shakes his legs out as if to indicate a problem with them; if only it were that simple. 'Thanks. If you don't mind, I prefer to stand.' He isn't allowed to sit in the waiting room is the truth, another order from above. Not before an appointment anyway. Today is not the day to break rules. He casually regards Susie's details on the 'Who Are We?' board: a person-centred counsellor, whatever this means. So long as it doesn't involve the maniac Freudian-type shit, he thinks, who knows? Maybe she'll be able to help him. Despite the monumental gap in time.

A few minutes later, Susie and he sit in the small angled room, rescued from the direct sunlight beaming through. Susie is, much to his amusement, all he'd envisaged. She rests upright but relaxed into her low-level chair without arms, a calm hand with a pen hovering over a lined notebook. She has a soft yet commanding voice; he feels himself drawn into her monotonous tone. It was suggested he saw someone so many times before; he could never see the point. But now, everything has built to a crescendo and his emotions overwhelm his ability to think straight. If he is to finally put everything to bed, maybe now is the time. He taps his right, then left foot on the floor alternately, twice.

'Where would you like to start, Gregg? How do you think I may be able to help you?'

'Now, there's a question. To be fair, sitting here now, I haven't got a clue. I'm not even sure why I'm here. I hope I'm not wasting your time.'

She nods at him, allowing him space to continue, reassuring him subliminally he can take his time. When he doesn't respond, she prompts, 'You're not wasting my time, Gregg; I can assure you. You begin whenever you feel ready.'

'I guess it's because I've things in my past, stuff I've never come to terms with, and I've now reached a point in my life when I really need to be able to… draw a line, I think they say. The thing is, it's been a stupid amount of time. Since when this all started, I mean.'

She nods at him. 'So, there've been issues in your past that you've not been able to talk to anyone about, and now you feel the time is right for you to talk?'

He takes a few moments, a little perplexed. Didn't I just say that? Resounded through his mind. 'Yes, that's exactly it,' he adds, a little unsure about her reaction hanging in the air.

'Good, Gregg, go on. You're doing so well.'

He waits for her to offer more but clearly the onus is on him alone. Again. He thinks how strange it is to be sitting in the unfamiliar room with a complete stranger about to discuss things he has never been able to talk about, even with those he loved the most. He has left it all too late.

'Where do you want me to start?' he asks, hoping for a prompt.

'Wherever you wish to start, Gregg; take your time and begin once you're ready.'

He looks down at his tightly clasped hands on his lap. Counting, then begins to unravel at ten. He breathes in deeply, then exhales. 'I can still smell the air. It was the end of summer, you know, when you can feel autumn poking its head around the door.' She nods at him to continue, pen poised.

'The ground was firm underfoot, start of the school autumn term, end of the summer holidays. I remember feeling really miffed because we'd had such abysmal weather during the holidays, with it raining for most of it. It seemed that way anyway. But that day, there was a brilliant blue sky.' He laughs through his nose. 'I was so self-conscious about the regulation long grey socks I was forced to wear, being fourteen, it wasn't at all cool.' She smiles at him, without articulating. 'It's not that I wasn't looking forward to school, I was kind of… if it wasn't for him, school was okay.'

'Him?' she urges.

'I'll get to it. The thing is, I enjoyed school. We lived in the middle of the Cotswolds, in the sticks, as my grandmother called it. Most of my friends lived a distance away, so I'd get fed up, lonely even at times.'

'It was not a local school, then, where you attended?'

'No.' He shakes his head. 'A grammar school, Walesby Grammar, about fifteen miles from where we lived. I used to walk a mile or so to the bus stop each morning, then pick up the yellow school bus.'

'You must have been clever, to get into the grammar school,' she encourages him.

'I guess, just not clever enough. I can remember the morning clearly, you know, when the letter came, advising me I'd been offered a place.' He lifts his head to glance out of the window, discouraging his wretched eyes from filling with tears. Where have they come from? Not now, he warns. He turns back to address her. 'Sorry, it's just, I don't think I've ever allowed myself to think about those times, not without pushing the thoughts away again, never mind talk about them.'

'You're fine, Gregg, take your time. You were saying, you remember the morning clearly...'

'Yes, you know, waiting for the letter, am I in? Am I out? The look on my grandmother's face – it meant so much to her, I knew it, that's the problem. My grandfather too, it meant so much to him. He didn't always say how he felt, but I knew anyway. Over the summer, we spent a lot of time together, me and my grandfather, I helped him dig over his allotment, in the rain mostly. That's when he'd talk to me, explain things; whilst he dug away, I'd learn how he felt about things. He, and my grandmother, hoped the opportunity of going to the renowned grammar school would change my life prospects, open doors, allow me to fulfil my true potential.' He smiles, then abruptly removes it. 'Huh, it certainly changed my life!'

'I can understand how proud they must have been. It isn't easy getting a place in a grammar school, especially as they're so few and far between.'

'Especially as they're abused by those they were not intended for, you mean.'

'Sorry; what do you mean by that?'

'No matter, ignore me. It's a personal issue I have with the system.' He shrugs. 'Obviously some students are there by their own merits. Some are only there because the family have enough money to tutor them to death before they sit the entrance exams. It defeats the whole point of grammar schools, doesn't it?'

'I understand what you're saying.' Susie appropriately sits on the fence.

He gazes around the room, whilst counting to six in his head. He didn't mean to go off on that point; it was a pointless track. That was life after all. Unjust.

'The point is, I knew how important it was to my grandparents. I understood it was an opportunity for me, one not many had. And I did intend to make the most of it, but life had other ideas.' He shakes his head. 'Or I just wasn't strong enough in the end. I failed, big time.' He regards his feet; he'd always believed this, but he'd never voiced it before. He didn't get the chance. He was told his parents would be so proud of him. Not that this mattered; he couldn't remember them anyway. His grandparents were his parents. That was more than enough for him, despite the cruel remarks. Cruel annotations made by a leader with many followers. The school coward, the bully.

'So you feel like you failed, Gregg?'

Didn't I just say that? Brings him back to the moment. 'As I said, one of the downsides of not attending the more local state school is separation, distance from your friends. I had a good group of friends, but I was especially close to Tom. He was an only child too; to be honest, we were more like brothers. Were, being the word here. Tom stayed with us for the first two weeks of the holidays whilst his parents were away. Which was great.' His eyes smile. 'We built a makeshift gym using various bits and pieces we found in one of the outhouses. Spent hours doing it, then worked out to music, sneaking some of my grandfather's ale in to help us along.' After Tom left for home, he spent many more hours pummelling his makeshift sandbag swinging from the log-store beam, with that bastard's face in mind. It helped. It was what bullies needed, he and Tom agreed.

'But the rest of the holidays dragged. There's only so many times you can play football against the wall. It was good enough reason to look forward to returning to school again.'

'So, you and your friend Tom were as close as brothers; but you were quite a lonely lad otherwise. And school helped with this loneliness?'

'That about sums it up, yes.' He regards Susie, waiting to see if she offers any more insight. Nothing, so he feels compelled to continue.

'But had I known then what I did by the end of the term, I'd never have got on the bus that morning.'

'It wasn't a good term for you, then?'

He sighs heavily, filling the air with regret. 'No.' He shakes his head. 'It wasn't, no.'

'Okay.' Susie nods once. That's it, no questions? he ponders. Not that he's ready for questions.

'If you don't mind, Susie, before you ask, I'm not ready to go over that stuff, not yet. As I said, I haven't ever spoken about it before.'

Susie's nude upturned lips reassure him. 'No, of course. I understand, it's going to take some time, Gregg. That's fine with me, of course it is. You're not ready to take the step yet so just continue with what you feel comfortable with.' She makes a note on her pad as he looks on, jotting down his first revelations. He wonders if she dines out on this book of secrets.

'Thank you. I'm not sure I'd be so patient with me. I really couldn't do your job. I'd want to tell people to just get on with it, for Christ's sake!' He notices her slight frown; she seems a little bemused by his comment. A quiet awkward moment for him but not for her ensues, occupying the room; urging him to fill it.

'The thing is, I mean, the reason why I find it so difficult is because it changed my life forever. It ruined everything. Or, more accurately and honestly, I ruined everything. If I tell you it was over twenty-five years ago, all this, and I still haven't recovered. It still keeps me awake in the middle of the night. It also completely changed the direction of my life, all of my ambitions gone.' He taps his feet on the silent floor. 'I think, worst of all, I lost all and everything

I've ever loved. I betrayed them, you see. I've never been able to forgive myself.' He averts his eyes back to the window, feeling his jaw harden, biting down on his teeth. 'I. Have. So. Much. Burning. Hate and. Resentment.' He stabs at his chest. 'Inside me. I can't ever forgive myself.' He looks back at Susie. 'I just can't let it go. The injustice of it all, knowing he got away with it. I know he's still out there somewhere, with no remorse at all. Some days, Susie, some days, it feels as if I'm being eaten alive.'

Susie nods, looks to her pad and scribbles away. It is easier than he imagined to blurt this stuff out. But he is so conscious of opening wide the doors in his mind he expends so much effort trying to keep shut.

No going back now.

He looks down at the oversized watch hanging heavy from his tanned wrist; his father's. A well-built man who spent his life in the forces. A cruel irony. A life devoted to the firing line, then killed in a car accident on his honeymoon. At the time, he was just a baby. He lost them both, his mother too, before having the chance to know them. His grandparents took over the realm. The two people he treasured most in the world. Them and Tom. He takes a moment to himself, conscious his time is running out for his appointment. His suddenly eager mouth has to wait, at least until the next time.

He pictures the moment again, waiting for his school bus, seeing himself throw his worn grey bag to the tarmac, plonk himself down on top; wriggling around to manoeuvre the contents into a more cushion-like, comfy position. With sight of his bus approaching, he dragged himself up from his squashed rucksack, brushed off the gathered dust.

'With a bit of luck that little shit might have left,' he muttered before beginning his routine banter with the driver.

He looks up, but Susie is still scribbling.

So much unnecessary loss. Pathways built to a never-ending road. September, 1986, the annual school trip, marked the twisting of destiny. Everything changed in Cornwall. The gravity of the consequences could never have been foreseen. He innocently found himself indebted to a cause searching for accountability and retribution. Fuelled by a potent measure of guilt, injustice and hatred.

He's suddenly aware of Susie's eyes studying him, rescuing him from his thoughts. 'So, Gregg, this is about all we have time for today. Do you want to make another appointment?' He really doesn't have any choice, it has strangely enough provided a strange form of relief, hearing the dreaded words rather than the constant mind-battering.

'Yes, I think I will, thank you.'

'Lovely. You have done excellently. I realise it hasn't been easy for you today.'

You have no idea, he thinks. But the end is in sight now. He doesn't care what anyone says, revenge is going to be sweet.

Back outside, he descends the steps, avoiding the last. Perhaps a wander through Truro will help clear the mind, he decides. He only makes it as far as the old market square, where local produce exhibits, the aroma of pasties from a local bakery, antagonise his hollow stomach. He stops to share a bench with an eagle-eyed seagull, allowing his mind to reopen the door now already ajar. After the school trip to Cornwall, everything turned horribly wrong. September 1986 – he closes his eyes, to revisit the oozing scars.

He rushed through the archway to his grandparents' cottage, throwing his tattered heavy rucksack to the floor. Thumped his way up the old staircase, before slamming the bedroom door. The piece of wood that separated him from everything he loved most. With no idea how to engage with it. He clouted his wardrobe before lobbing himself on the bed. Stoking the burning fire of hatred deep down in his gut. He couldn't, wouldn't, allow it to go out. Please talk to us, his grandparents pleaded. *Tell you I killed him. That I wish it were me who died. How can I?* he thought.

Alone in his darkness; blind to any route out. Drowning as his grandparents desperately stretched out soothing arms he couldn't quite reach. He scrubbed at the blood on his hands, but nothing ever worked. Nothing ever would. Night times were the worst. Banging a turbulent head against his pillow; desperate to eradicate the words, the faces, the images. Trembling, dripping cold sweat on flaming skin. His heart trouncing against cotton. As if he were still there, at the scene. The truth stuck inside him, while the lies consumed the air.

Cornwall. His first and last taste of freedom.

His friend, brother. Was dead. The setting was a lads' paradise. A youth hostel perched high on the cliff side. Turquoise sea views. A Cornish flag billowing above surf waves, miles of pale honeyed sand. Rocks. A boy's hallucination, twisted into his nightmare.

Because he quarreled with Tom. Sending him into the path of the school persecutor.

Who then led Tom to a spot on the map of pure majestic beauty. Skyscraper rocks; blue sky high, with crystal lagoon pools. But Tom couldn't swim. The bastard knew Tom couldn't swim. Then as the daylight began to fade the bastard swaggered back with his gang. The low sun just about holding on. *A test of loyalty*, the bastard bragged.

Red-hot anger. Quickly followed by guilt.

He sprinted acres over the headland to reach the spot. A helicopter flew over. Minutes later, from his viewpoint on the towering rock, he watched as a small limp body was laid on cold stone. A man pumping up and down on Tom's chest as his lifeless head lay in a backwards tilt. The man paused to blow air into his mouth. Over and over. Pumping, pumping. Until a soft hand appeared on the man's shoulder. It was over. Tom had gone.

He'd never be able to say the words, *I killed you, Tom. I did it.*

Chapter Nine

Cornwall 2016

Another day over. I pull up alongside the pretty Cornish wall and wait, in need of some thinking space. My eyes wind down the narrowing road where I can steal a glimpse of the frisking Atlantic. Warm memories of childhood holidays creep over. It's amazing how these feelings are still with me, despite life trying to warp and dissolve them. Memories create personal benchmarks, I explain to people, to measure life's experiences against. If children have unhappy childhoods, their benchmark is set sadly low. Was my benchmark set too high? Perhaps my happy childhood was not such an advantage after all. As much as I try, I can't relate the balminess of those memories to my present. I've lived three unconnected lives. Right now, I'm utterly detached from all three. I can see them; I can't feel them. I'm no different from my clients earlier today.

When I'm with people, I feel as if it's all happening without me being there. I'm not part of any of it. Is this normal? teary eyes enquired.

No, it is not. How can it be normal? I thought.

People talk to me, I answer. But it doesn't feel real to me. Almost as if I'm watching my words. Do you think I'm going mad? she asked.

No. But it's a short continuum from stress to anxiety to psychosis. Blurred boundaries can quickly diminish. Where am I on this scale?

Your bucket is too full. We each have a stress bucket. Some with a larger capacity than others. But as it fills over the day, it can be something quite insignificant to tip it over. The rising of cortisol, the depletion of serotonin, the need to ruminate, see to our disturbance of sleep. We wake shattered from too much active REM sleep, insufficient replenishing slow-wave sleep. We begin our day with an already half-full bucket, and so it goes on. A vicious circle. A rolling ball of destruction. If not managed. If not dealt with. If questions remain unanswered, I explained.

The light is lowering around me, casting atypical shadows. I notice a movement from the corner of my right eye. It's my neighbour, Gloria, bobbing up and down a couple of walls along, attending to her abundant garden. She's taken such a shine to Jack, his surrogate grandmother. When we first moved here she used to let herself in to greet him from school, staying with him until I was home from clinic. Now, she pops in from time to time to leave home-baked delights and fresh produce. Neither of us have other family close by. I reach for my handbag, just as an unmistakable rumble of an approaching engine grabs my attention. I freeze, my hand hovering. My stomach tightens as a blueish 911 Porsche slides past with centimetres between us. The images from last week voyage through my mind. It's the sound, the distinguished sound of a 911 engine, gripping my throat.

Last week, driving home late from clinic, that horrible feeling of being followed consumed me. A haunting ambience, in that in-between-light-and-dark condition. The lanes smothered by a dense sea mist. There was a car, far too close for the conditions, behind me. The headlamps burning my eyes through my wing mirror. Circular, amphibian headlamps. We continued for a while, just the two of us, each twist and turn heading back via Callestick from Truro. Was I imagining it, an innocent commuter caught up in my creativity, or did I know who was behind the wheel? I strained to catch a glimpse of the driver. It was hopeless; the frog-like headlamps dazzled my vision into a block white wall. I could smell danger. Should I find somewhere to abandon my car? Attempt to run, but where? Human habitation in the area was sporadic. By the shadow I glimpsed, I was as sure as I could be – the driver was male. Unsteady legs stumbled on and off the accelerator. A little voice whispered not to turn for home, reveal where I live. I loitered along, hunting for a suitable red herring. Eventually, I saw a large farmhouse with obvious lights ahead. At the last minute, I swung sharply onto the stone driveway. Nuggets flying everywhere, quarrying deep tyre grooves. I breathed out as the car passed by.

Now, I fumble for the keys I've managed to drop down the side of the seat. I need to follow the car. Swinging out ungracefully in the hope of catching up. How can I not? It's a dead end. But isn't this sheer, utter madness? Even so, I have to see for myself. I could be wrong, but I need to know either way. I roll down towards the dead end, passing Enid Blyton cottages and gardens, negotiating the seasonal stray end of tourists wandering in the middle of the road, seemingly without a care in the world.

As I draw closer to the seafront my stomach rolls in harmony with the waves. I spot the car already parked up. It doesn't make any sense; the car appears to already be unoccupied. Sod it! He couldn't possibly have gone far. I scan from left to right, then notice, Charlie, the parking attendant, casually propping up his hut. How the hell did the driver get away so quickly? I abandon my car in a truly obnoxious position, blocking anyone else from coming or going, scrambling to reach Charlie before he forgets. Secreting adrenal glands pushing me forward.

Waving like a crazy woman, I scuttle towards his salty lined face. 'Charlie. Charlie?'

'You okay, Evie? Not seen you for a while… you're lookin' pale, lovely,' he says. 'You coming to the pie and ale night, then?' A deep-rooted Cornish accent washes over me.

I've forgotten about the pie thing; I said I would, but I can't face it now. 'Oh, I'm not sure I can make it any more, Charlie. Something's come up.' I walk closer to him. 'Did you notice the guy from this car, by any chance?'

Charlie gives the car park a once-over. Come on, Charlie, switch on. He returns uncomprehending eyes. Please, Charlie, not today, think, please.

'This one, the blue one, Charlie, in front of mine, here,' I implore him.

'The blue one? Oh, yeah, that one.' He nods. 'The flash one. Proper job, isn't it?' he rolls out. 'Difficult to say whether it's blue or green, isn't it? Nice though, yeah, proper nice.'

'Lovely. But did you see who was driving it? Did you see the man get out?'

'Yeah, I did, yeah. Seemed in a bit of a hurry, he did. Needs to slow down. Gave me a fiver, then drove off before I could tell him, there's no charge for night-time functions. Mad.' He tuts to himself as if we're talking about hundreds of pounds. 'Mad.

Bloody emits. Need to learn to slow down, they do. Come down 'ere…'

I touch his arm. 'Where'd he go, Charlie? Did you see where he went?' No response; a blank look greets me. 'It's quite important. Try and think for me, please.'

'You know him, then, do you, Evie?'

'I don't know. That's what I'm trying to find out.' It's like pulling teeth.

'Oh, I see. Well, I dunno, think he went up over the footpath. Seemed in a hurry, like, now I think of it.' He nods to the footpath meandering out of sight towards Trevellas Porth. There's nothing in that direction, not for the non-rambler or rock jumpers anyway. So it's odd, to say the least. Why would you be going up there?

As if reading my mind, Charlie continues, 'Perhaps he's meeting his lover. You know how mad you girls get when us men are late.' He giggles. 'Didn't notice anyone else, mind.'

I lean back against my car; there's no way I'm going to follow him. I know the footpath well; I don't fancy it alone. I'd be out of view from the village and my head is knocking at the door telling me not to do anything foolish.

'Shit,' I whisper.

'You okay, Evie? Was he supposed to be waiting for you, then?'

'No, no, not at all. I'm fine, thanks.' He nods. 'Did you get a look at him, though? Can you describe him? Anything at all?'

'What? Aww, I dunno, love, all look the same to me. Quite 'andsome, I guess. Not my type, though.' He chuckles.

I can't help but smile at him, such a lovable guy. I just wish he could have tried a bit harder. But I'm doing it again, expecting everyone to be privy to my needs without bestowing the details. The bits that make my behaviours understandable. 'Okay, thanks, Charlie, not to worry. You take care. Catch you soon.' I squeeze his shoulder.

'Okay, my lovely. You too. Maybe see you at the quiz night, then?' I turn and wander back to my car. Charlie's voice echoes in the distance of my world.

'Odd, though, isn't it?' he calls after me.

I halt, then turn. 'What? Charlie, what's odd?'

'Well, him asking if I knew you, like, then you just turning up like that. I mean, he could've waited for you at least, couldn't he? No manners, you see. Got the car, but no manners.'

I freeze as an overwhelming sickness creeps up from my gut. Then my feet walk back towards Charlie. 'Go on, what else?'

'I told him, no, don't know no Eve Austin. We've an Evie, though. Evie Sands we have; proper clever she is. Then he said - that's what he meant to say, like, Evie Sands.'

I knew it. I catch my breath from running away from me. 'What else did you say, Charlie?' I realise from the startled look on his face I've worried the poor guy.

'Nothing, love. Well, just that you live up there, top of that hill there. But he said he knew that anyway, what with him already calling on you earlier. Didn't say nothing else. He asked if I knew you, like, then drove off, parked up, walked off without his money. A fiver he gave me. Weird.'

I touch Charlie's arm in reassurance of his worried expression and leave. I could wait to see who comes back but it's pointless, I know who it is. I feel like a child who's realised the game's up; I now need to face the consequences.

It's always only ever been a matter of time.

With a lack of awareness, I make my way home. Hoping Gloria has abandoned her garden. I really can't face the thought of conversation. Leaving my car against the wall, I gingerly open my gate, kicking over the silver candle lantern as I and everyone do, to creep to the sanctuary of my cottage. I feel violated. Each time I think I've turned a corner, I dare to breathe, something or someone blocks my way. I open the door to darkness, fumbling to locate the light switch. Jack's out for the night with friends, staying over. I wish he weren't. For a moment, I fight with myself not to call him, check he's okay. A paranoid mum. Passing through the front room, I put the TV on, the silence being all too much, then take myself upstairs. A cursory glimpse over all dark spaces.

I replace clinic clothes for lounge pants and patter back downstairs to pour myself a large glass of wine, before slumping into my squidgy sofa. Only to get straight back up – did I lock the doors? I'm sure I did but sure isn't good enough. Why would you go to Trevellas Porth, or along that pathway anyway? Did you think I would follow you? How do you even know about the path, Trevellas Porth – have you been here before, checked it out? Sitting back down, I pull my legs up under me, I flick absent-mindedly through TV channels, in need of light-hearted distraction. Anything to stop me thinking, listening for each and every alien noise. Why is there so much tosh on? It's either depressing or gloomy, mostly a combination of the two. For God's sake. Is it just me? Do people really watch this stuff? I've become so damn miserable without noticing. I opt for a film, not appreciating how sadly it is all going to end.

As I sip wine, I taste the familiar tang of blackberries combined with home-grown trickles of salty hurt. I quickly switch over to a documentary on crazy mothers-in-law; how apt. Have these programmes been especially chosen for me tonight? The thought of my mother-in-law crashes through my mind. I couldn't stand the woman. It still grates on me. I only met her once – why didn't it resonate more, as so obviously odd? Who only meets the mother-in-law just the once? She was vile. But now I wonder, was she trying to warn me? Help me? Did I get her wrong? Though she's never attempted to make any contact, even after you disappeared. I remind myself everything always feels worse at night. I tell others this, so it has to be true. But when it doesn't feel any better in the day, you know you've got problems.

I leave the TV running in the background as I begin to skim through my mobile; a craziness of missed calls, voicemails and emails. Go away; leave me alone. Then I notice the text; a withheld number again, but with a voicemail notification attached? I hurriedly dial my voicemail; skipping through to the relevant time. My fingers, not able to work quickly enough. 15.17? This isn't the usual time. Pressing my mobile hard against my ear, as if it may help me hear more, I strain to listen. Nothing. Silence. A distant breathing; a rising chest, a falling smugness... the foundations of a smirk. An evocative presence. No words; but so much passes between us. So, you're upping your contact to twice a day. Is this some form of sign you're getting closer? This isn't a client not wanting to speak. This is you.

It's definitely you, isn't it? I feel you.

The silence breathes a haunted murmur: I'm coming, Eve; not long now.

Chapter Ten

Before

My mind drifts back to the first time I met your mother. A whole new experience. I'd thought experiences were supposed to enrich, or at least inform. But then, on reflection, I guess it did the latter; I just didn't understand at the time. Talk about the need for alarm bells. I didn't think too much into it other than it was a little odd and perhaps not ideal for when you first meet your partner's parents. Your parents didn't come to our wedding. You refused to invite them. Providing such compelling reasoning, I even felt sorry for you.

Six months into our relationship we wandered hand in hand through the streets of Stratford-upon-Avon. It was nearly Christmas, the dark shut-up shopfronts lit up to reflect seasonal atmosphere. Medieval Tudor buildings hidden between recent repugnant appearances. Shakespeare hiding in the background. Or was that me?

'I don't get why they've put up that plastic tree at the bottom of Bridge Street this year. I'm really annoyed about it. Stratford's always had real trees. It's not the same, is it?'

'What?' You frowned at me. 'What are you talking about? I was enlightening you with the specifics of my new anticipated role. Why would I be looking at a tree?'

'Sorry. It's just, did you notice, they've used a plastic tree rather than the real one.'

You regarded me, a little flummoxed, holding your open hands out. 'I don't know, Eve. It's probably more economical. Anyway, who cares? It's a tree!' Clearly, I'd interrupted your flow with my trivialities.

'It's not just a tree! It's a Christmas tree. We've always had real trees in town. That's an ugly artificial eyesore! Where is your soul, Mr Austin?'

'It is merely a tree, Eve.' You squeezed my hand. 'I, on the other hand, have important news about a new appointment opportunity.' You studied me. 'Okay, if it's so important to you, I'll write a letter to the mayor. Or whichever other blithering idiot I need to, on the council. Tonight. Okay?'

'Okay. Can you also convey that half the Christmas lantern lights on Sheep Street are out, and the Santa they employed this year was super skinny and wearing a pair of Reebok trainers.' I confused you. As you gazed down Sheep Street, your expression communicated, *so what?*

'Why don't you put a list together? All the reasons you think the council have ruined Stratford at

Christmas. Just in case I miss something?' You winked at me.

'I'll do that, yes, good idea. Change isn't always for the best. This used to be a beautiful medieval town with sweeping willow trees lining the river! Now look at it. It was always about Shakespeare and Tudor buildings. Now, it's about betting shops, numerous flipping fudge shops, mobile phone and charity shops.'

'Eve, you are such an idealist. Come on, one man's progress is another man's nightmare. Not all of us are dreamers. Life's about moving, changing, always looking for the next step.' One look at my disagreeing face, and you laughed. 'Let's return to our conversation, shall we?'

You were particularly jovial; your annual assessment with the company partners had been fruitful. Rewarded with a huge bonus, with promises of great things to come. Apparently senior partnership looming. The long hours, commitment and networking were acknowledged. You were animated with plans and hopes for the future. At just twenty-eight, everything in the bag. No room for ifs and buts. At twenty-three I was still finding my way. I'd completed my undergraduate course at Warwick University with many further years of post-graduate learning and placements to consider. You talked of our future together, another done deal. You didn't ask me. A mixture of happiness and being marginally overwhelmed fused inside. How were you so certain of where our relationship was going without talking to me about it? We'd only been together a matter of months. We strolled on to the end of the street to view the billboards advertising forthcoming performances at the Royal Shakespeare Theatre. You nudged me. 'We've spare tickets hanging around the office, if you fancy it? *A Midsummer Night's Dream* springs to mind.'

'Lovely, of course.' I began to laugh.

'What's so funny?'

I wondered whether to share; sometimes our humour was so different. 'Nothing really.' You raised your eyebrow. 'I was just remembering a time, in a bar, earlier this year, someone asked Sam what her favourite Shakespeare play was. She said, *Robin Hood.*'

'Sorry, I'm not with you?'

The look of sheer bewilderment scrawled across your face made me laugh all the more. 'It's just, we'd seen it here at the end of last year. She got... a bit confused.'

'I see,' you said.

We drifted left, heading towards the Italian restaurant on the opposite side of the River Avon. It was a cold night and as you articulated your grand notions, I blew steam from my mouth. With no plans as such. Just to wander until we were hungry enough to eat. We'd end up at the popular bistro pub at the top of town. You knew the owners and, without exaggerating, at least fifty per cent of its patrons too.

I salivated as a waft of warm garlic smacked me across the face as we reached the large glass doors of the Italian. You pushed at my hand, directing me through the doorway. Odd? The Italian belonged to a well-known restaurant chain; it wasn't one of your approved-to-be-seen-in establishments. It smelt so scrumptious; the atmosphere buzzed with a casual warmth. The entrance adorned with boxes beautifully wrapped with metallic papers and iridescent bows. Italians are fine craftsmen at creating atmosphere.

'Lovely! We're eating here? Do you think we'll manage to get a table, or have you booked?' It was rammed.

You sniffed. 'Of course we're not eating here! Just something I need to do. It won't take long, then we'll be on our way.'

Your hand, firm around mine, pulled me through the bustling, raucous pre-theatre diners. Walking at the speed of a man on a mission, passing through somewhere unpleasant, making me stumble over my own feet a couple of times. Bumping into unsuspecting guests; kicking a couple of handbags along the way. No grace at all, just a clumsy elephant charging through.

'Who are we meeting?' I asked. But either I was drowned out or you chose to ignore me. Not that it mattered; clearly, I was going to meet them regardless. You impatiently scanned the room before eventually stopping at a table with two diners, I guessed in their seventies; both with white hair and fixed, stern faces. Hers, a little more so than his. They eyed you but didn't utter a word. The man continued with his meal almost gingerly; the woman glared at you, then looked at me, then back to you with a look of revulsion. Why were we loitering here? Clearly you didn't know each other. You hovered, mute. How awkward.

Finally, you broke the silence. 'Why are you dining here? How many times have I told you where to eat in town? The food's abysmal; why waste your money? My money?'

I was stunned by your rude outburst. Hardly a polite way to start a conversation and with no introductions. I couldn't help but feel a lot embarrassed. Remarkably the woman didn't bat an eyelid. She continued to chew on a piece of meat, eyeballing you. My eyes rolled from her to you. The hoary-haired woman slowly supped from her glass, still observing you, then picked at something lodged in her tooth.

Eventually she retaliated. 'Oh, shut up! What is it to you? Your father likes it here.'

Jesus, the penny dropped. Your parents? Surely not. I'd never have spoken to my parents in this manner, or anyone else. Why did, or how could, you? An unfamiliar expression of vulnerability flashed through your eyes as you twitched. I lurked on the sideline trying to decipher how best to act in such cringeworthy circumstances. Your parents; surely, I needed to make a good impression. Surely, they were intrigued as to who I was?

I squeezed your hand. Ignoring her remark, you shoved my hand rather gauchely in the direction of their table, in the manner of a sacrificial offering. 'This is Eve.' Your father smiled sheepishly in my direction, swiftly turning away before I could return his gesture. Your mother continued to glare, then made a deliberate point of noticing my red shoes. Sniffed, before returning her attention to her plate without so much as a nod. Another wasted smile on my part. I couldn't give up; they were your parents.

I offered my hand towards your mother. 'Hi, lovely to meet you both.' Another sniff followed. I withdrew my awkwardly dangling hand. 'Sorry, we're interrupting your meal. It's lovely in here, isn't it, the ambience?'

She cleared her throat before turning dark eyes to you. A shiver danced down my spine; those eyes, almost black in the subtle lighting. Perfect, that went well. The warmth in my cheeks crept upwards; I was aware that I was beginning to glow. Even better, cheeks to match my shoes. Like a gawky ten-year-old I hovered, fascinated by the obscurity in her eyes. Imploring you to make sense of the situation.

'When did you return home?' you asked, oblivious to my attempted conversation.

'Last night. Nice of you to ask!' she snapped.

'Did you do as I asked?' Ignoring her last gripe.

'Don't we always do as we're told?' she goaded you.

What were they talking about? Did what?

Your father didn't utter a word, continuing to munch at his dish indifferently. It was so odd. I don't think I've ever witnessed such a cold parental, maternal occurrence.

'What about the paperwork?' you persisted.

'At home. Thought maybe you'd come and see us one day. If you have time, that is. Or if you need something, more like,' she barked.

Paperwork for what? What had you asked them to do? You'd not mentioned anything. But then you'd not mentioned not getting on with your parents; or your mother, to be more precise.

'Fine. I'll have someone collect it in the morning. You did actually open it, didn't you?'

'The paperwork?'

'No. The bank account!'

What bank account? Where had they been?

'Yes. I just said we did, didn't I?'

'Good. Remember not to mention this to anyone.'

'Like who? We hardly see anyone any more, do we?'

You turned to me, smiling warmly. It threw me completely, the smile being so incongruent with the mood of our small gathering. I attempted another pathetic smile at your mother; she turned away, took a swig from her glass, opening conversation with your father. Our cue to leave. You turned away, ushering me out as brusquely as we'd come in. Back on the pavement I allowed the cold air to extinguish the flames encroaching my cheeks as we continued in silence, turning left up Bridge Street. What was that all about? I waited for you to enlighten me, your hand tense in mine. Instead you began to hum, without uttering a word for at least a further five minutes. Were you upset? I wondered. Finally, you found your voice.

You squeezed my hand. 'So, where to eat? I'm ravenous, are you?'

What the hell? Nothing? Nothing to say on the matter?

'Eve?' You playfully nudged my shoulder with yours. 'You hungry?'

'What the heck was that all about, Gregg?'

'What?' You looked genuinely surprised.

'What?' I asked. 'That, then, back in there with your parents. Why did you introduce me like that? Why did they behave as they did – or your mum, anyway? And what the hell were you both talking about? I mean, what did you get them to do?'

'Oh, I see. Listen, please don't take any notice. She's always the same. Rude. No etiquette whatsoever.' You shrugged off my horror.

'But you were pretty horrible to her too.' You ignored me. 'What have you asked them to do for you? What were you both talking about?'

'Nothing. It's not important. Forget about it.' The sound of our out-of-tune footsteps filled the chilly air some moments before you decided to embellish. 'She visited some properties for me over in Spain, on behalf of a client. He invests in overseas properties. That's all. I asked her to hand in some documents to his bank. Nothing more. I assumed it would be a pleasant trip for them, with it being an all-expenses-paid jaunt to Spain. But no, nothing makes her happy. Don't worry about it – she doesn't understand social conduct. That was normal behaviour for her.'

Your voice muted in my mind. Did you think the interchange was acceptable, normal or, despite explaining it away, were you perhaps as perturbed as me?

'But—'

'Please, Eve, not tonight. I've had some fantastic news today; this is tainting it for me. Please, trust me. Leave it be. She's not a pleasant person. It's unfortunate she's my mother, but so be it. So, for me, can we move on? Please.'

'Perhaps…'

'Believe me. There is no perhaps. Not with her.'

But why take me to meet them, if you knew how she would react? Knowing she would disregard me? How rude of her. It was more like some weird point-scoring ritual, than a mother-and-son get together.

You turned me slowly to face you. 'I am sorry you had to meet my parents at all, if I'm honest. There never would have been a good time. My mother is discourteous, unappreciative and embarrassing. My father is too faint-hearted to do or say anything about it. We rarely speak, ever.'

I couldn't even imagine how it had become so bad. My disappointment in you bowed to sorrow, such a sad situation. It didn't bode well for the future either. I didn't realise it then, but it would be the last I saw of them. I didn't realise it then, but they too were tools in your box.

Chapter Eleven

Cornwall 2016

Over time, despite my ever-watchful fight-or-flight response, my memory system very effectively boxed, then filed away, specific experiences. These boxes altered my perspective on both a conscious and subconscious level. They remain intact, undisturbed, until something you do, hear, smell, taste, touch or see triggers the opening.

I couldn't sleep last night for tossing and turning, listening for alien sound either outside or in. My eyes were heavy but my mind held me on alert. Then, at the rise of the sun, my mobile alerted me to two missed calls, incoming withheld calls at 03.08 and 03.12. What were you doing up at such an ungodly hour? Were you outside, watching? Did you really think I would pick up, or were you anxious for me to know you were thinking of me, even during sleep? I forgave Jack for his frustrating morning behaviours; I missed him not being with me. I couldn't run from the house quick enough. Whichever room I was in, whatever I was doing, I could feel you breathing down my neck.

Now, I draw up outside Lemon Street Clinic and peer down the street. No sign as yet of our overzealous traffic warden. I can't even use the old one of *being on call*. He knows who I am; I can't be on call at my own clinic. I've already tried. I've probably about ten minutes of safe time. He's on the larger size – it will take him a while to climb the street from the market area.

I burst through the clinic door.

'Hey. What's the rush? Could have made me jump, if I wasn't so knackered.'

'Traffic warden, I'm on borrowed time.'

'Running late this morning, by any chance, are we?' I squeeze past Ruan hovering in Reception and head straight for the filing cabinets.

'Slightly. Been stuck in the roadworks for the last twenty minutes. I wouldn't mind but as usual the workmen are invisible. I now have…' I glance at the clinic clock '… yep, twenty minutes before my next appointment in Mevagissey. I forgot to take the blasted files home with me last night, didn't I? All because I switched my briefcase yesterday for a lighter bag, then forgot my usual routine when I left last night, didn't replenish my stock of files.'

'That's not like you.' He smiles. 'Talk about cutting it fine.' He rubs tanned hands through his fair waves. 'Here, let me help. You're dropping stuff out the middle. I only sorted them for you yesterday.

And it took me most of the afternoon.' He hurries to me as I juggle all the silly open-ended A4 files in search of the only one I need. 'You're so going to be late.'

'Thanks.' I pile his open arms with files. 'It's fine. I'll make it, kind of, so long as I can just find this – oh, where is it? Why is it always the only one missing? I had it out before I left last night.' I continue to empty the entire contents of the filing cabinet.

'Wait. You mean the one for Milly Sanders?' Ruan quizzes me.

'Yes. Have you seen it, then?'

'You should've said. I've got it, haven't I?' He graces me with another childlike smile before casually wandering towards my room.

'Jesus, Ruan, are you trying to test me or what?' I follow him, half relieved, half exasperated. Ruan doesn't seem to have the words 'in a hurry' in his vocabulary. Is this a male thing? Between him and Jack, I'll end up with tachycardia.

'Hmm, no,' he utters slowly. 'You asked me to do some background work on it, remember? You know, the social media stuff.' His eyebrows rise.

A horrible sinking feeling – how did I forget this? It was only yesterday. Should I even be allowed out? 'Oh, God. I did, didn't I? How did you get on with it? Did you find anything interesting?'

'I've printed the relevant stuff off. You were right. Can you believe self-harming has its own clubs and signed-up members, the full monty? When did this become such a big thing? I mean, why would you?'

'It's complicated. A form of control, punishment, perceived relief, peer pressure. Also, one downside of public awareness: as much as we need to bring issues to people's attention, sometimes it can promote the condition, desensitise it in another twisted way.'

'There's literally so many websites, YouTube videos about it.'

'Hmm, somewhere along, it unbelievably became a with-it act, for some. Almost allowing them to feel part of a family. A cult-like membership. Not everyone obviously, but some. Those posting pictures online especially.'

'No shit. How come this stuff doesn't get taken down from the social media sites? Surely, it's policed?'

'You'd think so, wouldn't you? But you've seen for yourself. The "how to do it" guides are there for all to see. Exclusive memberships, the lot. Disgusting.' I flick through the papers. 'Thanks for looking into it for me. You know, I'm intending on contacting local schools with this. But the problem is, will they want to be involved? I mean, why open up new problems, to stretch the resources even further?

Pop it back on my desk, will you? I'll take a look at it properly tomorrow.'

'Kids are selling and buying drugs and smokes on these sites too, you know?'

I nod. 'Yep, prescription drugs, so-called brain-damaging recreational drugs, weed. At the hit of an emoji or a hashtag, I read about it.'

'Yeah. My niece was telling me, someone in her class has been suspended for handling drugs, weed.' Ruan says. 'She's thirteen.'

I shake my head. 'I can't tell you how often I hear these stories. It's a dangerous world for our teenagers. Suspension is hardly going to help, though, is it?'

'Not really. Only in pushing them further to the dark-side?'

'Exactly. These emojis; there's a fair amount of research out there about them. Teenagers are using them to communicate emotions, rather than use words. When we look at emojis, the same area of the brain is activated as if we're looking at a human face.'

'You're kidding?'

'Nope. So-called social intimacy.' I say. 'Helpful sometimes, for those who are struggling alone. But while there are emojis and hashtags – which are just as bad for self-harming, suicide and cyberbullying – we have a problem.'

'A proper problem.' Ruan adds.

I nod. 'Hidden coded languages, hidden dangers away from the eyes of the parents.'

My next client is Milly; eleven years old, referred for self-harming. I asked Ruan to check out any obvious links between her profile and online networks. I'm receiving frequent requests for help as self-harming and other similar problems become more common at such incredibly young ages. Some of these Internet sites have cult-like followings. Milly is one of the many I've seen; she isn't the youngest. Our previous case opened up an entire chamber of shocking shenanigans being channelled through various social media sites. Girls and boys in their teens and younger, actively scouting for followers as they demonstrated acts of self-harming.

Ruan moves away from my desk, hovering with something on the tip of his tongue. Looking at me in a fashion I keep noticing just lately. I brace myself.

'I've been thinking.'

'Go on.'

'I reckon you need a break.'

'Couldn't agree more. Just not possible, I'm afraid.'

A mock concerned frown creases his face. 'You should, you know. What is it they say? All work and no play makes Eve a dull girl.'

'Who are they, anyway? I often wonder who these voices of wisdom are, don't you? So-called experts on our well-being and life, clueless to context. How often do people use these unknown oracles to back up personal arguments? They say…'

He turns and walks away, wagging his finger at me. 'Just saying. I'll make you a coffee to run with,' he calls over his shoulder.

I finish putting together all I could possibly need. I could do with a break from my life in general. Perhaps even start again all over. I hear Ruan singing away; what would I do to spend a few weeks in his head? He dallies back with a flask of much-appreciated coffee.

'It's strong, I hope?' I ask.

'Yep, three heaped and a bit. I'll leave it on the window sill next to the front door. By the way…' he wanders off again '… you've had a referral come through from the PTSD charity.'

'Oh, yes?' I'm half listening, half concentrating. I really need to get going. Let me think, do I have everything? 'Can you just check out the window for me, Ruan, make sure our trigger-happy parking man isn't looming? What kind of a person is a traffic warden? Have you ever wondered? Where did it all go wrong?'

'Nope, you're okay.'

'One point to me, then, he's such a miserable guy. But I'd probably be too if everyone hated me for doing my job. Or does he enjoy the power, do you think?' Definitely the power. Ruan doesn't oblige me, he's still muttering about the new referral whilst stretching his neck to see further down the road.

'Where did I put those worksheets? Filing cabinet?'

'Yeah, so this referral, an ex-soldier or something similar. Sounds like he's in a bad way from what they told me – said they'll email you the details. He's been stationed out of the country for the last few years, I think they said, Pakistan, maybe? Retired now, though. I think so anyway. You can't fathom it, can you?' he continues.

'What?' I indulge. I really need to be more organised; this chaos drives me insane. My working memory is so stretched at the moment, stress, the ultimate memory enemy.

'That he's been out there, protecting us, fighting for his country, gets back and, well… nothing. Absolutely zilch! Dumped to get on with it. And—' Ruan continues. '—I know, it's outrageous. They're not offered any support really, our servicemen, expected to simply slip back into normal life. Too many of them are abandoned to deal with PTSD alone. Very sad.' It is so very wrong.

'Yeah, they mentioned PTSD. He's not from round here, apparently. He's from somewhere up-country. Warwickshire, I think it was, and he—'

'Aha, here they are. Right, love you and leave you, sorry, Ruan, got to fly.' I grab my magnificent hot coffee, push the front door open with my pointy impractical shoes, as always forgetting how heavy and solid it is. I run out onto the street, smiling to myself as I hear Ruan's voice fade after me.

'Oh, cheerio, Eve, have a great day! You too, Ruan. Oh, thank you, Eve. I much appreciate your interest. Let me—' he shouts before the door closes, rudely cutting him off mid-flow.

I precariously pile everything onto the passenger seat. Turn on the Bluetooth, so as to listen to voicemails from this morning as I drive. My car is becoming another version of my office. With each stretched to the maximum minute. But then, it's best this way, prevents my mind from wandering into dangerous territories. By the time I climbed out of bed this morning, my stomach was already gyrating around the room ahead of me. Vile familiar fluttering. Urging me to remember. You. I jumped out of bed as if it were on fire, busying and distracting myself as quickly as I could. But it never works, trying to push things from the mind; the imagination will not hear of it, insists we keep revisiting. A stretched elastic band, smacking you in the face, the further you attempt to push it away. I appreciate more than most, the only way is to grab it by the neck and deal with it. Reconcile, negotiate, or destroy.

Before I could stop myself, I texted Jack at his friend's too.

Morning - are you ok? x

Yeah Mum, why wouldn't I be? x

Exactly, why wouldn't he be? How can he be normal, when I behave in neurotic ways? He was twenty minutes down the road, for goodness' sake.

I texted Jack because I am scared. You will never let us go. Of all the decent men in the world, why the hell did I marry you?

No reason. Just saying hello! x

Cool x

But it's not cool, is it, Jack? Something tells me, you know – it's not. My little sponge. You're scared like me; neither of us wish to say. Speaking makes it real. I will not let him get to you, I promise. The hum of a 911 meanders through my mind. The sound of your breathing, the silent calls creating so much noise. Then the kitchen-door incident – no, that was fine; it was locked after all. I needn't have worried.

I flick through contacts on my dashboard computer. I'll have to call ahead; I'm going to be late. How do people manage to be so organised? Is it only me forever running around like the phantom headless chicken? I hear the other mums at school functions, talking of coffee, gyms, lunch dates and so on. How do they do it? How do they fit everything in? Are they up at 04.00? Not that I would do these things anyway: too many questions, too much gossip, not enough left-brain balance. I find myself slipping away from school gatherings of any kind. I like to keep my distance. Idle chit-chat, what's the point? Why would I want to know what Judy is hiding behind closed doors, what Sally has divulged to Julie? What Ann has manipulated out of Philippa. But what Philippa has over Ann, Julie, Sally and Judy? I can't be bothered. But it would still be nice to know how they manage their time.

'Good morning, Dr Fellows' surgery.' The super-efficient voice answers my call. Oh, God, what is your name? Think.

Got it. 'Sandra, hi, it's Eve Sands. I'm supposed to be with you, well, in truth – by now. Can you please let my client know I'm afraid I'm running a little late? Should be with you in about fifteen minutes, all being well.'

'Oh, hi. Of course. She's here but don't worry, lovely, no problem. I'll tell her for you,' she soothed.

Sandra goes on to mention something about a recent enquiry. Her voice shuffles to the back of my mind, a mottled voice in the background. I cut her off as quickly as I can. It's become an annoying noise. I'm not even sure if I said goodbye. I take my foot off the accelerator and let the car drift forward.

Warwickshire?

Ruan, definitely said the PTSD referral guy was from Warwickshire. He said he was from up-country somewhere, Warwickshire. I should have paid more attention. But thousands of people are from Warwickshire. Am I just being paranoid? No, someone has been following me, then last night someone was asking about me, knew where I live. Drove past my house, probably does so every day. But then, my details are all over the Internet. I advertise, encourage people to make contact. How stupid, careless. Maybe I'm just fusing one coincidental factor with my ugly past, and completely blowing it out of all proportion. It's not as if I've any hard evidence. Just a twisted version of reality. I'm looking for symptoms, so I'm finding them; every single ache and pain, inhalation and espying is attributed to the panic condition.

But deep down, I know the truth. My heart is telling me. My waiting is over. Time is never a true divide.

Ruan definitely mentioned Warwickshire.

Chapter Twelve

Hate is an insignificant word.

Despise. Scorn. Spurn. Utter contempt. The words circle, attacking me from above.

I do not sleep; injustice smarts deep inside my gut. Images scratched into my wretched mind. Each and every time I close burdened eyes.

I can't breathe, you're so near. I could have touched you the other day. Still, without conscience. No fear for consequence. Remember what they say, you son of a bitch: what goes around, comes around.

This I guarantee.

This isn't your kingdom; justice will be done.

Be waiting, I will catch you.

I'm willing to lay my life on it.

Chapter Thirteen

Cornwall 2016

I eventually arrive at the Mevagissey surgery. It gripes at me being late, especially as I'm seeing a child. As if they're not feeling nervous enough. I squeeze in beside the brand-new Audi, belonging to the new GP, Sandra divulged on my last visit, thinking it would interest me. She was wrong. I breathe in to inelegantly cuddle my car, climbing out in the eight-inch gap I've left. Pristine paintwork is an overrated liability living down here. I turn and catch a glimpse of my reflection in his glass. Thank God, it's imperfect. My cheeks are flushed from my overwrought journey, I feel dishevelled. I throw off my personal hat, replacing it with my clinician's.

Composed, I walk towards the seventies brick building. Leave it all at the front door, Eve. The words, fit to practice, spare capacity, echoing through my silenced mind. I shove them away. Life equals experience and experience equals a better clinician. Besides, I have no choice. Sometimes though, the responsibility of my work feels all too heavy and burdensome. Thankfully, most of the time, I'm a master of displacing my personal angst, boxing it away in the attic. Usually for night-time perusal.

I bundle through the heavy glass door, stealing a cursory glance around the waiting room, in desperate need of some TLC. I spot mum and daughter waiting, a partnership of apprehension. I smile in their direction then hurry on to sign in at Reception. I have the word 'psychologist' stamped on my forehead. I try my best to blur stereotyped suppositions. But we're still witch doctors for many. I'm not sure who looks more nervous, mum or daughter. The paradox, this child possibly feels so in control and mature partaking in self-harming behaviours, yet she now emits fragility and immaturity. Mental health symptoms proposing a mode of control, yet the truth is the absolute opposite. Lies, all lies. The conditions deceive and conquer, twist and distort the truth, then deactivate the mind they have thieved.

In my temporary room, I haphazardly abandon my briefcase in haste so to return to the waiting room. Taking to the edge of an inflexible seat, I perch next to the small girl. Blimey, these clinics don't always help; if I had to wait in here, I'd feel depressed too. I face the young, all-eyes expression, and smile. She looks to mum, as reality hits. I need to speak to mum but only once Milly has engaged with me. Knowing I've a very small window of time to build rapport, no second chances here. Her toned-down green eyes regard me before preferring to ogle her shoes. She is only a little younger than Jack, yet she already appears to hold the responsibility of the world on narrow shoulders. As does Jack at times. I feel a shooting pang in my heart for mum and daughter. Both of them wondering how they've got to this.

'Hi. Milly?' I ask, despite knowing.

'Yeah,' a falsely confident voice bounces back.

'I'm Eve, this must be mum. Clare?' I smile at mum. Milly nods after a swift peep at mum; as if to check she's still here.

She wishes for mum to take over, to speak with me instead, so I keep the conversation moving in her direction. A few moments later, Milly agrees to join me alone, wishing she hadn't agreed to being here at all. How can she explain to a stranger something she doesn't even understand? I make meaningless chat as we walk the corridor, her nerves buzzing around her like static energy. What connects us right now is the acknowledgment of her not wanting to be with me.

We sit opposite each other; her nails are bitten to the point of being sore, obscured by the chipped emerald-green nail varnish. Fleeting glimpses between me and clenching anxious fists. She has what look like marker-pen tattoos covering her right hand, and reaching up her left arm, as far as I can see.

I'm thinking, Milly is not normally an unconfident girl. Low self-esteem maybe, but not shy of craving attention. The nail-biting implies she is anxious, out of control of something. It's not just because of me, the undesirable stranger standing over her natural sureness. Her hair is cut in a modern style, requiring a degree of nurtured styling. She clearly cares about her appearance, yet chooses to disfigure it. Though, she may not view this as a choice, yet. A cry for attention, of any form. Insecure, definitely. Trauma, a possibility. Historic patterns, age, biology, behaviour and or environment? Last week, I visited a child of the same age, a mathematical genius, but her extreme left-brain dominance made normal daily social interactions so painful, she too turned to self-harm to escape her hostile world. Milly is different; her tattoos and subject biases communicate creativity, right-brain strength.

Confident enough to scribble all over her body, to wear bright green nail varnish, but she is at the moment insecure about something, someone. Did mum appear anxious? Has she learned this? She struggles with direct eye contact; this is in part her age, and also these unusual clinical circumstances. But mostly because she doesn't wish to be discovered, not by me anyway; only by the rest of her world. Her new temporary world. Often the most outwardly confident prove to be the individuals who seek the most affirmation and security. A confidence in acting the part, even the jester, paired with a low self-esteem. Confidence versus self-esteem. Often mistaken as the same. I'm confident in my ability as a therapist but my self-esteem hangs on something else, and has been smashed over the years. Milly is confident, but her self-belief system is on the floor.

I smile at her.

'Okay. Milly, tell me if I'm wrong, but I'm pretty sure you'd rather be anywhere else than sitting here with me right now.'

Wide eyes stare at me. Am I setting her a trap? I nod to assure her I'm not.

'Yeah, probably.' She nibbles on her non-existent nail.

'Yep, I think I'd feel the same too if I were you. Completely understandable, I promise you. Still, at least you're missing some time from school. That's got to be a good thing, yes?'

She allows the smallest of chuckles to escape.

We continue a little longer with informal chatter, until I receive a few more grins and nods. I already know a little relevant information to break the ice; I asked her mum to email me Milly's interests. Eventually the mature façade drops sufficiently for us to begin. Milly's hands have unclenched; she's gaining eye contact, despite shuffling in the uncompromising chair. But there is something else behind those eyes, an undisclosed heaviness. I have my concerns.

'Milly, can I just say, this is not the same as being at school. There are no right or wrong answers. I don't expect you to say or behave in a special way. I appreciate I'm a stranger, but I'm hoping, with time, you'll be able to talk to me about anything you want to. If I say something you don't understand, stop me, if I say something you disagree with, tell me, please. Deal?'

'Okay.'

'Great. So why do you think you're here today, with me now?'

She looks slowly to the ceiling, before back to me. Wondering what she is supposed to say, rather than saying what rolls off her tongue.

'Whatever comes first to mind, Milly.'

' ´Cos they… think I need help.' She shrugs her shoulders. 'I think.'

'They?'

'Yeah, Mum and her boyfriend. Miss James. They do.'

'Miss James, she's your school nurse?' I ask, making a mental note she referred to her mum's partner as *her boyfriend*. I already know they all live as a family, together. Does Milly not get on with him? I'll ask mum about this one, at some point. It could be Milly's way of reaching her mum's attention, or something more sinister. Or pure defiance.

'Yeah, she used to be, like, nice. But then she rang Mum. And it's caused loads of trouble at home. So I kind of don't think she's nice any more. She should have kept out of it.'

'Ahh, right, okay, I see. Do you think she may have been worried about you, though, Miss James? It's a difficult situation for her, Milly. I'm sure she thought she was helping you, that she was doing the right thing.'

'That's what Mum said, yeah.' She shrugs again, adjusting her seat. One thing I dislike about not being at the Lemon Street clinic. It's really hard to relax when you're so uncomfortable.

'Okay, we'll come back to why perhaps mum and Miss James think you need help. I'm only really interested in you and what you think. This is about you, Milly. This is your time. Do you think you need help? This is what is important to me.'

Milly's body language and demeanour tell me the answer; the words are almost irrelevant now. But then again, she needs to hear herself say it.

She shrugs, looking to her feet, inspecting them as they flex backwards and forwards.

'Milly, are you happy at the moment? As happy as you used to be? If you can think back to maybe last year?'

'Sometimes.' She pauses. I wait. 'But… no, not really. I'm not, no,' she divulges to the floor.

'Well, I'm guessing, it must be pretty horrible for you to feel unhappy?' I should know, I cannot help thinking. 'Even if it's only for some of the time. No one wants to be unhappy. But if there is a chance I can perhaps help you with this, Milly, would you like me to try, and help you? Together we can attempt to undo things, the bad bits, I mean. You needn't be alone. I will try and help you all I can. But this has to be something you are okay with.'

She nods, just a small child. I notice her algae-green eyes grow moist with tears.

'What do you do when you feel unhappy?' It's not always so obvious, when covered by layers of protection. Sometimes this is the first time the client hears themselves speak the behaviour; until this point, it is easier to ignore.

'I do stuff.'

I nod. 'Okay, what kind of stuff?'

'I hurt myself.' She subconsciously touches the tops of her thighs.

'So, when you're unhappy, you hurt yourself,' I repeat softly. 'What do you hope to achieve? What do you think hurting yourself will give you?'

'It makes me feel better about stuff.' She uses pain to relieve pain.

'Does it last, this feeling better?'

She shakes her head. 'No.'

'Do you believe it does help? You know, with whatever it is making you unhappy?'

'No.'

'This is what most people say, Milly. That little voice in your mind, the one that tells you you'll feel better if you hurt yourself. It tells you lies. It's nothing more than a bully. It cannot help you. It will only make things worse. But still, it convinces you each time, that it can help? Are you saying, it's the thinking about hurting yourself that sometimes makes you feel better, rather than hurting yourself actually stops you from becoming unhappy?' I expand in more detail on the difference.

'Yes,' she agrees.

'Who would you have turned to before, Milly, whenever you were unhappy, before this bully came along?'

'Mum.'

'So what has changed? Why not talk to mum now?'

'I can't tell her what I need to say.'

'What makes you think that?'

'I don't want to hurt her.'

'You think if you talk to mum, she'd be upset?'

'Mmm.'

So pain is better than the truth. How bad does the truth have to be?

'And by hurting yourself, Milly, do you think maybe that may upset mum, even more?'

'I suppose.'

There's something else she's not saying. Something she believes is even worse than self-harming. I feel sure. The things she won't talk about when I probe, I'm guessing are the root to her pain. The self-harming is a red herring. A very proficient one. It's not what we see with Milly that worries me.

Eventually, having explored other possible ways of seeking help, and prodding at potential triggers, I see Milly out and return to gather my belongings. Just as I'm refastening my briefcase, I notice the inside zip is open. I always keep it zipped; it contains business banking details and other personal information. I open the compartment further, to ensure all is still there. It is, but, strangely, so is an alien A4 envelope. Where's that come from? I remove it to investigate, but I'm interrupted by a resolute knocking at the door. Milly's GP pokes his head around the door for an update. I replace the envelope; it must be something I've forgotten about.

*

Following many more appointments and a particularly stretched day at various clinics along the English Channel, I finally retreat for home. Just as the dark is threatening to creep over, with the early stages of a most spectacular red and orange sunset fighting it for prime position. The coastal waters have taken on an almost charcoal colour and the intermingled sky, cast off the sunset, is coloured with pinks, silvers and pale blue hues holding on for dear life. The pinky aspects remind me of Milly. Earlier, having discovered the name of Milly's mum's boyfriend, I made a note to ask Ruan to do some digging. I could be wrong, but Milly's eyes were unusually bloodshot, especially given her age. She didn't seem to have the focus of someone I know to be bright, either. I'm hoping I'm wrong. But everything is caused by something.

Then, within an instant it all floods back, the issue of the PTSD guy from Warwickshire. I'd pushed it to a dark far corner of my mind. I need to speak with Ruan. I make numerous attempts to reach him on his mobile – no joy. I envisage him either propping up the bar in our local, The Wheal in St Agnes, or off contemplating waves. But then, with countless reliable haunts for mobile quiet time, where there is zero chance of finding a signal, and the reliable 'emergency calls only' words conveniently cover your tracks, the chances of reaching him feel hopeless.

Can I detach until morning? I'm so tired too, but an underlying protest from my belly impels me to deal with it. I refocus on driving, all the time willing

Ruan to gain a signal. Until then, just because I've a referral from someone who's relocated from Warwickshire, doesn't mean it has to be you. Does it? Am I totally losing all perspective? What will Ruan think of me quizzing him at this hour, especially as I practically ignored his earlier attempt to discuss it with me? But if I don't get hold of him, some point later, in the pitch-black dark of the night, my rationale will bail on me. I leave Ruan a voicemail, requesting him to call or text me. At the end I add, 'Ruan, this is important. I really do need you to call, tonight, please. Not your usual sometime soon. Oh, and I'm sorry for disturbing your evening.' Going on Ruan's past 'chill, everyone' demeanour, I thought I'd better communicate my urgency.

I cut away from the main route, opting to take the inland, 'have to be local or mad to drive' route. My wing mirrors are now outwardly devoted to both left and right hedgerows. Bracken scraping at my paintwork. I jump as my mobile buzzes from the passenger seat. With no obvious other traffic, I grind to a halt, relief daring to flash through me. Ruan must have received my message; he's texted me back. He's probably already swaggering up the hill away from the pub, plodding his drunken way to mine. I feel a tad guilty. He's so good-tempered – just as well with a neurotic boss.

I illuminate my screen. Strange, why is Ruan's caller ID displaying as an unstored mobile number? I don't recognise this number. Something to do with the poor signal? Fumbling to press the message icon, my fingers like sloppy sausages, I open it. My heart rate fast-tracks to the next beat. I impulsively fling my handset back to the passenger seat, as if it's on fire. Shit. The words trouncing my chest. The screen remains lit. I re-read the text, over and over, in case I've misread.

Busy girl, Eve. Not home yet. Jack is home alone again, I see. At least he has a friend with him. Don't worry, I'll keep my eye on them until you return. Drive safe, won't you? No hurry.

Chapter Fourteen

Before

Following the hiking expedition; life seemed to change so precipitously. The Gregg I'd fallen for; the Gregg I'd married, where did you go? I stumble across this situation in clinic, so how did I allow myself to fall into the very trap? The mélange of lies, an existence behind locked doors; the very same I assist other victims with. How many hours have I squandered since, attempting to justify my susceptible-beyond-belief behaviour? Still, I have Jack, and I would never change this, not for the world. Not even for my freedom.

All the same, as most of the others do, I repeatedly feel the need to defend myself. To others sometimes, but mostly to myself. How can an observant, apparently intelligent being behave so obliviously? How does a marriage fall apart in such a titanic way? So you didn't notice the gigantic iceberg? Nor the monstrous tendencies? *There but for the grace of God go I*; John Bradford could not have said it better. Cruel words and judgments may not always be voiced, but I see it in the eyes. Do people have the right to judge, with no idea of perspective?

I once made the mistake of opening up to a hospital colleague before we relocated. I don't know why I was so taken aback by her questions, given I'd already asked them of myself so many times. But when others probed, it felt more like an attack, accusation.

'I don't get it, Eve. Why did you get together in the first place? If he was as cruel as you say?'

Her expression morphed from one of sympathy to one of scepticism. I should have lied; said we'd come to a mutual agreement to separate. He was killed in our car accident. Anything but the truth.

'Obviously, he wasn't like that in the beginning! I wouldn't have married him knowing what I do now. If I'd seen what I do now, I'd have stayed well clear. I'm not stupid!' Or was I?

'He couldn't have changed that much, surely?' she prodded further, a slight frown running across her forehead. Slanted eyes scrutinising me. Wondering if she'd got me wrong. She had a point.

I could feel my defensive barriers begin to lower. 'Well, he did.'

'How, so quickly, then?'

'I don't know. Clearly, I was utterly blind to all the flying flags. Maybe I chose not to see.' A 'surely not' look cross-examined me. 'I was a fool. Okay.'

'Just like that—' she clicked her fingers '—he became a different person?' God, dog with a bone.

'If you're trying to make me feel any more wretched, it's not possible.' She jerked her head backwards, offended. 'Look, it's not so much that he changed. So much as I woke up, when he began to show his true colours. He didn't change per se; he'd more… kept his true self well hidden. In the beginning he was, I guess, acting, playing the part. Then, after it was all too late, I'd signed the dotted line, he quit the acting. Only then did I truly see who he was. As much as it grates on me to admit it, he's a very astute man. A master of disguise.'

'Why did you stay with him for so long, then? I mean years, wasn't it?'

My reasoning was not hitting the right places. Unless people have had dealings with a psychopath, it's so difficult for them to comprehend either of our motives.

'I understand why you ask, Emma, but, to be fair, it's because you're still considering us as – how can I put it? – two normal people in a normal marriage. Stand outside your own box for a minute. You're a psychologist. Come on. Sometimes it's not what we see, or what we're told, but what we don't see, what we're not told! People need to be more open to what defies the visual reality. I thought you of all people would understand, because, if you don't, what chance do I have? I didn't leave because I couldn't!' I was cross with her, which wasn't fair. This was why it was best not to engage in these conversations, I thought.

From then on, I'd allow such questions to drift yonder. My chronicles were at the mercy of, not what people knew, but what they didn't know. My truths were obscured, hidden by societal perceptions, which were discreetly manipulated by what they saw and heard. In the end, both you and I played our part in obfuscating the truth.

'Look, Emma. I explain this to people I see as the Egg Timer Effect. Initially, the dominant partner appears attentive, charming, kind. As the glass and sand is, at the base of the egg timer, the relationship is full, rounded, complete; perfect. Some time on, at the correct point in the relationship – once the psychopath has sufficiently ensnared its prey, bewitched the prey's allies – the egg timer is rotated. Furtively, gradually, the care mutates to control and ownership. The charm morphs to belittling and scorn. Changes ever so discreetly slither through bit by bit, until your world has dropped away entirely. From the outside, and this is where the psychopath excels, your timer looks exactly the same as it always has. Perfect.'

'Crikey. You wouldn't think it would be that easy, would you?'

'Indiscreet criticisms tiptoed by. References to my deviations; my hair, my weight, my posture, my clothes, my make-up.'

She nodded along.

'He'd say things like: "Are you really wearing that this evening?"

"That colour lipstick again; is the light working in the bathroom?"

"Perhaps you should try a new hairdresser. Or is it your diet?"

"Do you really think you should be eating such an amount?"'

'Nice,' she said.

'Constant little pointers to my inadequacies: my cooking, my time management, my messiness. Snowballing reproaches towards those close to me; friends, family.'

'Poor Eve.'

'Knock after knock. Day on day. One week after the other. A slow torture, weakening the soul. Dividing and conquering. Isolating. Slowly leading you by the hand up the wobbly pathway to psychosis.' I stopped to breathe. 'Then, the classic – *"Are you sure you're mentally stable?"*

I think Emma got my point.

But to you, I failed. I didn't fulfil your desires for me. I observed; I absorbed. I took your hand and walked so far. But I didn't walk on to the end of the path. I took shelter, regathered and bided my time, learning the rules of your game. You hadn't calculated for this; no one says no to you. No one.

It took patience. Heartache and forbearance.

Even so, the only possible outcome is that I will never be the same again.

*

Seven months pregnant, I sat, dumped in your golf clubhouse. Coaxed into being the chauffeur for the evening. Why did I go along with it? Because I was still walking along your path. Vulnerable with hormonal changes; being the dutiful wife. However, I learned valuable things this night. I situated myself in the corner; an antique wannabe fatigued chair took my weight. Beige in colour, anything but its pretentious aspirations. Where did they actually find this stuff?

I fetched my mobile from my handbag, but still no saviour text messages. No missed calls. Where was Sam? I glanced over to where you and your disciples were, propping up the dribbling, sticky bar. One man trying to outdo the other; you, as to be expected, holding pole position. Suddenly feeling wearily tired, I allowed my head to fall back against the headrest. Hoping it wasn't previously occupied by a Brylcreem-wearing golfer.

Attempting to clear my mind, I practised the diaphragmatic breathing technique I'd learned on a course that week. In through the nose for seven, out through the nose for eleven. It was supposed to initiate my natural relaxation response; reset my system to baseline. But just as I'd negotiated the only quiet spot in the room, a rather loud crowd of men decided they too wanted to get up-close and personal in the corner. Not so much next to me as practically on top of me. I was evidently invisible. I attempted to super-focus on my heartbeat; to blur out their voices and induce calmness. But their non-dulcet tones superseded any such intentions.

'My word, you were playing so well, Jonny boy! Game was practically over by the back nine.' A rosy-cheeked Jonny smugly accepted the gushing praise. Had I been magically transported to a Jeeves and Wooster set without realising? Surely people didn't genuinely speak in this manner? It sounded so uncomfortable too. A tray crammed to capacity with drinks chinked its way to their table, reminding me of how much I was gasping for a drink; clearly you had forgotten, and no way was I going to remind you of my existence in the room. Or push my way through the crowded bar.

Jonny rested his hand on the headrest of my chair, consenting to the offering of his free drink; desperately needing something to dilute the lashings of syrupy mutterings he was being showered in. If I could have been bothered, I'd have moved.

'For Christ's sake, I hate clubhouses,' I muttered under my breath. Though I needn't have worried; they were all far too self-indulged to hear me. It was every reason I'd refused to take up golf, these behaviours, and the appalling dress code. I checked my mobile again, in a desperate need to call a friend, ask for help. A horrible thought crossed my mind. Friends? I only had Sam left. It had been easier to let all the others go. In the end, I'm sure they, too, were waiting for me to release them from their friendship duties. Countless times I'd made excuses, stood them up, sent them home early from gatherings at home. Justified your abruptness; rudeness. It became such hard work to keep friends.

At the back of my mind, I still hoped this was just a phase with you. Perhaps you were simply feeling the pressures of work. Your hours had increased to something ridiculous; so many after-work dealings and meetings, sometimes into the early hours. Maybe you were stressed? Was I being unsupportive? But what about Joe? I was struggling to forgive you for what you did to Joe. Threatening him; not you personally – you contracted someone else to do it. I've never been able to grasp what went on; Joe barred my calls, though. He told Sam he didn't want contact with me anymore; he'd apparently had a lucky escape. One of your disciples made an impromptu visit to his home, the evening we were in the Lake District. You laughed it off when I confronted you on the issue.

'*You're better off without friends of his ilk; so weak. A loser"*, you informed me. *A true friend would defend his right to be so!'*

The following week I discovered I was pregnant.

I shifted in my seat, allowing for my discomfort at the memories.

I called Sam again. 'Jesus, Sam, come and rescue me, please. You said you'd be here by now. Where the hell are you?' This was the third voicemail I'd left. Either she couldn't face it either and was playing truant, or she'd decided she would rather slowly pull out all of her eyelashes, one by one. I wouldn't have been there either if you hadn't insisted. Which was an odd one for me. I was beginning to learn, when drink was at the party, I might as well not be. You were always oblivious to my company. Then, there was the point when I realised I became grateful for this.

My ponderings were rudely interrupted again by my adjoining crowd. 'How did you find it, Fred? Did your new spikes work out? Expensive, were they? Yes, thought as much. I wouldn't buy cheap either.' I found myself studying them with interest. Why did they insist on wearing such ghastly clothes at these clubs? If I had to look at one more pair of salmon-coloured trousers with coordinating shirt and—

'Can I take this?'

A ruddy-faced, boorish man pointed at a tub chair to my side. His entire party were staring at me in silence. *My gosh, would you believe it, there's a woman, alone in our clubhouse. Who the devil let her in? Where is her man?*

'Sure.' I nodded. But didn't you miss out those humble words, excuse me, please, and thank you? I thought. Still, no need to be courteous when you had lashings of ego. Ego, I pondered – ego or insecurity. I wondered, had he always spoken as if he had dog poo parked under his nose? How awfully unpleasant for him. I really shouldn't think so badly of the afflicted.

Jesus, where was Sam?

I resigned myself back into the headrest, deciding to listen to their conversations for research purposes. A possible paper on the battle of egos and the correlation of trousers, colours matching all the flavours of ice cream. Could I get a research grant for this? Probably, given the other ridiculous projects I'd heard of. The nation's favourite way of removing tomato ketchup from a bottle. Did bereavement have an effect on mood? And the likelihood of developing mild situational depression shortly after experiencing loss.

'I've just realised who that is at the bar,' I heard Jonny say, alerting me further.

'Who? You mean Gregg Austin?'

'Yes. But who's he with?'

They all craned their necks. 'Well, there's a story.' Raised eyebrows everywhere. 'No, seriously, you really don't want to know. He's...' He began to explain, but his voice became smaller and smaller, then he was interrupted. Wait a minute, the balding man with the offended face hadn't finished what he was about to say. I wanted to know who he was too. I leant in further to the group, but it was no use, they were speaking in reduced tones; typical. I managed to catch the odd word. Spain. Overseas. Buy-to-lets. Bank manager. But it was all too disjointed.

'Just stay away. I've heard, on good authority, he's bad news.' He tapped his potted nose. 'Seriously. Trust me on this one.'

With a mutual understanding of trepidation in the air, something I was beginning to feel akin to, they resumed their independent incoherent speeches. No interactive conversation to be had anywhere. No one listening; everyone talking. A wave of nausea washed over me. What did they know about you? Who was the man? And why for the first time in the evening did they feel the need to whisper? You didn't need to be up to anything, your reputation was sailing, or so I'd thought. Why would you do anything to damage it? Perhaps it was just jealous speculation. Dangerous hearsay. Sometimes these men could be gossipier than the females. All of them desperate to get one over on the other.

I changed my mind: I hated people-watching. Sam had better have a good excuse. I slinked further down into the beige velvet-imitation chair; reached my mobile for the last time, praying for Sam to pick up.

'You cannot use that in here,' reverberated a voice from nowhere.

I jumped in my seat and looked up to see an apple-red shiny-faced woman staring at me. Addressing me in a tone a five-year-old would have found condescending. To add to the insult, she was dressed like a character from a low-budget town-hall pantomime. Noddy sprang to mind. I wished I could have consumed alcohol. She continued to glare at me, then began a strange dance, waving her arms in my face. Did she think I was deaf?

'Are you talking to me?' A rhetorical question; I couldn't resist.

'If you want to use that—' pointing at my mobile '—then go outside. Phones are not permitted in the clubhouse. So, if you don't mind.' She jerked her eighties-permed head backwards towards the clubhouse door. Did she not have any friends to advise her? Though rich, coming from me.

Had I missed something? At what point did it become acceptable to be so blatantly rude, so completely obnoxious? Maybe there was a notice at the door informing no manners allowed in the clubhouse? I was the one being sensually abused from all imaginable directions. My ears and eyes subjected to an onslaught of invasively loud experiences from the ice-cream crowd, yet Noddy felt offended as I'd discreetly, minding my own business, pressed my mobile to my ear. If I'd been any more discreet, I'd have disappeared into the bland wallpaper.

Was it just English clubhouses or was this a worldwide golfing phenomenon?

I glared back at Noddy. I couldn't be bothered. She'd also successfully managed to draw your drunken attention in my direction. You began to orchestrate people and furniture to reach me; you didn't look happy. I ungracefully seized my belongings and left the sitting area as she observed, ensuring I did as I was told. I couldn't be bothered to discuss the incident with you, being such a social conformist if it suited. I quickened my steps to the ladies' toilet, somewhere you wouldn't follow, childishly pretending I hadn't noticed your advancement.

Why hadn't Sam at least texted me?

We'd been best friends since school. Up until the time I introduced her to you, we'd never had any real disagreements. When we were younger we spent hours talking about how we'd make our fortunes. But our career choices divided, orientating us in diverse directions. Sometimes, I still wished we'd followed our dreams. But life's tide swept us adrift. I followed the sciences, but Sam always had something I didn't: the gift of the gab; she moved into sales. We remained firm friends. Our only bone of contention being you.

'I don't get it, Eve. He's not right for you. I never thought you'd be with someone like Gregg. I don't mean to be horrible. You'd tell me, if it was the other way round,' she told me over a girl's night in. Chopsticks chasing rice around the silver container.

How could she say such things? I didn't understand either; I'd honestly believed she'd love you. You were probably more her type than mine, with all your showy charisma. You were at your most charming when the two of you first met. I didn't want to believe it, but I had to wonder if perhaps Sam was a tad jealous.

I put down my squashy container, catapulting the chopsticks across the already-food-smeared table, drawing my legs in closer to me. 'What? Why are you saying this? I don't get it. I thought you'd approve.

Really, Sam, how can you even say these things? I'm really surprised at you, to be honest,' I retorted.

'It's just something about him. He's a bit too…'

'A bit too, what?'

'A bit too full of himself.'

I did notice how the two of them eyed each other. Felt a little as if they were in competition for their place in my life. So many unsaid words between them. But I put it down to them both being dominant people. Behaving like animals, vying for pack leadership.

'I find him a bit, kind of, creepy. Smarmy.' She began to put her shoes on, avoiding eye contact. 'Look, at the end of the day, if he makes you happy, then great. Maybe I'm wrong. Like I said, I can't see him being the one for you…'

How could she be so harsh? I shook my head at her. 'That's because you don't know him. You've only just met him; you've hardly given him a chance. You know, I actually thought you'd be happy for me,' I snapped. It was important for me to have Sam's affirmation. But if she was going to be selfish, make me choose between them, I wouldn't appreciate being backed into a corner. 'He's such a confident guy, maybe this makes you feel, I don't know, uneasy?' She did always seem a little uncomfortable around him, when I thought about it.

'No, Eve, it's nothing to do with that. Do you even know me? I can speak to anyone. I used to work in cold-calling, for God's sake. It's really not that…' She reached for her jacket thrown over the sofa.

'Well, you're wrong. Look, you may as well leave. I'm pretty tired anyway. It's not as if you have anything nice to say – what's the point in you staying? We'll talk about it another time, or not.'

'Eve, you asked me for my honest opinion. You should have said if you wanted me to lie! If you want the absolute truth – I don't trust him. Okay, that's what it is. I don't think… I don't think you can be happy with him. What you see, maybe…'

'Just go, Sam, please.' I turned away to the sound of Sam's under-breath mutterings then a slammed door. I threw away the Chinese remnants, sat up, waiting for you to return home.

It was just before midnight when you found me asleep on the sofa. 'You're better off without friends like her,' you whispered. Where had you been? You were only supposed to be meeting a colleague for an hour after work.

I would like to say they reconciled their differences after a while, but they didn't. On the surface they had a relationship built on a mutual respect for each other's position in my life. But it was cold being in the same room as them. I had to accept they didn't and probably never would see eye to eye.

You told me Sam was a bad influence; it made me giggle. You said you couldn't trust me when I was with her. Strange. Sam claimed I couldn't trust you. It was simpler not to be with either of you. I didn't grasp this was exactly what would happen anyway. Sam went first; then you later on.

She'd let me down. She wasn't going to come and rescue me from the toilets.

Lost in thought, I found myself slumped in a 1980s rejected pastel armchair, in the corner of the ladies' room. The alternative being Noddy and co or a drunken you. I'd have left, but I knew you wouldn't call a taxi; you'd still drive home despite the alcohol. A previous bone of contention between us. I made myself as relaxed as possible, my bag and coat scrunched on my lap in a defensive manner. I must have dozed off, as I was woken by the persistent voice of a concerned toilet visitor. She obviously thought I'd fallen into a drunken stupor, despite my huge bump; she was speaking to me in a loud, exaggerated voice. The same voice people used when speaking to someone of a foreign tongue.

'Are. You. Okay?' A crinkly finger belonging to an orange face prodded my arm. 'Do. You. Need. Me. To. Fetch. Someone. For. You?'

I quickly sat myself up. 'No, I'm fine. Thank you, though, for asking.' I answered her as eloquently as I could, stuffed in the toilet chair. The last thing I needed was more attention. However, she was insistent on there being a problem, continuing in the same tone.

'Oh. Are. You. Here. With. Someone?'

I was tempted to reply, 'No, I'm not. I often find myself asleep, alone in golf-club toilets. Do you think it's unusual? Doesn't this happen to you, then?' But I gave her what she needed to carry on with her own business so I could continue with my evening, in the toilet. When I thought about this, it was becoming a bit of a habit.

My watch assured me it was 1.10 a.m. Thank God, surely it was time to leave. I needed to be up at 6.00 a.m. for work, just a few hours. Odd, you hadn't attempted to find me? Maybe you'd texted me and I'd not heard my phone. I really hoped not; it would infuriate you. I checked. Strange. Nothing from you, no excuses from Sam either, yet I had full signal. I dragged myself out of the surprisingly comfortable chair, checked my reflection in the mirror, before leaving to find you. Again the feeling of sickness crept over me. Surely at seven months pregnant I should have been tucked up cosy in bed. I placed my hand on my stomach; in response to the floaty, fluttering sensation. Normal? Or was it butterflies?

Leaving the safety of my den, I was sorry to see the party still in full swing. The ice-cream brigade noticeably louder, even more animated. Odd though, as I made my way to the bar area, there was no sign of you. I crept and stumbled around the drunken bodies with matching puerile behaviours, nothing worse when you were stone-cold sober, until I exhausted every possible dark corner. You were definitely missing. I felt a momentary feeling of relief. Shouldn't I have been worried if you were okay? Did I need to be concerned? I'd be in trouble again, if you thought I'd abandoned you. My stomach churned, though my head questioned the audacity of you. I decided to leave alone. Holding on tight to the impetuous feeling, knowing it could surreptitiously slip away by the morning, turning to trepidation.

After a slow, thoughtful drive home, I pulled through the black iron gates onto the stone driveway. I was surprised to see we had company. The house was not in darkness, as I'd anticipated. Two unrecognisable cars sat outside. Should I be worried? What if they were intruders? I was about to waltz in with no concern. I hesitantly dragged myself from the car, my heart all the time picking up pace. Should I retreat, go to Sam's? Try your mobile again first? What if it wasn't you inside the house?

I stood for a while hovering from foot to foot at the front door, wondering what to do. It must be 2.00 a.m. Who on earth could be inside? Wasn't this the most common time for burglars? Then through the glass side panels, I noticed lights from the study at the opposite end of the reception hall. I peered further in, maintaining a reasonable distance. My heart moving up into my mouth, mingling with the sickly feeling. I could see dark silhouettes of masculine figures with their backs to me; I couldn't quite work them out. I didn't instantly recognise them. On the other hand, they were not exactly ransacking the house. So, unlikely to be burglars. Then, I saw you. You were there. Gesturing and articulating. Relief flooded through me, followed by annoyance. What about me, your pregnant wife? Thanks for giving a damn!

For one stupid moment, I considered stomping through the party, making a scene; demanding you explain yourself. Would you still feel so clever and powerful in front of your disciples? Then I thought better of it. I ever so quietly opened the door and stepped into the hallway, softly closing the door behind me. Holding my breath, I slipped off my shoes so as to tiptoe across the hall towards the sweeping stairway. At least I could go to bed, pull the duvet over my head. But then, halfway up the stairs, I stopped in my tracks. Something gripped my throat, choking me. Who were those men in my house? Because I know I didn't imagine it – one of them just mentioned a gun. I stiffened, unable to remove my hand from the rail, though I couldn't hear anything over my heart. A gun?

Frozen to the spot, I lowered my head to listen. More laughing; then something about a done deal. You were talking about your firm's partner's son? Who was based in the same office as you; something about him being fresh, nineteen, workable. Poised footsteps on the hard floor alerted me, emboldening me to move. Upwards quickly. I reached the top, but slightly wrong-footed the final stair, my handbag clunked me on the back of my head as I pushed my arms forward to break the fall. I held my breath for the worry of being heard. In my own house. Nothing, so I gingerly stood, thankful for the acoustics of a galleried landing. I waited, lurking in the shadows of our bedroom door. Chairs shuffling. Someone was leaving, saying their goodbyes. I stepped back further into the dark of the doorway. I saw one of the unidentified men open the front door, whilst turning to speak. It was the man I'd seen you with earlier at the bar. The same man the loud group next to me were whispering about. What the hell were you up to?

Without caring to undress, I fell into bed. What had I got myself into? More to the point, what was this baby going to be born into? My mind hurtled down dead-end options. Maybe it would all feel better in the morning. You would have a perfectly reasonable explanation for the entire evening and the strange man. But you didn't even know I'd arrived home. You obviously didn't care. I'd kind of come to terms with this in the last few months. A painful acceptance of hurt. I just didn't know what to do about it.

But something else felt so very wrong.

Alarm bells calling.

Why would they mention a gun?

Chapter Fifteen

Cornwall 2016

Oh my God.

You are there with Jack.

You are watching Jack.

You could by now be with Jack. In our home.

What if you have taken Jack?

Please, someone help.

I'm thirty minutes from home. Jesus, I need to stop for petrol. Why didn't I fill up this morning? Idiot, Eve. I glance at my fuel gauge, begging it to have acquired extra fuel from somewhere. Flicking through computer options on the steering paddle, I see the fuel has fallen from twenty-five to five, in a spin of a coin. Metallic essence sits on my taste buds as blood surges to vital organs. Why tonight? After all this time, all these years, the night I'm not there, Jack is alone, the dark shadow finally returns. Missing, hoped dead, all this time. Why tonight?

My foot presses firmer on the accelerator. Conscious of being restricted by the lanes I'm travelling, I recklessly tear along. Fifth gear to second gear feeling each sharp twist, making the most of sporadic straights. I swear I'm moving further away.

An oncoming car senses my urgency – I'm not stopping for anyone – and obligingly reverses into a gateway. Come on, come on, faster, hurry up, I urge.

I reach out, grabbing at my disappearing mobile. Damn, it slides off the passenger seat, clattering down the side of the door. For Christ's sake. I need my mobile to get hold of Jack, check he's okay. Should I tell him, warn him? Or are you bluffing? No, how would you know Jack is home alone, has a friend with him, if you're not watching him? Keeping my eyes on the road, I stretch to my left, desperately trying to grasp the mobile; my fingers skim the smooth surface, pushing it further away. I jump on my brakes, release my belt, and begin to frantically scratch around in the darkness. Got it. The screen illuminates the text. The text that changes everything. Years of wondering; hoping. Subliminal waiting.

Stupid, stupid woman, Eve. I knew you'd catch us. How have I allowed this to happen? Bumbling fingers flick through my contacts in a 'more haste, less speed' fashion until Jack's face is looking back at me; I hit the green call symbol. Blasted, blasted voicemail. No dial tone, just a flipping voicemail.

Who else?

My hands quiver, making clumsy mistakes; dialling people I haven't spoken to in years. My mobile responding to me, with a delayed reaction. I eventually locate our landline number; I cannot for love or money recall it. Nobody uses our landline. I momentarily picture the last time it was ringing. Jack and I sat on the sofa, staring uninterestedly at it, then at each other. Deciding it was odd, couldn't be important, then opting to ignore it. Irresponsible! Why hadn't I taught him to pick up? It could be important.

Please, please, Jack, please pick up the goddam phone. I call it three times.

He doesn't pick up. I try Ruan again in vain. What's wrong with everyone? I set off, mobile grasped in my left hand on the steering wheel. Before long, a bright fluorescent light looms, an oncoming petrol station; approaching far too fast, I brake hard to swerve in. Filling my car just enough to reach home, I dash in to pay. As I'm jumping from foot to foot in the small queue, I think of Bea. She lives on the Porthtowan crossroads with her boyfriend; it's only eight minutes' drive from our house. I throw a note on the front desk, explaining I'm on an emergency call, and dash back to my car to locate her number, as I leave the garage at speed.

'Hi, Evie?'

'Bea, oh, Bea, thank God.'

'Hey, what's up? What's wrong, lovely?'

'I'm trying to get hold of Jack. I'm really worried about him. He's not answering his mobile or the landline. But I know he's at home. I've tried Ruan –

he's not answering either. Please, I'm so worried, can you get over to mine now? Find Jack for me? I'm still a while from home, you see. I really wouldn't ask if I wasn't desperate. I'll explain later. Please.'

'Oh, Evie, is everything okay? What's the problem? He's probably not got a signal, that's all. You know what it's like living here. I'll go, though, sure I will, it's not a problem at all, but why are—?'

'Bea, sorry. I can't go into it all right now. I'm really scared – I wouldn't ask you otherwise. Please can you get to mine? It's urgent. Trust me.'

'Sure, don't worry. I'll go now. But what do I say to him? To Jack when I find him?'

'That doesn't matter. Please leave now. Call me when you have him.'

'Okay. I'm on my way.'

'Oh, and, Bea?'

'Yes, lovely?'

'Is Matt home with you?'

'Yes, why?'

'Take him with you. Don't go alone. Don't go without him. Promise you'll leave this minute. With Matt?'

'But—'

'No, Bea. Now's not the time. Leave now and take Matt.'

I hang up. The adrenaline rush burns at my cheeks as the shivering spreads from my hands towards my feet. I'm really hoping Bea understood my urgency and doesn't hang around, matching shoes and jackets et cetera. I hate myself for sending her blind into the situation. The only consoling thought is you wouldn't touch Bea or Matt. Would you? You'd hide in the shadows, observe maybe, but I'm as sure as I can be you wouldn't confront them. It's not your style. It's me and Jack you want. Or is it just me? But you know Jack is your only pathway to me.

I frenetically make my way home, silently imploring someone to make contact, to reassure me. It flashes through my mind: I'm not really sure what I'll do if, when, you and I come face to face again. So much time has passed between us. I haven't set eyes on you since the night of the car accident. No one has. My stomach somersaults as I have absolutely no idea of what I am driving into. I'm lost in panic when a shrill noise eventually pierces the air, causing me to jump. My mobile, vibrating through the rigid left hand – please, God, let this be Jack. I squint to make out the caller ID. It's Bea.

'Bea, are you there? Have you found Jack?'

'We're at yours, yes. We've been knocking for a while. There's no answer, Evie. The lights are on, though, downstairs and upstairs. What do you want us to do?'

My chest tightens; the in-breath hurts. 'Shit. Have you looked through the windows? There's no sign of Jack at all?' Of course, there isn't; she just said so. She's not stupid. It's not as if we live in a huge house, and he's unable to hear the knocking. Why the stupid questions?

'Try not to panic. Matt's going over the wall now, to get to the back of the house. He'll check the back door, and make some noise on it, see if Jack hears him from there. Where are you? How far away?'

'I don't know, ten minutes maybe. Can you ask Matt to smash the small panel of glass in the kitchen back door? He'll be able to put his hand through then, and turn the key. We usually leave it in the door.'

'Really, Evie? You're that concerned? You'll be home in a minute with a key.'

'I'm out of my mind, Bea. Please, just ask him to do it.'

'Look, Jack could be upstairs. You know what he's like, listening to loud music, and can't hear us knocking from down here.'

'Can you hear music, then?'

'No. But… hang on, just a sec, Eve.' I listen to Bea's muffled voice speaking to someone, thanking them, '*no, everything's fine,*' she's advising them, and no, they don't need any help. 'Sorry about that, Eve, just some random guy asking if there's a problem.'

Surely not. Surely even you wouldn't be so barefaced. 'Who? What guy? Where is he?'

'No idea. He's gone now, I think. Anyway, I'll go and find Matt, tell him what you said. Just get yourself here safely. Okay. Don't be driving like a lunatic. Eve? Eve? Are you still there, Eve? Hello?'

A strange intermittent buzzing disrupts our conversation. I take the handset from between my shoulder and ear, pulling the screen into focus. Jack's face. It's Jack. Jack is calling me. Oh, thank God. I cut poor Bea off without explanation.

'Hello? Hello, Jack? Jack?'

A torrent of warmth drains through me, as I'm greeted by a gruff oblivious voice. 'Yeah, Mum, were you trying to call me? I've got loads of missed calls from you.'

'For pity's sake, Jack. Where are you? Why haven't you answered my calls?'

'At home, why? What's the problem? I didn't know you were calling me.' As soon as he says this, I picture him slumped on his bed, back against his wall, playing on his Xbox with an online friend, with headphones on. Ignorant to the outside world. Unaware of my sheer state of dread. Unconscious of you, looming in the shadows.

'Are you on that game? With your headphones on? On your own?'

'Yeah, why?'

'No matter.' You were wrong, then; you didn't know after all – you said Jack was not alone at home. 'Just thought you might have brought someone back with you, nothing more.'

'No. Oh, yeah, Fyn came back for a bit. He's just left. Why? What's wrong? Why are you being weird?'

I didn't want to hear this, Jack. I really didn't.

'I'm not being weird. I worry if I can't get hold of you, you know I do. Doesn't matter now. Forget about it. I'll be home in a jiffy.'

I tell him to go downstairs this instant, to let Bea and Matt in, make them a cup of tea, and have some form of conversation until I arrive. I hope to God he does this before Matt smashes any windows. Now I'm able to catch my breath, I understand I've so much explaining to do. What on earth am I to tell Bea and Matt, Ruan too? I must have dropped a further three or four panicky voicemails on his mobile, he'll pick up any time soon. I didn't care at the time, at the mercy of my emotions. But then this is how you took control in the first place, isn't it? Have me reacting like a paranoid, hysterical woman with no obvious motivation. A heavy feeling starts to weigh me down, the aftermath of a surging adrenaline and cortisol party. A most debilitating hangover without the associated frivolities.

As I arrange my car alongside the wall, I notice a dark masculine figure marching swiftly towards me, intent in his stride, seemingly gaining pace at sight of my arrival. I remain still, too frozen to move; my eyes too tired to make him out. I haven't planned what happens next. I don't know what to expect or what to do. The sharp end of my car keys buries into the flesh of my hand, as I squeeze tight in a fight to regain some control. Straining to distinguish the approaching ghost of a figure. Should I make a run for my front door? But my legs are paralysed, unwilling to budge. I'm sitting prey. It's the recurring nightmare, trying to run from something sinister, my legs refusing to cooperate, stumbling and falling. Vulnerable and exposed, I await my fate.

The figure begins to wave a hand at me as it draws closer. I exhale, as I just about determine the expressions of Ruan. My encumbered head falls into my hands, I'm so exhausted. All I want to do is retreat, lock the doors and hide away in the dark. Stick my head in the sand with a glass of something strong. Keep dreaming, Eve. I reach for my briefcase and climb out of my ticking, clicking car, the acrid whiff of hot metal and rubber being yet another reminder of a regretful past.

Ruan is now a few yards away, a worried look decorating his manifestation.

'Hey,' he calls out, slightly furry with alcohol. 'What's the problem? All the messages, what's going on?'

'Ruan. I'm sorry, I was just about to call you again, let you know everything's okay.' I sigh out. I don't have the strength to discuss it tonight. I've run out of steam. I smile as convincingly as I can. 'It's all fine now. I panicked when I couldn't get hold of Jack. My silly mistake. I'm really sorry I've dragged you away from your night.'

'Panicked? Err. You could say that. Come on, Eve, what is it? What's going on? You sounded well scared on the messages. What's happened?'

'It's all far too complicated.' I nod at the front door. 'Bea and Matt are inside waiting too. If you don't mind, I just need to get in.' To see Jack with my own eyes. Ruan calmly joins my side and takes my briefcase from me, frowning at me as he does. 'Sure,' he says. As we start to walk the path I steal a look around us; are we being watched? Eyes smug, exultant with the reaction you've created tonight. Are you still here?

For a moment, I see them, your eyes, dark, deep, forceful, yet void.

I shiver to shake off the image.

We crash through the front gate. Jack is peering out of the front-room window, watching us approach, then he disappears to open the old oak door. A sudden feeling of emotion falls over me. I smile at him, attempting to convey a million words without leaving them with him. I want to wrap him in my arms and sob into his messy hair. He understands more than he lets on, I know he does.

He doesn't need to utter a word; I see the haunted glimmer running through his eyes. The look you gave him. Not again. I hoped I wouldn't see it ever again. A pain shoots through my chest. Jack still doesn't speak; he knows. But what does he know? How much does he know? And for how long has he known? Do you remember more than you let on, Jack?

'Forget the kettle,' I say, looking through to the kitchen, noticing Bea at the tap, filling the yellow kettle. 'I need a drink. There's a bottle in the fridge, Bea. I'll be back in a minute.' I deliberately avoid any direct eye contact as I head upstairs for the bathroom. Wishing I could leave them all to it, hide up here with Jack, curled up under my winter-warm duvet, watching rubbish on the TV. Through the floorboards, I gratefully hear gentle banter as if the ridiculous and harried events had not just happened. Isn't it comparable to days of old, when weird happenings are explained away as normal, everyone unassumingly carries on?

Moments later, I reluctantly return downstairs and take the coward's way out, opting to use Jack as my excuse for not wanting to discuss my behaviour. Pulling Ruan and Bea to one side, I hold my hands out to them. 'What can I say? Other than, I really cannot apologise enough about tonight. I realise my behaviour must look a little odd,' I attempt.

'That's one word for it, I guess,' Ruan affirms, knocking back his bottle of beer, leaning up against the beam.

I nod. 'It's extremely complicated, though, if you don't mind, it's not for everyone's ears.' I gesture in Jack's direction; they both glance over. Subtlety or discretion not being either of their best points.

'A clue maybe?' Ruan urges me.

'His father,' I whisper. Ruan's not going to let go, despite Bea elbowing him in his ribs. Saying father has made my skin crawl.

'So? Do they not get on, then?' he whispers, leaning off the beam, genuinely surprised. All my fault; I never speak about you. Why would I? I want to forget you ever lived, hoped you were dead.

Bea exhales heavily. 'Well, obviously not. Leave Eve to tell us tomorrow. She's right, now is not the time!' She comes to my rescue. 'Are you okay, though, Eve? Would you like me to stay with you tonight? D'you think there's a chance he might turn up here later, then?'

Too many questions, not enough answers. I don't know what happens next. 'No, thanks, we'll be fine. I don't think he'll come back tonight.' I don't know this, but it would be too clean cut, too obvious. It wouldn't be any fun; timing and entrance are everything to you. 'I'll need to talk to Jack tomorrow first. He has no idea.'

My words do nothing to convince me. I'm not so sure of this anymore. I look over at him, sitting flopped back on the sofa, mobile in his hand, scrolling and apparently texting. Completely engrossed. Isn't this normal, what all teenagers do? Stop being so paranoid. He looks up at me, as if feeling my concern, and smiles. It was so much easier back then, the cover-ups, the lies, the protection.

'He needs to know the truth first, then I'll do my best to explain to you two.' I'll do my best to articulate, strictly on a need-to-know basis, excluding the darker fragments lurking in my mind.

I'm just about to change the subject when Ruan pipes up again. 'Hang on.' His face lights up as he leans closer in. 'I didn't think anything of it at the time, but a guy called the clinic this afternoon, some guy. Didn't get his name, though.'

'Go on,' I urge him. 'There must be more to it than just some guy calling the clinic?'

He nods at a tentative-looking Bea. 'I told you, Bea, didn't I, remember?' Moments pass, leaving me hanging between the two of them.

'Oh, yeah,' Bea said thoughtfully. 'Yeah, you said it was strange at the time, didn't you?'

'What? What was strange?'

'This guy called, asked for you. I told him you were out of clinic. Then he asked me if you were coming back to the clinic, and did you do late appointments. I told him, yes, sometimes, and no, I didn't think you'd be coming back because it was already 17.45 and you were still, as far as I knew, in appointments. That you would be for at least another hour or so. I asked him if he wanted to leave a message for you, but either we were cut off, or he hung up.' Ruan shrugs. 'I don't know which – the line seemed okay. So I checked, but he'd called from a withheld number. I didn't think anything of it after I mentioned it to Bea. D'you think it could have been him?'

'No idea, Ruan. No idea at all.' My mind drifts off to the text you sent me earlier. This changes things. Maybe you didn't know for sure then that I wasn't home. Ruan had told you I wasn't. Maybe you don't know where we live. But then how did you know about Jack having a friend here? A lucky guess? Could have been. I don't even know for certain it was you at all, do I? The text could have been from anyone. Other than the manner of the wording: precise and smug. Why would anyone else send me such a text? It wouldn't make sense for it to be anyone other than you.

After more drinks, and despite the relief of casual banter, I'm still unable to shrug off the dark feeling tormenting me. I always knew you would be back, but to have it confirmed is something else. Jack knows too, I know he does; it shines through his eyes. There's something unsaid in his persona tonight, something he needs to unload. But now is not the time.

I close the door after they all leave, checking it is securely locked; then check the kitchen back door again. For the first time since we moved here, I wish I had curtains, blinds, anything. I thought about it initially, but decided against it; nobody overlooks us and the windows behold charismatic features. But then I hadn't considered what it would feel like to be watched. Every move I make in the kitchen, every step and each breath I take in the front room, I feel your eyes on me. Violated by your perceived presence.

I make for bed as soon as I can, thankful for the higher floor level. Somewhere to escape your eyes. Checking in on Jack as I pass his room, I stand and watch, waiting for his chest to rise and fall, just as I used to when he was a small baby. Petrified he was going to stop breathing. Feeling helpless; his safety, his fate out of my hands. For a moment, I once again consider sleeping next to him, or at least on the floor at the foot of his bed. I cannot go back to living this way again. I can't. Across the room, I notice his mobile, a light indicating it's charging on his chest of drawers to the side of his window, beckoning me. Should I look at it? No, how could I even contemplate it? Anyway, it has a password and I've no idea what it is. Why is this? Since when did I become such a suspecting, untrusting mother? I just want to keep him safe.

Oh, God. What have I done?

Should I have gone to the police with what I took back then? But I couldn't, I can't. Not only is it my weapon, our defence. It doesn't tell the whole truth. And whilst you don't know I have this, it keeps us safe. But does it? Is this why you have come looking for me now? Who else knows of its existence? Lies, so many lies. I stare at Jack's peaceful face; why did I tell so many lies?

I rouse early, ahead of the sun, just in time to catch the moon before it magically disappears into the pastel sky. It's cold; condensation has gathered on the old leaded windows, obscuring the view to the outside world. Time for the heating to kick in. A sleepy Jack follows me downstairs sometime after, as normal without much more than a courtesy acknowledgment of my presence. We both understand mornings are not our thing, and a mutual respect for quiet, other than the TV morning news programme, is fully respected. I busy myself picking up, straightening squidgy cushions and wiping kitchen worktops. Jack is huddled protectively over his bowl of cereal, staring absent-mindedly at the news channel. So he takes me by surprise when he initiates conversation.

'You know last night, Mum?'

Here we go. My stomach performs a customary flip. 'Mmm,' is all I can manage.

'It was about him. Wasn't it?' My stomach cartwheels, followed by a triple somersault. Jack didn't ask me a question. It was a statement. He knows.

'Him? What do you mean, Jack, "him"?' Why am I saying this? He's not a fool, so why am I treating him like one? Still trying to protect and shield him. But he needs to know. My protection could put him in danger. When am I going to face facts? He's not stupid, but I am being so.

'You know, him. You were thinking something to do with him, last night. Weren't you? That's why you were so upset.'

'No, why do you say that?' What am I doing? I still can't help myself, can I? Tell him, for goodness' sake! But it makes me feel so sick. I still, even now, keep hoping that if I don't talk about it, it isn't real. Total bullshit, and I know it, so why am I making this so extra hard?

'I saw it in your eyes, Mum. It's the only reason you'd behave like you did last night. Panicking as you did. I'm not stupid. I remember how you looked before, back then. I've seen it all before. You think I don't realise what's going on. It's okay, Mum.' I feel his eyes pleading with me as I start to fill the dishwasher. Trying to bide my time, to decide how best to handle this. Hoping something intelligent will come to mind. But it's a little too early. Jack continues for me instead; I wonder who is the adult here.

'There's something else too. It's not just about last night. There's something else.'

I turn slowly to look at him. He doesn't look up from his breakfast.

'What? What else? What do you mean? What are you not telling me?' I probe.

'I'm trying to.'

I take a seat at the table with my coffee. 'Go on, sorry, Jack.'

'It might not be anything. It's just odd. I keep getting these requests, invites, on Facebook and Instagram.'

'What do you mean? What do they say?'

He shrugs. 'Nothing really. They're just friend requests. But from someone I don't know.'

'But isn't this normal, happens all the time? As in, can't random people just do that anyway?'

'Yeah, I suppose so. But I dunno, there's something not right about them. Then last night, it all made sense. When I saw you like that, again. You think he's back too, don't you, Mum?' He looks up at me, searching for answers, but ones I know he doesn't really want the truth for.

I think about telling him, of course I don't think he's back. I think about lying. But then, Jack's right, he's really not stupid. I should give him more credence and respect than to lie to him. Most importantly, if you are back, Jack needs to know. I need to keep him safe above all and everything else. Lulling him into a false sense of security is not going to help. But what if I'm wrong and I reignite all of Jack's dark past, for no reason at all? I simply can't take the risk; I need to warn him, gently. Is this even possible?

By the way Jack, I think your psychopathic father has hunted us down, he's watching us, waiting for the right moment to corner us, but try not to worry about it too much. What are you up to today anyway – got anything nice planned?

'I'm just not sure. He could be, but I really don't know for certain. I don't want to frighten you, but you must be aware from now on. You know what I mean – be watchful. I could be wrong, you see. I know what I'm like, my imagination, I mean.'

'Mmm. But it's more than that, isn't it? It's kinda creepy, but I can sort of feel him. You know, it's like I can feel him near.'

An icy shiver runs through my bones with his words. I know exactly what he means. 'What do you mean, Jack? It's really important you tell me everything you know. Is there or has there been anything else? Other than the odd friend requests?'

Jack shrugs at first, then glances back at his empty bowl, and begins to play with the spoon. He's about five years old again. Vulnerable and scared. I hate myself for bringing him into this horrible world. I take his hand in mine over the table. 'What is it? You need to tell me, please.'

His blue eyes take on a grey tinge. 'The other day, when I was walking up from the beach with Fyn and the others, a car drove past us really slowly.'

'Did you see him – the driver, I mean? Was it a man?'

'Yeah, it was definitely a guy, but Fyn's head was in the way when he drove past us, I couldn't see his face. Loads of cars drive slowly there, from the beach. I didn't think anything of it at first.'

'So, what happened? Why did it suddenly worry you?'

'Dunno. ´Cos, I guess, he was obviously looking for something or someone. It's not the holidays anymore, so down where we were, it's mainly locals, we know them. But it was the way, after he passed us, he sort of stopped, adjusted his rear-view mirror. Then, he… he stared straight at me. In the eyes.

When he saw me looking, he drove off really slowly, still staring at me, then accelerated, like pretty fast.'

'When was this?'

'The other night, not last night but the night before.'

The night of the 911. Charlie's words bounce through my mind. 'But you were at Fyn's house that night.'

'Yeah, but we'd gone down for the surf earlier on.' He shrugs at me.

'Jack, what car was he driving? Can you remember?'

'Yep. That's what made me turn in the first place. It sounded so cool. A Porsche 911, a blue one. I kinda recognised it, the sound of the engine.'

I squeeze his now-clenched fist. 'Jack, I don't want you being alone from now on. Not at home, not walking back from anywhere, for now. We might be wrong but until we know for sure, okay? You are not to go or be anywhere alone.'

He nods at me. The expression in his eyes rebukes me. How could I have allowed this to happen to him? Why can't he just have normal teenage worries, typical teenage thoughts? I need to find a way to allow Jack to move on. I thought I had, but clearly it's not going to be enough. I should have known better. I've once again put my beautiful boy at risk; I thought back then it was hard enough to protect him, but now, with his growing independence, it's all the more frightening.

Chapter Sixteen

Before

I don't think anyone can prepare you for your first child. I didn't realise it was possible to love so wholly. Conflicting emotions of utter enchantment yet absolute fear smothered me. Scared of not being able to protect and provide all this bundle of joy could ever need; terror of not being able to shield him from the life I was rapidly being submerged by. Sad with the understanding he would be short of all the precious subtleties of life I wanted him to have. A growing awareness over the previous months that I did not know who my husband was; I didn't know what he was up to; for most of the time he was an unmitigated stranger.

My beautiful baby boy, Jack.

A newborn; into a world I no longer recognised or cared for. How was I in a position to guide and shelter? Alone; cut off and insecure. How had it all snowballed so quickly? In such a relatively brief period of time? The first time I held Jack, the old me walked out of the door, a new me seized control. My priorities changed, my wishes, wants and the focus of my drive and motivation aligned with them. Jack was so unbelievably perfect; I was terrified I would let him down or accidentally harm him in some way. I'd read all the books, attended all the classes, but even so nothing had prepared me. Uncertainty and self-doubt tore through my conscience, shredding my confidence further.

We sat together, I just grateful of her presence, Janet, my health visitor, oblivious to my thoughts. How could I tell her? She would have doubted my ability to be a fit mother. I'd heard the horror stories of social services taking children into care, asking questions later, realising they got it wrong. I couldn't risk it, ever. She gently touched my hand and smiled with soft eyes as she spoke.

'Don't worry, Eve, it's completely natural to feel this way.' She didn't know anything really. Perhaps I hadn't kept it as covered up as I'd thought. 'Many of the mums I speak with feel a little low in the beginning.' She dipped her compassionate head.

My eyes welling at her kind words, I wanted nothing more than this show of humanity but I couldn't cope with sympathetic words. They stung deep inside, forcing me to ache all the more. I yearned so many times for understanding and gentleness, but it only deepened the open wound. I was perhaps scared of compassion, realising it would then feel worse to be without it. It was easier not to be reminded of the loss.

I regarded her caring hand still on mine. 'What do you mean?'

Slim lips turned upwards. 'You look lost, Eve. A little overwhelmed. I hope you don't mind me saying. I thought it might reassure you to hear lots of mums feel the same in the beginning. You're not alone.'

But I was. I couldn't have been more alone. 'Thank you,' I snuffled. 'It's okay. It does help a little, I suppose. It's easy to presume I'm the only one.' I pushed my head back to stop tears from falling. Urging the threatening globules to retreat.

'Here.' She offered me a tissue. 'You don't need to hide those from me. It doesn't make you a bad person. To cry.' I didn't dare start though; I wasn't sure how I would stop if I did. I desperately attempted to avert my mind to trivial housekeeping thoughts. I found concentrating on the practicalities, despite not being able to address even a fraction of the list, some form of comfort. Left-hemisphere distraction.

'You know, you're really being rather hard on yourself. You've only been home...' She counted, nodding her head. 'Wait. Just two days! This little fella's only three days old.' She pulled at his pure-white-cotton-enclosed leg, Jack gently kicking back at her touch.

I fixated on Jack's minuscule creamy dimpled hand clamped firmly around my finger, his eyes closed tight. Unenlightened to his world; secure in my arms. I marvelled at the trust he held in me. I'd indulged so many of my hours, holding him, watching his tummy rise and fall with each reassuring breath as he slept. Hypnotised by his virtuousness. But then I would often fall asleep too, shattered.

You left us alone on our first day home from hospital, returning to discover us curled up asleep on our bed. '*What are you doing? It's the middle of the day! Why is there crap all over the kitchen worktops? A dirty nappy on the floor?*' Luckily, I'd been too dog-tired to make myself anything to eat; else that would have been on our bedside table too. I'd tried to reason with you. I was completely exhausted. I couldn't seem to find the time; hours rolled away from me, despite my chase. '*Pull yourself together, sooner rather than later. Pathetic excuses*', was your response. But my to-do list grew to ridiculous lengths. I couldn't remember the half of it anyway. I was torn, dog-tired and anxious. Apparently, I was also '*pitiable, lazy*' and '*disorganised*'. And worse, making you doubt my child-raising capability.

'Eve, can I say? You look so very drained. You really ought to have stayed in hospital longer than you did. The nursing staff wanted you to, asked you to, I understand.' She lowered her head to me; she wasn't being critical, more concerned, given the long and difficult birth.

I wished I could divulge to Janet, my kind-hearted caller, but I was afraid she'd interpret it the wrong way. Was there a right way? On reflection, I was embarrassed. I too had wanted to remain in hospital, more than even I could understand. I'd originally anticipated I'd be desperate to get home. I felt safe in hospital, everyone was so kind to Jack and me. Allowing us to feel special, important even, with no need to worry or think about anything. The midwives and nurses allowed me to believe I'd achieved something amazing, something to be proud of. I didn't wish for it to end.

The day you arrived to collect us, the day I'd played out in my imagination numerous times the previous six months, crushed all my hopes. Despite grasping, deep down, it wouldn't have been any other way. I tensed at your voice approaching, charming its way past the nurses' station before you pushed open my door. At your insistence, I was isolated in a private room, despite looking forward to the company of other mums. My appeals caused an argument; you stormed out of the house and returned blindly drunk. Despite my being nine months pregnant, us living in the midst of the countryside. You said I was hormonal, so particularly argumentative. I was simply expressing my opinion.

You then insisted I was to return home the day after Jack was born, regardless that he was born in the early hours of the morning; it was only a matter of hours. Against the advice of the clinicians. You refused to listen, arguing I should be at home; you offered assurance we'd be looked after. You appreciated it had been a difficult birth and I was appropriately weak. They didn't mean weak in the way you understood it; it wasn't expected to be a criticism.

I still picture you lingering at the foot of the bed, mobile in hand. 'You two not ready yet?' You frowned. 'I did mention this morning I'd be returning at eleven. What have you been doing since then?'

'You did…' I pulled my tender body up from my supportive pillow '… but I had to wait for the consultant to speak to me, then he woke Jack up, and—'

'Right, well, come along, then. I've only thirty minutes on the ticket,' you said whilst picking Jack up clumsily from his sleeping state.

'Careful, Gregg, he'll be hungry again if you wake him.'

You glared at me, indignant. 'He's my child too. Don't start.' You began prodding at his tummy, as if to encourage a reaction.

'I'm not, it's just… well, you're the one in such a hurry.'

'Here we go again. You are always so… in the right, are you not?' You continued to poke at Jack as if he were some kind of toy you pressed to release a sound. 'Your mummy is becoming such a bore, isn't she? You'll learn, Jack. You'll soon find out.'

I cursed myself, feeling my eyes well up. 'Can you pass me my bag, please? It's behind you.'

'What for? Why do you need your bag? There's no time to be fussing with hair and make-up. This morning was your time. We need to get going.' You smiled to yourself. 'Do you not think you may need a little more than a hairbrush and lipstick anyway? I take it you've not had sight of a mirror as yet?' I bit hard on my lips to stop the tears from falling. I wanted to tell you how much you had changed; how spiteful and hurtful you had become. But I didn't. You already knew, didn't you?

I stood tentatively to gather my belongings from around you, each slight movement hurting. I imagined the discomfort akin to having been in a car accident. Battered and bruised. Although I had no lacerations. Then it dawned on me, despite your promises, reassurances to the clinicians, you were in your work suit.

'Have you been into work already this morning?'

'Not as yet. I will be, as soon as I've dropped you two off. Why?'

'Do you have to? I really wanted to have you at home with us today. I thought it would be nice, with it being our first day,' I pleaded; I'm still not sure why I did this. Was I still hopeful things could revert to how they used to be? Nonetheless, the idea of suddenly being all alone for the day frightened me.

'No can do, I'm afraid. Far too much on. You need to learn to be on your own at some point. No time like the present.' You shook your head impatiently. 'I'm simply not able to drop everything on a whim. As you are aware, I'm working on the McKenzie case. It's essential I go in.' You clap your hands, making me wince. 'Come on, let's get to it.' You reached for Jack's pristine, all-singing-and-dancing car seat, slotting him in as if packing a parcel. My stomach smarted as I picked up my overnight bag. As a new family, we left my safe haven. I stopped briefly to thank the staff at the nurses' station; they wished us good luck. Moments later we walked out into vulnerable skies to the car, in silence. Their wishes were never going to be enough.

The whole experience felt so far removed from who I am, the person rapidly becoming hidden deep inside me. I told myself not to be such a dreamer, such a romantic, but still I couldn't fight the feeling of it all being so wrong, such a waste. The joy of this beautiful baby being smothered by the sterile atmosphere. Where had I gone wrong? Had I just become a whinger? Was I depressed?

'You okay, Eve? You drifted off into your own world then.' Janet squeezed my hand, eyes smiling at me.

I nodded. 'I'm fine, just a little tired. Nothing some rest won't fix.' Who was I trying to kid?

She glanced at her watch, 'I need to get going. Would you believe it's gone six already? Will your husband be home soon? I think you're going to need some TLC tonight.'

'Yes, of course, you should. Thanks for coming, then staying for so long too. It's very kind of you. I hope I haven't made you too late.'

She must have mentioned about the TLC because it would be the normal thing for a partner to do. All the other new mums must have this kind of support. Was this what happened behind other closed doors? And those who didn't have a partner at all, were they better off too? Because then at least people knew they were alone. I lived a lie.

As Janet stood pulling on her coat, she unwittingly dealt another blow. 'Do you have any other visitors, Eve? You know, people who can help you, family or friends?'

I looked to her concerned face. Did she think I really wasn't coping, then? Had she guessed the truth? I turned away, grasping for Jack's blanket I'd carelessly dropped on the floor. What was the truth anyway? Mine? His? The truth was, I couldn't ask my mum, the only person I'd want with me, because it wasn't worth the heartache, the inevitable ensuing rows. I couldn't ask for my friends because I no longer had any; contact with them had long ceased. I'd not seen Sam for months. Following her no-show at the golf club, we had another disagreement about you; I reacted defensively. Why did I do that? Defend your horribleness? To save my own face?

The truth, Janet, was no; I couldn't and wouldn't have visitors. But this was to be my secret, my lie. For the time being. Pushing myself up to meet Janet's eyes, I fibbed, 'Yes, yes, I do. I'm lucky, I have several people to call on. Please, don't worry, I'll be fine, really. Gregg will be home soon too.' I pointed to the hall clock. 'Any time now, in fact.'

'Good, super,' she said. 'I'll be off, then, love. See you next week. You know where I am if you need me, but I'm sure you'll be absolutely fine!'

True to word, you came home early, just gone seven. I was in the bathroom, giving Jack his first home bath. A sentiment of dread gripped me as the crashing of the front door reverberated through the solid floors. Then silence. I'd made the decision after Janet left not to give up; perhaps I was being overly sensitive, reading into things I didn't need to. Jumping to silly conclusions. 'Gregg? Gregg, are you there?' I called. 'Come and look. Quick, come and see Jack. He's having his first bath!' I hollered. Nothing.

I could hear you downstairs. At first it sounded as if you were opening post, something you always did as soon as you walked through the door. Then, the familiar sound of you muttering away to yourself. Banging around. It wasn't a good sign. I was about to call out again when I heard the trill of your mobile. Blasted phone; such an intruder of time. I could tell by your tone, whoever it was, whatever they were saying, was not something to please you. I half attempted to eavesdrop, but Jack was so blissfully distracting, kicking his legs around to the familiar feel of water. Until your voice began to rise.

'Where are you? I told you not to discuss this in the office. Far too risky.'

I smiled at Jack as I dribbled warm water over his tummy.

'What the…? How did he get involved?' you continued. I strained further; what had happened?

'Right, listen to me. You need to smooth this over. Call him now, tell him we need to meet tonight.' The word 'tonight' crushed my intentions. 'Then, book a flight for later this week. I can't go, not a chance, far too dicey. You need to go.' Who was he speaking to? 'Not interested, change it. I'll be there in an hour.' Silence.

I continued to bath Jack, aware of my heart pumping against the bath panel. It was a good few minutes before you thundered up the stairs. Your twitchy body materialised in the doorway. 'What the hell have you been doing all day?' you snapped, in total ignorance of your son.

'I've been here all day. Why? What d'you mean?' Was I supposed to have done something?

'The house is a pigsty. You were at home all day.' You kicked the door with the side of your foot. 'You might be okay living like this, but, I. Am. Not. I work really hard. Keeping the house is all you have to see to. What have you prepared for dinner?'

You knew I hadn't, else you wouldn't have asked. Jack flipped around in his new-found joy, splashing water into my eye, blurring your angry face.

'Well, I—'

'Perfect. I'll eat out, then. You need to get a grip. Sort yourself out, Eve. It's truly, truly embarrassing. The state of this place. What if someone had come back with me?' You turned away, shaking your head, pulling the door behind you.

'Gregg, please,' I pointlessly implored as you stomped your hard-done-to way down the stairs to the sound of the jingling of your car keys. Moments later came the ricochet of the front door slamming.

'Gregg, please,' I whispered to Jack, 'we really need you to be here tonight.'

Jack thrust at the water again, splattering my eyes; I wasn't sure if it was runaway splish-splashes, or whether the tears had finally burst their banks.

Chapter Seventeen

In my dreams I see a woman slumped. Her heavy head suspended by threadbare strings. Feet lightly tap the shifting floor. Primed for flight. She examines them to avoid eyeballing faces behind the glass screen. Yearning for things to be different. She contemplates leaving an empty seat, the easier option; she should know. She feels hollow, yet heavy and helpless.

Wait, I recognise her.

She's me.

Another woman moves slowly towards me. I look up. Her hand held out as she smiles, but I cannot feel it. In return my eyes peek out from under heavy lids.

I sense I know her too. Perhaps she is my last chance. Perhaps she has come to help me.

A concealed sadness saturates my dark hollow eyes as I stand slowly to contemplate hope. Legs too exhausted to carry the encumbrance. My lifeless hand meets hers; it has no strength. I know this hasn't always been so. Words spike my dry throat, a nod suffices.

I follow her, trapped in a trance-like state, a few steps behind. Feeling so utterly out of control. A puppet reacting and responding. I sense she feels the weight of me behind. Yet I am so slight. I ooze desolation, debilitated by unyielding meaningless thoughts. An emotional hijacking in progress.

But I'm not alone; depression thieves many prisoners, clouding perspectives, intimidating and isolating its prey. I ask of her, 'What about the dark? I'm afraid of the dark.'

She tells me, 'The light is dimmed, but not gone. It's not always been dark. Your reality now is not the truth. Hold this small pebble to your eye, see how it distorts your view. Your memories do the same. The dark obscures the truth. This is not your truth, Eve. You need to fight back.'

Wait, I remember, I do recognise her.

She is me too! She's all I have; my last hope.

I am alone, me and now Jack.

I wake.

Chapter Eighteen

Cornwall 2016

A slow wistful walk up Lemon Street, a million consternations resting heavy on my shoulders. I take a deep nasal breath of crisp autumnal air. It's such a beautiful day, I was coerced to the beach before clinic this morning; the sea beckoned me down. In need of the kind of perspective the turquoise waters always allow me, I followed. Switching off the ignition, I remained, transfixed, stretching my gaze as far as I could out to sea. What was happening the other side of those waters? Maybe someone was looking back at me, wondering the same? Mesmerised by the mélange of blues, greens and frothy whites, lapping marbled silver slate rocks. Thrashing waves, gradually creeping closer, pilfering our beach. But what was happening beneath the shifting surface? I tried to remind myself of its vastness as my world began to close in once again. My concerns were a drop in the ocean. I couldn't drown, not now.

Fresh tides washing away the deeds of yesterday – why couldn't life do the same? A moving figure caught my eye, making me start as the shadow knocked on the side glass: Charlie. He giggled, waving, oblivious to my startled response, before ambling away to his seemingly uncomplicated job. Unlike mine, loading already encumbered shoulders. How did life become so complicated? Didn't we sometimes miss the point?

Now, crispy golden leaves float beneath my footsteps, as I feel each tentative tread on solid grey ground. An unusual seasonal warmth joins me, gifted by the perfect blue-skied day. Why did you have to come back? The cathedral bells peal behind me, advising me to quicken my step. I'm going to be late. Normally by now I'd be aware of my scheduled appointments for the day, have planned for them, rereading my notes. But today, I'm not sure if I've forgotten the plan or if I'm just without one. Ruan will bail me out. By the time I arrive, the reception will be warmed, the air filled with the aroma of freshly brewed coffee. I've explaining to do. My stomach hardens, with the thought of Bea and Ruan; they'll want to understand what drove me to the insane behaviours last night. They'll question me about you, my reasoning for being afraid. In the cold light of day; I wish I hadn't created the stir. But I was truly scared. I thought I'd be ready for you, if and when the day arrived. I was wrong. After all this time, you still have such impact on my nervous system. Screwing it up, wringing it out.

I clasp the cold iron handle, stretching my foot towards the clinic door just as it moves away from me. 'Here she is!' A beaming smile. 'Told you she'd be here. Late as ever. Gosh, you look rough, lovely!' Bea adds.

'Thanks, Bea. Here, take these.' I dangle the slightly moist paper bag under her nose. 'Inhale. Croissants, hot out of the oven.' I withdraw the bag. 'But that was before you told me I looked rough!'

'Hmm. Can I retract that particular comment, please?' She grins, snatching the bag from my hands.

'Thought we could do with some sugar this morning. It's also a small, though delicious, peace offering.' They regard me. 'For last night?' I know they're being polite, that they were probably talking about it before I arrived. Like, I needed to remind them.

'Mmm. Absolutely. They smell so, so good. You know, you really don't look quite so rough in this light, anyway.' Bea hugs me, clutching the bag to her side. 'You certainly don't need to provide peace offerings. Silly.' Letting go, she plants her face in the paper bag, breathing deeply, in then out. 'Thing is, though, I did intend to be good today.' She sighs heavily. 'Oh, well. Tomorrow's as good a day as any. Anyhow, you can't rush these things, can you? Rome wasn't built in a day, was it?'

'Exactly,' I say.

'Here, Ru, grab one while it's warm. You've got hollow legs anyway. Git.' She orders him to take a croissant whilst shoving the end of another into her mouth. Flaky crumbs everywhere. I try my hardest not to glance at the floorboards. The now flaky-pastry floorboards. 'Don't worry, I'll fetch the vacuum. You can't bring croissants, then worry about crumbs!' She rolls her eyes.

The sickie feeling overrides my hunger as I walk towards my room. 'I've had one already so feast away,' I say before Bea begins to guilt-trip herself further. Despite my stomach being empty but for the caffeine. You always were the best diet around.

'Can't you help her with that?' an equally full-mouthed Ruan blurts.

'What, making a mess?'

'No. Her diet thing. Does my head in. I don't get it. It's simple, isn't it? If you're hungry, eat, if you're not, don't. Why's it need to be such a deal? Couldn't be bothered.'

'Hey. Cheeky sod, Ru! What you trying to say – you think I need help, do you? Need to lose some weight, eh? A bit on the chubby side? You should've said before.' She nudges him fondly.

'Me? No. Never said anything. It's you – it's all you think about. Talk about. Imagine how much extra time you'd have if you stopped thinking about eating, and just ate. Must be exhausting. No wonder you're always hungry.'

'God, you're such a simpleton sometimes.' She turns to me, pointing her mostly demolished pastry at me. 'Could you help me, do you think, Evie? You deal with eating disorders, don't you? Perhaps I should book myself in. It's not such a bad idea despite it coming from him.' She nods at Ruan.

'For God's sake, you two. Don't you think I've enough of this during clinic hours? No, Bea, you haven't got an eating disorder, okay? You're just like the rest of us. Someone who worries and thinks too much, likes her food, beats herself up about it, so feels bad about it, so wants to eat more to make herself feel better. You don't need therapy to work that one out. Join the proverbial club.'

'Yeah, I own the bloody club,' she hoots.

'What I'm actually saying is, you're normal. Normally abnormal. Normally imperfect. Great just the way you are. Not overweight. Okay?'

'Okay. If you say so.' She nods at Ruan. Two rivalling siblings.

'Yeah, whatever she just said, I agree, if it helps,' he adds.

Bea rubs her greasy fingers through Ruan's hair before he can pull away. 'How d'you get your hair like that anyway? So much body? D'you gel it?' she asks him.

He runs bronzed hands through natural blond waves. 'All natural, of course.' He flicks his head back, smiling. 'Courtesy of the sea. Never wash it after I've been in. Salt water. The best and it's free.'

'I hate you. Look at your eyelashes too. What a waste.'

I leave them to it, continuing to the haven of my room. Though aware of the eyes on my back as I do and the conversation going on between them without words, about me. They'll have to wait. I need to switch into clinic mode; no room for personal twitterings. I turn to pacify their expectant faces. 'Later.'

'What?' they say together, as if surprised.

'We'll talk. About things, stuff. Last night.' Two heads nod back in unison.

I hover over my desk, flicking through unopened envelopes, trying to ignore the rushing of my heart. I hate even talking about talking. The front door opens as I hear Bea greeting her next client. 'Ruan, have you got my list? For my first appointments today? Please.' He quickly reaches my side, handing me today's list with the relevant files.

'Certainly have. First one, Dr Jakes.'

'Yep.'

'Second one, umm, here, it's the new-referral guy.' A fist seizes my stomach and twists. What's the problem? New referrals are a weekly occurrence. What's up with your heartbeat?

Ruan bumps his head back. 'What's the look for? I did tell you. Or tried to anyway. You know, the PTSD guy. The one from up-country.'

With the antics of last night, I'd forgotten all about this case. A sick sense reminds me it's a worry. 'Warwickshire?' I ask.

'Yeah, the soldier, the ex-soldier now, from somewhere in Warwickshire, wasn't it? He must be living down here now, then. I mean, to be able to get a referral for here. Isn't that how it works?'

'Or at least residing here for the time being,' I correct.

'Should be interesting. Wouldn't mind sitting in on this one?'

How could I have forgotten? I glance at my wall clock, ignoring Ruan; Jesus, he's going to be here in an hour and twenty. If he turns up, that is. There's always a chance he won't. Here, in my clinic after all these years. How come you're still alive?

'Hello? Earth to Eve?'

'Sorry. Not today, you can't. I haven't asked his permission yet.'

'Pity. Here's the others, then. I'll leave you to your preparations.' Ruan places the remaining files on my desk and I watch him leave. The rule book filed away in my head fleetingly questions my ability to work ethically this morning. I'm hardly feeling calm and collected. The responsibility of my appointments feels like gigantic boulders, hurtling towards a rickety thoroughfare.

I remove my overflowing diary, full of needs-attention household paperwork, from my briefcase. Each day I undertake that I'll go through it, but the ruler separating pages reminds me nearly nine months of broken promises have passed. Then I notice it, the brown A4 envelope sitting solitary in the unzipped pocket; the one I was to open after seeing Milly at the GP surgery yesterday. Something else I'd completely forgotten about. I flip the envelope over. No postal mark – it's obviously been hand-delivered.

STRICTLY PRIVATE AND CONFIDENTIAL

EVE

How strange – no surname? I open it quickly, suddenly aware of muffled voices; the doctor's arrived for his appointment. Cautiously easing out an A4 sheet of photocopied assemblages of newspaper articles. What the hell? Swallowing hard. Who could have done this? Who has access to my briefcase to be able to plant it? Me, Ruan, Jack, Bea? I don't get it. I clumsily examine the sheet, then again, the envelope, as the titled words repeat over and over, hurtling through my mind.

Partner's Son, Latest Victim of Money Laundering Fraud. Just Nineteen. Tragedy, Enquiry, As He Takes His Life.

I drop it on my desk. No. Please, no. Who has sent this? What are you trying to tell me? Why now? The articles are as old as my story. Is this your idea of a bilious joke? Ahead of your appointment? Shaky hands shove it back in the envelope, out of sight, temporarily out of mind. I don't have the space to think about it now.

Fifty-five minutes later, I show the doctor from my room, pondering about his lucid exchanges. He's a self-referral, seeking help for a severe alcohol addiction, but I'm undecided if he wants to be helped, more, he knows he should pursue help. The pretence of taking action enables him to fulfil his consultancy at the hospital. A consultancy he clearly struggles with, partly due to the addiction, partly due to the stresses and unfair demands of the job, but mostly because of the turmoil both of these have caused at home. Yet for all his candour, morality and obvious intelligence, he lies. He lies to me, he lies to his consultancy, to his wife and family; but most of all, he lies to himself. In love with his addiction but doesn't wish to be realised as an addict. But for his alcohol dependency to be an accepted member of his life and family. Smacked by the king of motivation, a huge dopamine release, each time he even contemplates alcohol.

Ruan follows in soon after him, swooshing the air with both hands.

'Quick, help me get this window open. It stinks in here.' As I grapple with the heavy sash window. 'He assured me he hadn't touched a drop this last week. But I'm already inebriated on the fumes. How long have I got?'

Ruan stands back from the open window, grinning towards Reception. 'About ten minutes, I guess.'

'For Christ's sake, that's all I need. I'm going to be branded as the clinician who's partial to a little intoxication.'

'Matches?' suggests Ruan, on the hunt towards Reception, then he returns. 'Here, light the candle thing, always works. That's what I used to use at home.' He laughs. 'Let's just hope I'm not about to blow us up.' He lights the candle.

I snatch the matches from him. 'Glad you find this so amusing. Go out into the street, then come back in.' I give him a gentle push.

'What? Why?'

'To make sure you can't smell the stale alcohol any more. We've probably just acclimatised to it.'

He rolls his eyes as he heads off out onto the pavement in a theatrical manner then bursts back into the reception. 'No, it's definitely okay. We're in the clear. Can I put this down as valuable work experience? You know, tricks of the trade, kind of thing? The art of discretion? Why didn't you just tell him straight when he denied it – he reeks of the stuff?'

'You perhaps need to work on that art of discretion. No. I didn't, of course not.' I've already asked some clients if they're happy for me to discuss their cases with Ruan, whilst he's gaining work-experience hours. This is one of them.

'Does he think you're stupid or what? I mean, does he even pay attention to what you say?' He throws himself into the tub therapy chair, a leg hanging over the side.

'Ah, well, he listens with interest, nods and agrees. But no, I'm not convinced he really hears me or engages. He's a smart guy. He uses selective hearing with a "this doesn't apply to me" attitude.'

'So what's the point in him coming?'

'Good question. He needs to be seen to be doing something. But he's not ready to give it up yet; believe it or not, he doesn't believe it's a problem. As others do, he uses it to fill many voids, you see.'

'You're kidding? Not a problem? I thought I had a drink problem. So what did you talk about?'

'Willpower, how addictions of any guise cannot be defeated with willpower alone. We talked of stresses, coping skills, sleep cycles and unfulfilled needs; all being fed by the alcohol. The thing is, he tackles his bucket of stress with inflammatory alcohol. But as it's a depressant too, talk about inappropriate legions. It's also a chronic disturber of sleep, a booster of cortisol. He wonders why, despite knowing he can't possibly feel better or even consider a life beyond it.'

'So if it can't be beaten by willpower?'

'More often than not, it's the expectation of what the addictive behaviour provides rather than the actual behaviour that keeps the person addicted. The brain is coerced by the behaviour to feed lies. For the addict, the expectations are then always positive and rewarding, the harmful reality of the behaviour is boxed away.' I look at Ruan, swinging his leg, taking it all in. 'The truth is ignored.'

He nods. 'Yeah, makes sense. Who wants to think about the bad stuff?'

'Exactly, so the lies need to be uncovered, acknowledged, then challenged. But it's almost impossible if the individual refuses to accept responsibility, doesn't want to see the lies. Refusing to consider the reality of misuse, not what it gives them but what it takes away.'

'So many addictions are fought on willpower, though, aren't they? If you think about it. Even all these weird diet clubs. It's always willpower.'

'Hmm, but willpower can rarely succeed against lies, against little pots of hope and expectation. The doctor knows this really, but he's not ready to hear it or ready to accept it. I wonder how far he has to fall before reality hits.'

'Why would you? You know, lie to yourself like that?'

'Life, Ruan. Sometimes people get themselves into situations. Before they know it the boundaries between lies and truths are too blurred. Telling lies to get to the truth, whatever that is. We're not here to judge, though, are we?'

'Me? Never.'

'Did you have any joy, by the way, with that name I gave you, Milly's mum's boyfriend?'

'Oh, yeah, I knew I'd something else to tell you. Sounds like he's quite a local dodge pot. Mevagissey's answer to Mafioso, by all accounts.'

'What?'

'Nothing online, I could find. But my mate's mate's mate's dad – well, he runs The Black Sheep pub in the town. He knows of him all right. In fact, he barred him last year.'

'Go on?'

'Let's just say, he has things in common with the kiddy catcher, or the Pied Piper, or the—'

'Okay, Ruan, I'm getting the gist. He's bad news.' I look at the clock on the wall. 'This will have to wait.' I'm aware of my heart quickening. 'I need a few minutes before my next one, if you don't mind.'

'Sure thing.' Ruan retreats to Reception, leaving me to think some more about the envelope. Before long, I'm snapped away from my daze at the sound of the front door, opening and clunking shut. I freeze; I'm five years old again. I'd really expected a no-show. Actually that's not true; I'd hoped for a no-show. I hear Ruan acknowledging him, as a deep masculine voice hums in response. I strain to decipher the tone of his voice but the walls are just too thick. Is it you? Direct confrontation was not your style. Certainly not with an unknown audience. At least it didn't used to be. I creep across the room to listen from behind my slightly ajar door. Shunted up against the bookshelf, I urge my feet to step forward, but they don't respond. I hear my heart thumping, feel my mind haze, but I can't move my feet.

Eventually, Ruan peeps around the door. Arching his eyebrows, he whispers, 'What are you doing, Eve? He's here, your next appointment. Why you hiding behind the door? You okay?'

'Shhh.' I gesture for him to come in and shut the door behind him.

'What's up? What are you doing?'

'Who is that?' I ask, jerking my head in the reception direction.

'What d'you mean? You know who it is. Your next appointment, William Adams. You know, the PTSD referral, the one—.'

'Yes. I know who he says he is. I mean, who is he? What does he look like?'

'What the hell's going on?' A look of puzzlement shapes his face. 'Oh, God. D'you think it's him? Jack's dad?'

I don't respond. The words snag in my throat. Why didn't I cancel this appointment? Because, I didn't think you'd actually have the nerve to come, because I pushed it to the back of my mind, but also because I don't know it is you, do I? I could be making a complete fool of myself again.

Ruan regards me, clearly concerned, obviously not knowing how to help. 'Look, he's just a normal-looking guy. Kinda does look like an ex-soldier, to be fair. Tallish, darkish, biggish build, I suppose. Quite softly spoken. What else? D'you want me to take a photo then come and show you?'

'This isn't a joke, Ruan.'

He moves further away from the door, lowering his voice. 'What is it about him anyway? Why d'you look so frightened?'

I breathe in deeply through my nose, realising how ridiculous I must look. I shake my head, then usher Ruan out of the room, and prepare to follow in his footsteps. I'm probably just being stupid and it isn't you anyway. The only true connection I have is that *he* is from Warwickshire. That's not a lot to go on. He's referred under a different name, but that doesn't mean anything; I wouldn't put a name change past you. I've changed Jack's surname, after all; from Austin to Sands, before we moved to Cornwall. You're also a pathological liar, so anything we've already been told doesn't mean anything. Ruan's description fits you well, but then it would also be appropriate for many other men. And, given it's Ruan's description, he could actually be small and blond. Then, a quiet, softly spoken voice – no, you had a commanding, sardonic voice. But then, you could be, it could be, whatever you wanted it to be, in any given situation.

Counting to three, I step out from the security of my room, forcing the fixed, unnatural beginnings of a smile, into the open reception. The man has already stood up and made his way over to the far side. He stands nonchalantly, hands in pockets, looking out onto the street. Is this because I've annoyed him, keeping him waiting? Or is it because he doesn't want me to know who it is just yet? He doesn't want me to see, recognise his face? He's planned this moment, wants to be in total control at the point he decides to reveal himself. He will only turn to face me when the instant is right for him. For you. I take in his physique, his stance; a perfect shadow of you stands before me. A gush of sickness upsurges from my roiling stomach as I hear the words fall inelegantly from my anaesthetised lips.

'William?' I request of his back. I secretly will him not to turn around. Why am I playing along with your game, calling you William? I imagine you simpering at the window. I urge him to answer me whilst still facing the outside world. My legs begin to subtly quiver; someone has removed the muscles. My pen slips from my sweaty, unsophisticated hand. It drops, but I dare not move to pick it up.

Ever so steadily, he coils towards me. At full twist his dark eyes seek immediate contact. A look of knowing satiates them. Blood drains from my limp body. I notice how his shoulders capitulate. An impression grabs me.

He has found who he is looking for.

Chapter Nineteen

Before

It seemed often I would hear people remark on how quickly time passes when having fun. My time passed painfully slowly, watching and learning. I stopped walking your path; I just didn't tell you. I wasn't ready for you to know. All I could do was safeguard the happiness of Jack, riding the waves of loneliness and heartache. All the time, the lies were stacking up. I couldn't afford to trip over them. Why did I still not leave? It was compulsory I played the game, or you'd always be with me. A creepy, climbing plant, strangling its support system, tightening its grip, obscured, unnoticed. All the time, sucking away at vital nutrients. No, I needed to be cleverer than you.

*

'Oh. My. God. A chauffeur-driven trip to Wimbledon. Centre Court tickets. A three-course lunch, wow. How amazing! I'm so jealous!' She assumed much, while juggling the arms of an octopus into his coat at the end of Jack's music group. She asked, so I told her; I wished I hadn't. She was nice, kind and funny, but I kept her at the required distance, our conversation couldn't go any further than surface-level banter.

I tackled Jack to the ground, still wriggling, wedging his shoes onto chubby feet. 'Hmm, I suppose.' I could understand where she was coming from; I wanted to be excited. The thought saddened me. She thought she knew me, but she didn't.

'Well, don't sound so happy about it, will you? Listen, I'm more than happy to go in your place, you know. Just give me the nod,' she jested.

If only she knew. But how could she? I needed to make connections, join the obligatory groups for Jack's sake. He was two years old, needed to be amongst other children. I, too, needed to be around other adults, other females. But it was tangibly painful. Gradually, I developed methods for hiding the truth. Not just from others but myself too. It was my only way to cope, a desperate attempt at normality. I daren't allow anyone to get too close; for their protection and mine. Expert in dodging questions, ignoring invites, imaginative excuses. Friendships were amputated anything beyond the acquaintance stage.

From the outside we looked like the ideal family unit. So much so, sometimes I'd catch myself querying, was it me who was the problem? Did I overreact? Were you correct in suggesting I was mentally sick? Could it be a case for postnatal depression? But then, why did the other lives, the ones I watched and heard about, look so normal and simple? Why did I crave so much, for these lives? Ironically, others often articulated their envy of our life; it was purely a conceptual envy. They didn't know of the life, the other side of the front door.

It was irrelevant how they saw us; they only had an obscured pinhole view. By then, I'd pushed myself so far into the corner, I couldn't figure out a feasible escape route. It was harsh, cold and isolated. The veiling of my life and constant pretending so brilliantly disguised the facts and hid the evidence. So much so, a cry for help would appear fraudulent. It wasn't that I didn't consider leaving. I thought about it every day. But it was hopelessly complicated. Alone in the midst of night with a two-year-old child, a self-esteem buried somewhere under the rubble; it felt unbearably impossible. Day by day, week by week, and month by month, increasingly cut off. Jack was my only living reason to keep my flame alight, but also the reason I needed to be more than sure of my decisions, my timing.

*

You stood upright and tall, checking your reflection in the full-length mirror on the galleried landing. An apparent piece of fluff on the arm of your dark suit catching your attention. How could you care about such things? In the beginning, I found it quite sweet, but these ways soon became peculiar and abhorrent. I turned away, conscious of my lack of time to finish getting myself ready. I fingered the soft silk of my cornflour blue 1950s-style dress. You'd reactivated my credit card, so I could choose a suitably expensive dress for the occasion. Your corporate occasion. I hadn't realised my cards were cancelled in the first place, until an incredibly embarrassing moment at the children's farm with other mums. They'd had to pay for me whilst I'd fumbled for feasible excuses.

'Don't worry about it, it happens to me all the time. The next one's on you.' I bet it doesn't happen to you, I'd thought. Not like this. Not as a punishment.

Kind words to soothe my blushing cheeks. How could you have done this? To teach me what exactly? There was always a lesson to be learned in all these actions. I'd called you as soon as I'd managed to free myself from the group; maybe there had been a genuine problem with our account. You always took charge of the finances; I was not to be trusted.

'Gregg, I'm at the farm, my card's just been declined?'

I'd felt the smirk before the words had come. 'Yes. It will have been.' I'd imagined you sitting, self-preening, satisfied. I'd wished I hadn't called.

'Why?'

'You know why, Eve.'

'No, I don't!'

'The matter of the missing supermarket receipt. From your last statement?'

I'd bitten my tongue. Visualising wiping the smug expression from your face. 'Why didn't you at least tell me you'd cancelled them?'

Your voice had been muffled. 'Thank you, Patricia. I don't know what I'd do without you,' you'd oozed to some poor fool in your office. Her slinking away with your compliments. 'Where was I? Oh, yes... now, if I had warned you, how would that have taught you a lesson, Eve?'

I'd been able to feel my cheeks reddening with blood pressure. 'You've taken all the cash from my purse too!'

'Yes. Actually, no, that's not quite true, I left you enough change for parking. Perhaps next time you'll make sure you keep all your receipts. Everything has consequences, Eve, everything.'

I didn't spend a fortune on a dress; what was the point? Just another way of dressing up the lies. But I did want to make an effort; not for you but because I desperately needed to feel nice. I was off to

Wimbledon for the first time. I slipped my feet into bronze-coloured high-heeled strappy sandals, admiring them from each angle. So pretty. I felt your eyes on me, saw you smirking before walking away, shaking your head. Pulling myself up, I blushed with the thought of being girly and silly. Clumsy and awkward was how I felt next. I observed my reflection in the mirror. Even my make-up, especially my signature coral-red lipstick, now appeared puerile. Reaching for a tissue, I dabbed at my mouth to make it less obvious. I tucked my shoulder-length ashen strands behind my ear, exposing diamond studs, a present from my parents. You didn't like them. But they allowed me a surreptitious closeness to my memories of warmth and love. I loosened my hair again, to cover them up.

I could hear you downstairs, parading up and down the oak floors whilst charming our babysitter. A perfect gentleman. You knew how to make people feel good about themselves. Jack was giggling away, chatting in an animated, jumbled-up, nonsensical manner. He was happy; that was enough for now. I imprisoned my finger with my wedding and engagement rings. I only ever wore them in public. They made me feel bound and suffocated. I always took them off as soon as I walked back through the door. You never noticed, or at least you didn't comment on it. Or perhaps you just didn't care.

A few minutes later we were collected from our over-elaborate statement gates by a black funeral-like car. Thankfully, David and Sue, a senior partner at your company and his wife, were already in the car, so some animated conversation with good-humoured banter covered for us. I knew the couple reasonably well from the numerous corporate events, enough to relax a little. Still, the feeling of it all rolling out before me, around me, as I watched life go by out of the window; such a façade, all of it. How long could I keep it up for, fake smiles, forged banter? Was I becoming as good an actor as you? I was aware of a muffled you, floating over my semi-conscious state; talking about me, us, in a vivacious manner. As if you thought of me in a positive light, as an intellectual equal. My skin was beginning to crawl.

Sitting back against the leather seats, I listened as you enlightened them how I was due to return to the hospital soon, to work within the brain-rehabilitation clinics. So this was what it must feel like to have true appreciation from your husband; for a moment, I tried to embrace it as if it were real. Fascinated at your eagerness to express your appreciation of my work, your compassion for the unfortunate families and loved ones. I could feel myself slipping between the two worlds again, a twisted form of reality. Was I on the edge of psychosis? I caught your dishonest eye before returning to the world outside the window. Only yesterday you loomed over me, mocked me for even considering returning to work.

'What?'

'I'm thinking of returning to the hospital. Not full time, a few hours each week. They called me last week, asked me to consider it. So, I've given it a lot of—'

'Huh. Really? You seriously believe it's a sensible move, given your state of mind at the moment? You in a position of helping others?' You guffawed. 'I've heard it all now. No wonder so many people die in our hospitals. Bloody public sector.'

'Actually—'

'Have you told them?'

'About what?'

'Well, I think you'll find they've only asked you because they're assuming you're as you used to be.' You snorted. 'They have no idea.' You swaggered back over to your desk, flipping your Apple screen into action. 'Why you'd even want to is beyond me. Especially on your salary.'

Your mobile trilled, cutting through the air. 'Hold a minute, will you?' you said to the caller.

'What about Jack?' you said to your Apple screen. 'Have you for one minute considered him in all this babble? You are, then, able to live with yourself, knowing full well you'll be sacrificing his needs for your own selfish ones? Grow up, for Christ's sake. You've responsibilities. Poor Jack, whatever did he do to deserve a mother like you? Seriously, you are bloody unbelievable.' You returned to your call.

It was on the tip of my tongue to remind you how you had refused to have any relationship with your own mother for the last three years. But learned self-control took a grip, so as not to cut off my nose to spite my face. I needed to win this one; I turned and walked away. The seed was sown for the time being. I felt your eyes follow me out of the room. Your mobile ringing served me well. You wanted a fight; I didn't want to play anymore. Things were changing. You knew it, didn't you? You knew you needed to up your game in order to renegotiate some respect. Power and control. I shuddered at the thought of what might come next, but I also knew it was essential.

How could anyone switch so transiently from black to white to now articulate these words tripping from your mouth? I was caught between not allowing myself to be surprised by such turncoat behaviours, and ensuring I kept them at arm's length. Otherwise they would become my norm too. How would I escape then? The daily disgust and astonishment kept me within the realms of lucidity. I lived the lie, but I knew it was a lie. I knew it was so wrong in every conceivable way. I wouldn't ever let go of that. I was brought back into the moment by you kicking my foot, realising I'd absconded from the conversation.

'Heavens, Eve, this is wonderful. Your work must be unbelievably recompensing. So worthwhile. I'm not sure how you cope with the heartache. I honestly don't think I could.' Sue looked from you to me.

For a passing moment, I wasn't sure whether she was referring to my home life, or the hospital; either way my response was apt. I smiled at her earnest face. 'It's hard at times; I'd be lying if I said otherwise. I try and focus on what I can do, rather than what I can't do.' Your eyes bore through me, sending me a warning. 'We see some really sad cases; you wouldn't be human if they didn't touch you. But, I've come to realise, there's always hope for change. Even when it seems truly hopeless. Good things can come from bad. I've seen it happen, lots of times.'

I wanted to add to this: Look at Jack, for example, I'd never be without him. You continued to eyeball me, trying to decipher any hidden meaning in what I'd said. Anything you would be obligated to deal with later, when we were alone. Your dark eyes piercing mine. Then you smiled that smile at me. 'All very good, Eve, my eternal optimist. I'm afraid hope is a little too ambiguous for me. I need concrete facts. Charming, though. Really it is. I've always loved that about you. Always hanging onto something or other.'

'Yes, she is, isn't she? Good job some people keep hope, Gregg,' Sue added, smiling at me.

You tapped on my leg as you smiled back at her. Sending me a message. Making me squirm at your touch. Please, God. I sat, silently fuming, feeling as small as any adult possibly could. How come no one ever saw through your performances? So cringeworthy and insincere. Was it a case of them not wanting to see? Ignoring all the signs, because it was easier to do so. Wasn't this human nature? To avoid unnecessary hardship and confrontation, especially if they had nothing to gain by it. Or was I becoming increasingly cynical of the world and its people?

After a couple of hours and plenty of traffic, we eventually arrived. Only ever having seen Wimbledon on the TV screen before, I couldn't help but feel a slight stir of disappointment. In my mind's eye, I'd imagined it somewhere much grander. I hadn't realised we were approaching the entrance on just another suburban residential street. Pleasant, but fit for any ordinary sports club. Within the grounds, and the streams of people, it vaguely reminded me of a lavish village fete; just busier. How the imagination is so proficient in plugging the cavities with what it desires or needs to see. We were immediately guided by David to the marquee-adjoined restaurant, where we would mingle and be served lunch, ahead of the Centre Court excitement.

I sneaked off to call home and check on Jack, before rejoining the swarm for polite conversation. I hovered from foot to foot, aware of an edgy feeling, my confidence threatening to bail. I didn't recognise myself any more. What had I possibly to talk about? Eventually, we were shown to a white-tableclothed circular tables adorned with unnaturally fixed arrangements of white lilies. I hoped this wasn't a bad omen. The embarrassing decision of who should sit where, while you scanned the room for the most influential dinner-party partner, was thankfully addressed: set named places awaited us. The only downside being I'd been dumped next to you. The alcohol would be flowing in abundance. We had a chauffeur; you would be under the influence, amplifying the volume levels before long. At least I wouldn't be travelling back with you alone, in your inebriated body and mindless state.

I was starving and keen to satisfy the low-sugar shaky feeling, so consumed the minuscule smoked salmon starter with speed. Reaching for the basket of bread as you scowled briefly, inconspicuously. I made polite conversation with my left-side companion as my second course arrived. You leant over me, continuing conversation across the table, then glanced up to the hovering waiter holding a bottle of ruby wine. 'No more here. Not for my wife, thank you,' you added, covering my wine glass just in time to prevent it from being topped up. The waiter seemed slightly taken aback, as I probably did too. He glanced nervously between us.

'Oh, so sorry. Would she prefer white instead? I'll fetch another glass?' he asked you, obviously thinking I didn't have a tongue, or a mind. Strangely, I too found myself looking at you to hear your response.

'No. No, I mean, no more wine. Of either kind. Thank you.' You turned away from the poor lad, who offered me a consoling half-smile. You continued conversation with your pompous-seeming neighbour. An influential figure, I was later informed.

I was aware of my rising heart rate. 'What did you do that for, Gregg?' You completely ignored me. I tapped your arm. You turned to me as if to an annoying child.

'What?' you said under your breath.

'Why did you say I didn't want any more wine? Speak for me?'

You smiled at me, then at the prim-looking lady across from us. 'Because you've had enough.' You attempted to turn your back on me, so I pulled at your arm. My head told me to back off, my heart urged me otherwise. I was pushing my luck. But sometimes it was so unbelievably testing to follow your path.

'One glass, that's all I've had. I'm not driving, so why not?'

You regarded me as if I were a simple-minded idiot, and you needed to spell meaning out to me. 'For Christ's sake, Eve. Stop drawing attention to yourself...' you slunk closer to me, lowering your voice '... making a fool of me. Keep your voice down. You have Jack to look after later. Remember Jack, your son? The child you left at home?' You tapped my arm gently, as if consoling me. 'Stop creating a scene. You're downright embarrassing,' you whispered.

Causing a scene to embarrass you was exactly what I felt like doing, self-important idiot. I pushed back my chair, placing my napkin on the table, avoiding eye contact with my fellow diners. Counting in my mind, zigzagging my hurried way through the room towards the ladies. Passing the raucous laughter, drunken slurring and people generally enjoying themselves. A glass screen between them and me. Self-loathing swatting at me all the way. Did I imagine the look from the other diners as I left?

Poor Gregg, his wife really is a handful. He's so lovely too. Shame. Did you see how she reacted, all over a glass of wine. Maybe she has issues. Maybe she has a drink problem? I do feel sorry for him – she's clearly out of control. That poor baby they have. How can she possibly be capable of looking after him? Poor Gregg.

I freshened myself in the ladies. Why was I bothering? I was merely a decoration in the guise of a wife, a disliked one at that.

I returned in time for dessert, which I pushed around the plate. Strawberries felt so incongruent to my mood. A flashback, of a time strawberry-picking and abundant eating with Sam, reminded me of how far removed I was from me. Later that night we'd made summer cocktails with frozen strawberries for a pop-up barbecue with friends. The laughter and carrying-on. I sipped at my tepid water. Sober, and sad. You, on the other hand, downed liquor and became merry and merrier. I wished I could up and leave. To add insult to injury, the balls of my feet were pulsating – one thing to wear uncomfortable heels when having an amazing time, another altogether when your experience was soul-destroying.

Eventually, you were beckoned over to another table. I recognised one of the men; he'd visited our house in one of the several after-work congregations. I'm sure he introduced himself as a bank manager, or did he work with you? I decided I didn't care. He clearly worshipped you, whoever he was. I reached for my bag, took my chance and absconded. Funny, I thought, I'd believed we were at Wimbledon to enjoy the tennis, but no one else seemed to be budging. Intent on mingling and consuming as much free alcohol as possible. Anyway, polite small talk was very overrated.

I perched on the edge of my Centre Court seat, with dejected empty seats to my left and right. Another waste. You and your cronies stayed in the marquee, by then probably downing whisky shots. The atmosphere on Centre Court was thankfully as I'd imagined. Exhilarating and upbeat. It crossed my mind, if I could, by observing the ball pace left to right, de-traumatise myself with a little EMDR therapy. Or maybe hypnotise myself into believing I was happy, having a great time. I remained until the very end, half watching, half dreaming of what ifs, should haves and wish I hads. Still empty seats surrounded me.

I stood as the sweaty players left the court. I had no excuse but to try and find you; assuming you were still prowling the marquee. I fought my way through the inter-court passage, wondering why I always seemed to be travelling in the wrong direction, pushing against the swarms. I pressed on through until someone stopped abruptly in front of me, blocking my way. His entire face smiled softly, an ordinary male with benevolent eyes. I couldn't help but return his smile. An amiable voice asked me for the time; I glanced at my Rolex, a gift from you on our wedding day. My pulse upped a pace – God, I'd been missing in action for ages. Too long, you'd be furious again. Hopefully you were too blotto to realise. I shared the time with the stranger, he thanked me, smiled then sauntered away. I rotated to allow my eyes to follow him, touched by his apparent gentleness.

Stupid. I hadn't realised I was being surveyed. Was I set up? I now wonder.

Once, I'd never have believed such an innocent interchange could have consequences, would require me to be taught a lesson. The flame to ignite the noted list for all my other evident indiscretions during the day. I continued along the passage, oblivious. Moments later I was jolted back in my tracks; a sharp pain in my small wrist, squeezed tightly as if to crush my delicate bones, my arm yanked at the socket. I spun around in a flash, twisting my ankle over my heels, creating a burning-hot sting. I didn't need to ask; I didn't need to face you or look into your eyes, I already knew. I knew what I'd done wrong, in your sick eyes. I understood, tomorrow I would ache with the marks of tonight. Something told me the wounds would no longer be superficial. Something in your eyes had changed.

Why did I have to wear my watch? But then I was unaware I was being stalked.

Why did I need to smile at the man? He only needed the time.

It was a quiet journey home from Wimbledon, despite the full car; a little civil conversation but you struggled to hide your icy intentions towards me. Your dark eyes attempted to catch mine from time to time. I deliberately avoided them, choosing to natter quietly to Sue instead. All the time the knotting in my stomach squeezed further, a slight shaky feeling seeping through my limbs. The two-hour journey flew by. Before I knew it, we were back at our gates, then imparting goodbyes to our babysitter. I was informed Jack was fast asleep, but as I trod my way up the stairs to check in on him you summoned me to the study.

You lingered at the foot of the stairs. 'Before you go upstairs, Eve…' You nodded towards the study and made your way there. Why did I follow? Because it had to happen, one way or another; I would rather have it over and done with. It was dark outside; only the hall light illuminated the room, the air we shared thick with trepidation. Daggered shadows scattered the floor as I stood on unsteady legs, facing your back. Waiting for you to turn. Your dark frame, deliberately facing out of the window. Casual, hands in pockets. Black was all you could see. The whiff of alcoholic fumes burdening the attitude.

Silence deafened the tone as the clock ticked intrusively, fixed to the wall. I observed the second-hand circle, until I could no longer cope with the slow torture.

'Gregg?' I appealed.

'Shush.' You stamped your foot.

I understood; I must await my fate.

Were you smiling to the outside world? Waiting for the perfect moment? Not wanting to begin, for fear it would be over too soon? Pure excitement pouring through your blood. Your moment to be in control. Finally, you slowly revolved. Deliberately. Calculated. Ominous opaque eyes sought mine. You had decided on my next lesson. My punishment. Just a few premeditated steps forward, you stood in front of me, not uttering a word. There was no point in my running. Where would I go? Jack was asleep upstairs. It was too late. Your hands reached out in slow motion. I was frozen to the spot. I did not protest; I had already shut down. Aware of being walked backwards.

My head whacked hard against the intolerant wall, as I magically slid up it, defying gravity. Defying my self-worth.

Your masculine hands at my throat. My feet floating.

I still did not speak. I couldn't.

I gasped; fighting for air.

You smiled, then dropped me. I fell to my knees.

Not long now.

A crushing pain gored my ribs, your shoes making the strikes all the harsher.

I dropped flat, then curled up like a fallen leaf, so as to protect my head with my arms.

Blow after blow. Thinking only of Jack and our new life to come.

Then hush, as you inspected your work, looking down on me. You crouched down, to whisper to the child you reluctantly disciplined. 'When will you learn, Eve? Why do you insist on doing this to us? Take some time, think long and hard. Consider your behaviour. I should not have to do this, but you leave me no choice. You are sick. You do realise this, don't you? Sick, Eve.'

Hard-done-to footsteps departed the room, the door steadily closing behind them. Darkness but for the moon watching over; I was alone.

My heart banging on the floor, I urged it to keep quiet; it was not the time. I lay listening as the clock ticked on. Then the footsteps trod down the stairs. I hadn't heard them go up, I'd thought you were still lurking in the hall, listening for my next move. The front door slammed, vibrating shock waves through the floor as the realisation dawned: had you taken Jack? I lay immobile, curling into the shape of a kidney bean to let the blackness take me.

I wondered, did that man understand how much his request would cost me? Did he know his smile would punish me? Why did people have to be nice? Why couldn't they leave me alone? Through the silent tears I could see the remains of time, my watch; silver crushed to hundreds of tiny pieces. Elements sparkling in the moonlight on the floor next to me.

The gift of our marriage smashed forever.

Time was a great healer, they said.

But time was a parasite of my sanity.

Chapter Twenty

Cornwall 2016

The adrenaline pumps subaquatic sounds through my ears. I'm conscious of heat illuminating my cheeks and aware of Ruan's eyes spearing my back. But time seems to stop, for a moment, as we all remain immobile without words. Frozen in time. Eventually, he returns my forged smile. I'm unsure if his is a genuine one. My ability to read people's intentions momentarily deactivates. I watch as his eyes search my face. Deliberately checking off my features as if from a list. A mental detailed list he prepared earlier. It's a while before he opens his mouth to answer me, closing it again. Instead, he holds out his tanned hand to greet mine, looking so small in comparison.

I do not know this man; but I suspect he knows me. A disconcerting awareness shrouds me as I wrack my mind. Who are you? A strange unidentified atmosphere fills the room. Then a cough from behind breaks through as I feel the eyes of Ruan moving between us.

'William?' I tender again, shifting my feet to steady myself.

He shakes his head as if waking himself from a trance. 'Yes. Hi, sorry. I was miles away.' He steps closer to me as my feet automatically step back one. He still has hold of my hand; he's also invading my personal space.

My heart is still pumping wildly; I was sure this was you. From behind the resemblance is uncanny. 'Not to worry.' I step forward again. I'm hardly behaving in a welcoming manner. 'I'm Eve, by the way.' I pause for a moment, waiting for him to say, I know, but he doesn't. I am as certain as I can be he's thinking it. Am I just being paranoid again? This could be a genuine case and my distrust is stripping me of any composure or practised etiquette. He smiles at me knowingly; he is self-confident yet there is something so unsettled about him. So many unsaid words sitting on his shoulders. But not in the usual fidgety, anxious manner I've become so accustomed to.

'Please, come on through, William. It's lovely to meet you,' I lie, wishing I'd refused to take the referral whilst I still had the chance. I'm also aware as I say this, he hasn't yet released his grip of my hand. His clasp is firm, touching my skin, almost trying to communicate something. I cannot shake off the uneasy feeling, but then, given the recent rush of stress hormones, it's to be expected. Perhaps it has nothing to do with this William, and I'm simply filtering down again from the battered boxes.

I slowly pull my hand from his and spin round to face the room. So conscious of each footstep he takes behind me. 'Come on through.' My shoulders tense ready for action. I glance at a perplexed-looking Ruan and try to transmit to him: I don't even know where to begin but please don't leave the clinic, please stay close; just for the next hour.

We step into my room, and I shut the solid wood door behind us. There's no glass in this door, to protect people's privacy. But with no way for Ruan to observe and without the reassuring alarm buttons I had in the hospital, I feel decidedly vulnerable. I watch him glance around the room. Most people avoid averting their eyes from me, their feet or the floor. Next, he regards my desk and I realise he's looking at the brown A4 envelope containing the newspaper articles. Why is he looking at it? I'd meant to hide it, not that he appreciates what it contains. Or does he? I notice a flicker of acknowledgment in his eyes before he returns his eyes to me. Did I imagine it?

I direct my hand towards his chair. 'Please, take a seat, William.' We both sit. For the first time, I realise it's me who sits awkward and with apprehension of what's to come, rather than my client. He slouches back into the depth of the chair, spreading out his legs as far as he can without touching mine, as he alternately flexes and taps his feet. Self-certainty emanates from him but it's not arrogance. I feel a little bad – he's come to me for help, and so far he hasn't received the best of my attention. He's been referred through a professional body, but something is not right.

I smile at him uneasily as I reach behind to gather the paperwork from my desk. I feel his eyes wash over me, studying me. Perturbed, I shift in my chair, thrown completely as to how to begin our appointment. Why am I allowing him to make me behave in this manner? *People can only affect us if we allow them to*, runs through my mind. Now look at me. But he's good, he has discreetly managed to shift the balance of therapist and client, and a bad therapist at that, one who wishes to have control. I need to break the cycle.

I feel my throat scratch with dryness. 'Can I fetch you a glass of water? Or a coffee perhaps, before we make a start?' Desperately hoping he'll say yes, so I can leave the room to have a word with myself. Re-establish some self-control, and cease behaving like such an amateur.

But he smiles at me whilst pulling a bottle from his jacket pocket. 'It's fine, thanks. I always carry water with me.'

'Always prepared, I see; must be the soldier in you.' If you are one, that is. 'Would you mind, though? I've such a dry throat today; I'll pop for some water, if that's okay with you?'

'Sure, of course, please, carry on.' He watches as I stand. Should I move the envelope before I leave the room? Why am I allowing him to get to me so much? I decide it would look ridiculous; I've already wasted enough time. Even so, I leave the door ajar behind me, and scuttle across to the water machine, listening for any possible movement. I glance over to the front-desk area where Bea has now joined Ruan; I half smile, half grimace at them. Drumming my head against my hands, I take a gulp of cold water and count to ten. Get a grip, Eve. I head back for my room. Ruan calls after me.

'Eve, just to let you know – your next appointment has just called in. Cancelled. Said she can't make it, her partner has insisted she join him instead, something about needing to visit his son. Said you'd understand?'

I don't, but it will just be something else I've forgotten about. 'Fine,' I tell Ruan. I re-enter my room, leaving my anxious state outside the door, Bea and Ruan undoubtedly confirming to each other that my behaviour is becoming more insane by the hour.

'Sorry about that. Right, so, William, I've received this referral—' I flash the piece of paper '—and you are ex-forces?'

'Yes, I am.'

He's not giving anything away. 'Okay. Let's start with the here and now, then work our way back.'

'Okay.' He settles further into his chair.

'Okay, this referral states PTSD. What is your understanding of this, or, more importantly, can you tell me what your symptoms are? How they affect you on a day-to-day basis. I mean in today's terms.'

'How long do you have?' He smiles. Almost teasing.

I return his smile. 'As long as you need.' I note, despite mentioning his diagnosed condition, he's so together and calm. 'It's perhaps easier to start with – how you believe your life has changed because of any symptoms. So, if we were to look at yesterday, what did you do or not do, feel or not feel, in comparison to perhaps twelve months ago, two years ago or, if you've been suffering for some time, ten years ago. Go back as far as you need to.'

He spends time relaying debilitating symptoms: sleepless nights, panic attacks without warning and the most lucid flashbacks and anxious tendencies – these he keeps well hidden, except for the obvious. A constant wired feeling, always feeling on the edge. Clearly, this isn't going to be a one-off appointment.

Despite empathising with this man who sits in front of me, who has been through experiences which would force you to turn away from a TV screen, I still feel quite uneasy about him. Something doesn't add up, but I can't put my finger on it. I admonish myself, but it wouldn't be too difficult to research and relay typical symptoms of PTSD and trauma-related disturbances, so to manipulate a referral. He continues, composed and precise, conferring with a smooth, educated, but not a la-di-da voice. After a while, I can't dispute this man has suffered trauma in his life. He is genuine; I'm now as sure of this as I can be. It's horrifying learning what these servicemen go through; how can they possibly be expected to readapt, without help, into everyday society? But there is more he's not telling me. Something buried underneath.

'You're from Warwickshire?' Merely articulating the W word sends shivers down my spine.

He holds up a finger. 'Was,' he instantly corrects me, as if it had the same effect on him. 'Sorry. I mean, I was from there, yes. I no longer have any connections to the area.' This is the first time I notice a flicker of guardedness in his attitude. I watch him as he shifts position in his seat, back to the same position again. Eyes locked on mine.

'Okay, so now you're living in Cornwall?'

He shrugs. 'Kind of, yes, at the moment I am anyway.' Have I touched on something here? His confident eyes are reflecting a little caginess.

He clearly feels uncomfortable with this line of discussion, but it's not exactly relevant to his treatment. I decide to leave it, for the moment. Maybe the referral team can throw some more light on the matter. Though it's odd something so everyday can evoke this reaction. We continue to discuss his symptoms, how they impact on his health and quality of life, then I talk through the treatment options for trauma, the neurobiology of how it manifests and subsists. At all times, William is polite, appearing to take an interest. We talk about the brain and its many disobliging behaviours, physical and psychological; he listens with interest. Perhaps he is here with genuine needs.

'Interesting,' he utters.

'The thing is, I believe, if people have a better understanding of the science, why they're feeling, reacting the way they are, it allows it to feel more correctable.' He nods. 'Your brain is a most powerful computer; your ultimate control centre but also a creature of habit. Like all new learning, we can also learn bad things, even build new neural pathways to support the bad things. Yours possibly manifest from trauma of some form. Not allowing you to move on, always alert. Always hyper-vigilant. Sitting dormant waiting to prod you into action.'

'Can you change these pathways? Or am I stuck with them for good? Knackered?' he asks.

I nod. 'Yes, definitely you can. Your brain's like a malleable chunk of plastic; it can be moulded and adapted to new learning; new responding and new thinking.'

'And the old bits? The bad pathways?'

'Like the old adage says, if you don't use it you lose it. That said, we need to deal with the trauma first.'

He tilts his head to one side. 'But what if I don't want to talk about it?' I've the message loud and clear: he doesn't want to discuss his traumatic experiences with me. This isn't unusual in itself. It's not exactly pleasant conversation and, in some respects, discussing the bad things can make the trauma worse; especially if the client is anxious at the time. Creating yet another anxious-to-be-avoided experience can only compound the trauma further.

'It's not a problem. We can treat the trauma specifically; there are techniques that do not require you to discuss it with me. Non-invasive techniques. You will still need to recall the experiences in your mind's eye, though. I'll give you more information about this before you leave so you can go away, think it through.' I wonder why he's so anxious about sharing it with me. He asked for the referral himself. He must already know I've worked with many serving and non-serving people. What could be so bad? Or what did he not want me to know?

Eventually, we move on to talking about historical patterns. How we learn to respond and react to circumstances and people, based on past patterns of behaviour. He crosses and uncrosses his legs, intermittently swigging from his bottle of water. Little beads of sweat appear on his brow. Where has the self-assured man gone who entered my room? This isn't supposed to happen in this order. Something I've said has triggered his response and he's struggling to refind his footing.

His left leg jigs up and down in time to his tapping heel. I can't ignore it any longer. 'Are you okay? Before we go on. You seem a little on edge. Is it something I've said?'

His eyes dart from me, to the desk and back. 'Yeah, I'm fine.' He tugs at the collar of his polo shirt. 'It's pretty warm in here.'

I'll oblige him. 'It is, isn't it? I'll open the window.' I begin battle with the window once again, conscious this is not the cause for his anxious moment. It isn't overly warm at all. We'll both be freezing in a minute. I sit back down, deciding to change the subject.

'What about family, William?'

'What about it?' he challenges.

'Do you have any close family or friends to support you at the moment? A partner maybe?' I've noticed the absence of any ring.

'Nope, I don't. No family. No partner,' he shuts me down.

Interesting. Why such a sensitive topic? Another one.

'Okay. Any close friends? Anyone to help you through this? Someone you can talk things through with?' He exhales, lifting his chin to me. 'It's not a problem. This is simply background information. So I have an understanding of your support system.' He sits tense, almost defiant, as if I'm judging him. I'm not.

'No.' He sighs deeply, rubbing his outdoor hand through thick dark hair. 'Look, if you don't mind me saying, I can't really see how this helps. But, in answer to your questions, no. I don't have anyone. A life in the forces can do that to you.' I'm not mistaken; his eyes take on a deep look of sadness. I think we've encountered another knot in the tissues here.

I hold my hands up to him. 'It's fine, William, we can move on.' A glimmer of relief washes over him as he physically relaxes into his chair. 'Just so you know,' I say, 'you're not the only one. Many people are without support. It must be tremendously difficult to build relationships when you never really know where you're going to be based. Always on the move, overseas, out of the UK so often.' Or sometimes people choose not to involve friends or family. It's not too often I come across people who are completely alone in the world. How sad. 'Anyway, that's what I'm here for, so it's no big deal. Let's just move on.'

Clearly he doesn't wish to talk about his family or his past. It could be a personal privacy issue, but I sense this time it's more than that. I stand to give him a moment. 'Think I'll pull down the window now, if it's okay; it's getting a little chilly in here.' I begin to bump down the pig-headed window.

'My parents are dead,' he blurts at my back, so as to get the stuck words to release. I turn to acknowledge him but remain silent. I don't want to interrupt his flow. I nod at him whilst sitting down. A few breaths later he adds, 'The thing is, I've never known my parents. They died before I got the chance to know them. I can't even remember them. Sometimes I think I see them. Hear them too in my memories. But I'm not sure if they're actual memories, or if they're just in my imagination or my dreams. Other than that, I'd rather not talk about it, if you don't mind.' I smile and nod at him. Before he adds, 'I can assure you, though, it's not really a problem for me; I've had plenty of time to get used to it.'

The sadness I witnessed earlier is no longer with him. I think he probably is okay with it. 'Of course, whatever we talk about has to be because you want to, or need to. Not always the same thing.' He would appear to have no history, no roots and no current base. It's not what he's saying, but what he's not saying, that concerns me. I glance at the clock on the shelf to the left of the door, purposely placed so I can keep my eye on time without alerting the client to it. 'Do we have an address for you, William?' I flick through my paperwork. 'For some reason the referral form was incomplete.'

'No, I don't think I had a fixed address at the original meeting.' He rubs his hand through his hair, still in the same position from before. 'I told them I'd be heading down to Cornwall anytime soon for a while. So they suggested I booked in with you.'

'Fine. Can you please give Ruan your full details before you leave? It's quite important. Are you registered with a GP down here?'

'Nope.'

'Can I suggest you do, when you have a moment? Whereabouts are you living – in Truro?'

'You can suggest I register at the GP's, yes.' He grins; confidence is back in the room. 'Just outside Truro, on the outskirts.'

'I'll get Ruan to set up our next appointment and then—'

'What kind of experience do you have with trauma, Eve?'

'I've worked with trauma cases for many years. What would you—'

'No, I mean personal experience?'

'I see. Sorry, William; I don't express details about my personal life in clinic. It's a—'

'I just wondered as you appear to have such an innate understanding.'

I feel the beginnings of a blush. I could be wrong, but it sounds as if he's challenging me; digging at something. 'That will be my training. That, and my experience of working with it,' I explain.

He nods, smiling. 'Understood.' He jumps to his feet, holding out his hand. 'Well, it's been… insightful, Eve; thank you.' I stand to shake his hand. He embraces my hand for a moment too long, before adding, 'Do you have anyone to support you, to talk things through with?' I stare blankly at him; what is he trying to say, imply? He continues, 'Of course, I'm referring to the difficult cases you must work with.'

But this is not what he meant at all. What does this man know about me and who is he? Does he know you? Have you sent him? 'Don't you worry; I can look after myself,' I tell him.

'Yes. Yes, so I believe. Thank you, Eve.' He turns and leaves my room, before one last turn, his eyes meet mine. Unsaid words meet somewhere in between us, and he closes the door behind him. I fall down to my seat, rest my elbows on my desk and place my head in my hands. What the hell was that all about? My eyes fall once again to the A4 envelope.

A few minutes later; I'm broken from my thoughts by a gentle knocking at my door, followed by Ruan's head.

'Coffee? You've time now for a quick break.'

'Please, Ruan, thanks.' He backs out of the door.

'Ruan?'

'Yeah, I know, strong! Already on it.'

'No, not that. Did William leave his address, before he left? Did he give you his details?'

'No. Should he have?'

'Yes, I asked him to.'

'No. He just said, "Can you tell Eve I'll be in touch?"'

I have no way of contacting him, no mobile number, no address. I know nothing about him. Was he even a genuine PTSD referral? More importantly, what did he mean, 'tell Eve I'll be in touch'? Was that a threat or a genuine comment? Why do I feel as though he came here under false pretences? All that outlandishness – have I ever experienced any trauma? – what was all that about?

I prod to silence the rumble from my empty stomach. I feel too nauseous to consider food. I finger the brown envelope, hoping for enlightenment, then tug the insert out again. Tell me, does this have something to do with you? Along with the phone calls, the car following me, and those dark shadows I feel at night. But how could it have anything to do with you, given I unearthed it in my briefcase? The only people with access to my briefcase are the people I care about and trust the most in the world. I can't go down this dodgy road; I can't allow myself to suspect any of these people. But if they didn't plant it, either I'm losing my mind and I put it there myself, or someone else has gained access to the clinic or, God forbid, my home, without my realising. For the life of me, I cannot see how it could be possible.

I jump and turn as Ruan kicks the door open with a mug of coffee in one hand and a box of Jaffa Cakes in the other. The sheet of A4 paper floats in slow motion to the floor.

'I forgot to mention...' He places my supplies down on the desk. 'I'll get that, don't worry.' He begins to bend down.

'No, it's fine, leave it. It's for the bin anyway.' I bend forwards to scoop up the sheet, before he attempts to help me again. 'What did you forget to mention?'

'Someone got hit this morning.'

'Hit?'

'Yeah, by the cranky traffic warden. Made his day, probably. The best thing was, the woman was sat there for ages. I thought she was coming in here to begin with. She was looking our way for some time.'

'Sure,' I respond, but Ruan's words are drifting around the room, as I only have eyes for the sheet of paper now in my hands.

'About… thirty minutes, I reckon. She must have decided to run down to the public loo. She was only gone, what, five minutes…'

'Really.' For the first time, on the back of the sheet, I notice a handwritten note.

'Then, he hit her, didn't he? I tried to intervene, but he wasn't having it. She must have been back literally seconds after he got her. She didn't look very happy.'

'Oh, dear.' I quickly shove manila folders on top, to cover the paper. I'd recognise that handwriting anywhere. 'I bet she wasn't.'

'Eve, are you even listening to me?' He sways back to get a better look at me. 'You okay? You've gone real pale.'

'I'm fine. I was listening. What a shame, poor woman. Bet she wasn't expecting that the moment she wasn't looking.' I stand, reaching for my jacket. 'I'm just popping out, won't be long.'

'You sure you're okay?'

'I just need some fresh air, Ruan. I'm fine.'

I'm not fine. I wasn't expecting this. How did I not see it before? It doesn't make sense – why now? I crash out onto the pavement, a deep breath battling for space within my constricting chest as I fight back the rising taste of bilious disorientation. How would she even know about it? Know about you?

It doesn't make any sense at all. After all this time.

Chapter Twenty-One

Before

Over time, I became less absorbent, more unflinching by the *lessons* I was taught; the rules I was required to learn. The punishments, though painfully damaging, had a perverse numbing effect on my conscience. It needed to be this way; to be my coping mechanism, essential for reaching my 'get out of jail' card. Fortunately, your incredibly protracted work hours gifted me and Jack bursts of normality, left to our own devices. The interludes that kept me afloat. The nights were the worst as the ghosts of past and present desolation made nightly visits, just at the point my head merged with the pillow. During the daytime, I became expert in burying our living reality deep beneath the surface, invisible to the naked eye; only known by the heart. Always holding my breath.

If you knew how I felt, how I saw you, what I was thinking, you didn't show it; I suspected it was more because you didn't care. So long as I behaved myself and played the part; and from time to time showed gratitude for the life you provided us. Most of the time I obliged your rituals and behaviours, plodded along with your conditions. I tried as best I could to keep any consequential upsurges private. It was part of a giant learning curve. I soon learned of the penalties of doing otherwise.

Deception and lies. I became as practised as you. I almost forgot who I was.

My sanity and Jack's well-being were running on borrowed time. As Jack developed so did his need for regularity, decent archetypes. I found myself continually monitoring him for unwelcome signs; praying that so far, his environment hadn't tarnished his memory templates, and misinformed his psyche of how to behave. I desperately wanted him to feel ordinariness but didn't want him to absorb his environment as normal. I decided to go ahead and return to work on a part-time basis; much to your disgust.

'Pathetic. Preferring to spend your time at the hospital, than time with your son.'

'Can you not see how it may help us – my ability to hold adult conversation? I'm referring to the many corporate events, every other week. I don't feel I offer anything near intelligent conversation.' I lied through my back teeth. I didn't give two hoots about your corporate events. It was going to kill me being separated from Jack. But somehow, I had to rebuild my confidence in an alien world.

'Your life is somewhat dull. Now you mention it, what do you manage to talk about?'

I don't, I thought; you just don't notice. Or, I lie mostly. I'd noticed how I would blush, feel a slight tremble, be aware of my quickening pulse; I was becoming so self-aware and so horribly distanced at the same time. Losing ground.

Returning to work was essential for the steps I needed to take, but a total wrench; we'd become such a close unit, Jack and me, I cried myself to sleep the night I informed the hospital of my return. I hadn't cried for a long time, not externally. The following morning, I sat Jack in his favourite spot, on the kitchen work surface, our usual wrestling match tying the laces on his soft boots. Chaotically kicking his legs about, chortling at me trying to catch them. I tried to explain to him as best I could; he was after all just two and a half.

I gently lifted his chin, so his brilliant blue eyes met mine.

'Listen, Jack; Mummy has some exciting news. I've something important to tell you.'

'We're gunna go to de farm?' His eyes lit up further.

'No, not the farm, sweetheart, not today. Maybe on Friday though.'

'Doh, me loves de farm.' His little angel-like face fell sullen as he shrugged his shoulders dramatically.

My heart panged. 'No, listen, it's something else, just as exciting. Mummy's going to go back to work, Jack. Just for a little while anyway. Not every day.'

He raised his eyebrows. 'At de hopipal?'

'Yes, that's right, at the hospital.' He searched my face for clues, with no idea what this meant for him. I wanted to tell him not to worry, I'd changed my mind; I wouldn't be going anywhere. But I couldn't do that, not for either of our sakes.

'I don't want to leave you, Jack. I will miss you so-o-o much.' I knew his understanding was limited, but I needed to try, for my own sake. Especially as I couldn't explain to him just how much hung on my decision.

I tapped his tiny button nose. 'You may not understand now, but I hope you will one day, when you're a big boy.' I smiled as he sat up straight, pulling his shoulders back and holding his head high. 'Yes, a big boy, just like that but even bigger! This is very important for Mummy to do, but especially for Jack.'

'Speshaly for me-e-e,' he emphasised, without any real idea of what I was talking about.

I kissed his soft pink nose. 'Yes, speshaly for you, my beautiful boy!'

I continued, despite knowing it would go over his head. 'It will give Mummy lots of strength and all the confidence you and I are going to need soon. Okay?'

Soon? What was my plan, other than to escape? It had to be one to also benefit you. The normal routes of leaving a broken marriage were not an option. You would never let us go, would you. Unless it was in your best interest.

'Okay. So, Mummy, Be Strong,' he exaggerated at me. I picked him up and snuggled his warm body tightly.

As we walked towards the patio door, I promised him. 'One day soon, not too long away, Mummy will take you away from all this.'

'Mummy, Jack go on olerday.' He beamed.

'Kind of like a holiday, yes. Then we can be happy together. Okay?' He gave me one of his crushing smiles before nuzzling his head into my hair.

He had no idea of the true meaning of my words, so it didn't matter that I voiced my motives. We had an unspoken understanding: mine was to make essential changes and his was to place his trust in me. It was a huge ask, given his angelic face still lit up at the sight of his daddy, since he didn't realise the truth. He wanted to love him; I wished it were possible. He naturally assumed the things he witnessed and heard were standard. This was my greatest fear of all. Jack could grow up thinking his dad was normal.

Just the night before, I was giving Jack his tea in his high chair in the kitchen when you arrived home unusually early. The slam of the door caused us both to jump. 'Eve?' you bellowed from the hall.

'In here; giving Jack his tea.' Why did I always hope today would be different? Even when I knew it couldn't be. Your leather shoes tapped on the wood before you sauntered into the kitchen, pulling at your tie to loosen it, dropping your suit jacket onto the side.

You stopped in the tracks of Jack's chortle-filled smile. 'There you are.' You pointed back to him, smiling. If only this were how you could remain, I ached.

Jack's little face emitted splashes of joy and mischief. Then he picked up his apple and flung it to the floor, giggling, 'Daddy!'

You moved towards him, scowling as you bent down to pick up the apple segment. 'Don't do that, Jack, it's naughty! Does Mummy let you do it?'

I watched as Jack's upturned plump lips levelled out.

'He was just excited to see you. Over enthusiastic.'

'He has to realise this is naughty. Not acceptable.' You glared at Jack as if he were an insolent teenager.

Shame your parents didn't teach you the rights and wrongs of life, I thought.

I was keen not to let the situation escalate. Constantly playing the arbitrator, trying to prevent a fall-out over the most insignificant issues. 'Do you

want Daddy to finish giving you your fruit, Jack?' I
asked him.

'Ye-e-s-s-s.' He kicked his happy-again feet
against the leg rest. I turned to pass over to you, but
the look on your face told me I was a fool.

You held out your hands. 'No can do, I'm afraid.
I've a meeting tonight.' You prodded at your mobile
screen. 'Everyone will be here in… around an hour.
I've notes to prepare yet.' You turned away to
swagger over to the glass unit, reaching for a whisky
tumbler. You didn't address Jack again. He simply
disappeared.

'Who's coming here?' I asked you.

You shot me a quizzical look. 'Why? Of what
relevance is it?' I didn't respond. Pouring yourself a
large whisky, swirling the burnt orange liquor in the
glass, you replied, 'Work colleagues; usual gang.
Important stuff.' You gulped back indulgently; I was
wishing you'd choke. 'Can you dig out the Thai
menu from the drawer in the utility room?'

'What about the lasagne I've made?'

You topped up your glass, smirking. 'Eve, come
on? I can hardly serve up…' you smirked '… lasagne.
This isn't a cosy soirée.' Your mobile pinged. 'Dig
out the menu, there's a good girl.' You didn't look up
from your screen but continued to noisily gulp the
honeyed liquid. I bit my tongue. I could feel my
blood pressure rising. So, was this how crimes of

passion occurred? I welcomed another night away from you, but you made my blood boil with your brazen, rude arrogance. I turned away to take a seat next to Jack, who had withdrawn at his father's lack of interest.

You moved to the other side of the kitchen, and began to rummage through the pull-out larder cupboard. 'Can you make sure Jack is bathed, in bed on time tonight? He can't be making a noise, running around when I've people here,' you conveyed to my back.

'Sure.' Why didn't I tell you, it's Jack's home, not theirs? Because it would have damaged our chances; patience was compulsory. 'Shall we read your favourite book tonight, Jack? The one with the flying chair?' Jack beamed, nodding enthusiastically.

'For Christ's sake.' I could hear you taking items from the larder cupboard, tossing them on the floor. I tried to ignore you. I already knew what your grievance was.

'What adventure do you think they'll have this time?' I asked Jack. You continued to empty the entire cupboard of jars, packets and tins into a heap. My stomach curdled at the sound, as I felt your frustration building by the moment. A ticking bomb.

'To a new land!' shouted Jack.

I could sense you were standing still. 'A new land? Like what?' I knew you were staring at me; willing me to turn around.

'EVE!' you shouted, making me jump despite knowing it was coming. I turned to see your incensed expression. I didn't need to ask; I'd been shopping that morning and, in the rush to get Jack out for his swimming club, had placed the grocery items in the appropriate cupboard but without care; not in the correct order or position. Careless.

'Well?' You stood looking from the carnage on the floor to me and back again. 'Do you not have anything to say?'

'Not now, Gregg, you're worrying Jack.' I looked back at Jack to see his bottom lip beginning to quiver.

Then, lots of scuffing and thudding noises behind me as you booted various packages over the floor, spewing contents, hitting the kitchen base units. My shoulders tensed with trepidation but it still took me by surprise as my head pounded forward, jarring my neck. The taste of iron filled my mouth as I'd bit hard down on my tongue. From the large tub of Marmite that now wedged itself between my backbone and the rear of the chair, having rebound from my skull. Thank goodness for plastic packaging, ricocheted through my mind. I took Jack's innocent hand in mine, in some rough attempt to soothe away his concerned look. Some time ago, I'd probably have apologised to you.

'I'm going to shower. Ensure this mess is straightened out. I mean, for pity's sake, what have you been doing all day? You're right, you should return to work. At least then I'll be able to employ someone competent to sort the house.'

I could quite easily have reached for a kitchen knife. I counted to ten; time, Eve, time.

With inflexible eyes bearing into me, you snatched up the bag of whole nuts you were obviously looking for, along with your whisky tumbler, before making your way back to the door, grabbing your jacket from the work surface as you passed.

It was then I saw the bulky envelope drop from your jacket pocket, the contents clearly visible. Two abundant wads of cash staring back at me. There must have been thousands of pounds lying shadily on the floor. Where on earth had it come from? Why would you, a professional man, be walking around with thousands of pounds' worth of notes in your pocket? You bent down and casually picked up the envelope, smirking at me, before back-stepping into the doorway.

'Make sure packets, tins and cartons are separated. In a logical content-related order; via the sell-by dates, so the product label is clearly visible.

NOT THE CONTENTS LABEL!' You stomped away from the kitchen, wittering to yourself, 'It's really not that difficult, or too much to ask, surely.'

I desperately needed to be free from my marital shackles. Why did I have to marry a psychopath? Someone who'd never give in, give up or accept. In your eyes, bit by bit, we were increasing your levels of frustration. So, forcing up the gravity of the lessons you required to teach me to keep control. An outlay I was required to pay. My prize would be bigger. From my point of view, you were becoming weaker. The jurisdiction in your eyes tightened, but in mine it was crumbling. Eventually, this would force you to make mistakes, let down your façade to show your true colours. I didn't ever truly consider how far you or I would be willing to go. We were on a path to somewhere without a map and only a vague idea of destination.

How it pained you if, when you returned in the evenings, Jack was not already fed, bathed and in his pyjamas. If he was downstairs and not upstairs. If I'd forgotten to turn off the TV before going upstairs; if the main light was visible in Jack's bedroom, instead of his bedtime side lamp. If I'd spilt some of his milk on his side table whilst putting his night-time beaker down. Or if for some, God-forbidden reason, I'd left out the toys from where we'd been playing together on the lounge floor.

Your work colleagues arrived just as I was settling Jack off to sleep. I lay with him, recounting a favourite story as he twiddled strands of my hair with heavy eyes. It was not long before I heard bulbous voices, followed by car doors slamming, then animated back-slapping greetings from downstairs. Why were you even holding these meetings in our home? Why did you no longer use the plush offices or one of the many lavish establishments you used to frequent in Birmingham? Jack stopped twiddling my hair, his pale eyelids shut tight. I tiptoed over to his bedroom window overlooking the driveway. One of the cars I recognised. I'd seen it on the driveway following the disastrous golf-club night and several times since; the other two cars were unknown to me. Were these people something to do with the cash? His strange and repulsive behaviour?

As I crept from Jack's room around the galleried landing I caught sight of one of the men, lingering at the study door. Except he didn't look like a man, more like a young lad. He couldn't have been more than twenty. Strange, why would he be here? To take the minutes maybe? Perhaps he was a legal secretary of some kind. I loitered in the shadows, trying to listen. Then, you must have closed the door. So, I decided to make the most of the peace and quiet, retreating to the bathroom for a long deep soak.

Sometime later, I re-emerged to check out of the window again; one of the cars had left. With you and co out of sight behind the closed study door, I slunk through to your dressing area, where you hung your suits. A pressing need to check your jacket pockets hit me whilst in the bath. I couldn't shake the feeling of something iniquitous happening. I ruffled eagerly through your jackets, but you had so many, I wasn't convinced which one you'd been wearing earlier. I found nothing. No envelope, no wads of cash. Where would you be likely to hide it? If it wasn't unlawful, why hide it anyway? I rummaged through your work outfits for a little longer to no avail. All your pockets were empty, not so much as a handkerchief or a lone receipt. Why did you have to be so goddam methodical?

I peeped over the landing to ensure the coast was still clear. With one last idea of where you might have hidden your stash, I stole off to one of the spare bedrooms. A rickety timeworn chest of drawers sat under the window full to the brim with your memorabilia and certificates. I wondered if I really wanted to be sneaking through your things. I had to. I quickly moved through the drawers from top to bottom, resisting the musty smell, with one drawer remaining to check. But unbeknown to me, it was locked, so as I hurriedly tugged at it, it shunted the whole chest forward. The mirror, being precariously balanced on the top, catapulted in slow motion over my head before smashing to the hard floor. Sending shards everywhere.

I held my breath as my heartbeat spiralled, waiting, frozen. It wasn't long before I heard footsteps, controlled but gaining-pace footsteps moving up the stairs. I remained paralysed, fearful of the situation I had created, until a dark shadow loomed in the doorway. You sneered. I shivered; that smile was always the worst.

'Cleaning? Surely not. Especially at this time in the evening?'

'I was looking for Jack's red medical book. Have you seen it?'

'And why would it be in here?'

'I thought, you or I might have put it in this chest, to keep it safe.' You shook your head; why was I even bothering to pretend?

Two more footsteps before I was yanked to my feet by my arm. Your unyielding eyes penetrated mine. My soul thumping at my ribcage for reprieve as you glared down at me. A few icy quiet moments passed before you walked me like a naughty child around the galleried space, squeezing my arm tightly. All the time being aware of your guests quiet in the study. You shoved me through our bedroom door, backed me over to the bed until it hit the backs of my legs, forcing me to sit. One last knowing smirk. Then you paced away. 'You are unbalanced,' you told me as you removed the only key from the oak door, locking it behind you.

'Gregg. You can't lock me in. What if Jack wakes up? You're downstairs in the study – you won't be able to hear him.' But you didn't care, did you?

'Shhh,' you said behind the locked door.

I heard voices radiating from the hallway. Should I shout, bang loudly on the door? Create a scene, let them know what you're really like? No, it wouldn't work. You'd make me out to be a lunatic somehow. You thumped something, your hand, I presumed, as a warning on the door. 'Don't you worry, darling.' The words being unnecessarily loud, obviously not for my benefit. 'Of course, take yourself off to bed. You're sick. Don't worry, I'll take care of everything. Relax for the evening.'

I considered the room for something to do, to distract my humming mind and the building anger. I couldn't blow all my hard work; as much as it pained me, I needed to wait. I picked up my Kindle and read and reread the same couple of paragraphs, each time forgetting to focus on the narrative. My eyes followed the words but my mind could not engage.

How could anyone hate anyone so copiously? How could I have married someone I now wished dead?

Chapter Twenty-Two

Cornwall 2016

Slow shilly-shally steps down through the village towards the sandy cove. My mind deliberating over what I need to spill; all I can afford to leave out. It feels so odd now – how did I ever exist in that life before Cornwall? A story of two distinct people; or is it? Maybe it's not so removed. Can anyone ever be totally detached from their past? My mouldable brain still reflects the past trodden pathways carved so deeply. New neural pathways for new experiences exist; yet the gentle foliage is not sufficient to disguise old dirty tracks. Several times, this week alone, I've woken in the early hours; my skin damp and hot, my heart running on overtime, my mind subservient to old templates.

Now, as I amble towards The Wheal, I think back to last week, when I decided to clear out the spare room. It had been nagging at me for a while and we could do with the space. I opened the door and cautiously peeked in before being transported back in time, face to face with two crates crammed with A4 ring binders. Each binder bursting with legal document after court order after personal statement after antagonistic solicitors' letters. Thousands and thousands of pounds' worth of absolutely pointless court orders and legal representation. They take your money but they don't tell you these orders are often not worth the paper they're typed on. Why did I bother going through a divorce? I knew it would never be the end.

I quicken my step, thinking of how I needlessly fed the fat pockets of so-called family solicitors and honourable barristers. Poor Gloria had popped her head around the door to catch me humping stuffed black bin liners that I'd emptied the crates into down to one of the outhouses. I'd promised her the liners didn't contain amputated limbs, but they may as well have.

I arrive at the entrance to the pub, knowing Bea and Ruan are waiting inside for me to spill the beans. When I agreed to come, I'd forgotten Jack would be at football training. I've sent him a couple of texts and he hasn't as yet replied. I push worrying thoughts from my mind as I enter. I duck my head ever so slightly to avoid the battered *Mind the Beam* sign. Drifting between oak-beamed low ceilings is the scent of onions, homemade pastry comforts and what smells like some kind of casserole, making my stomach groan. Nooks and crannies everywhere are already filling up for the night; the atmosphere dances with the usual buzz of local chatter.

I spot Ruan, casually leaning over the pumps chatting to Ted, the owner; he'll be there a while. Bea has found her favourite table tucked away in the corner with a view onto the road through the leaded-light window. I zigzag through the tables to her, tapping Ruan on the back and acknowledging Ted as I pass, hoping this will serve as a reminder to Ruan to stop chatting and hurry up with our drinks. They both give me a nod, before continuing with what I'm guessing to be idle chatter.

I'm feeling jittery, knowing I'm to disclose fragments of my past; after last night, I no longer have a choice in this. I'm about to open one of the locked doors in my mind; behind it is a dark room with a fading fire. The pungent smell of smoulder, blocking my airways, stifling my breath. I'd rather throw a cloak over, smother it, but I can't. It will simply catch alight again. Whilst smouldering embers are manageable, what comes next may not be. I know you're out there. It's not just the building evidence, it's also my super-sensitive sixth sense. I can almost smell you getting closer.

I kiss Bea on her cold cheek. 'You got here quickly. Did you come across the fields or something?' She smells of honest salt air; the human contact is comforting.

Her full lips upturn. 'Ha, you know me, when on a promise of alcohol. Got here just in time to bag our favourite seat...' she searches the room '... in case anyone else had plans for it.' She reminds me of a small child.

I rub my icy hands together. 'So I see. Well done, you. I must admit I could kill for a drink tonight.'

She takes my hand, rubbing it between hers, then blowing on it, as I used to do to Jack. 'Are you dead?' she asks me. 'You're colder than me. Cold hands, warm heart, that's what they say, isn't it?'

'Or bad circulation,' I offer.

'I prefer warm heart, Eve. You keep it at bay, but I see it, every day.' She smiles affectionately. 'A hard day for you?' She lets my hand go and places her elbows on the table to rest her face in her hands.

A sigh escapes me. 'You could say that. I seem to be having quite a few of them lately.' I look out of the window as my words run out on me. I can't quite fathom what to say next. What's wrong with me? I'm behaving like a teenager who has something awful to divulge to her parents. I'm supposed to be an adult, for God's sake. But my brain has just left the party and walked out of the door.

She lifts and tilts her head. 'You do look ever so tired, Eve, if you don't mind me saying.'

I shake my head. 'It's fine. I recognise I'm looking a little rough at the moment.' I smile at her. 'And some have already pointed this out to me this week.'

'No. No, I didn't say rough.'

'No, you didn't, but only because you're too polite, this time. Anyway, you didn't need to. Unfortunately, we have mirrors in our house.' We smile at each other.

'How's that adorable boy of yours? I do love him; he's so gorgeous.' She tactfully changes the subject.

I smile impulsively, thinking of him. 'Still being a pain in the arse in the mornings; still leaving his gear all over his floor for Mum to pick up. Other than that, he's mostly lovely.'

'Matt still does that, probably because he had a mum like you. Doing everything for him,' she adds.

'Probably.' I nod.

'Oh, well, if that's his only vice, you're doing pretty well, I'd say.'

Briefly, I think of Milly again. It seems I might have been right, from what Ruan has revealed. The day we met, I was sure she had been smoking weed. 'Except for being glued to his mobile twenty-four-seven, it is really.' I don't say I'm concerned by how secretive he seems to be with his mobile recently. Slightly angling it away from my view, rarely separated from it. This business with Milly hasn't helped. Ruan has made further shocking online discoveries looking into self-harming behaviours. Even when we think our children are safely behind the locked doors of home, in their eyes, in their thoughts, they can be anywhere in the world, connecting to dangerous parasites. And then, there's you, on the hunt.

'Oh, that's normal, isn't it? My nieces and nephews are just the same. My brother's always going on about it. Constantly scrolling, flicking, texting.'

'Hmm, the problem is, it's an accepted part of the world they live in. What do you do? If you ban them, you make them freaks, but it's so difficult when you're exposed daily to the damage it can do.'

We exchange a look. 'So, what do you do? What's the advice?' she enquires.

'I tell him, or nag him as he'd tell you, the same as other parents have to, in the hope that at some point the penny will drop. Usually while he's transfixed on his game. Silly as it sounds, it's the best time to get anything through to them, whilst they're super-focused on something, you know, in a trance state almost. I drop little snippets of information at him, then walk away before he's time to disagree. I live in hope that at some point he'll use it. Anyway, as you've probably already worked out, it's the least of my worries at the moment.' I hope.

Moments pass between us; two close individuals, with a sudden gawking gap between them. Bea shifts in her seat and pretends to adjust her cosy cardigan. Ruan always teases her; it's supposed to be me who wears the cardigans. He says I'm at risk of damaging years of valuable stereotyping by not wearing them.

It's exactly why I think I can't bring myself to, as if I did I would also be required to wear loafers and be peering at people above my half-moon spectacles. Then I'd need to keep enquiring, how does that make you feel?

Bea's attention is now somewhere else over my shoulder. She turns back to me, whilst lowering her head. 'You see that guy over there.' She nods in the direction over my right shoulder. 'Him, quick, look now. Quick, Eve, he's going. Quickly. Quick, you're going to miss him!' She's not the most discreet, so I ignore her and turn slowly so as not to be blatantly rude. But too slowly evidently, as I only catch a calf, an ankle and some form of trendy shoe-like trainer as the rest of the body escapes the opening door. We're hit by a cold rush of air as the person in question exits, sending a chill through my muscles.

'Didn't see him. Why, who is it?'

Bea tuts and sighs at me. I'm so not good at this gossip stuff. 'No idea.' She sighs again.

'What? So what are you fussing about, asking me to look?'

She rolls her eyes. 'For that very reason.' She smiles. 'We've no idea who he is, or where he's from. That's the point.'

'So?' Confused, I am. Why do people always insist on talking around the point?

'So? So, we know who everyone else is in here, at least this time of the year we do. Except him. No one's seen him before.' She nods back over at the now empty chair.

'We?' What's the big deal? This is a locals' pub, granted, but even so we do get unknown people in here; lots of them in season.

'Oh, God, Eve, all of us in here, no one knows him. I've asked just about everyone; nobody knows who he is. Ted, Lizzie, Karl, Matt, Abi and Frank so far.' She leans into me again, as if to reveal some dark secret. 'Apparently, he first appeared last Monday night on Frank's shift. Out of the blue. He came in, alone, ordered a drink at the bar, sat at a table for a couple of hours, alone.' She pauses, then flashes her eyes over towards the bar, nodding in their direction. 'They said he's always dressed casually, but smart; usually in dark colours. Each time, he's sat there, by the fire in the gallery room.' It's referred to as the gallery room as each and every inch of wall space between the oak beams reflects the work of local artists and photographers. I shrug at Bea; sometimes she can be so local. I let her ramble on for a little as she's clearly enjoying herself and it's a welcome distraction from where I need to be. Eventually, she comes to a stop and looks to me as if she's just revealed some highly sensitive, shocking disclosure.

'Really! I mean, how bizarre. Someone visiting a village *public* house, buying a drink, then sitting at the table by the fire on a cold evening. Not once, not twice, but possibly now for the third time. I see what you mean. Really, Bea.' I laugh. 'Come on, please.' Then it occurs to me; why didn't it before? Is this you? Have you been stalking my local pub, sussing out the area? Have I just been sitting with my back to you for the last twenty minutes, after all these years?

Bea leans in again, and whispers with a frown, 'You're doing that thing again.'

'What's that?' I say as I begin to stand.

'Firstly, behaving like a migrant from up-country,' she pauses. 'And, secondly, thinking you're an expert on human behaviour.' She winks at me. 'I don't care what you think. It's odd.'

I press my face up against the window, but it's too dark to see outside. 'Am I?' I say, sitting back down. I'm being ridiculous. It wouldn't be you; drinking alone in a local pub would never be your thing.

'Have I missed something?' Ruan asks, gently placing our drinks down so as not to spill the precious contents.

'No, you haven't. Just Bea being Bea. Thinking she's Sherlock Holmes. Searching for clues, then condemning and hanging poor unexpected tourists for daring to enter a bar without introducing themselves first.'

'Oh, you mean that guy.' Ruan turns to point. 'Where's he gone?' He dramatically spins around.

'Oh, for God's sake, don't you start, please. Sit down and let's just have our drinks, shall we? You two are so blinking base sometimes.' Ruan shrugs and takes a pew next to me, in a youngster way, perched on the edge of his seat. He takes an enormous slurp from his pint glass, moans out a sigh of relief before slumping back into his chair to outstretch his legs.

'That's better, I needed that,' he informs us.

My throat feels constricted, despite my rationalising. Have you been trailing my local haunts, gathering information? Did you only leave, having noticed me?

'What did you say he looked like?'

'Who?' Bea asks.

'That guy, the one you were pointing out, speculating about. Describe him.'

Bea and Ruan exchange glances. 'Only seen him from behind,' said Ruan.

Bea tutted. 'You're useless,' she tells him. 'Like I said – good-looking, smart-casual, kind of elusive.'

My heart bounces up my body. I reach for my mobile; still no word from Jack. But then my signal here is so hit and miss.

'I'm just going outside to try and catch a signal, call Jack. Be back in a minute,' I tell them, and leave.

It's pitch black. The light taken by stealth as the winter nights move in. Rendering me on edge, for things hiding, lurking in the shadows. Are the shadows watching me? Watching Jack? A twitchy feeling of being observed crawls over me like an old jumper. I jerk my thoughts away just in time to the purring tones of a 911 passing at speed, only to turn itself around in the car park across the way. I stand frozen as it faces back up the road, preparing to pass by again, away from the cove. I steel myself to gain a glimpse of the driver, stepping slightly back into the porchway so as not to be noticed, but as the car draws level a group of locals bumble and jostle their way in through the doorway, obscuring my viewing point. Then, it's gone. Did the driver only come down here to turn around? It's possible. Or did it come with purpose? At a guess I would say the former. It didn't attempt to slow; it was leaving the village, not coming.

Jack's face flashes into my mind, quickly I call his number again.

Thank God, it's ringing. 'Jack?'

'Yeah, Mum. I've loads of missed calls. I told you I was at football tonight.'

'I know, I was—'

'Anyway, I'm here now, outside the gate, talk to you in a sec.'

'No, wait. I'm not at home, Jack, I'm at The Wheal.'

'Cool. Just presumed you were in, as the front-room light's on.'

It can't be. I'm sure as I can be I turned it off after I left, just an hour ago. I remember wishing halfway down the road I had left it on, for when Jack returned home.

'Jack, stop. Don't go in!'

'What?'

'Don't go in the house.'

'Why?'

I don't want to panic him, but I'm still shaking from the sighting of the car, and something doesn't feel right. 'Come down and meet me, would you? I'll not be too much longer here with Bea and Ruan, and I could do with the company to walk home after. I'll come and meet you halfway now.'

'But—'

'Please?'

'Okay, see you in a sec.'

I need to keep him on the phone. It will only take a few minutes for us to meet. 'So how was football?'

'Yeah. Good. What's wrong? Why you being weird?'

'I'm not. It's called conversation.'

'Yeah, but I'll be with you in a sec. Something's happened, hasn't it? To do with him.'

We can't be far away from each other now. 'Not sure, Jack.' He comes into sight and we both hang up.

As we meet, we turn around and start walking back to the pub together.

'What's happened? The truth, Mum?'

'Did you see that car again, a few minutes ago?'

'What car?'

'The 911!'

'No.'

How could he not have seen it? It must have passed him, either coming down or driving back up. 'Are you sure? It must have passed you. How did you get home?'

'A lift.' He pauses. 'Seb's dad, like I told you earlier. He dropped me back.'

'Did you? Well, I can't believe you didn't notice the 911.'

He shrugs. 'Dunno. Maybe we passed it when I was changing my boots over to my astro's – would have had my head down.'

'You still would have heard it, surely?'

He shrugs again. 'Probably not. Seb was playing his dad's eighties CDs really loud.'

I let it go as we reach the entrance to the pub. I turn to Jack. 'Actually, I'm quite tired, I think we'll leave after all, Jack. I'll just get my things. Bea and

Ruan are over there. I'll ask them to come back with us.'

'You think someone's in the house?'

'No, of course not.' I must have left the light on when I left.

Jack pulls an 'of course, yes' face at me. 'Hmm. That's why you wanted me to come here, isn't it?'

I close the door behind us. 'Stop it, Jack. I told you, I wanted some company, thought I might stay on here a little longer. I've changed my mind that's all.' Jack bites down on his bottom lip before making his way to the gents. I carry on to our table where Bea and Ruan are finishing their drinks.

'There you are. Jesus, how long does a call take? Ted was looking for you, by the way. Did he catch you?' asks Ruan.

I shake my head. 'No, he didn't. Look, sorry about this, but a slight change of plan. I've brought Jack back with me. Could we do this at mine? Talk, I mean.'

Bea speaks first. 'Only if you want to, Eve, if you want to tell us.'

'Yeah, only if you want to. Be good to know why you were freaking out big time, last night,' Ruan expands.

I raise my eyebrows at him

'You've got to admit, Eve; you've been acting really odd lately. I mean that in the nicest way.' He looks to see if he's overstepped the mark with either Bea or I, but we love his blunt talking. 'I mean, you've been even odder than usual,' he adds with a grin before going on. 'To be honest, no messing about now. I'm really worried about you. You looked like you'd seen a ghost. Vexed us all right out.'

Bea stands and touches my hand from across the table. 'You do know you can trust us. I know we tease, and mess about, but we're always here for you. We're just worried you're in some kind of trouble. Is this all to do with Jack's dad? It's just you mentioned him last night,' she said.

'Please don't call him that. Biology does not make a dad.' I'm snapping at the wrong person. I know it's not fair; how else could she have referred to you? I mentioned you only last night. But somehow, whereas the title of father is painful, the title of dad is like a dagger through the heart.

'Sorry, Eve, I didn't mean to—' she offered, lowering her gaze like a chastised child.

'No, it's fine. I didn't mean to snap. I'm sorry, it just grates, you know.'

'Sure. I understand.'

'Shall we call him "you know who", or "he who cannot be named"?' Ruan suggests with a deadly serious face.

I kicked him with the tip of my stiletto under the table.

'Ouch. Just jesting. Just jesting.'

'Well, don't. This isn't funny.' Bea scowls at him.

'I promise, this has never been about me not trusting either of you, because I do, implicitly.' I feel myself blush slightly as the envelope in my briefcase comes to mind. How I queried them in my confused mind, considered that one of them could have planted it. But the fact remains, someone has planted it and I still don't know who. I notice Jack swaggering over towards the table.

'Ready?'

'Yeah,' he says.

I leave Bea, Ruan and Jack chatting, while I hunt out Ted through the crowds. I catch him laden with dirty empties and tap his arm. 'Ted, were you looking for me?'

'Yes, love, I was.' He tilts his head towards me and lowers his voice. 'Just thought I should mention, a couple of people have been asking after you.'

'Really?' My stomach rolls.

'Didn't think much of it, but then when two different people asked, who were, I assume, unrelated...' he shakes his head '... just found it a little odd.'

'Who was it, Ted? What did they ask?'

'The first, a few days ago now, was a woman, proper glamorous, didn't look local, asked if I knew you. I said I did, but then we were interrupted. I looked for her but didn't see her again. Then, earlier tonight, a guy, who we've seen kicking about recently, he asked of you. I asked him who he was, who was asking, like. He didn't seem to like it. Just said, "No reason," and walked off.'

I thank Ted, tell him not to worry, lots of clients ask after me. But why would they ask here? It's not like you, is it, to show your hand publicly, so what are you up to? As for the woman, this must be a coincidence, a client, or a connection to a client. Just bad timing surely? But what about the note? Sam? Why did she send me those excerpts, with the note? I've not heard from her in years, not for fifteen years. Has she been looking for me? There's not a chance she's had access to my briefcase, so who else has she been speaking to about me? Who else knows what she's up to? She hated you with such intensity, it makes sense she'd want to warn me, but what does she know and how?

'Mum, we're leaving.' Jack's arm curls around my shoulders, bringing me back to the moment. We step outside the pub as I visually comb the area. I must have left the light on; you wouldn't be that obvious. My head is spinning with surely, buts and anxious questions, as the amicable banter passes over my wired mind. You're getting inside my head again. I need to fight it, except it's not so easy if you're changing the game plan. I'm banking on understanding your every move, but these latest incidents are not what I would have anticipated.

Chapter Twenty-Three

Before

I had lain still on the bed, eyes closed, wide awake, listening to the dulled tones from below in the study. An hour after I'd been locked in my room, you came back and unlocked the door. I knew you would if I didn't create a scene. You wouldn't see to Jack if he woke, not whilst entertaining your cronies and the mysterious overweight greasy man. Who was he? And who was the younger lad? I knew you were up to something, but why? Your career at Havers, Walker and Jenkins was all going so well. You didn't need to be up to anything, whatever it was. I didn't need you to be up to anything; it complicated my plans for escape. Made our home life feel all the more dirty.

I didn't leave the room again, despite you unlocking it; I wanted you to think I was asleep; I didn't need another argument. Not that being asleep would have stopped you; it wouldn't have been the first time you woke me to be abusive. I contemplated using the key to lock my door from the inside. Chances were you would be looking for the fight. Then thought better of it. Eventually, louder voices and joviality in the acoustic hallway signalled their leaving. Not much longer after, I lay motionless in bed, my heart hammering, listening to your footsteps climbing the stairs, holding my breath as you reached the top, then stopped.

My brain starved of oxygen, my body became a stiff corpse for the moments you deliberated. Until your footsteps continued across the landing towards the spare room. Then, thankfully, the edge of light around the doorframe disappeared; you turned the landing light off. Thank God; I could fall to a version of sleep. I glanced at the alarm clock. Just three and a half hours probably before Jack would be awake again, ready to play. What had you all been talking about until the early hours? I should have made more effort to eavesdrop. I wanted to know but, then again, I didn't. Jack and I led three distinct lives. Our one of playful love and shenanigans; our out-of-home pretend one with other normal people, and the one when Daddy was home. It was hard work. I hoped it was only apparent to me. That Jack was sheltered, others were ignorant. Only those who knew me really well could ever have suspected. But then, the people who knew me well were few and far between, or, more correctly, non-existent.

How had I allowed it to happen? My best friend, Sam, didn't even get to meet Jack. In the end it became so very tricky and tiresome to divide myself between her and you. Too much juggling. I allowed our friendship to drift apart. It was my fault entirely. I took the easy option, if there ever was one to take. One day I hope I'll have the opportunity to explain; maybe she'll find a way to forgive me. With Sam gone, any other peripheral friendships didn't stand a chance. My parents were isolated from me too. My doing again. I was so fervent in my need to protect them from my life, I fooled them into believing I was happy. In the end, Jack and I didn't get to spend much time with them. It was not worth the stress and complications that always ensued. Worse still, I'd hear my parents talking of the exciting and enriched life Jack and I had, and it didn't matter we didn't get to see each other too often, as long as we were happy.

Undoubtedly we were. Not.

It was so much easier before Jack could talk; I could even visit my parents' house. Eventually, as Jack became able to recount his day's events, it became too dangerous. In the beginning, I stole precious hours at their home on the pretence we'd been to the park; nowhere in particular, nowhere verifiable. I made it my business to find out about all local events and activities, being potential alibis for my deceit. Knowing you would check them out. Being locked out of the house at night, or denied an evening meal, fuelled my eagerness to do this. But as Jack became more knowing, began to talk, I stopped visiting so often, unless I could justify beyond doubt my need to visit. Or if I knew you wouldn't be home for at least a night and day, enabling me to pack in new, sufficient, exciting activities for Jack so he'd forget visiting Nannie and Grandad. On the odd occasion, I shamefully encouraged Jack to lie: it was a game, not to tell Daddy where he'd been. Hindsight showed me how downright peculiar this was but at the time it was my normal.

I returned to work, so we employed a child-carer recommended by a colleague of yours, despite my parents being delighted at the prospect of looking after Jack. By this time your parents were removed from the family picture. Since mother and son refused to back down on a matter unbeknown to me. Something to do with them turning down your offer of another trip to Spain. I can't say I was too disappointed about this, despite it being completely unnatural and odd. You didn't speak of them to Jack. You made reference to them from time to time, to affirm your embarrassment of them; how ungrateful they'd been. You intended not to have any further contact; they needed to learn the consequences of their actions. Did she think in the same way? Her denial of Jack and me made me assume so. Like mother, like son.

My parents decided to move to the sunshine. After all, Jack and I would be well looked after. How could I tell them we wouldn't be allowed to visit? I didn't; I agreed how wonderful it was going to be. I was genuinely happy for them. It also lifted the pressure a little. I'd stop feeling so torn, needing to make excuses about my infrequent, cut-short visits.

Lying in the darkness, my mind refusing to sleep, I thought back to the day they'd left. 'Why do they need your help? How selfish, expecting you to give up your time and ruin Jack's day. It's his music group day. It's simply unacceptable for him to miss. I cannot believe you're even suggesting it. Selfish beyond belief,' you retaliated.

My stomach knotted. I'd planned and played the day down for weeks. But Mum had innocently let it out of the bag the week before. 'Eve, love, are you sure you want to bring Jack over next Thursday? We'd love you both to come, but it's going to be extremely manic, cold too for Jack, with all the doors open and no heating.'

I'd felt my cheeks burn, my pulse accelerate; you'd quickly turned your gaze from Mum to me. She'd blown my cover. But then, how could she possibly have known it had needed to be kept secret?

'Oh? What's this, then?' you'd enquired, trying to keep the antipathy out of your voice. But I'd been able to see it saturating your eyes.

'Mum and Dad moving out on Thursday, you know, leaving for Spain the next day. Thought I'd go over and help them. Well, not so much help as just, say goodbye, before they leave. Jack will love it, the huge removals van. You know how he loves his trucks and vans.' I'd grasped at straws. You hadn't said a word, just gave the glimmer of a bogus smile. But you wouldn't say anything with an audience, your silence had said everything I'd needed to know.

'Don't worry about that now, Mum. I'll talk to you about it in a few days. Have you got everything you came with? It's becoming cold and icy outside. You'd better get yourselves going.' I'd begun to usher them towards the front door.

'Yes, okay, love. Speak to you in the week.' She'd bent down to pull Jack into her arms again. He'd giggled at the noisy kisses she'd planted all over his face. I'd felt you physically tense; I hadn't dared gain eye contact.

Despite not broaching the subject again, you made sure we didn't attempt to defy or deceive you. You chose to work from home that day. I hotfooted it around the house, clumsily picking things up unnecessarily, putting them down again. I watched the time tick away, knowing I needed to come up with a feasible plan. I really wanted to be there even though they didn't expect me to be. Why did I feel so pathetic? It took a while to spit the words out. 'I'm off now, to Mum and Dad's. Leave you in peace, since you're so busy. I'll take Jack with me so you can concentrate. We won't be gone too long.'

You were sitting with your back to me at your desk, your favourite seat in the house. You made a point of looking at your watch. 'It's 11.20, Jack's music group is in just over an hour, so it's not possible, I'm afraid. He can't miss out because you want to see Mummy and Daddy,' you scoffed.

'It's no big deal. As I've already said, Jack will love seeing the big vans, watching their furniture being loaded. I've already told him all about it.'

You held up a hand. 'You do what you like, Eve.'

I scurried away despite my cortisol-engulfed shaky body. You'd taken it better than I'd anticipated. Not exactly a warm sending-off, but at least you hadn't put up too much of a fight. I darted around gathering our bits and pieces so as to get away before you changed your mind. But I'd left Jack's jacket and hat in the study with you. I should have been more prepared. I could hear you chatting on the telephone, so took my opportunity to sneak in behind without you noticing. But just as I picked up the clothing, you swivelled slightly in the leather chair, then began waving your arm up and down, signalling to put the items down.

'Owen, this will have to wait. I'll call you back in a few minutes. Don't go anywhere, I'll literally be a couple of minutes.' You replaced the telephone to its base, before swivelling to me with antagonistic eyes.

'Where are you going with Jack's coat?'

'You know where I'm going, Gregg. What do you mean?'

'You're not going anywhere with Jack.'

'But you just said I—'

'No. No, I said you do whatever you like, *Eve*.'

'Yes, exactly. I need to leave now before—'

'Yes, you run along to Mummy and Daddy. But Jack's going nowhere. Like I also said, Jack has his music group, so I will stop what I'm doing, working, earning the money, because you're too selfish, and I'll take him myself.'

'For God's sake, why are you being so awkward? You don't have to do anything; I'll take Jack with me.' I knew I'd just made matters worse.

'Jack is not going to miss out just because he has a self-centred, irresponsible mother. Go, just go, enjoy yourself.' You began to call, 'Jack? Jack? Come in here with Daddy. Daddy will look after you today. Come on, Jack.' I knew Jack would be oblivious, sitting engrossed with the Tweenies. I wasn't going to win. With a thumping head, I turned, resisting the urge to clout his smiling face as I left the room.

I was so upset leaving Jack behind. Although they wouldn't admit it, Mum and Dad would be sad he wasn't there too. I'd make the obligatory excuses and get through the day. A bittersweet day: I was going to miss them, but I couldn't have the relationship I wanted anyway.

It was dark and late when I returned home. The house was in darkness. I'd called only a couple of hours before to say goodnight to Jack, but apparently he was having too good a time to speak to me. As I approached the house, I could just make out the flickering lights cast from the TV, then your shadow appeared as you jumped up, the TV lights disappeared. A light appeared on the landing upstairs, then the house submerged into complete darkness. You'd gone to bed. I crept up the steps to the front door and attempted to turn my key in the lock. It was pointless; the top bolt you insisted upon was locked. I knocked lightly on the wood so as not to disturb Jack. I don't know why I bothered. This wasn't a silly mistake; you'd deliberately locked me out. Again.

It was frosty and freezing but at least I could shelter in my car. I slumped myself back in and attempted to call you on your mobile. It diverted to voicemail. I wrapped my coat tightly around me, I wasn't sure if the shivering was from the cold, or the nervousness I felt inside. Or maybe it was anger in its purest form. After a couple of minutes, my mobile buzzed on my lap.

Thank you for your help today. Hope you're home safely now? Speak to you in the morning. Love you. Sleep tight xxx

I replied,

Pleasure. Home safely now, don't worry. Sleep tight. Love you.

Xxx

Thank God they didn't know the truth. I closed my eyes to avoid the inevitable tired and hopeless tears, just as a further text alerted me.

Why do you think it's acceptable to come home so late? IT IS NOT.

You need to learn some responsibility. Jack and I have had a great day without you. But now you need to learn a lesson. You only have yourself to blame.

In a normal world, I'd have called a friend, called my parents, told them the truth. Left to stay somewhere, anywhere warm. But I couldn't do that. I was not in a normal world. You had my bank cards again, so a B & B was out of the question. My world was horrid, insecure and unbearable. A world I was so ashamed of, I hated myself for allowing it to smother everything I was, everything important to me. A world that needed to end.

I remained in the car until the morning. My hands, feet and face being shades of pink, blue and white. Your silhouette eventually appeared behind the door, unlocked it without opening it. Your shadow stalked away from the glass panel next to the door. Upright and head held high. I sensed you humming your way around the rooms. Triumphant in your genius methods of punishment. Busying yourself with Jack as if all were normal.

Just another morning. Just another day. Another lesson taught. But for who? Me or Jack?

Chapter Twenty-Four

Cornwall 2016

I don't want to worry you, Mum.

I'm scared about making you frightened but I'm scared too.

It was probably nothing after all. The floodlights were so bright but when I looked up, I saw a dark shadow. I carried on playing football, but when I looked up again, the shadow wasn't a shadow anymore; it had become a man. A man in black. Dressed as a shadow. He was looking straight at me. I stopped and stared but someone ran into me. I stumbled to the floor. Bang; he was gone.

But I don't want to frighten you. I don't want us to go back to how it was before. It was probably nothing after all. My imagination, jumping from all the other stuff.

Why did this have to happen to us? Why did it have to happen to me? All of my friends have dads, not shadows. They all have memories, not nightmares.

I don't want to run scared of the shadow any more. I want to be normal.

I hate him.

I wish he were dead.

Chapter Twenty-Five

Cornwall 2016

As we clear away dinner plates I find myself gazing out of the window, over towards the holly shrub. It's grown. Jack and I planted it the day we moved in, such a deep hole I'd needed to dig. The holly shrub, my nan once told me, is a symbol of defence. Ironically, the woody stem is sometimes also used to make chess pieces. My dad taught me to play chess. I never did realise just how important this would prove to be.

I feel a little more human for eating, and for discreetly searching the house when we first got back. I must have left the light on – nothing seems amiss. We move to the comfort of the front room, the warmth of the glowing log fire. Jack leaves us and jumps the stairs three at a time. I still hold my breath. Seconds later, he returns for his mobile abandoned on the kitchen table, crisis averted for the reunion. Our stairs are so shallow and crooked, I wait for the thud of his fall. Then the smooth hums of music feeds down through aged floorboards.

Bea sighs heavily. 'He's such a gorgeous lad. I could eat him all up. You're so lucky, Eve. He's a real lad, but has that lovely sensitive side to him too.' She squeezes my shoulder in passing. 'He loves you to bits,' she says, slumping herself deep into feather cushions. 'Can you imagine, being on your own with him, if he was a little git? My brother was. So bloody annoying. We're okay now, though. I suppose, he's not so bad. Funny how life changes how you see people.'

She turns to look at Ruan, who has thrown his head back and closed his eyes, stretched out like a contented cat. She nudges his supporting arm away, jolting him back to the moment. 'Do you get on with your sisters, Ru? I don't know why, I always think of you being close. But you never really can tell, can you?'

You have no idea, Bea.

'Are you asking or telling me, Bea? As in, d'you want me to add to your running conversation or are you happy going it alone?' Playfully slapping her leg.

'Cheeky! I'm asking you, of course. Just wasn't sure you were still in the room with us. What with the snoring.'

'Get shot, I so wasn't snoring.' He shrugs, sitting up.

'And dribbling.' She raises her eyebrows at him. 'So, do you get on with them?'

'Yeah, guess so. We still have our moments. Any more beers in the fridge, Eve?' He stands up at the same time, making his way to the kitchen. He knows I have.

'Help yourself.' You're probably going to need it with what I'm about to divulge.

He's already opening the fridge door. 'Anyone else while I'm here?' he calls out. 'Mmm, cake, nice one, don't mind if I do,' he chatters away. 'What's this cake, Eve? Is it edible?'

'Course. Home-made. Apple and cinnamon or something like that, I think it is. Gloria made it the other day, popped it round while I was at work. I'd forgotten about it. It will be good, try it.'

'Proper job! Anyone else?' he calls.

'God, no, thanks.' I couldn't stomach any more food; my gut is already twisting and turning, bound in a tight knot.

'Yeah, I'll have some. Make sure my piece is bigger than yours. I'll be checking.' Bea taps her stomach in anticipation.

We make idle chat, delaying and putting off the very point of my two closest friends being here. I'm worried my past is about to dirty my present, soiling its purity and changing it forever. I jump up and pad to the bottom of the stairs. From here I can just make out if Jack's bedroom door is still closed. It is. I return to the warm shadows of my sanctuary, wary of my quickening heart rate. I open my mouth like some kind of gulping monkfish but nothing comes out. The room takes on an icy chill, yet the fire still burns.

Ruan wanders back, balancing plates, while he samples a forkful of cake.

'Okay, you two, so this is what you've been patiently waiting for, the juicy gossip.' They glance at each other. 'It's fine. I can understand where you're coming from.'

'No one understands where Bea's coming from – even she doesn't get that,' Ruan interrupts. Bea slaps his leg, scowling at him.

'Go on,' she urges me.

'Can I just say, despite my flippancy, this really is so tough, I can't possibly relay how badly I didn't want to discuss my past? I or we, me and Jack, needed desperately to move on, to push it all to the backs of our minds. But obviously, I no longer have the choice. Poor Jack, he's already been through the unthinkable.' Neither Bea nor Ruan move or speak, both studying me with despondent eyes. Whilst I appreciate the care, the sympathy hurts all the more.

'I've been silly not to have explained before now. Selfish, I guess, too.' Even so, as I prepare to disclose I'm only too aware of how skimpy with the details I propose to be. No more lying, just withholding details; especially the darkest ones, the depth of my pain with it. Unsure who I'm protecting – them or me? It could alter their perception of me, forever. How would I cope with this?

'Even Jack hasn't spoken much on the subject, since we arrived in Cornwall. It was supposed to be a clean break. I hope you can both understand. On a daily basis, I see, behind the eyes, the damage our past has done to Jack.' Sometimes he reacts to situations, people, in a certain manner, slightly out of context, but I understand why. But does he? Although I've always reassured him he can talk, he hasn't. 'He's needed the time to heal and grow.' The memories will always be lodged deep in the emotional brain; anticipating, lingering just in case. Filed away like a ghastly nightmare. As if it were a disturbing horror film we've shared, since then we've striven hard to distort the images, sounds and words. A temporary façade, a sleeping monster. Smaug.

'Oh, Eve, has it really been so awful for you both?' Bea breathes out.

'To be honest, I'm not even sure where to begin. I can't quite find the words.' I turn my attention to the amber flames of the fire, reaching high up the chimney. 'Perhaps, if I begin with the end, the last time I saw Jack's…' The word glues itself to the back of my throat. But it's who you are.

Bea bails me out. 'Him, Eve, him. We know who you mean. Go on.'

I nod. 'You must have thought it odd, I won't have him mentioned or named. You don't need to answer that, by the way, I know. I see it in your eyes.' They both nod. 'The thing is, we didn't simply part company. Things happened.' I'm trying to get to that last night we saw you, but my words seem so small in comparison.

'I must stipulate, it was anything but a normal relationship, ever. I speak on both our behalves. It was vile. He was, is, vile. The calculating, unscrupulous rule of his rendered our lives hell. He was also cunning, powerful, exceptionally shrewd and an engineered social god. Eventually, he did leave, but not in the fashion you suppose he did, or in the way I've expressed. To be honest, if I dare use the phrase, the fine detail here isn't necessary. It would take too long to substantiate, for one thing. Nor am I up to it.' Here I go again, shut-door policy. Although I may now benefit from some support, as I did last night, ultimately I'm alone with this. You. I'm also far too ashamed to entirely divulge.

The room is quiet except for the crackle of the fire and the hum of Jack's music. Am I betraying him all over again? He should be down here, involved in this conversation, but I don't want him to be. I cannot contemplate yet another embezzled night for him because of you, bastard of a so-called father. I want to leave him in blissful ignorance, for all I can.

'Did he hurt you, Eve?' Bea softly enquired.

'I'm not sure hurt pays it justice. This is the problem – anything I relay to you can't possibly do it justice. Not when you're existing as we did seven days a week.'

'No, of course not. I understand.'

I know she's being kind, but those last words are the precise ones to shut the door. How can anyone understand unless they've been in a comparable situation? I smile at her; she's sincere in her concern. I am grateful for this.

'There's no simple way of saying this.' I look at Ruan, who has finished his cake, now removing the remains of imaginary crumbs from his mouth with the back of his hand. 'So, the last time we saw him. We were already divorced, had been for some time. Dragged through the family courts, the financial courts, you name it.' I shake my head. 'Another story. Then, out of the blue, one night, he turned up at our house, forced us into his car.' I see Bea open her lips to speak but I press on. I need to spit this out. 'Things happened, he crashed the car. Then vanished,' I splutter. It's out, the first time I have ever articulated this story. Done. I take a long breath in, filling my lungs with resigned air.

Ruan sits forward, rubbing his forehead. 'He crashed the car?'

I nod. 'Left us for dead.'

'He left you for dead? Jack's dad did? What, on purpose?' Bea struggles.

The expression on Bea's face smacks of reality. How have we lived alone with this for so long? 'Jack's father, yes, Bea. Crashed the car then left us. Ran off into the night. We were badly hurt and alone.' I taste metallic terror as the memories of the night flash at high speed through my mind, a train pummelling tracks through a Tube station. Blurred images everywhere. I've opened one of the doors, now the flashbacks pick up pace, as the smell of burning rubber, the sound of screeching tyres hammers at my consciousness. My chest tightens; I fight to breathe. Someone is sitting on my chest. I breathe out but cannot breathe in, my torso constricts with the grip of the seat belt. Tighter and tighter. The oxygen leaves my head as it floats away with the images. I'm struggling. Drowning, submerged under deep icy water. Shivering.

Breathe. Breathe. In through the nose. Five. Out through the nose. Seven. Count, for God's sake.

'Eve?' A low and distant mottled voice calls. Bea's voice. But it's so distant. 'Eve?'

Heat everywhere. I'm burning now, on fire. I try to stand; if I get myself moving, I can break the hold of panic. A soft hand takes mine. 'Sit back down, Eve,' she gently advises. But I need to walk. I clamber through to the kitchen, open the back door; the cold air slaps my face. Leaning in the doorway, I begin to slow my breathing. I stand in silence for a while, looking out into the dark. Are you there? Smirking, high on my low? I slam the door, treading back the few steps until I'm back in the front room. Safe. But for how long?

Ruan kneels down in front of me clutching a glass of water, offering it to my lips, as if I'm a small child. And that's how I feel. Again.

'Thank you.' I take a grateful sip. Silence. 'That was the last time we saw him.'

'Eve?' Bea shakes her head. 'Sorry, nothing,' she says.

'It's okay, Bea. What were you going to ask me?'

'You said he forced you, so he took you against your will? So he what – kidnapped you? Then there was a car accident?' probes Bea.

'Not an accident. I meant what I said – he crashed the car. I can't be completely sure he intended to kill us, but my heart tells me he did. But, yes, he took us against our will. Call it what you like.'

'Oh my God, Eve! Did you go to the police? That's kidnapping.'

'I didn't go to the police, no. For several reasons. I'll get to why, soon. Also, I did get into the car of my own accord, but only because I had to.' This is what happens, and another reason I couldn't go to the police. When you only speak in half-truths for self-protection, other issues, such as why I couldn't go to the police, look odd. To go to the police after three years and report an abusive marriage, having attended public events, apparently lived an entirely carefree and normal life, without so much as a mention, is somewhat discrediting. Once you begin to lie, the truth will never look the same again.

Ruan catches up. 'What a t—'

'What happened to him, after the crash?' interrupts Bea.

'No one knows.' I roll back to be caught by my comfortable sofa, curling my legs up tightly under me. Shit, what have I done? 'I should have told you before. I've been so selfish. I didn't mean to be.'

Ruan jumps up. 'I'll grab a bottle and some glasses.' We don't put up a fight. Bea makes herself comfortable, now sitting in front of me on the floor, perched on an oversized cushion. Ruan saunters back from the kitchen with his incongruent playful yet comforting smile. He offers me a glass full to spilling. I take a hefty slurp and gulp. He then lavishly fills the other two glasses. 'I don't care what you say, this is the answer to this kind of shit,' he says.

'Steady on, Ru, I can only have a sip. It's okay for you, I've to drive later. Or, I suppose, I could get Matt to pick me up, get hammered instead.' I can tell this is an appealing consideration for her. To be honest she looks as if she needs it more than I do.

She leans forward to look me in the eyes. 'You're such a funny one, Eve. Why, oh, why haven't you told us before? Actually, second thoughts, silly question. You're such a flipping private person, aren't you? You'd never have told us, would you? Unless...' She pauses.

'Unless what?' Ruan helps out, slopping back on the sofa, the bounce spilling my wine.

'Unless you've a damn good reason to. Unless you thought you had to.'

'I...'

'I'm not upset with you. It's just you, isn't it? How you are, my lovely. But come on, you have to let us help you now. Whatever it is. I mean, it's over now, isn't it? It can hardly get any worse, can it?' Her thoughtful accent offers warmth. I gladly accept and hold on tight. But deep down I twist with the knowledge, despite her or their genuine intentions, they cannot possibly help us. This is something I need to do alone. And despite her beliefs, it can very easily get worse.

For one thing: if you did intend to kill us, you haven't yet achieved it.

We're silent for a moment, Bea and Ruan both waiting for me to spill more. Me wondering how much more I need to reveal; how much I can leave behind. Bumper to bumper, the words ricochet up in my throat. Colliding with one another. I need someone to push me. I'm back in clinic with divided thoughts; those I'm thinking and those I need to articulate. Occasionally leaving behind the truth. Delivering only what is required.

Ruan breaks the silence, his face holding the frown of a small child. 'I don't get it. I mean, I know some people have crap marriages, relationships… whatever. But why would someone want to kill their partner, husband, wife… whatever; why not just walk away?'

Good question. 'I'll come to this, Ruan; sorry for the cliché, but it's complicated. All I'll say is, Jack's father is a white-collar psychopath, so normal rules, behaviours and such do not apply. Come on, Ruan, you know this – they don't accept failure, are incapable of accepting responsibility and they never, ever give in. The word *no* doesn't exist in their vocabulary, unless they're the ones utilising it. It's textbook.'

'Yeah, now you say, I've read about this stuff, I think. It's pretty interesting, isn't it?'

Bea gives him a shut-it glare.

'Shit, sorry, Eve. Wasn't thinking. I meant, it's interesting to read about; not so good if you're living it though – eh?' He smiles at me.

'Don't worry, it is fascinating, if you're looking in on it, rather than locked into it.'

'So, can you expand? Because, I've got to tell you, I don't get it, at all. The hows or whys. Psychopath or not,' says Bea.

I take a long swig of tepid wine. 'To cut a ridiculously hideous long story stupidly short, that last night he arrived unannounced at our home, reeking of alcohol. Like I said, we were divorced, and after our stint in the rental flat, we moved to a cottage outside of the town. He took me and Jack in his car. Let's just say, he had an agenda, we didn't have a choice in this. But it didn't go to plan; then his driving became scarily dangerous. The conditions were horrendous. The car left the road. The police later reported we may have skidded off the road. Perhaps this is why after a while they quit searching for him. They didn't appreciate the truth. And I was too afraid to tell them.'

'Why?' asks Bea.

'Because how could it be proven, especially with those road conditions? It would have been my word against his, a professional man. I could have used the fact he was over the limit but... oh, I don't know, at the time I was, I guess, too scared of any recriminations. Extra recriminations. And a part of me hoped he had run and would keep running. A part of me prayed he was dead. I was too afraid to move, either way, afraid of him, afraid of going to the police. I didn't have anyone to turn to for rational advice. It was just me and Jack and if there was a chance he was gone…'

'You took it,' says Ruan.

I nod. 'But it wasn't an accident. He drove us into the tree – I'm as certain as I can be. I woke up in the ambulance, with Jack in the one behind. The police advised me the driver was nowhere to be found by the time they arrived. How he wasn't badly hurt too I'll never know, or perhaps he was, we don't know. He left us with some nasty injuries – me and Jack were both knocked out for a little while. Jack can't really remember anything. He says it's as if he has missing fragments of information, a temporary black screen. Thank God.'

'Jesus, Eve. I'd no idea.' Ruan leans forward, rubbing his hands through his hair before throwing himself back against the cushions again.

'I can't believe all this happened, yet neither of you have ever mentioned it.' Bea swallows a mouthful of wine.

'Jack was so young, Bea; just a little boy. It was a few years before we relocated to Cornwall. It's not the kind of thing you drop into conversation. Then, as time goes on, you manage to push it away to a point. It's not something you choose to recall at will.'

Bea nods.

'So where could the bastard have gone?' asks Ruan.

'We don't know. For a while, I told myself he'd wandered off hurt, died somewhere. We were in the middle of nowhere, incredibly wooded. But then, after some time when the police searches didn't unearth anything, I had to accept he had literally crawled away somewhere. That he was still out there, in hiding.' I find myself staring out towards the front window into the darkness. Could be anywhere, watching us.

'What about his job, I assume he had one?' Bea asks. 'Did he abandon that too?'

'He did, a good one. He was a solicitor, a partner, never quite made senior partner.' This was my fault, in your sick eyes, wasn't it? 'But that's another convoluted story. For now, all I'll say is his days were numbered. His reputation shredded, the other reason why I think he disappeared into hiding.' This slice of the story is irrelevant to what Bea and Ruan need to know. Not even Jack knows; I don't think he does anyway, although he did ask an odd question the other day. Something about corporate fraud cases, whether the crimes carried prison sentences. Apparently, it was a debate they were having at school. The problem is, I've become so suspicious of seemingly ordinary questions, normal conversations, I'm continually searching for hidden agendas.

'So, are you saying, he may have tried to kill you both because he lost his job?' I can tell Bea is struggling with the concept of you.

'It's considerably more complicated, unfortunately. Remember what I said about the psychopath: failure and responsibility are simply not possible. Around the same time things began to fall apart in his professional life, our marriage, if you can call it that, collapsed too.' I'd planned to see you settled in your senior-partnership role, to leave by the back door, escape to Spain to live with my parents. You should have been happy with your lot... you could have blamed the whole marital split on me. People would even have felt sorry for you. But you had to ruin things, didn't you? Greed. Power. You didn't need to do it. 'He knew his practising days; his intended recognitions and promotions were in jeopardy. Not long before this time, we'd trawled the courts, battling over Jack. Him wanting ownership, me wanting to protect him. I knew who he was, what he was capable of... but the courts only ever saw a professional man. They didn't understand his status was about to be called into disrepute. Eventually, the decree absolute was granted and...'

'And he'd lost everything. Was devastated about losing you and Jack.' Bea nods.

'No, Bea. No. He hated me for saying no to him. He blamed me for his professional demise too. He'd failed on both counts; he needed to hurt someone, me.' I can't afford to reveal any more. It's like trying to write a synopsis for the bible.

'God, he's one messed-up guy,' she tells me, though putting it far more politely than I would. Ruan leans forward, then again collapses back into the cushion, clearly uncomfortable.

'The thing is, from my perspective, that night was merely the final episode. The tip of the iceberg from the many years before. It's one of the reasons I don't talk about it, because, as you just were, Bea, people are horrified, yet I have to believe it was... simply a shit period of my life. Something I don't think people can appreciate is, to us it had to become normal living, to act as a protective anti-trauma ruse. It's the only reason we remained sane.' I notice the rising of Ruan's eyebrows as he half smiles at me. 'Well, kind of sane, anyway,' I add.

'But you told me things hadn't worked out, and in the end he'd gone to live abroad, that was the end of that. He didn't want anything to do with Jack. Never sent any cards or tried to call, anything. End of?'

'Yes, I know I did. Please believe, I'm truly sorry I lied to you. I see now, it was a mistake, but at the time I believed I was doing the right thing.'

Bea nods solemnly at me. I do feel bad but how do you ever bring this kind of background into new and normal conversations? What was I supposed to say?

'I'm sorry to you too, Ruan.' I squeeze his leg, now sprawled all over my side of the sofa.

'It's okay,' soothes Ruan. 'It's really not the kinda thing you want to drop into conversation. I get why you had to almost pretend it didn't happen. But, Jesus, poor Jack. Bloody hell.'

Bea's eyes fill with tears. 'Poor little thing, how come he's so lovely?'

'I know. It literally eats away at me. Every day.' It still hurts, more than I can ever express. 'I think I'll carry the pain and guilt with me for the rest of my life. In the end I couldn't completely protect him. As a mum, it's a daily torture.'

'I bet.' Bea nods. 'So, if you don't know what happened after the car incident, he could be anywhere now. I mean, he could be here in Cornwall.'

I nod. As the years have gone on, it's all become muddied. I struggle to distinguish between what I remember, what I've been informed of and what I've since dreamt or had nightmares about. I'm about as reliable as an eyewitness to a crime scene sometime after the event. The mind fills in blanks and confuses, becomes highly suggestible. I've never said anything but I'm also as sure as I can be we were not alone that night, on the road. Someone was following us. Two shards of light, spearing the dashboard from behind. But after the blackout, can I even be certain of that?

'How badly hurt were you?' Ruan asks. 'After the…' he waves his finger '… you know.'

'I woke in the ambulance, my head pounding. I'd several facial cuts and—' I lift a section of my hair up, about an inch below my middle parting '—a nice little gash. A few broken ribs from the side airbag. The front airbag didn't release; it had been disabled. His released though. Concussion, and a serious case of whiplash. We were both lucky apparently. The terrain broke the speed, before impact.' You knew what you were doing, didn't you?

A high-pitched whistling and a swoosh of the shrubbery against the front window makes us jump. It's so dark outside, and blustery as the coastal wind approaches a crescendo. I can't see beyond the shadows and the promise of a new moon.

'The wind's picking up again – think we might be in for another stormy night,' Ruan comments in an exaggerated Cornish accent. Bea glowers at him. 'Sorry, Evie, go on.'

'I remember coming to. It was like a reverse plughole effect, images circling me so rapidly as my head spun. I panicked because I didn't know where Jack was, then apparently became hysterical, screaming out his name. Then it was black again. When I came back to, they told me Jack was fine, remarkably unhurt but in shock. He also had minor impact injuries from the side airbag. He was in the ambulance behind as they needed to take him in for observation.'

'But he'd gone,' clarifies Bea.

'Yep. He'd gone by the time the ambulances arrived.'

'Who called for the ambulance, then?' Ruan presses.

'I don't know. The police said it was a woman, said she'd discovered us but she'd left before the emergency services arrived. We're not sure who it was. They couldn't trace the mobile number either. It was a pay as you go; it didn't lead to anyone.' Both Ruan and Bea nod. 'He conveniently seemed to disappear off the face of the earth. I didn't hear anything, until I received an odd phone call a few years later, a man's voice, advising me he was living abroad somewhere. Somewhere being Spain, then he hung up. I don't know who that guy was either.'

'Bizarre. But why? Why would he do that? Why move to Spain?' Bea asks.

'Oh, Bea, it's so convoluted. For the moment, please can we leave it at my ex-husband, Jack's father, was a manipulative, cruel machine? Made our lives hell, then things started to go wrong for him. He slipped, while I grew stronger; he knew it too. He lost control, before I was ready.'

'Ready for what?' interrupts Ruan.

'My plan. Years of planning our escape. Jack and me needed closure, not this. Always trying to forget, always hiding from our imaginations, from thinking the worst, watching the shadows, listening for noises. Sleeping with my car keys and mobile phone. Always wondering when, always waiting. I didn't get the chance to put my plan into place. We've not been allowed to break entirely free. He was supposed to be content with the life he made, a successful partner, to become senior partner; Jack and I would have stood a chance to escape. It wasn't supposed to end this way.' It hasn't ended, has it?

I'm drained and exhausted and it's only just beginning.

'But it still seems so bloody unreal, to want to kill you both?' Bea continues.

'Bea, please don't try and make sense of this. Rational behaviour is not relevant here, so rational reasoning will get you nowhere. Like I said, I don't know for sure he did. He may have only wanted to teach us a lesson, to hurt us, scar us. If we were dead, he wouldn't get to see the results, we wouldn't pay for our mistakes, so I'm not convinced he did intend to kill us, just that he meant for us to crash. Though, as the front airbag had been disabled and he abandoned us, if someone hadn't called 999, we or at least I could have been in trouble from the amount of blood loss. And it was cold, so, so cold too.'

I also had his flash-drive, whipped last minute from his laptop in his study, but that's remaining my secret. Our secret. It may once have been reason enough to keep me alive that night. But now? I'm not so sure. You know I have it, don't you? But why now, why is it only now you've come looking for it? Or is it something else? Is this simply twisted revenge?

'Lucky, he didn't take Jack with him,' adds Ruan.

'No. It wasn't luck, he didn't want Jack. Jack was an asset for the future. He only wanted Jack because I needed Jack. Jack was his only real power over me. If I'd died, he'd have been stuck with him. Wherever he went, wherever he was going, he knew he couldn't take Jack. Jack was nothing more than another one of his tools.' This is what I hate you most for.

'But why did you stay with such a lunatic, Evie? Why didn't you leave him before then?' Here we go. It's a reasonable question but it can't possibly be answered in a reductionist manner.

'Exactly, why? I ask myself the same every day. Because hindsight makes me ask it. But context always wins the day, always. I didn't leave because I couldn't. I just couldn't.' I can feel myself becoming defensive.

Bea's not being judgmental; this must seem so very far-fetched. The strange thing is, it does to me too, or it did until a few weeks ago, before it was brought abruptly back into my life. A horrible thought hits me: I may know who the articles in the envelope were sent by, but not who put them into my briefcase? I assumed nobody had been in the house because the back door was locked when I checked but what if I'm wrong? If someone else has been in our home, have you too? Technically, you could have come through an unlocked back door, locked it, then left through the front door – it has a dead lock. I feel sick. Have you been in our home?

I feel them both silently eyeballing me. 'Sorry, Bea, I didn't mean to snap at you.'

'It's fine,' she graces me. 'I just feel awful. I didn't know any of this.' She leans forward and touches my hand.

'You have nothing to feel bad about, please. How could you have possibly guessed?' Bea is still looking at me with a mixture of shock and sadness. 'You know, I sometimes wonder if he intended for Jack to die; for me to survive and for Jack to die. He knew it would be my ultimate punishment; the only actual means of destroying me.'

They look at me with horror etched across their faces. 'It's so hard for any normal person to compute the workings of the mind of a psychopath. I mean, why would anyone kill their son to punish their ex-wife, how sick? I, on the other hand, identify; I've learned all too well we are all merely pawns on a chessboard to men like him. Used and sacrificed as needed to achieve an end. It's easier for me. Over the years I've needed to learn, to think and dissect in his terms. Kind of mechanical. To be honest, the fact I can do it so successfully frightens me.' Does this mean I can never be normal again? Can I ever truly unlearn the rules of chess?

'Jesus Christ.' Bea sighs out.

We sit in silence for a couple of minutes. 'Ruan, would you chuck a log on the fire, please? I'm feeling a little chilly.'

'Sure.' He jumps up to poke around with the fire. It must be a man thing; I only asked him to put a log on it.

'Eve?' Bea pauses, and something tells me I'm not going to like what she's about to ask. 'Why did you get in the car that night, you and Jack? If you knew he was so horrible, why get into the car with him?'

I think about this for a while, not because I don't know the answer, but because it's difficult to answer without sounding like a complete idiot. Who willingly gets into a car with a psychopathic ex-husband looking for revenge on a dark stormy night? How could I have been so context blind? I witness these incidents on the news and think to myself, well, what did you expect? How did you not see it coming? What made you suddenly become so stupid? How do

I answer without giving away anything I need to withhold? I trust them but, when the lives of Jack and me are the very things at stake, I can't afford to trust anyone completely. Has this not always been the case with my story? It's not what you see, it's what you don't see. It's not what you know, it's what you don't know.

We think we know the truth; what we saw, what we believed. But the truth is, our perceptions have been so contaminated by our past, can we trust our original observations and decisions? I was desperate. I wanted a way to end the living hell. So I watched and learned and gathered the evidence. But there are gaps in my evidence. Not to mention cracks in my moral conscience. It all seemed to make sense back then.

I hate hindsight.

'I didn't have any choice, Bea. I had to get in the car because he had Jack.' He had Jack because he was using him as a bargaining tool for the flash-drive I could never let him have; our freedom depended on it. Or did it? I'm not so sure any more.

As I swill the blackberry liquid around my glass, I'm startled out of my skin by a loud thud at the front door. Spilling the juices down my front. Bea follows suit, choking on her mouthful, spraying my legs with the remnants. None of us move. The letter box opens as a large brown envelope falls to the floor.

I wipe the wine from my face, trying to ignore the quickening of my heartbeat. I tentatively find my feet, Bea looking to me for reassurance.

'I'll get it,' says a confident Ruan.

'No, it's fine.' I'm already making my way to the front door, sick with the awareness of these familiar feelings. I used to dread the sound of the letter box, the sight of the poor postman, wondering what nasty letter would be dropping to my floor. I veer off towards the front window. I need to check if anyone's there. But no one. I'm aware of Ruan moving towards me as I open the front door.

'What are you doing?' shrieks Bea. 'Shut the door, for God's sake.'

'Shhh, Bea.' With my heart in my mouth, I step out. It's pitch black, the wind has died down and a silence surrounds me, other than the hum of the Atlantic behind. Our front gate has been left open. Was this to help someone make a quick getaway? I tread to the end of the small path, expecting someone to jump out, then gaze down towards the low wall bordering the road.

I can feel you breathing; you are watching me, aren't you?

I could have missed you by a few steps but I'm certain you're still here. I freeze. My words jar as my entire body quivers. Something hanging in the air; a familiar scent smothers my nostrils. 'Eve?' Ruan's voice echoes around me. I cannot speak. 'Eve?'

I turn to face him as he takes my arm. 'He's been here. I'm not imagining it, Ruan – he's been here tonight. I know he has.'

He turns me around, ushering me towards the door. 'Come on, you don't know this, do you? Not for sure. Let's go in, open the envelope; it's freezing out here.'

I step back over the threshold to pick up what has been dropped through my letter box. Scanning the envelope for signs, who the envelope is addressed to, a giveaway postmark, hoping it's simply an innocent redirecting of some wandering post. A neighbour has dropped it off.

Nothing.

I sniff the envelope.

It was hand-delivered. I can smell you.

'Eve, what is it?' Bea asks.

'Shush, please!' I glance at her worried expression. 'Sorry, Bea, give me a moment.'

I pull out two A4 printed sheets with eyes half closed, my head wispy with the lack of oxygen. With trembling legs, I walk further into the light of the fire to make sense of what I'm holding. A copy of our marriage certificate, and a copy of Jack's birth certificate. Then, I notice your additions; in black thick lettering scrawled diagonally across each of the

309

sheets. On the birth certificate the word MINE, on the marriage certificate the words TILL DEATH DO US PART, glare back at me.

I instinctively turn back for the front door, throw it open, ignoring the cries of Bea and Ruan; I stagger towards the gate, now closed. It's so dark, my eyes struggle to adjust but I manage to catch a glimpse of a disappearing dusky shadow, without a question of doubt – belonging to a man. He does not move at speed; to the contrary, he walks with a slow, sure confidence. I consider for one stupid moment running after him, but my feet refuse to budge. Then I'm grabbed from behind by Ruan.

'He's back, he was right here, within a couple of feet from me, a few moments ago, we were side by side pretty much.'

Ruan doesn't respond as I fall against him. My body stiff with fear, then anger.

At least I now know for sure: you've found us.

Chapter Twenty-Six

Before

Anyone would have thought we were short of money. I stood at the till, counting out coppers. I only wanted some fruit for Jack. I'd made the stupid mistake of not including it on the online grocery shop, with only one chance to include all the items I needed. Once all the items in the basket were added for checkout, you would comb through, removing any frivolous non-essentials, as you saw them. Usually, this was anything personal for me, skin-care items, hair products or similar. Even though I was working part-time, my earnings were minimal compared to the monthly outgoings of mortgage, car payments et cetera. You considered I didn't contribute sufficiently, insisted my salary was paid entirely into our marital joint account, all of which was allocated, other than the small amount you gave me each week to use for Jack. This, though, I'd stashed away, for future needs.

You were unaware of my intentions, so what on earth were you scared of? But then, it was never about fear; it was about control and power. Were you becoming scared of losing these, even before you did?

I reached into my pocket at the trill of my mobile.

'Eve?'

'Yes.'

'Where are you?'

'Out with Jack, why?'

'Obviously, but what are you doing?'

'I promised him I'd take him to the park, why?'

'Right.' I could hear your mind ticking. 'Then, are you heading straight home?'

'Yes… of course; why wouldn't I be?'

'Thought, maybe for a treat you could take Jack for a pizza. But if you're going to be argumentative about it, I—'

'No. Wait, don't say this. How am I being argumentative?'

'There you go again, can't help yourself.' You sighed heavily into the handset. 'I can't be dealing with you, if…'

What were you up to? Trying to cause an argument, so I'd become submissive, then you could get your own way. For whatever it was you'd really called me for. This transpired so many times; I knew how to play the game. You were definitely up to something, I needed to find out what.

'I'm sorry, Gregg; I wasn't meaning to argue with you.'

'Well, you were.'

'Okay, in that case, I apologise.'

'Good.' Your smugness seeped through my mind. I bit down hard on my teeth. 'I was going to suggest you take Jack out for his tea, to the new ghastly American diner place, near Warwick. On the industrial estate, by Sainsbury's.'

Oh, how joyous. How kind of you. 'Mmm. That would have been lovely, but how can I? I don't have my cards or any cash.' You should know.

'Not a problem. I'll call the restaurant now, leave my card details. They'll be happy with this.'

You really thought you were doing me a monumental favour. What were you planning so important to need to gift us a treat, to keep us away from the house? 'Okay. Thank you. Great.' My words were like razors at my throat. How dare you? How dare you call me to give permission to take my son for pizza, and expect gratitude? I felt my blood flood with adrenaline; all I really wanted to do was tell you where to stick pizza. It was becoming harder and harder.

'Sorted, then. I'll call them now, see to the bill. In fact, why not make a night of it? Don't rush. No need. Jack can have one of those atrocious American sugary ice creams for afters too.' You chortled into your handset like a father who cared.

'Yes, he'd like that. Yes, okay. I'll see you later, then.'

'You may or may not; I'll be back home shortly but heading out again for a late dinner meeting around eight. Like I said, take your time.'

I could tell from the echo you were still on the train, on your way home from Birmingham. Clearly, with plans for the evening, but not just the meeting; you wanted me out of the house until you left. Did you actually believe I was so stupid? For someone so astute, you really hadn't worked me out. Or had you? Was this a trap?

I squeezed Jack's hand. 'Jack, do you know anyone at all who would love to go for a special tea? Pizza or burger?'

'Me-e-e, me-e-e. Jack does!'

'Shall we go for a little treat? You and Mummy?'

'Yes-s-s-s. Mummy and Jack go for a treat.' He began jumping up and down, yanking on my arm. 'What's for treat, Mummy?'

As much as I wanted to dart straight home, I couldn't deny Jack the opportunity of this rare treat. The last time the three of us visited a restaurant, all themed for his birthday, you eventually turned up, tanked-up, in a terrible mood and were as obnoxious as possible all evening. I quietly cried in the toilets; the whole experience was so far removed from your wishes for your child's birthday. For some godforsaken reason, I'd hoped it would be different. What a fool. Other parents often took their children for tea, after our clubs. I was invited, but how could I go without money? I needed to go along with the meal; you would undoubtedly check on our arrival with the restaurant. I'd hurry it along so as to return to the house before you left for the evening.

The dark was drawing in by the time we turned down the lane towards the driveway. As expected, we had company. The same cars as before, except for one that was conspicuous. Unlike the other more sophisticated, valeted, this-year's-model cars; a more tasteless, loud and old, white saloon-type car with blacked-out windows sat behind the others. I loitered at the bottom of the driveway behind the gates, which were closed. I glanced at Jack, who'd fallen asleep. Did I really want to take him into the house? I'd a bad feeling about it. But I also needed to find out what you were up to.

In the end, I tucked the car into the small layby just to the side of our gates. I didn't want to take Jack in, but equally I couldn't leave and miss this opportunity. Slightly opening my window to relieve the misting glass, I sat and waited, feeling my chest rapidly rise and fall. You'd stated you'd be leaving around eight and would be expecting me home at some point, so I reckoned I hadn't long to wait. Eventually, the hall light illuminated shapes across the driveway, indicating movement in the house. I ever so quietly released my car door so as not to wake

Jack, discreetly squeezing myself through the gap up against the hedge.

A small break in the privet allowed me a viewpoint. I could just about make out the elevated area before the front door. The sound of raised voices hit me, despite my distance. The front door opened as the security light shone down. I crouched further into the hedge as the electric gates opened. My blood turned cold as the action unravelled before me. The young lad I'd seen at the house once before was punched out of the front door, before tumbling head first down the few steps to the driveway. I gasped too loudly; my legs began to wobble. He was gagged, with hands tied behind his back. Not capable of breaking his fall or with any chance of defending himself. What the hell was I involved in? This was someone's son. I hated myself for even being there. The others laughed on, as if it were some form of drunken prank. You didn't laugh but towered above with a half-smile. Jesus Christ, what should I do? I knew what I should do but what about Jack? I couldn't risk it — shouting out or trying to help the lad could put Jack in danger.

Even I hadn't thought it would come to this. But why hadn't I, given the lessons I was taught? I'd known all along what you were capable of. But this felt worse; the images would torture me for a long time. Who the hell were Jack and I sharing our lives with? What kind of a monster? But why? I watched in horror, the lad being roughly pulled to his feet then bundled into the boot of the white car, hitting his head on the hard edge. My body threatening to vomit, my mind racing.

I couldn't chance being caught as a witness. Would we be next? I staggered back to my car with jelly legs, hands trembling trying to open the door. Once in I flicked the central-locking button switch. I swallowed at the pizza threatening to resurface and waited until I could hear the turn of a car engine. I turned the key in the ignition, so to be synchronised with the sound of the thug's car, hoping to God my headlamps didn't come on. Slowly I reversed – until the rear of the white car began to edge out of the driveway. Quickly, I slipped into first, then second and picked up speed to pass the car and driveway as if I were an innocent passer-by, praying you didn't notice us. As I approached the driver of the white car he politely tucked into the hedgerow to let me pass. What the hell? I sped on as if our life depended on it.

Where were they taking the poor lad?

A few hundred meters further down the lane, I bumped the car on to the grass verge. Allowing myself to breathe again. I sat and waited. What should I do? How could I possibly go home, but how could I possibly not? Should I call the police? But that could ruin everything, all my planning, everything, Jack's life from here on, our freedom. The worst surely had already happened for the lad, whatever they were up to. I'd read about these things in gory crime thrillers – often carried out to scare people only, warn them off, stop them from talking. About what? The worst for him had already happened, please. They would let him go, dump him somewhere; he'd have learned his lesson. But what had he done?

I restarted my engine still feeling so close to the house. I drove around, circling the area for the best part of an hour, the images replaying over and over. Feeling sick to the core. Reliving the scene; wondering where the lad had been taken. Was he okay? Then chastising myself – of course he wasn't okay. It was 8:15 p.m. Jack would wake soon; I needed to return home. Please let you be gone. I couldn't face you, not now or ever.

Some time on, I arrived back to an unoccupied driveway. The house in darkness. A huge sigh of relief. I carried Jack's heavy body up the steps, all the time seeing the face of someone else's son scraping down the slabs; the look of absolute fear in his eyes. I had to go in against my will; with nothing other than my mobile with me, I had no choice. But I knew at that moment, my plan needed to be brought forward. There was no way we could continue to live under the same roof as you. A line had been crossed;

time to leave. I'd prepare the necessary belongings and leave once you'd left for work in the morning.

I fetched the blanket from a spare bed so I could sleep in Jack's room in the chair next to his bed. With me I grasped my car keys and my mobile. I'd spent a couple of hours gathering supplies, nothing that wasn't essential, all mostly Jack's. I hadn't planned for this yet; I didn't even know where we'd go. A refuge maybe? I looked up the number for the Citizens Advice Bureau. I would ask to speak to a voluntary solicitor in the morning. I researched reasonable cheap bed and breakfasts in the not too close area. I could use the money I'd stashed away, until I knew my next move. The solicitor I'd consulted a few weeks ago had assured me I could apply for some emergency funding in court. It wouldn't take too long to achieve, he'd promised. I'd make my way to the courts in Leamington Spa in the morning to file my application. I was already exhausted but the adrenaline fuelled my hypervigilant state.

At some point, in the early hours of the morning, I heard you return, slamming the front door with force. My neck stiff with tension, I could hear you staggering around as items clattered and clanged on the floor. My stomach twisted and turned; I could see my legs physically trembling as I imagined your drunken black mood. Why hadn't I taken the opportunity to leave that night? Then, I listened intently as you consciously climbed each moving stair. Please, don't look for me. Please. I rubbed my sweaty palms on my jeans, baulking at the taste of bile. Seconds later, I stopped breathing, aware you were standing on the other side of the door, listening. My heart missing a beat as the door opened slowly, I slumped low in the chair, feigning sleep.

Your thuggish self staggered towards me, kicking at toys on your way. A robot began to bellow instructions. I didn't dare glance at Jack. I squeezed my muscles tightly, worrying I was going to lose control of my faculties. The game had changed tonight. You were far more evil than even I'd believed. My heart jumped to my mouth. I felt sheer fear, sweat glistening at my brow as you loitered, soaring over me. You kicked out at my left foot. I pretended to stir in my sleep before slumping lower in the chair. How did you not notice me shaking? I only had the alcohol to thank. Heavy fumes smothered my lungs as you exhaled in my face. Chortling to yourself. My eyes scrunched tight. I was petrified – you must have realised I was awake?

'Pathetic,' you whispered in my left ear.

I held my breath.

'Absolutely, sodding pathetic.' You switched to my right ear, stumbling, thumping down hard sharply on my lower arm. 'Look at the state of you!'

Your face millimetres from mine. Hot breath tickling my tortured face. Before swaying back, still leaning hard now on my wrist with your full weight. You flicked my face with your fingers. It stung, bringing tears to my clamped-shut eyes. I resisted flinching. 'Look at the state of you,' you spat in my face. 'No wonder you've no friends. No one. Even your interfering parents left you.' You snatched my mobile from my tightly bound fingers, hurled it, smashing it against the wall. Jack stirred. Please, God, no, Jack, please.

My chest ached, ready to explode. You hovered, glowering at me. Your eyes burning through my soul. Then you spun, kicked my right foot, before staggering back out of the room. No key for this door, I thought. I stole a gasp of air.

Please, God, let this be the end. I'd got away lightly this time.

Chapter Twenty-Seven

Cornwall 2016

'Come on, Jack, for goodness' sake; have you seen the time?' How many times do I utter this statement? I wonder.

'Yeah; I know, I'm coming!'

'No, you're not, though, are you? Else I wouldn't need to shout. I'll see you in the car. I'll turn it around, ready to go.'

Moments later, Jack shoots down the path towards me, his huge sports bag bouncing off his back. I catch myself at how grown up he suddenly appears; as if when he hit fourteen, he fell asleep as my little boy, then changed to a lad overnight. He gives me a big teasing grin; he understands it will prevent me from having a go for taking his time. He opens the back door, hurls his bags across the seat, then slams the door, making me wince. At the same time his mobile catapults, landing in the footwell of the back seat. I reach back for it.

'It's fine, Mum; I'll get it,' he says, all too quickly. As lovable as Jack is, he'd normally have me bending in all positions to pick things up for him. Old habits die hard.

'Okay. I was just trying to help.' I glance at him eagerly twisting back for it. 'Stroppy pants.'

'Yeah, it's okay. I'm on it. Thanks.'

Catastrophe over, he pulls the sun visor down, adjusting his hair in the mirror.

'It's fine; looks gorgeous, in fact.'

He pans it back. 'What?'

'Your hair – looks great. Don't worry.'

He relaxes in his seat and smiles. 'Yeah, whatever, Mum.'

'Did you pull the door to properly, and shut the gate?'

'Yeah, I did. What's the big deal with the gate? You never used to bother shutting it, before.' I take my eyes from the road to observe his almost defiant eyes. 'Anyway, Allan's bound to leave it open when he drops the post, so what's the point?'

I have no right to challenge him. 'I know, just feel better with it closed.' I notice his tensed fists. 'You're right, no big deal.'

The mood instantly changes in the car, away from light, normal school-run banter to a feeling of something heavier. But then what did I expect, given the recent revelations? I don't know how to tell Jack about last night, but I'm going to have to, later maybe. In the end, I stuffed the second envelope into the wooden chest in the kitchen. Why didn't I set it alight on the fire instead? I remained awake for most of the night, moving between moments of sheer fear to red-hot anger; then an overwhelming sadness. When are Jack and I going to be allowed to move on?

'You okay?' I squint at him.

'Yeah, think so.' He looks straight ahead. 'Are you?'

'Yes, of course I am.' I feel his eyes on me, looking for clues. 'It's going to be okay, Jack. Everything will be okay.' Who am I trying to convince?

I can tell he's psyching himself up, as he used to as a small child. 'Will it, though, Mum?'

'Why wouldn't it be?' What a stupid question – what is wrong with me?

'You know why. I'm not stupid, you know.'

'I know you're not. Anything but.' He looks out of the window as I reach for his clenched fist. 'We've talked about this. We just need to be vigilant, you know, be sensible. That's all.'

'Right, so that's normal, isn't it?'

'What? Being sensible?'

'No, having to be vigilant. I'm fourteen, but I can't go anywhere alone. We live in Cornwall – it's supposed to be safe, you said. All my friends will think I'm a freak! No, sorry, Seb, can't meet you at the beach, because Mum isn't here to hold my hand and walk me down. No, sorry, Jake, can't meet you in Truro because it would mean walking to the bus stop alone, then travelling on a bus alone! Yeah, that's not weird at all!' He sighs loudly. The pain in his eyes does not go unnoticed.

'I know, Jack, I know. I'm sorry. But it's only for the time being. Just until—'

'For the time being, okay, so how long is that going to be? And then what? What's he going to do? What are we going to do? Shouldn't we talk to the police? Isn't this what normal people would do?'

'No, Jack. No, we can't do that, not yet.'

'Why not?'

'First of all, we've nothing to go on.' I think about this, as it's not quite true: I have the certificates and the other envelope; not to mention the other stuff. But it still doesn't prove unquestionably they were from him. I don't have any proof he's been stalking us. To the police, he hasn't actually done anything wrong. Yet. 'Look, it's not that simple, take it from me. Going on past experience, the police only want to know if you've hard evidence. Suspicion and observations are simply not enough, Jack. It's wrong, I know, but they only get involved once a crime has been committed.'

'Smart, so he has to kill us first. Great!'

'Jack, don't say that! It's not what I meant. That's not going to happen. Don't say such horrible things.' My stomach flips. He's right, though. How can it be that my child is even having to think in this manner?

It's happening again, the feeling of not being able to protect him, against all my most basic instincts.

'Come on, Mum, we both know what he's capable of. Or have you forgotten?'

I'm a little taken aback, as Jack doesn't know the half of your behaviour. He was too young, yet his words tell me otherwise. Could he have been digging, researching? I've blatantly avoided doing the same. Stuck my head in the proverbial sand, pretending ignorance is bliss. Perhaps Jack now understands more than I do. His mobile bleeps; he turns it over to read the screen. Like a paranoid mother, I instinctively lean over to take a look.

He moves the mobile out of view. 'What are you doing?'

'Who is it?'

'What?'

'The message, who's it from?' What am I doing? Invading his privacy, like some kind of controlling mother.

'What's wrong with you? It's just a Snapchat. Why do you want to know? Jesus!'

'Sorry. I didn't mean to be nosey. I'm just worried about you. You'd tell me, wouldn't you… you know, if you knew anything?'

He nods and turns to look out of the window.

The car fills with an uncomfortable silence. This is how you get under our skin. You're not even here, yet still creating tension. Don't let him in, Eve; you're better than this.

I take Jack's white-knuckled fist and squeeze. 'Unclench your hand, Jack.'

'What?'

'Unclench your hand. It's bad for you.' He straightens out his hand without argument but returns to look out of the window. 'I'm sorry. We'll sort this out, just give me some time to think about how best to handle it.'

'Okay.' He nods. A mishmash of love and hatred burns through my gut. Someone give me a knife, a chance to stab you slowly over and over.

Half an hour later, I make my way to the multistorey car park in Truro, having dropped Jack off at school. Right on cue, as I leave the concrete blot, it begins to spit. A glance upwards informs me it's a passing shower; I scurry into the small coffee shop for a shot of caffeine and wait. I place myself in the window, cradling a double black Espresso, to watch the world go by.

I don't feel like clinic today – too much buzzing in my mind – except I'm booked up, including a trip to see Milly again. She's just eleven years old. Her mum's boyfriend is the local pot dealer, by all accounts. Recruiting children as young as and including Milly to sell his wares. Offering her freebies as payment. What initially gave her an enormous high sent her crashing, stretching her right-brain imagination into the frightening land of paranoia. Her way to escape was to descend into the dark world of self-harm. With a little help from the world of elusive hashtags and manipulative emojis.

I wince further at the recall of the certificates I received last night. You haven't changed; I sense you feeling hard done by. Betrayed and forsaken by your son and wife. You blame me. You will never grasp the truth, an even further distortion of the imagination, this time held captive by the left-side dictator. You are dangerous.

A deep Cornish voice breaks my thought. 'A penny for them!' he says, tapping my shoulder as he shuffles by with his stick. You wouldn't want to know, really. I smile back at him. The rain begins to ease so I prepare to make a run for clinic. But I'm momentarily stalled in the doorway as I spot the familiar figure, casually strolling in the fading shower, running his hands through damp hair. Before turning to deliberate the steps, one by one, missing the first. William Adams? Yes, I'm sure it is; I've his image implanted in my mind's eye. Why is he going in there? The Truro counselling place? How strange.

A minute later, I walk past the entrance, to confirm I've the correct building. Why would he be visiting there, when he's already booked in with me?

Has he switched? Thought I was useless? Given my state of mind during our appointment, this wouldn't be difficult to believe. There's something peculiar about this man. Am I simply reading too much into it? After all, he didn't leave his contact details, so maybe he did think I wasn't up to the job. But there's more to this than meets the eye, I'm sure of it. I walk on by for now, but I'll return later. Besides, professionally I should know if he is seeing someone else at the same time as me. After all, we could undo each other's work, a conflict of interests. I know the practitioners fairly well here; it shouldn't be too difficult to find out.

My morning's appointments pass slowly. A fear of flying and an antidote of exposure therapy via guided imagery. A teenager who is bombing out of school, another victim to a boarding routine. A further OCD case; why is this becoming so prevalent? Is it a case of clutching at control in an increasingly insecure society? Finally, a case of domestic abuse. Should I simply relay my story? Don't wait, get out now, there is no such thing as an ideal time to leave. Don't play the game, just get out; and especially if you have children.

I pull up outside the GP surgery in Mevagissey to see Milly, wondering how she will be today. I had an interesting phone call with her mum in between appointments earlier. Circumspectly, stepped my way through it. Was she aware of her boyfriend's antics? Of Milly's involvement? I could very easily have made matters worse for Milly too. It makes me shudder to think this is even possible, but it is. Turns out, her mum was aware of her boyfriend's pot-dealing, just not that her daughter has been sucked in. Milly isn't aware of her mum's knowledge; it is for me to encourage her to open up to mum. The boyfriend will hopefully be gone by tonight, probably move back to his own residence, the pot hole.

I watch Milly as we talk. She's warmer today, not so wary of me, talking openly about her week. She's listened to me, and has managed to abstain from harming herself, relaying how she's used other distraction techniques, as we'd discussed. I'm praying this wasn't the weed.

'The thing is, Milly, it's a lot tougher to struggle through this alone.'

'I have you,' she says.

'You do. But, I mean, at home, it's tough when you're at home, to feel alone with things.'

She regards her feet and shrugs.

'It's even more sad, Milly, because you're not alone. You have mum.'

'Used to,' she says.

'Has mum told you you're not to go to her with your problems?'

'No. Not as such.'

'Has mum changed towards you in any way?'

'No. Not really.'

'So, why do you think you don't have her any more, to talk to?'

'Not sure, just don't.'

'Tell me if I'm wrong, but… is it you who has changed maybe? What with everything you've been going through. Is it perhaps this bully in your head, the very same telling you to harm yourself to feel better – is it this, telling you not to go to mum?'

She looks at me, eyes slightly bloodshot. 'I don't know,' she says.

'From what I understand, mum would prefer to know; whatever it is frightening you, upsetting you, she would want to know. This bully will be weaker against the two of you.' I watch as her eyes glisten. A gentle knocking on the door prompts me. 'It's mum – she's waiting outside now. Can we let her in, Milly?'

Burdened eyes look back at me. She nods.

*

Ruan watches me as I run back into the clinic, dumping my briefcase, belting up my coat. 'Hey, where you off to in such a hurry?'

'I need to pop to the counselling place across the road. Do you want anything while I'm out? Sandwich? Pasty?'

'Mmm, tough one. Go on, then, since you asked so nicely, pasty, please. Why the counselling place? Thinking of booking yourself in?' He grins.

Much truth said in jest, Ruan. You probably think I should. 'Yes, actually, I am.' His smile disappears as quickly as it arrived.

'Oh, bum. Sorry, Eve, wasn't thinking.'

I smile at his awkwardness. 'What do you think? Can you really see me, of all people, attending counselling? It would be an extremely quiet session – can you imagine?'

'Ha, I did wonder. Thought you'd finally lost it.' He genuinely looks relieved.

'I won't be long, just something I need to check on, for a client, that's all.' I reach out for the front door. 'Ruan?'

'Yeah?'

'You didn't put a hand-addressed envelope in my briefcase, did you?' I find myself studying his face for a guilt-ridden reaction. I don't want to; I can't help it.

'An envelope? Nope, no, not me. Why? Wait, do you mean the one from last night, when we were with you?'

'No, a different one, not related.' He genuinely appears perplexed. 'No big deal; just found something in my briefcase, not sure how it got there. I wasn't sure if you'd slipped it in for me.'

'No, not guilty. Could it have been Bea? What was it?'

I open the door. 'Nothing, really, don't worry about it. I won't be long.' Why don't you tell him? He knows more or less what's going on – why the secrecy now? Are you really beginning to mistrust those closest to you? Haven't you just pulled Milly on this? Do I have any choice though?

I bustle down Lemon Street on a mission, take a left turn through the quaint indoor market, breathing in deeply as the smell of sweet garlic engulfs me. A few moments later, I reach the pedestrianised street of terraced houses, standing in line like soldiers. Such a pretty cut-through. I rush up the steps and through the door of the counselling place.

'Hi, Maggie, how are you?' She looks up from her salad in a plastic bowl. 'Sorry, I'm interrupting your lunch,' I say to the receptionist.

'No, lovely. Not at all. I'm well, how are you? Not used to seeing you in here.' She looks a little muddled, worried she's forgotten something pre-arranged.

'Yes, all good,' I lie. 'Busy, you know how life is.' She nods, taking another forkful. 'I need a word with someone about a possible mutual client. Who's in today, Maggie?'

'Oh, I see.' She stands and moves towards the clinic diary. 'Yes, now, then, Dr Willow's here. Steven, the acupuncturist, he's in. Just a minute.' She puts her glasses on and moves her finger down the list in front of her. 'Lara Maidwell, Dr Burns and David, the physio, they're in, oh, and sorry, Susie Hammond, she's in too. That's it until later, Eve.'

'Okay.' Who would he be likely to see? Maybe he's here to see the acupuncturist or the physiotherapist and I've got this all wrong. 'Hmm, it's difficult because I need to talk to whoever it is seeing this mutual client, I'm just not sure who it would be.'

'Oh, quite, yes, that is difficult. Can you give me a name?' Can I? Is this ethical, confidentiality and all that? Yes, because there could be a conflict of interests here, and something is definitely odd about all this.

'I can. It's a William Adams.'

Her forehead forms confused lines. 'William Adams? William Adams.' She looks back through the diary.

'It was today, Maggie, if it helps. This morning, he was here this morning.' She nods, still searching the page. 'William Adams, William Adams. No, Eve love, can't have been. We don't have a William Adams.' She looks me in the eye. 'The name certainly doesn't ring a bell with me either. I've been here all morning too.'

I was not mistaken; it was definitely him.

'That's so strange. The thing is, I saw him this morning, walking into your reception. I know I did.'

'Really? Yes, how strange.' She looks back at her list, puzzled. 'But I was the only one here this morning. I'd remember his name, I'm sure.'

'Yes, of course you would, you're right. Look, don't worry about it.' I can't push her any further; it's as though I'm doubting her. Maybe I did get it wrong – wouldn't be the first time. My stressed brain is beginning to bail on me.

'What does he look like, love?'

I picture him from this morning. 'Six-footish, dark hair, quite distinguished, nicely spoken, quite well built. Oh, and he was wearing black jeans, tan trainer-like shoes and a navy bomber-style jacket?'

Her face lights up. 'Now then, that rings a bell; a nice man, pleasant he was, didn't want to sit down though. Had a problem with his legs, I believe. Yes, I remember him. Yes, he's been here before too.'

Bingo. I move closer. 'Thank goodness, thought I was seeing things.' I laugh. 'Who did he come to see, then? I could do with having a word with them, please.'

'Yes, okay, love, but just a minute because his name wasn't William Adams.' She looks up as footsteps move down the stairs behind us. 'Oh, Susie, good timing.' Maggie looks from Susie to me. 'It was

Susie who saw this man. It's her you need to talk to.'
Maggie nods towards Susie, who's looking thrown.
'You know the man you saw for your first appointment this morning? Eve needs a word about him.' She taps her nose, making me smile.

'My first appointment, yes, I know who you mean.' She smiles at me. 'Eve, lovely to see you. What is this? What do you need to talk to me about?' She joins us in Reception.

'Sorry about this. I was just asking Maggie about a mutual client we have, apparently. Do you have a moment?'

'Sure, come through.' We walk into a freezing cold side room; I can't help but shiver.

'So, it's to do with the gentleman I saw this morning?' I remember now how prim and proper she is, and feel a little bad for putting her on the spot.

'Hmm.' I run through the description again for Susie's acknowledgment. 'I don't wish to know any specifics, obviously, it's just, he didn't tell me he was seeing you, during our appointment. I mean, perhaps he was meeting several people, checking who he felt he could work with best. But it's just mine was a very specific referral. Look, I've a gut feeling something is not right here, is what I'm trying to say.'

'I see. Well, he didn't mention to me he was seeing anyone for anything either. He certainly didn't mention being referred. But perhaps he's seeing us for different reasons?'

'Yes, that's possible, of course.' After all, counselling alone may not satisfy his trauma-related issues. 'But the odd thing is, when I mentioned his name to Maggie, she told me it wasn't the name you had for him.'

Susie raises her eyebrows. 'Really? What name do you have, then?'

'William Adams. This was the name on the referral too.'

She shakes her head. 'No, that's not right. No. Are we sure we're talking about the same man?'

I ignore her; my instincts tell me we definitely are. 'So what name did he book under with you?'

'In confidence, Eve?'

'Of course.' I nod, the suspense killing me.

'Gregg. Gregg Austin.'

Dear God. I was not expecting this. My legs wobble as adrenaline rips through my body. No, no, no. How can this be so? I'm sure Susie is speaking to me, but my ears can only hear humming.

'Eve?' I hear. 'Eve. Are you okay? Do you need a glass of water?'

I can't get the words out; I want to curl into a ball on the floor. Is this some kind of sick joke? Why does he call himself Gregg Austin? My mind is frantically running through the details. What have I missed?

Susie gently takes my arm. 'What is it, Eve? What's wrong? I thought you knew him already?'

'I do,' I manage. 'Well, clearly, I don't. I don't know anything about him.' I take Susie's arm. 'What did he come to see you for?' It's worth a try.

'Come on, you know I can't divulge this!'

'No. No, sorry, I know you can't. I shouldn't have asked.' At least this means he can't have told her he's about to commit murder on behalf of the person he claims to be. She would have been ethically bound to tell me then.

Moments later, I wander back through Truro, distracted by the cobbles I repeatedly wedge my heels between. Why do I wear such stupid shoes?

So much information rattling through my mind, so many disjointed facts and uncertainties. I can't figure it out. Only one thing is for sure: whatever his game is, this William Adams, or whoever he is, he's telling lies and he knows you. But how well does he know you? Has he been sent by you? Is this, then, the shadow that has been following me? Is he the bearer of unwanted gifts too? Absent-mindedly, I accidentally bounce off someone lurking in the street. 'Sorry,' we both mutter. She looks at me, a face overwhelmed by gigantic sunglasses, despite the clouds. She turns quickly from me, in a knowing way. An ex-client maybe? She does look vaguely familiar. She totters off in a hurry, before turning to look back once more.

My thoughts return to William Adams. The more I think about it, you never used to relish getting your hands dirty, did you? You thought you were above it, too clever, but it makes you a coward in my eyes. So have you sent me William? To follow me, frighten me and begin to break me down, before your grand finale? I wouldn't put anything past you. I can't afford to.

Who are you, William Adams? And what do you know?

Chapter Twenty-Eight

Before

I awakened in the rigid chair to the slam of the front door, a cramp-like ache in my neck for company. I didn't know the time, but it was still dark. Jack hadn't stirred so I was guessing it was not much after 6 a.m. Why did you leave so early this morning? You could only have had a couple of hours' sleep. Still, it suited me well. If you were gone, time for action. I crept past Jack's bed. With no time to lose, I needed to shower, dress and get us out of here. My stomach fluttered at the thought; a mixture of nervousness but also a timid excitement – we were finally leaving.

An hour later, Jack was dressed and sitting eating breakfast. It was then, I spotted the note.

I will (reluctantly) order a replacement mobile today. Why do you always have to push me? Not home until very late, plenty of time to think about your behaviour!

Perfect. I had time to gather our belongings together. Perhaps make a few phone calls before I left since my mobile was in hundreds of pieces. I would do the sinful act of putting Jack in front of his favourite TV programmes and use the unexpected time. I then booked us a room at a bed and breakfast near Chipping Campden, somewhere remote, difficult to find. Somewhere to breathe for a while following our escape.

I sat with a coffee, pen and paper, time to go over all I'd packed for us, being not a lot. I hoped this was going to be a short-term solution, until we'd taken the next legal steps. What was I doing? Was it fair to be taking Jack from his home, all he knew, all his home comforts? Why, despite everything, did I still feel so guilty? Terrified too. It reminded me of the first time I'd abseiled, a team-building exercise; stepping blindly off the cliff edge, too scared to pay too much attention to where I'd end, should I fall. The first step off the so-called secure ground was always going to be the worst. I had no choice; we had to leave. For everything we had lived through, for all I'd witnessed; and for all my heart told me was to come.

Jack's red medical book; I shouldn't leave without it. I ran up the stairs to the spare room, I kept it in the drawer of the old pine wardrobe. With book in hand, I turned back towards the door; a perfunctory scan of the room, just in case. I noticed the bottom drawer of the old chest; the locked one, except it wasn't locked, it was ajar. You must have opened it the evening before, and, in your drunken state, forgotten to lock it again. I couldn't resist, sure I'd find the wads of cash. Boy, could I have done with some cash to take with us. Wrong. Most likely illegal. But principles wouldn't keep us safe.

I slowly bumped the rickety drawer further out.

My heart missed a beat. Oh my God. Nausea crept upwards. Jesus Christ. I wobbled from my crouched position onto precarious knees. Pressing my hands hard to my temples. Wads and wads of cash. Thousands and thousands of pounds, but it was what lay beneath that shocked me; petrified me. My mind raced back to the conversation I'd heard the evening of the golf-club event. I'd dismissed it – why? Because I didn't want to believe it? I was too weak to confront it? A most convenient oversight? Then images of the previous night; the poor beaten lad tossed down the steps.

A gun.

Jesus Christ. A gun. In our home.

Think, Eve, think. What to do?

It took me a while to remove myself from the chest and room. I glanced at the hallway clock over the galleried landing. I was taking far too long; I needed to get out. Why was it taking me so long to leave? I'd planned to leave hours ago. Still, you said you wouldn't be returning until very late. I ran down the stairs, gathering and hurling belongings into the boot of my car. Not wanting to transfer my panic, I decided I would offer Jack refreshments before the start of our journey. My heart jabbing at my T-shirt, I couldn't stomach any food, despite being aware of my cortisol-filled light head.

'Come on, sweetheart.' I held out my hand for his. 'Milk and a biscuit?'

'No, Mummy, want it in here. Please. This, my favrit bit!'

Normally, he wouldn't be allowed to drink or especially eat crumbly biscuits in the sitting room. But this was time to mark new beginnings; new rules, or just fewer of them.

'Why not, sweetheart? Why not? Mummy will bring it to you.'

I made sandwiches to keep us going; selected some other nibbles and drinks. Checked my bag for one final time, whilst willing Jack to hurry; I was beginning to feel exceptionally jumpy. I needed to leave, but didn't want to unnerve Jack any more than absolutely necessary. What was the panic? I'd plenty of time, I reassured myself. Everything was packed, ready, all I could need, just in case. So one more mendacious act couldn't possibly hurt.

I placed our shoes and coats next to the front door. Then made my way to your study. I'm not sure why but a gut feeling whispered in my ear to take your flash-drive. It was still there. You usually kept it under lock and key, with your mobile. Jack would still be a few minutes. I decided to check – no point in taking something to anger you unnecessarily, if it held no use for me. Your laptop was password protected, so I fetched the family laptop from the kitchen, booted it up and inserted the flash-drive. Hopping from foot to foot, willing the process to speed up. Finally, the option to open several files appeared. The latest with the date of the previous evening. I clicked it. One minute later, I closed it down as my body temperature soared; I couldn't bring myself to observe any longer. I needed to get out of the contaminated house. You were evil, and the flash-drive could prove useful. Protection. Proof of something I didn't want to know about.

'Mummy's just going to the bathroom, Jack. Then I'm afraid we need to turn this off.'

'Oww,' a small voice came back.

'I know, sweetheart, but we're going on a surprise adventure. Remember; a kind of holiday. How about that for exciting?'

'Yay. But Daddy's not coming, is he, Mummy?'

'No, Jack, Daddy can't come.' Please help me God.

I was drying my hands upstairs when I heard it, the thump of the front door. No, please, no. You cannot be home, I silently prayed. I tentatively crept around the landing, then slowly moved down the stairs as my worst thoughts were confirmed. I could hear you, shuffling around in the study, muttering under your breath. What were you doing home?

'Eve!' you commanded. I didn't need a scene. If I cooperated, you would leave again, I hoped. Then it struck me: what if you were looking for—?

'Eve!'

'Yes, Gregg, no need to shout. What is it?' I took steps into your study.

'Have you touched my laptop?'

'No, why would I?' I lied.

'Because something is missing.'

I felt the beginnings of a blush. Why did I have to be such a bad liar? You moved from your desk to take my chin in your hand, tilting it backwards. Your lips a millimetre from my cheekbone, you snarled, 'You're a liar.' I stumbled backwards; one sharp move away from snapping my neck in your grip.

'Gregg, please. I don't know what you're talking about.' Please don't find my handbag, I prayed.

You released me and stalked back towards your desk. Picked up the glass paperweight, then hurled it at the oak door. You were losing control; you didn't understand the alien feeling. It was more frightening for me too. As you turned without words and moved back towards me, I tasted each step draw closer.

Not now, not now, please. I'm so close to leaving.

The force of your recoil flung me to the remorseless floor; my already bruised ribs ached with repetitive strain. Don't let go, Eve, don't let go, you're nearly there. I sheltered my face as usual, repeating: *not long now, not long now. Do. Not. Give. Up. Now.*

I opened my jaw and released it, to check my face was still whole. Through the haze I heard a small voice, shrieking from the doorway, then it froze. You froze. You didn't want Jack to find out who you were, did you? Everyone immobilised. I took my moment. I somehow stood, swiped up Jack, scrambled through the hall, bouncing off walls, and managed to finally sling open the front door.

Jack held tightly in my arms, I ran as quickly as my bare feet would allow. Why hadn't I put my shoes on first? Because time wouldn't have allowed it. We ran, half focusing ahead and half with eyes behind us in fear you would be following. We had no time; we had to get away. We had nothing, Jack and I, nothing; no time to collect our things, no time to collect our coats. It was freezing outside but I don't think either of us felt it, at that point.

I had no car keys, no house keys, no money, no bag, no change of clothes for Jack, no food and no phone. But then who would I have called anyway? I didn't have anyone left to call. Not strictly true – there were people to call; it was more, no one was aware of my situation. Anyone I'd have called would have been deeply shocked, requiring explanations. Stories, the lies, years of covering up and more, all the unimportant matters I didn't want to be concerned with.

I felt Jack's chubby hands holding on tightly to my hair tied at the back of my neck. It pulled and stung but didn't matter; at least I knew he was with me. He was heavy to run with but it didn't matter either. He didn't speak, neither did I, not for a little while. We just scarpered, clinging onto hope. I didn't even know what I was going to do, or where I was going to go. I only focused on increasing the distance between us and the house. Listening all the time for the roar of your engine. I knew if I could keep moving at a pace, I would eventually reach our nearest neighbour; about two kilometres away. Once I cleared the immediate parameters, I would need to put Jack down; he quickly became too heavy for jelly-like legs. The fight or flight borrowed charge would run out at some point. But I was worried Jack would not be able to move his little legs quickly enough, especially without his shoes, on the cold harsh tarmac.

Eventually, I buckled and positioned him down in front of me, taking his tiny hand in mine. I peered at his pink frightened face. I didn't have much time. I needed him to stay as calm as he possibly could. Not easy, especially as I was anything but calm. Focused and determined, but inside the panic gripped. He looked deep into my eyes. I recognised the expression: unadulterated fear and bewilderment.

'It's okay, Jack, Mummy knows where we'll go. Everything's going to be okay. Trust me, darling, please. I promise, Mummy will sort it. Please try not to be scared.'

He didn't speak; he didn't know how to or what to say. He simply nodded. I pulled him in for a hug. As I did, I noticed my bare arms, turning from a pinky red to a blueish purple. I hated to think what my face looked like. I wished I could have explained it merely as the effect of the extreme cold and inappropriate attire, but it was, I expected, more to do with the beating. The pummelling and the booting. A vile metallic taste of blood and a slow-motion flashback of hard knuckles to chin bone. A new form of attack. Just how far were you going to go this time, if it weren't for Jack? Would it have been lights out for me?

It didn't matter anymore; we were free. Nearly.

Hand in hand we set off again, a couple of shoeless waifs and strays. I silently prayed; please let someone be in at the neighbour's house, please. I didn't know their names; how particularly humiliating for this to be our first formal introductions. A couple in their forties or thereabout, whom I'd only ever waved at in passing from time to time. But as the imposing grey granite house came into view, I heard the inimitable rumble closing from behind. It was possibly still a few hundred metres away, thankfully out of sight; obscured by bends in the country lane. I couldn't let you catch us. We couldn't go back now. Or ever. Irreversibly, you had overstepped even your concealed mark, and poor Jack; Jack had witnessed, heard far too much. Things that would without any doubt inhabit his conscience for the rest of his life.

I clutched Jack's cold arms, yanking him up to me. And ran.

'Jack, quick, we need to hide; we need to find somewhere to hide. I can hear his car, sweetheart. I'm so sorry.'

At the first opening, I trudged through thick gummy bog as the ground tried to suck us under. The cold sludge squelched between my toes as we slipped and stumbled on. Sheer bloody resolve mixed with terror allowed us through. We continued down the edge of the field before I plunged us both deep into the thick hedgerow. The week before, Jack and I had stood the other side picking cobnuts. Those same branches scratched at sore arms. Biting at my purple bruising. The first drops of blood appeared and smeared against Jack's taupe trousers. His little face, horrified, as he tenderly touched my bottom lip, holding up his finger to show me: we matched. He appeared so abnormally calm but I could feel his heart thrashing out of time against mine. But we were together, and alive.

'What we doing, Mummy?' he eventually whispered. 'Is Daddy goin' to get us? Is he goin' to hurt us, Mummy?' I heard him; I didn't know how to answer. I didn't know the answer. I couldn't afford for him to feel safe just yet. I didn't want to frighten him either. I bit my tongue as it longed to reassure him.

'Shush, darling. We need to keep very, very still. Shush now. It will be okay as long as we keep very quiet, very still.' Words no three-year old could possibly be expected to understand. Let alone the circumstances. 'Like a game of hide and seek. It is so important we keep very quiet. Try not to move, Jack. Try your hardest for Mummy, please.'

As I kissed the top of his head I heard the murmurs of a silent cry. Then a whimper. I held and squeezed him as tightly as I could without crushing his small icy body. As from somewhere behind, slithering over us, came the shadow of your dark car, ever so gradually creeping by. I stopped breathing. It slowed to a forbidding stop. No sound. I couldn't even hear us breathing. I couldn't feel our heartbeats. I waited, we waited, not a word was uttered between us. We both fully understood the importance of what hung on the next few moments. Shivering, as I felt my body temperature rise. Freezing, yet sweating. Still silence.

I caught the release of a car door. Then, more silence. I gripped Jack firmer. I could feel your cool anger through the bracken. Could you smell our fear? I couldn't see anything through the density but your closeness was palpable. Standing a few feet away on the other side. A few menacing inches away. The smell of your aftershave assaulting my senses. I held Jack's head tightly to my chest, shielding his ears. I pictured you in my mind's eye; with one narcissistic foot touching smooth tarmac. Leaning on the immaculate roof of your low-slung Porsche. Scanning the area, listening. Attentive and waiting. Just another sick game for you. A game you needed to win. But I needed to win more.

Jack unsurprisingly let out the start of another terrified whimper. I stifled his mouth with my hand, hoping he hadn't been heard. Clasping his cold cheeks in my hand, I kissed the top of his head, staring into his blue eyes, silently pleading him to hold on. Trust me. I couldn't speak; it was far too risky. We crouched together for what felt such a long time, holding our breath as if submerged under water. We needed to resurface soon. We couldn't go on for much longer. Jack especially.

I heard movement from the other side. You were out of the car. Your self-assured footsteps prowled to my left. Making their way towards what I could only imagine to be the field entrance. Where we'd lumbered through just moments before. Could you make out my footprints? Why hadn't I thought of that? Holding an already fully constricted Jack, I somehow managed to squash us down even further into the abrasive undergrowth. As if without bones. Desperately attempting to time any noise of our movement with the noise of your leather soles on the tarmacked lane. Please, God, someone help us. Please, let us be invisible.

Your X-ray eyes surveyed our proximity. Glaring in our direction, directly at the shrubbery. I could feel them. I didn't dare look up. I didn't need to. Just one further malevolent step forward and I was sure you would see us. We were drowning, held down by your presence, your being. Sinless fear. Dark and darker. I felt myself slipping. I felt Jack slipping; his body became a dead weight. Was it the shrubbery? Was it the terror? Or had we finally passed out? A trickle of sweat and a further sniffle from Jack hurled me back to the moment.

What were you waiting for? Enjoying the moment? Knowing you didn't need to move. Standing watching us. Biding your time. Laughing at our pathetic actions, our attempts to escape your prison. I pictured you looking at the boggy field entrance; understanding your dilemma, trying to decide if it was worth ruining expensive shoes for. Looking at my bare footprints, realising you didn't need to do anything. You simply needed to wait. Prolong our agony and wait. It would soon be dark. I couldn't survive without you for much longer, could I? Why spoil the fun? After a few moments your footsteps retraced. We took a gulp of air.

Then, the words, 'I know you are there, Eve,' stole my heart.

I was beaten, with no choice but to relent, despite my resolve to escape. My fear for Jack. The cold air, our isolation, thieved our options. I convinced myself it was only me you would hurt. Not Jack. But then Jack was your weapon. Your pawn. You knew the only true way to hurt me, to control me, was to hurt Jack. But with no phone, in the freezing plummeting temperatures, I would have to walk into the lion's snare. I hated myself for it. I was trapped. As always. I dragged exhausted legs back through the field entrance and surrendered. You were sitting in the car, reading a newspaper, until your eyes met mine in the rear-view mirror. I saw you smile. Jack sobbed as you climbed from the car to greet your family, looking to my feet in disgust. Your car had not long been valeted. You calmly strode towards us shaking your head, tutting.

'You took your time, Eve,' you said, reaching out. 'Come to Daddy, Jack. What has your mummy done to you?' You clasped Jack's waist, and he dug his feet into me, tightening his grip around my neck. I swayed him away from your touch.

'Don't touch him,' I reproached.

'Stop being so fucking stupid. What else will you do? Catch a bus maybe? Call a friend? Your parents perhaps?' You smiled in a sympathetic manner; a true impressionist.

Before snatching a defiant Jack. With Jack in your hands you dealt another blow, another lesson. My already bruised ribs crunched on the ground as Jack squealed. I felt nothing, as pain and cold numbness mingled, knowing this was just the beginning. You turned away with your traumatised son and strapped him into his seat. I pressed upwards. I couldn't allow you to take Jack without me. Please forgive me, Jack, I had no choice.

We drove back in silence, you humming a cheerful tune to yourself, whilst Jack remained frozen behind. Why did you have to come back to the house? When I had everything ready to leave, why did I take so long, faffing? We could have escaped. As we turned into the driveway, I couldn't believe my luck, seeing the unknown but familiar black car, the fat, balding man leaning up against it. He looked rougher than I did, nearly. A fleeting glance at you informed me you were not amused by his presence. You had an agenda for us, didn't you? You thumped your palm on the steering wheel, knowing there would be a delay in my punishment.

'Wait here,' you instructed me, jumping from the car. I watched the frustrated, hostile exchanges before you returned and leant into the car; you hurled the keys at me. 'Don't do anything stupid. I'll be home in a couple of hours. I mean it, Eve. Do. Not. Betray. Me. The world is not a big enough place for you to hide.'

Thank you, God. Thank you. I watched them speed away before I dared move. I turned to Jack, sitting stunned in the back, and reached for his hand. 'It's okay, Jack. It's over now. Come on, let's get ready for our adventure. We need to be quick, sweetheart.' I left him, running into the house, only to retrieve my keys, bags, shoes and coats before slamming the heavy door behind us. No going back.

Chapter Twenty-Nine

Cornwall 2016

'So, Milly. I'm so happy you and mum are communicating again.'

She nods. 'Yeah, it's good. We've been over all the... stuff. He's gone now, Mum's boyfriend. I was scared that he'd come back. But Mum's said she'll go the police again if he does, so I'm kinda okay with it now. I got myself all worked up about it.' She pulls back her sleeve. 'Couldn't get it out my head. I did this, the other night.'

I'm looking at a nasty cut, on her arm. 'Okay, thank you for being honest.' I smile at her. 'Can I ask – what played through your mind when you hurt yourself? What did you tell yourself? Take your time, put yourself back in the exact moment, think about where you were, what you were wearing. What were you thinking, Milly?'

'That I'll feel better when it's done. That I'll be okay.'

'Okay. And did you?'

'Not this time. I felt guilty.'

'Guilty?'

'Yeah. ´Cos of Mum. I promised her. And she's really sad already.'

'She is, but mostly because she's been so worried about you. Perhaps you can see now, it's the thought of harming yourself, rather than the actual act of doing it, that makes you feel better, for a moment?' Two lost eyes search my face. 'The expectation of what the harming will give you. Not the actual harming itself. The actual harming hurts, I'm guessing?'

'It does, yeah.'

'It probably hurts even more now, because now you realise Mum is there; is going through all this with you.'

'Probably.'

'The harming, it stops you from working out what makes you so unhappy and, more importantly, what to do about it. The bully, remember, the voice in your head, it tells you what to do, that it's the only way and for the best. It's the very thing that has locked you into a world of hurt. It lies to you, Milly. Prevents you from working through any problems, so it can keep control of you. For good reason, because if you fight back, stop listening to it – it will lose power, die. Does this make sense?'

'Yeah.'

'So today, let's knock out the lies, and replace them with truths. Put a plan together, decide on a better way to deal with problems.' She nods at me. Her happiness has fallen prey to the bullies in her life, aided by the Internet. I can't remove her from this social world she now lives in, only help her to stay in control of her choices.

I drive home, thoughtful about Milly and the many others. Is this another victim of the instant satisfaction society? I've a problem; it needs instant resolution. I don't want to think about it, wait and sort things through. But then, if I'd taken this approach instead, maybe Jack and I would be free by now. I had a bully in my head, I heard it and, on the surface, obeyed it; but I also repelled it. Needing to get close enough, in order to be rid of it. I always kept in mind just how convincing the lies were becoming. That bullies are cowards, and at some point they need to be faced. I'm fearful but also weirdly excited with the thought of being rid of you. Petrified of being in your presence again, but I'm stronger now; I'm as ready for you as I'll ever be. I hope I'm doing the right thing. Last week, at 08.10 sharp, you called my mobile. Only this time, for some reason, you forgot to withhold your number – was this deliberate? Whilst sitting with Milly, I decided – tonight is the night, I am going to text *you*.

My journey home is lost in thought. Then when I arrive, straight away I notice Jack is not back yet. The house is in darkness. Where is he? He was supposed to be dropped home after football, before now? I call his mobile; it diverts to voicemail. Though I'm as sure as I can be it was a deliberate rejection. Why would he do this? He knows how worried I quickly become. My imagination begins to fire: is he with someone he shouldn't be with? Doing something he shouldn't be? Or has someone else taken his mobile from him? I drop my briefcase to the floor, suddenly aware of the weight. Should I go and look for him? I sweep through the ground floor, flicking light switches. My mobile pings in my hand:

Back in 5. Stop worrying x

My breathing begins to move down my chest – but why didn't he pick up my call in the first place? I gather up my coat and briefcase; at least he's safe. It's all that matters. I clatter through the front room, towards the stairs as Humphrey bounces down the last step, meowing, twirling his soft fur around my legs.

'At least I have you.' I drop my briefcase again to pick him up, as he nuzzles his cold nose against my cheek. But there's a scent of something. Not in the air; a foreign scent, not unpleasant, more – unknown. I sniff at Humphrey's fur again. It's on him, the strange smell. He must have been in all day, with no way out. Yet, someone else has stroked him.

A subtle smell of something woody, slightly sweet, hand cream? Aftershave? I tread through the kitchen; everything looks the same. I try the back door; it's locked. I scan the room looking for deviations; nothing as it shouldn't be. Then it occurs to me, how is Humphrey in the house? When I left this morning, he was outside. I'm sure he was, or was that yesterday?

'Mum?' Jack calls from the front door. I start, turning to face him.

'Where have you been, Jack? You're really late!' I spot his mobile flashing in his hand as he flings his bag to the floor.

'Yeah, sorry. It went into extra time.'

'Extra time? I thought it was training tonight?'

'No.' He tilts his head. 'I did say I'd a match, not training. This morning.'

Did he? Am I really becoming so absent-minded? I'd normally have made the effort to go and watch. Or is he just making excuses? 'I don't remember. Even so, how long is extra time? You're still really late.' Why am I doing this? Because I'm angry with myself for forgetting? Because I'm so stressed? Or because I'm so frightened for him?

'What the hell, Mum? The usual time, then penalties. How about, did you win, Jack?' He stomps past me.

'You don't look very dirty.' I follow him.

'Oh, I'm sorry, I'll go outside now, roll in the mud, shall I?' He turns back from the kitchen, grabbing his bag from the floor.

'I'm sorry, baby. Come here, give me a hug.' I throw my arms around him, drawing him in to plant a kiss on his cold cheek; he smells of fresh air. 'I'm sorry, Jack, I didn't mean to be horrible. I just get so worried. How did you get on? Did you win?'

'Yeah, 3-2 after penalties.' He walks through the kitchen to pour himself an obligatory glass of milk.

I follow. 'Brilliant; that's great, well done. Wish I could have been there. I'll make us something nice to eat, shall I?'

He nods. 'Please, I'm starving.' His mobile vibrates on the table; he lays it face down, disregarding the alert. I warn myself, stop reading into things. Trust.

'Bet you are. There's some cake left in the fridge, if you can't wait. I'll go and get out of these work clothes first.'

'Nah… it's fine. I'll wait, thanks.'

'Put the TV on, please, can't stand the silence – oh, and can you feed Humph, please?'

I'm halfway up the stairs, when he calls out, 'There's already food in his bowl. He's eating it now.'

I halt, remembering the scent from Humphrey's fur. Remembering swilling out the food bowl, leaving it empty on the tray on top of the tumble drier, before I left this morning.

'Is this window open for a reason? Can I shut it? It's like an ice box in here.'

'Which window?'

'The one in the utility. It's flipping freezing. Thought, Humph wouldn't use the window? That's why we needed a cat flap, you said?'

He doesn't. He's always refused to use it, even when I showed him how. He'd rather sit and wait on the window sill, in defiance, feeling sorry for himself.

I scramble back down the stairs to join Jack in the utility. 'Let me see.' I squeeze in beside him, with literally only enough room to swing a cat in here. I study the window. If someone was intent, they could have squeezed through it. It opens upwards on an angle; it's just about big enough. But I didn't leave it open; I know I didn't. I wouldn't have – for what purpose?

'Just close it, please. I must have left it open, yes.' I wander back into the kitchen. I should go and check upstairs. I don't want to alarm Jack, so I take my chance whilst he's busy with Humphrey.

I start with his room, throw open the wardrobe, look under the bed, all clear. Then the bathroom: nowhere to hide in there. The spare room is empty. Then my bedroom: no one under the bed, no one in the wardrobe. They'd have a job, with all my stuff crammed in. I sit on the edge of my bed, that feeling again. Am I reaching the edge of psychosis here? My dreams and imaginings are beginning to blur with reality. Is this you? I shiver at the thought. Surely, you wouldn't fit through the window? Who else would it be, though? Whoever planted the envelope in my briefcase?

Jack sticks his head around my door.

'By the way... and don't start panicking.'

My heart skips a beat. 'What, Jack? What is it?'

'That car went past again.' The look on his face tells me he's obviously worried about it too.

'That car? You mean…'

'The 911. I'm pretty sure it was the same reg plate as the one last week. You know, coming from the beach?'

'Where, Jack? Where did it pass you?'

'Just outside now, heading down towards the beach. When I was walking through our gate.'

I jump up. 'Stay here, I'm going to look.'

'No way, Mum.' He holds his hands out. 'Please don't.'

'Jack, I have to. Stay here and lock the door.'

'No, Mum, no. If you're going I'm coming with you.'

'Not a chance, you're not.'

He stands blocking my doorway. 'I'm bigger than you. I'm not letting you through without me.'

Those worried eyes, the same eyes as before. 'Okay,' I tell him. What am I doing? What I have to do.

We fasten our seat belts, no words between us, and set off for the beach. I haven't even considered how I'm to handle this, if you're there. You may have already left, be somewhere else by now. I flashback to the night I met Bea and Ruan in The Wheal; my blood runs cold. The mystery patron – to think we could have been sitting back to back. Then last night, a mere few steps away from you. All the dark shadows, outside the windows, every night since the start of the phone calls. In all honesty, each and every night, since I last saw you, you've never actually left my side, have you?

We pull down towards the cove, slowing to a crawl. I glance through the pub windows as we pass. The usual suspects loiter, but if you're sitting at the table I won't see you anyhow. Next to me, Jack clenches and unclenches his fists.

'There.' He points.

My stomach floats away; I see it. 'I see it.' A Porsche 911, sitting proud in the unattended car park overlooking the beach. What do I do now? I'm not quite ready. I wish to God Jack weren't with me but, then again, I'm so relieved he is. I didn't ever want for him to have to face you again, but maybe he needs to. We edge closer to the car.

'There's no one in it,' he says.

A brief sense of reprieve flushes over me.

'What now?' he asks.

I look at him. 'Not sure,' I say, crawling at a snail's pace. I park up, not more than fifteen feet from the Porsche. I can't get any closer; this is too close as it is. 'I'm going to have a quick look round.' I undo my seat belt. 'You stay here, Jack, please.' Jack unfastens his seat belt, reaching out to release his door. 'No, Jack, please. I promise I'll not move more than a few feet from the car. I'm only going to have a quick look.' He ignores me, stepping from the car anyway.

Together we walk the few feet to the steel railings overlooking the beach. It's dark and so difficult to make anything out. I scan as far as I can along the beach and pathway beyond, dimly lit by the half-moon. Nothing. The Atlantic lashes at the rocks to our side, warning us to take a step back. I'm about to suggest we leave, when Jack taps my arm, making me jump. Placing his finger to his lips, informing me not to speak, he nods to the level below us, to the bench looking out to sea.

I lean over. Straining my eyes, I can just about make the solitary figure out. What? Why sit down there? What are you up to? Is this a coincidence? Or are you the driver of the car?

I indicate to Jack to backtrack and follow me back to the car. We ease the doors open, despite appreciating the noise of the sea will drown out anything we do, and climb inside.

'Promise me you'll stay here.'

'Why? What now? It's not him, so where are you going? Who is it?'

'I'm not going anywhere. Well, only to confirm it is who I think it is, but you don't need to be with me, okay. Lock the doors, though, after me.'

'Who is it?'

'It's okay – it's only one of my clients. I'll be a minute or two, that's all. Just need to check all is okay with them, so you can't be with me. Do you understand? This time you stay in the car.'

He nods. 'But I'm only giving you a few minutes, then, if you're not back, I'm coming to find you.'

Gingerly, I tread the moonlit steps down towards the clash of the waves. Praying and hoping I'm doing the right thing. That Jack locked the doors as I told him to. That I'm correct in thinking, assuming, he was definitely alone down here? Or did I miss something? I catch my breath as a gust of wind pushes me off my track. Yesterday, I had my suspicions, standing with Susie. What am I doing? Did I miss something, a few moments ago, looking down in the dark?

You?

Chapter Thirty

Before

No going back, I said. And I didn't, wouldn't. Not even, as I told you… if it meant living in a shed, in a box, anywhere, anyhow.

Though I didn't quite appreciate I was to spend so many hopeless years in the metaphorical box. It was edged with six walls. No windows, no natural light. Stale air hung low. The smell of foreboding suffocated. The taste of doom delivered bile to my dry throat.

But to touch vulnerable air excited you. An inward smile, an outward aura of invisibility.

We sat divided by the truth. The judicial process.

The perception of truth; the prostitution of morals. On one side, a tailor-cut jacket smothered your broad shoulders. On the other, a reduced form; grasping onto a version of hope. For you, the threat of ignominy; for the other, me, the threat of entirety. Both exposed to ruin. With motivations so poles apart.

I sat fossilised, hands trembling, heart thumping my ribcage, only eyes for the ground. Why did I choose these shoes today? So inanely incongruous.

My ears buzzed, struggling to clear dense fog. A surging mishmash of imperfect thoughts fed my deep limbic system. Caught between fight or flight, in sight of my predator. I tilted my head back to avert portending droplets. Outward vulnerability was never an option. But my eyes failed me, exposing the painful truth. Only a heart full of Jack saved me from falling.

You sat calm yet aroused. You could taste frigidity. Something of old, galvanizing your ego. Your game continuing. Humming a tune of flawlessness, winking an invisible eye at the typist. A game with one winner, you thought. One conceivable outcome. You being the king, me being the *pawn*. A matter of time.

For thine is my Kingdom. God, how you hate me. The power and the glory. God, how I hate you. The domination of weakness.

A black-robed grey head strode into the box, and commanded.

'All rise.'

Together we rose. The beginning of the end.

I had no idea, that the courts and entire divorce process would be such a hostile, caged box. I had no idea, at the time, it would take years, not months to cleanse ourselves of you.

Chapter Thirty-One

Before

I spun the car in the driveway, trembling, desperate to get away before you returned. Drunk on norepinephrine, we accelerated away from the house, retracing the twists and turns Jack and I had run along earlier. My dashboard dinged, alerting me of a below-freezing temperature. I flicked my lights on to full beam, to guide us and potentially blind any oncoming car. You. It was unlikely we'd pass anyone else. I called ahead to the bed and breakfast in Chipping Campden, worried they'd let our room go, for our lateness. It struck me, this was when I should be calling Sam. Have somewhere, someone to turn to; it even crossed my mind for one silly moment to try her. She'd understand; she hated you too. But too much water had gushed under the bridge. Our pre-booked room would serve us well for the time being. Even if it did mean paying with illegal cash, at least until I was able to secure some funds.

The following week was painful. We spent so many days, Jack playing with the few toys I'd gathered, and me making phone calls to legal bodies, desperately trying to work out where to go next. The dirty money wouldn't last forever. My mobile was constantly dinging. I refused to answer the irate texts from you; threatening, if I didn't return. They left me trembling, wanting to vomit. You almost scared me more then, than you ever had before. A hunted animal, in hiding. I hardly slept; the thought of food turned my stomach. I kept promising myself, it would get better. Time would heal.

In a blur, the week passed by. All the time I could see you in my mind, out, trailing local areas, searching for us. We belonged to you, didn't we? We had no right to leave. In the eyes of the law, I had no right to keep Jack from his father either. In one of your texts, you said you'd report me for kidnapping. That you had evidence I was mentally insecure, not fit to be taking care of Jack. That you were going to report me to the police. Then, had reported me to the police. You convinced me, in my desperate state, the police were looking for me.

I became scared to leave the bed and breakfast. Too afraid to go to police myself; you had already blackened my name with them. They had no prior knowledge of our broken marriage; they'd take your word over mine. You were so credible. I had your dirty money, but I'd also been using it – maybe you could implicate me? I couldn't think sensibly. You could afford the best lawyers. I obtained advice mainly from researching, and occasionally from a sweaty, red-faced, legal aid solicitor. I was terrified, mostly, from all the horror stories I'd stumbled over on the Internet – if I decided to go to the police, they would involve social services, and Jack could be taken from me.

The following week, the red-faced man, wearing a waistcoat, advised me I must make contact with you. It was in fact true – I couldn't simply disappear with Jack, despite his understanding of my position. He asked about my then-yellowing bruising. Advised me to go to the police. I couldn't. I didn't tell him about the cash I was using, what I'd witnessed but not reported. How would I explain I'd done nothing? Apparently carried on with my evening, to bed, with no conscience? The flash-drive I'd stolen? What if they believed you? I was mentally unstable. Jack would be taken into care, or taken by you. I asked the red-faced solicitor to make a note of my injuries, but informed him I didn't wish to involve the police. Only hindsight confirms I was a fool. Together, we drafted a letter to you. Two days later, he received your reply from your London solicitors. Threatening, accusing, demanding.

I was on the edge. I thought I'd got through the difficult bit. I knew you always had been and always would be beyond any law. You were one of them, for a start. Two further weeks, we stayed at the bed and breakfast, on a special long-term rate. After that, with the help of my solicitor-cum-only-friend, we were awarded emergency funding. Enough to cover the rental costs of a flat on the outskirts of Stratford-upon-Avon. Divorce proceeding were initiated. Then, terrified, I was no longer able to withhold my address from you. I chose a flat, because it was cheaper but also because it had an intercom, and several surrounding neighbours, on the Shipston Road. Until the day I most dreaded: you were finally granted contact with Jack by the Court.

In the reductionist, biased eyes of the court, from the financial court proceedings to the family courts, it was the cruellest, most degrading of journeys. How did I stand a chance against you, the professional? Justice and humanity followed somewhere behind in the distance. Despite a child's life being at stake, despite the truth radiating from each meticulously prepared court document. The only truth the numerous judges entertained was that you were a member of the club. Many more thousands of wasted pounds on legal representation. The court finally ordered for the sale of the marital home; several months after we were able to purchase a tiny cottage on the edge of Wilmcote village. You didn't like this, did you? You then saw to the diminishing of my funds, very quickly eating and meeting the bills became a weekly worry. Our financial child-maintenance agreement counted for nothing, the

CSA being just as inadequate in the pursuit of someone who knew every loophole, with a limitless supply of cash. Justice and integrity were no more than a white-collar illusion, courtesy of a black-gowned elitist boys' club.

I sat through hours of lies, weeks of manipulation and months of distorted and perverted arguments. Arguments for the rights of him, regardless of his intent; his wants; I questioned in vain about the rights of the child. Cafcass were weak, too afraid to challenge, choosing to rest on the fence or to side with a course potentially most coercing, more threatening. Jack was interviewed by cardigan-adorned strangers, in dowdy, unfriendly environments. Asked to draw pictures, interpret scenarios and fill in the gaps of the same procedures used for each and every different child. And even so, the most prevalent and telling of these findings were ignored, for a wish to calm the waters.

Jack's was the unheard voice of a child.

Chapter Thirty-Two

Cornwall 2016

I stir with the smell of the sea; a lock of hair resting across my cheek. Images of me battling the elements, trying to make sense of the man in front of me, a mere stone's throw from where the tide lapped, flashing through my mind. Over and over throughout an agitated sleep of a kind. It's the white, dense fluff smothering me now. In the early hours of the morning, I recognised the man was you. All over again. The proverbial bad penny. I can't afford to let you into my mind.

Later, I'm going to meet that man from the bench; try and get to the bottom of of who he is. How he knows you. What his business is with me. I'll cancel my morning's appointments, whatever they are. Last night, me and the bench man agreed to meet, at the café above Waterstones in Truro, impartial, but not conspicuous. Bustling, so safe. He told me, today he would explain things; but now I wonder, do I want to know? The cotton wool is closing me down; urging me to retreat into a ball. If it were not for Jack, maybe I would.

'Mum?' Jack's just-woken squinty-eyed face appears in my doorway.

'Hi,' I manage.

'You not getting up?'

Shouldn't I be the one saying this? I drag myself limb by limb from the bed, only to sit on the edge. 'I'm up,' I say. 'You want some breakfast?' I hear myself; I'm normal in words, such a good actor. Just like you.

'I'm on it, thanks; shall I make you a coffee?' Christ, I must look bad.

'Oh, go on, then, thanks, Jack, that would be lovely.'

He moves over and plonks himself down next to me, bouncing me on the bed. 'Are you sure, Mum, about the meeting today? I mean, are you sure you should go? Shall I come with you, just in case? What if he's a—?'

I laugh, and slap his leg. 'You'll do anything to have a day off school, won't you?' He grins at me, still not wide enough to hide his concern.

'You know me. Seriously, though, I was thinking, I should come with you.'

'No, Jack, really, there's no need. It's just a chat, that's all.'

'But what if—?'

'No buts; it's fine. I promise; we're meeting in a very public place. Please, don't worry. I'll tell you all about it tonight. Besides, I already know him. Kind of.' I don't though, do I?

'You always say you'll tell me stuff, then you never do.' I look at his troubled face. I've been so stupid; in trying to protect him, I've worried him more. Keeping him in the dark has made him feel more vulnerable. 'What if he upsets you?'

'People can only affect us, Jack—'

'If we allow them to. Yeah, you said.' He laughs. 'Like, every day.'

'Am I boring?' I ask.

'A bit.'

I pull him into me, give him a squeeze, kiss his head. He pulls his obligatory 'don't be so sloppy' face. 'Good. Now, go, get yourself ready. We're going to be late, again!'

A couple of hours later, I stroll into the familiar book store. Why do bookshops always have a restful atmosphere? I wonder. An air of calmness, an antidote to how I'm feeling. I repeat to myself, as if I'm the most confident person, as if I'm the most confident person, no one knows any different, act as if I am so confident, posture, walk, expression. Why am I doing this? Jack was right. What's wrong with me?

I move towards the lazy escalator, before deciding to count my way up the winding steps instead, good for left-brain control. Bumping into shoppers, already breaking my personal space barrier. At the top, I turn in full view of the open café. He's there, sitting up, confidently gazing over the cobbled street below. He already has two coffee mugs in front of him. So he does think he knows me. What else do you know?

He spots me, seconds after, and stands at my approach. Nice manners. I pull at the chair as we both regard each other. This time, I'm offering no words. Is he nervous too? Of me or his environment? 'Were you early or am I late?' I look at my watch, expecting it to be the latter. I'm bang on time; there's always a first.

'No problem,' he says, sliding the mug of black coffee towards me, then the milk jug. 'I'm always early, no matter what.'

'Black, thank you.' We study each other, looking for clues. 'You know, out of clinic – making conversation with a stranger suddenly feels so odd.' I sip my medicinal coffee.

His eyes seem to crinkle with his smile. 'I can imagine.' He stirs his already stirred coffee. Twice.

'So, without all the normal rules, who goes first?' I ask.

'I guess, I should? The question is, where do I begin?'

'Well, clearly, you know who I am; but how about we start with you? Who are you? Your real name, what is it?'

'You already know my name.'

He thinks I'm stupid, clearly. 'Do I?' I raise my eyebrows.

'Yes. I didn't lie to you. My name is William Adams.'

'Okay, so it wasn't me you lied to about your name. But to say you haven't lied to me? Really?' Too soon for aggressive talk, I tell myself.

He sighs. 'No. I haven't lied to you. At worst, I've...' he looks around for inspiration '... well, I'd prefer to put it as, I've not told you the whole truth.' I open my mouth to speak but he holds his hand out to me. 'But it doesn't necessarily mean I've lied to you. Does it?' He maintains assured eye contact; if he is lying, he's very good. But haven't I been here before? Accomplished liars are brilliant at what they do. Aren't you? I think back to my mum: you can catch a thief but you can never catch a liar, she would advise me.

'Don't play word games with me. This isn't a game. I'm anything but amused.'

'Sorry, you've a right to be pissed off,' he says.

'So, the referral? Your background? What's it all been about?' I challenge.

'Look, Eve, I know I haven't helped myself. But that was all genuine. I am ex-forces, I have been diagnosed with PTSD, amongst other things too, you've probably—'

'Generalised anxiety, manifesting as acute OCD; a sleep disorder, co-morbid depression,' I suggest.

'Exactly.' Slightly disenchanted eyes regard me. 'Is it really so… obvious?'

'Afraid so. Do you always choose a seat near the window, against a wall, rather than in the open? Eye up possible escape routes? Stand rather than sit if given the option? Take two sips of coffee rather than one or three? Align the mug handle to the angle of your body? Count your steps in and out of a building, always needing it to be an even number? Wear trainers with laces tied to within an inch of their life, so you don't need to re-tie, or touch, what has been in contact with the floor?'

He smiles. 'See. You do know who I am.'

'Here's the thing, William, I don't know you at all, but you apparently know me. Don't you? Shall we get to the point now?'

He smiles. 'Can you call me Billy? I don't like being called William. Only my grandmother called me William, if I'd been naughty.' He takes two sips of coffee. 'I know who you are, Eve, yes. More importantly I know who you used to be: Eve Austin.' He looks for affirmation; I'm not giving him anything. I sip my coffee and wait. 'The thing is; I think you may be in danger.' He lowers his voice.

Tell me something I don't know. 'I'm in danger?' I say. 'What is it to you? Who are you? I'm not referring to what you call yourself. I want to know why you're saying this. Please, try and give me a straight answer.'

'Fair enough.' He leans forward, lowers his voice. 'Gregg Austin,' he says. 'Let's just say I know, or, rather, I knew Gregg from way back. We were at school together, grammar school. I also know, he's good reason to come looking for you.' He takes a swig of coffee, then another. 'Also, he's not the only person who has reason to want to find you.'

I say nothing. Others? My stomach rolls.

'Look, Eve, I understand, he's dangerous. What he's capable of. I need to get to him first. That's all there is to it, really.'

'Hang on a minute – you knew him from school, that's it?' I laugh, despite not finding this funny in the slightest. 'You think that makes you an expert? Without being rude, your school years, well… that was some time ago,' I say. 'What do you think you know about his current motives? And while we're here, what is it to you anyhow, if he finds me? Are you trying to tell me you're here as a good Samaritan?'

'It's complicated.'

'It's odd! Have you been in contact with him since school?'

'No.'

'So you don't know him at all, do you? I'm sorry, but I fail to see—'

'People like Gregg don't change. Evil traits run through their blood. He's no different now from back then, just feels he has more power.'

'How would you—?'

'I've never stopped watching him, even from a distance,' he says. This is becoming more sinister by the second. He glances at his watch. 'How much time do you have?' he asks.

'As long as it takes.'

'I'll try and explain,' he says. 'My grandparents brought me up; my parents were killed when I was very young. I was accepted into the local grammar school. My grandparents, it meant the world to them. Gregg was in the same year as me. I hated him. A complete bastard, bullying and manipulating. Most of the kids were either scared or in awe of him.' He turns his attention to his mug; it's pain I see.

'Go on, Billy,' I say softly.

'There was a school trip to Cornwall. We stayed at a youth hostel, just down the coast from where you live.'

'So, this is why you were hanging around at the beach.'

He nods. 'My best friend, more of a brother.' He clenches his fists and takes a moment's breather. 'We were close, but he was weak in the presence of Gregg. On the last but one day, we argued. He said he was going with Gregg and his mates over to Trevellas Porth, probably to spite me; said I was a jerk. I didn't try hard enough to stop him, I let him go. I was angry with him. But, as the sun went down, he didn't come back. I was starting to feel bad, worried. Gregg and his gang returned without him.' He shakes his head and pauses.

'We had a fight, Gregg and me. I wanted to kill him – if it hadn't been for his mates, I may have. That… smirk, I still see it now. I knocked him to the floor, when I pulled his head up towards me, all I could see was the hard rock behind. I'm pretty sure I would have smashed his skull back on it, in that moment. But I was pulled off. I ran as fast as I could across the cliff path to where they'd supposedly left Tom; as I was running, a red helicopter flew over. I stopped, puked up, then continued on.' I see tears in his eyes. This is the trauma memory, nothing to do with being a soldier.

'I looked down from the cliff; saw a small body being pulled from the water, someone giving him mouth to mouth. CPR. Then, I saw the guy shake his head. He was gone. Just like that, gone forever.'

Now, it makes sense; Billy must have walked the path from St Agnes to Trevellas Porth, the night Charlie spotted him. 'Gosh, this is awful, Billy, really. It was Gregg's fault too – you're sure?'

'Positive. He bragged about it.' He shakes his head. 'He knew. Knew Tom couldn't swim. Thought he was clever didn't he? Said Tom failed the initiation activity, laughed in my face.'

'Oh my God, the bastard!' Why am I surprised?

'The thing is, Eve, he was responsible, yes. But I was to blame. Tom was like a brother; I let him down. Let him go.'

'No, you can't think like that, Billy. You were not responsible; you were a child yourself. What were you – thirteen, fourteen?'

'Fourteen. After this, I dive-bombed out of everything. I couldn't get my head around it. So much hate inside me; I couldn't sleep, couldn't get the images out my head. I rejected everything I had, worse still, the two people who I loved most. My grandparents. I couldn't reach them, you see, the guilt. I hated the world, I was so angry.'

'That's so understandable; you needed help.'

'I wouldn't let anyone near me. They tried, my grandparents. I went off the scale, ended up signing up, leaving the country, for years to come. Eventually, moved into special services; channelled my anger, but always running away.'

'Makes sense. I wonder how many end up in services, only to get away. What about your grandparents?'

'I let them go. Never had the chance to speak to them, to put things right. Every night, I go to sleep knowing they died with broken hearts. I did that too.' Now I see the real reason for his traumatised brain.

'Oh, Billy; this is all so sad.'

'So, this is why I'm here. I've waited for my day; all this time, to have my time with him.' He clenches his fists. 'I've waited too long.'

'I can only imagine how hard it's been for you. But surely you realise, whatever it is you intend to do, it won't change anything, other than land yourself in trouble. Is it worth it?'

'Yes, 100 per cent it will be. Anyway, I'm a professional. I don't intend to be caught.'

I completely understand where he's coming from. 'You said something about others wanting to find me too?'

'I think you know who I'm talking about.' He raises an eyebrow at me. Do I? I feel myself blush. I ignore his comment, not wanting to dig a deeper hole.

'Remember, I've been tracking him for years; he was never far from my thoughts or radar. When I returned to the UK, earlier this year, I dug some more. Seems he was a very naughty boy some years ago, wasn't he? My feeling is, you know all about it.' I remain mute. I'm not giving away anything yet; I need to know what he's discovered.

'A partner of Havers, Walker and Jenkins, wasn't he?'

I nod; even the mention of this sends shivers down my spine. 'Why are you asking these questions?'

'Involved in a money-laundering scam; by all accounts he masterminded the entire affair. Unsurprisingly, he walked away, relatively untouched.'

'He lost his practising certificate, his reputation. But, yes, that was the extent of it. I feel I need to say... I didn't realise this at the time, by the way. We'd split up by the time this all came out, other than his contact time with my son, Jack. I purposely didn't involve myself in anything to do with him. It was some time after, when he returned to, shall we say, pay me a visit, before I found out.'

'Sure. How much do you know about what happened, when the shit hit the fan?'

I shake my head in honesty. 'The bare minimum. Through Chinese whispers. It sounds lame, but I really couldn't bear to—'

'It's okay, I get it,' he says. 'The other partner involved, he went to prison and the young lad...' he coughs '… committed suicide – yeah right!' God, no. 'Gregg got away relatively scot-free.'

I feel sick. Images of the young lad being flung down the steps from my house, whilst I looked on, did nothing, now intimidate me. Why didn't I go to the police? I could have saved his life. But I truly didn't think he was going to end up dead. I had no idea at the time what it was all about. Should I have tried harder to find out? Do I ultimately have blood on my hands? I could have changed the outcome.

'I should have known,' falls out of my mouth. 'Should have done something sooner. I knew he was dangerous.'

'How? Come on, no one could blame you; give yourself a break.'

'I knew he was up to something, something bad.' I still can't bring myself to admit it, but it was this lad's plight that finally made me flee. Or worse, my mind floats back like a feather to standing in the study, loading your flash-drive. I stopped it after thirty seconds; after the lad was headbutted to the ground, blood leaching from his nose, I couldn't watch any more. I fled. All this time, I've had the crime scene in its full glory on the flash-drive at home.

'Hey,' Billy urges me. 'I perhaps more than anyone understand how he operates. You became one of his victims too.' He's being kind, but it's too late: I do blame myself. At the time I could only think about getting Jack to safety but, now I look back, it wasn't enough.

'Who was the lad? What was his name?'

'Toby Jenkins.'

'The senior partner's son? I knew them; met them. I didn't know he even worked there. I went to Wimbledon with his parents, Sue and David Jenkins.' What have I done? They didn't deserve this, no one deserves to lose a child.

'I met up with his father, David, last month. Apparently Toby didn't choose to work within the company; he'd bailed out of university, from what David told me, he didn't have a say in it. They employed him as the MLRO. As you can probably guess, he's full of regrets.'

I shake my head. 'MLRO?'

'Money laundering reporting officer, someone who looks out for any dirty tricks. They had a vacant position. Toby was far too young for it. It was more a case of the partnership being seen to be doing the right thing, rather than his suitability. Unfortunately, for him, Gregg took him under his wing.'

'Dear God. All the secret meetings, the wads of cash.'

'It had been going on for some time; Gregg, another partner, who was also believed to be under the spell of Gregg, Toby and – can you credit it? – a bank manager from overseas.'

'The fat, balding guy. Now I think of it, he definitely looked like a bank manager.'

'Err, right, maybe. He vanished off the face of the earth, when everything kicked off. Whispers are, he's somewhere in South America.'

'How did they even, I mean why...?'

'They took over a buy-to-let company in Spain. Reckon, Gregg did a deal with the insolvency practitioners after it fell into administration, except it wasn't in his name. They used another scapegoat for this. It's thought Gregg's cut of dirty money was paid into a bank account in the name of Pat and Dennis Austin.'

'His parents – so that's why he kept sending them to Spain, but surely this was proof enough of his involvement?'

Billy shakes his head. 'They knew he orchestrated the entire thing, but only had proof of a third-party involvement. Admitted to wheeling and dealing but not to money laundering. He'd covered his tracks well, hired the best lawyers. Lost his practising certificate, but they couldn't pin the rest of the shit on him. The Spanish buy-to-let company operated as a façade, a workhorse for collecting in illegal monies, paid into the solicitor's client account, then back out to the bank account in Spain, then distributed accordingly. On the surface legitimate monies would be paid out of the account for the deceptive purchase of more properties. Dirty money, all of it. A whole tangled grid of corruption. Toby, unfortunately, was made the scapegoat. His father believes he was murdered, he didn't take his own life.'

'Oh, God. No.' I don't want to hear this. 'How did it happen? How did he die?' I really don't want to know the answer; I've a sick feeling, I already know.

'He was found dead, taken an enormous quantity of pills.' I don't properly hear the next words; how had I not worked this out? 'It was recorded as suicide but he'd other serious injuries. They thought he'd been in a fight beforehand. Likely story, more like – someone held a gun to his head, forced him to knock back the pills.'

'Oh, please, don't say that.'

'A professional job. But his injuries were not sufficient, no other out-of-context DNA, nothing. Unfortunately, he was known in the bars for getting himself into brawls, a bit full of himself, mouthy. At the end of the day, the injuries were not what killed him, it was the pills. They closed the books.'

'Why do you say a gun? Did they find one?' I truly hope they did.

'No. But someone has it somewhere. Toby's father, David, visited the partner in prison. He said

Gregg had mentioned a gun, but he'd no part in it. Or no idea of its whereabouts.'

What have I got myself involved in? 'Billy, you said others were looking for me – who?'

'I'm just getting to it. This partner also told David they'd all met at your home, the night Toby was beaten, then died. He reckoned Gregg recorded the "meeting" on his laptop. The idea was to pay Toby off, bribe him into carrying the can. He intended to record evidence of his fake admission, but also to suggest his father, David, had full knowledge, sanctioned the dirty dealings. Then, Gregg could have used the evidence to blackmail his father, or at least encourage the company to cover up the scandal, leaving his practising certificate intact. But it all went shit-faced. Toby refused to implicate his father.'

Suddenly so much makes sense. No wonder Gregg was so angry, when he couldn't locate the flash-drive. I should have watched it beyond those few seconds. I'm so ashamed; I didn't want to know the truth. The deception was so much easier to live with.

'So the recording holds the truth?'

'So it seems.' Billy shuffles uneasily in his seat. 'They believe you may have it, you or Gregg. The flash-drive.' He's searching my face for answers. What if this is a ploy, and Billy's here on your behalf?

Is this why he's hunting me – for you? No, I believe him. He wants revenge; I see it in his eyes.

'So David Jenkins is looking for me?'

'No. I am. He sent me, well, not quite true. I offered – nothing would make me happier than to finally get my hands on the bastard.'

'So it's you who's been following me all this time?'

'For a couple of weeks, yes. I really didn't mean to frighten you.'

'And the referral?'

'All true and legit. Although, I think I'm beyond help. It was, though, a great method of getting close to you.'

'Susie, the counsellor?'

He at least has the dignity to lower his head. 'Again legit. I thought it may help me come to terms with things.'

'But why call yourself Gregg Austin?'

'Oops. Yeah, sorry about that. I made the call, and when I was asked for my name, I realised I couldn't give mine because of you. I was put on the spot.' He stretches his lip. 'It was the first name that occurred to me. Stupid mistake.' He nods his head at me.

'Did you follow me home last week, a couple of times?'

'Guilty, yep. As I say, I didn't intend to panic you. I needed to find you.'

'So all this time; when I've thought I was being hunted by my psychopath ex-husband, it's mostly been you!'

I say mostly because it was you who delivered the envelope the other night; I could smell you. I need some air. I push back at my chair to stand up. I'm shocked, upset, angry and feel so incredibly guilty. 'I need to leave,' I tell Billy. I steam away from the table; he catches me up, grabbing my arm from behind.

'No, Eve, please don't leave. I want to help you.' His touch is firm but gentle as I pull my arm away from him.

'I have to go. I've appointments to attend to.' I've still a couple of hours before I start, but I need time to rethink. 'You want to help me? Do you have any idea what you've done? Creeping around? Me and my son have been petrified, thinking our days were numbered, and all the time it's been you.' I know this isn't completely true; it's been both of you. I tap at my whizzing head. 'Have you any idea at all what I've been thinking, preparing, running through in here?'

Billy steps ahead of me, blocking my way. 'Look, I'll give you some time, but I need to see you again.'

'I've told you, I had no idea about what was going on back then. It's the truth.'

'I understand that – no one knows better than I how he operates,' he says. 'But I do have reason to believe you may have what they're looking for.' He raises his eyebrows at me. 'I need to see you again.' He pulls me aside from the eager passers-by. 'Eve, it's not just me. Gregg is following you. He's been so close to you, many times, a mere whisper away. I've been trailing him, observing you both.'

I shiver. Is he lying to me? Deep down, I understand he's telling the truth.

'Have you been near Jack?'

'No. Come on, give me some credit. I wouldn't do that. But he would, and he has. You're in danger, Eve, both of you. He's a broken man; nothing to lose. I wanted to get to you before he did. You have to trust me on this.'

He removes a stumpy pencil from his back pocket, then scribbles his mobile number on the back of a pay-and-display ticket, thrusting it into my hand.

'Please, for both your sakes. He's close enough to touch you; it's a matter of time. I'm telling you the truth.'

I turn away, running down the steps to the ground floor. I know you are. Each day I feel you getting closer. Bigger. More frustrated. I bounce off an assistant kneeling down opening boxes of Christmas cards; surely it's not here again yet? So many discordant memories of Christmas bounce through my mind, causing an ache in my chest. As I rush out of the exit, falling onto the pavement like a crazy woman, appreciative of the cold air, a glass screen descends around me. People busying about their day – I'm no longer part of this world. It exists without me. Is this really happening all over again? But then, after all these years, the beginning of the end; a chance to finally be free. Isn't this what I've been waiting for?

Chapter Thirty-Three

Before

I jumped at the metallic din as my car door thrashed metal against metal. I hadn't meant to be so heavy handed. My feet stood frozen on cold grey concrete. I felt somewhat compassionate to it, worn, used and trodden on. I struggled to engage myself sufficiently, bright sparkling lights bouncing off glass shop fronts momentarily confusing me. What was with all the dazzle? Then I remembered: Christmas. A mere few days before the big day. The most wonderful time of the year. I loved Christmas, didn't I?

I glanced over the lantern-lit street, everything happening around me. A crowd of cheery people pushed past, laden with brown paper bags; did they not notice me? Had someone forgotten to tell me I'm dead? I pinched the bare skin peeping between my tan mitten and fur-trimmed sleeve. I knew how it should feel, so maybe I imagined the pinching sensation, maybe I couldn't really feel it. The blueish tinged skin turned a pale shade of pink; chances were, I was alive. It was only the blackness stopping me from noticing.

Jack? He should have been with me. All excited, in awe of the twinkling lights, of the most magical atmosphere I could see. Where was he? What was he doing? How could a mother not know where her son was at Christmas? I looked at my watch; 23 December, it told me. Could inanimate objects lie too?

All around me, everyone, happy faces and Christmas cheer.

It was all black, except for a few flickering stars and the trails of Christmas lights. Everywhere. Music. Loud intrusive melodies; carols of all things. Please, God, don't let them sing 'Silent Night'. I headed through the town, avoiding eye contact with passers-by, full of joyful merriment, as I fought back the tears, breathing in sharp, frosty air. It would be more bearable once I got inside. The tones of 'Hark! The Herald Angels Sing' circling me like voracious birds of prey, I quickly yanked at the glass door of Starbucks. The aromas of Christmas hit me: cinnamon, nutmeg, eggnog and all the memories of family Christmas past, then present. I hadn't truly appreciated the numbness of the last few months was sent as a friend; I'd resented it. Pushed at it, allowing its nemesis – pain – to squeeze in, crushing its way through my body like a frightened beast. Numbness was sometimes the only way – only a general anaesthetic would serve better.

I unearthed a table tucked away by the toilets, where no one else wanted to be. A cold bolt of air shot over my shoulders as I unbuttoned my coat. I glanced at the ceiling – the only table beneath an overzealous air-conditioning unit, pumping away, regardless of the sub-zero temperatures outside. Patting my groaning stomach, I slunk over to the glass counter. Despite the sickly sensation, I needed to eat. I decided on a wrap containing a concoction I was not entirely sure about. Should it be eaten hot or cold? How could such a simple issue throw me?

'Can I help you?' the glummest-looking reindeer asked me. How could she, when I couldn't even help myself?

'No, but a large Americano will be fine, thank you.'

'Sorry?'

'Sorry, ignore me. I was thinking of something else.' I tapped my head. 'Must be the time of year. Christmas – head's everywhere.' The reindeer half smiled. 'A large black Americano with an extra shot, please. Actually, could I have two extra shots, please?'

'Your name?'

'Sorry?'

'Your name. To put on your cup.'

'Oh, sure, Eve. Thank you.' As I handed over my loose change, a brash voice thundered from behind.

'Eve?'

I knew who it was without turning. Another reason we needed to get away from Warwickshire. Too many people, thinking they understood. Blood-sucking leeches in the guise of sympathetic beings. The overbearing woman from your office. I'd forgotten she lived near here; you used to give her a lift, sometimes, what with being such a gentleman. The ultra-sleek dark-haired woman grabbed my arm from behind, spinning me, to commence her air-kissing routine. Emerging from the cloud of perfume, I decided she must have been mugged by the fragrance-squirting patrol at the department store across the road. But, for the life of me, what the hell was her name?

'Eve, I can't tell you how good it is to see you!' Expensive-clad arms gestured. She never did need to work; it was her hobby. Office gossip. 'We've all been so worried about you, you know, since… you know. Only the other day we were talking about you.'

I bet you were. Enjoy yourselves, did you?

She was on a roll. 'Such dreadful stuff, all this. Messy, I heard, the divorce.' She leant in close, keeping her voice unnecessarily loud. 'How are you coping? I can't imagine. Poor you, and Jack. And Gregg, what is he up to now? You still friends, you and him? I know it's difficult, but it's best for Jack isn't it, in the long run? We were saying, such a lovely little family, how sad, none of us could imagine… you know.'

I bet you've had a good go, run through every conceivable scenario, with the limited information you managed to steal. Since when had gossip been redefined as conversation? Jack eventually rejoined a nursery, whilst I was at work. I avoided any cliques there too. I hated small talk, hated gossip; I tried to disappear as best as I could without it impacting on Jack. So many children had their friendships dictated by parental groupies and social networkers. There were limits to my invisibility cloak, but I still chose to stand on the wall of periphery and watch, dodge and avoid.

'Sure,' I said.

'So, honestly, now. How are you?'

'I'm good actually,' I lied. A look of disappointment traversed her heavily made-up face, pencil-lined lips forcing a slight smile.

'Really? Wonderful. Really. Quite remarkable, I'd say. Given you had such a ghastly time of it all.'

I didn't answer her; what would she know? I reached behind me for my coffee, taking a sip.

'As if a marriage break-up isn't quite bad enough. To have all that… you know, with Gregg. Leaving the partnership, as he did, under a black cloud.'

I nodded.

'We were saying, it wasn't too clear, did he go on, you know, to pastures new?'

'I don't know,' I said in honesty. I didn't see him. The next day he collected Jack from nursery and dropped him back to nursery. A stipulation of the court. Apparently, it was only me Gregg was harmful to. 'You'd have to ask him.'

'Oh, you're not on speaking terms, then.'

'It was lovely to see you… but I really do have a lot of work to get on with.'

'Oh, super, you returned to work.' She tapped my arm. 'I guess you had little choice, what with Gregg losing his practising certificate like that. Terrible business, authorities crawling all over the offices, for weeks.'

So she knew you hadn't gone elsewhere. I tried not to look taken aback; I had no idea you'd lost your practising certificate. What the hell had you done?

'As I said, I really have no idea. I'm really not interested in the lives of others… Gregg. Only me and Jack, right now. And we're absolutely fine.'

'Eve, come on.' She lowered her voice. 'You don't need to be brave with me.' She regarded her bling watch. 'I've just time for coffee with you. You should know more than anyone, it's much better to talk, not keep it all in. A problem shared…' She tapped her nose. 'You'll end up with that thingy disorder if you don't, you know, PSSD.'

I so wished I were PSSD.

'You mean PTSD,' I said. 'But, really, I'm good. Nothing to report, nothing to be talked over. We've moved on fine, me and Jack. There's really no point in going back over things…' A frown struggled from her Botox brow before she bowed down in defeat. 'If you don't mind, I really ought to get on.' She threw her head backwards as if I'd headbutted her, widening precision-black-lined eyes.

I returned to my seat, alone. A kind of strong Americano nestled in shaky hands. My mind attempted to go back over you, and whatever you'd done so bad to lose all you'd worked for. I pushed it away. Not being able to bear thinking about you. My first Christmas without Jack. He was with you. I could have coped, if I'd believed Jack was having a lovely time. But I knew he was somewhere feeling alone too, worse still, afraid. Being told untruths about Santa not being real, that Christmas was about the biggest, most expensive presents. Left to his own devices to build his memories of Christmas. Memories capable of haunting him for life. The family court, advised by Cafcass, insisted on alternate Christmases from here on. Despite the evidence finally submitted by my ruddy-faced solicitor, photographs of my bruising, written statements of life with you, despite Jack's obvious fear of his father.

The courts left us exposed, in a position where Jack was so vulnerable. The only reason you kept your grip on Jack was to spite me. Your only remaining control; the last piece of the tattered and crumbled jigsaw. Last week, Jack asked Santa to please let him stay at home for Christmas with his mummy. Santa eyed me, over his head. We both knew, this year he'd stop believing no matter what. If only I could have bridged the gap. The gap between childhood and reality. But I couldn't. It was beyond me. I failed.

I too struggled to believe.

I opened the files in front of me. I'd allowed everything to slip, already only a few months back at the hospital. Small globules splashed, smudging the words into irregular shapes, as silent oblivious tears rolled, long overdue. I discreetly swiped them away, lowering my head until the threat of more subsided.

'It's no big deal. You simply have your Christmas Day on another day. It's only one day, after all!' the opposing, hard-faced barrister had informed me. My appeal on Jack's behalf had been futile. You and her, smug at the thought of another case won, another injustice served on a child with a huge fee tag. Hearts replaced by pound signs and ego. Since when had Christmas ever been about one day, to a child?

The image of Jack sitting on my knee as I'd explained to him he had to leave for Christmas swamped my mind. He hadn't said a word, only nodded in acceptance. You would think this would have made it easier, but it didn't; it made it all the harder. His silence was not normal; it hurt. I wrapped my arms around him, and we didn't speak for some time.

How had I allowed this to be? Powerless as a mother.

Jack, would you ever be able to forgive me?

Because I was certain, I never would.

Chapter Thirty-Four

Cornwall 2016

I half walk, half scamper back towards my car. Is it me, or have I become invisible? I'm like the ball in an old-fashioned pinball machine. Why is everyone bouncing off me? I steal a look over my shoulder. Am I being followed? I feel eyes on me. I subconsciously tuck my hair behind my ears, and increase my pace. Is it you I feel? You breathing down my neck? I quicken my step, as far as I can, without running. An overwhelming urge to get hold of Jack, keep him close, swamps me. But he's safe at school. I hope. With a sense of foreboding chasing me, I weave myself between oncoming people. If I run, you'll just run faster. Nothing to be gained.

You have nothing to lose, Billy said.

But I have everything to lose.

Entering the car park, I spot my car at the far end. Hearing the click of each step across the concrete, I scramble to locate my car keys in the depth of my bag, my brow becoming damp. I daren't look back; it's too soon. But I know you're there. Coward. I feel you. You've timed your footsteps to match mine; you don't fool me. My heart rate has alerted me to your proximity.

Pressing the button to release the centrally locked doors, I keep my finger on it for too long, and all four windows lower in perfect harmony. Jesus Christ, not now. Not now. Go back up, you bastards. You're getting closer, but I'm not looking.

Fear then fury, terror then sheer resolve to protect engulf and seize me. Jack's face plugs the wide gap.

I throw my mobile onto the passenger seat, with my chest hammering like an irritated woodpecker. I turn the ignition. I'm waiting for the passenger door to open. I see it opening in my mind's eye as you nonchalantly slide in next to me. I raise the windows, before grinding the car into gear; accelerating towards the exit. My hands clammy on the steering wheel. I still don't look, but out of the corner of my eye I see you. I see your obscure shadow calmly walking towards me. A smirk worn on a resolute face.

You didn't want to get hold of me though, did you? If you did, you would have. It's too soon for you too, isn't it? You're not ready to move yet; you need to close off any possible escape routes first, break me down as much as you can first, a fly vomiting on its sustenance, before you move in for checkmate. But have you considered, what if? What if I take you first? Have you thought of this? Maybe I wasn't running from you but pulling you in closer. Maybe I've a plan; perhaps you're playing my game now. Both of us profess to be experts of the mind. But whose game is it now, Gregg? Who was it who finally divulged to you where to find me? Once I suspected you were on my tracks, you left me no choice but to turn and face my fears. Have you stopped to consider where the control truly lies?

What if the vengeful psychopath has finally met his match? And I've waited so long to be the one to teach you the final lesson. Maybe, sometimes, you do get it wrong; possibly, you're not as clever as you think you are. I'm not the dupe you took me for. Am I watching you, or are you watching me? Years and years of meticulous planning have prepared me for this.

If you've nothing to lose and I've it all to lose, which one of us is the most powerful? Which one of us is the most dangerous? Or have we reached a deadlock?

I didn't think I'd be able to hit the send button, for the text, but then, when I finally had your number, I knew I had to take the opportunity. My hands were shaking violently; I knew there would be no going back. But then, the moment I married you, the route for return evaporated.

I head away from Truro, fighting my instincts to collect Jack; I turn for home. My meeting with Billy

Adams playing back over my mind. The poor lad; someone's son. Toby. How must his parents be suffering? Do they believe I've known all these years? Money laundering; why? Blackmail? Murder? How can anyone become so obsessed, so consumed by greed and power, to press their own self-destruct button? Someone so apparently intelligent yet so completely stupid. Was the gun, hidden in the chest, held to the head of a terrified Toby? Forcing him to take such a massive overdose? What about my part, my ignorance, then the burying of evidence? Evidence which might have given his parents some twisted form of peace of mind.

How was I not privy to the controversial findings of this case? So consumed with Jack's protection, I both intentionally and ignorantly turned my back on anything circling your world. But then, that night you came for us, after our decree absolute was granted, shouldn't I have guessed there was a reason for you to be so desperate to get your hands on the flash-drive? Curbed at the back of my mind – did I really not suspect? Was it then just easier for me to remain ignorant, fearing it would threaten our escape? Billy mentioned Toby's parents lay low initially, grieving for their son. But now they understandably demand answers, after David's meeting with the partner. You must have heard whisperings, and panicked knowing someone, somewhere, held your fate. All these years, you've believed you got away with it. A tiny contraption suppressing the big fat truth.

You knew, didn't you, we survived the crash? All the possible searches, Her Majesty's Services included, could not place you in this country after that night, or for the years that followed. The random silent call of Spanish origin I received, I knew it was you. You couldn't let go, could you? I didn't want you found; whilst the bumpy waters of the English Channel divided us, I could breathe. I lied to myself, you were dead. Until I received the call, confirming you were in Spain – was this Billy? I wonder. Immaterial now, but until then I fantasised you were dead. It was only when you returned to the UK, you withheld your number – did you think it would confuse me? Do you then still think I am so foolish?

I can't put it off any longer – too many questions. I pull over in St Agnes. Grab my mobile.

Hi Billy, sorry for earlier. I need to meet you soon as possible please.

Today? Eve

A woman walks past singing nursery rhymes to her toddler, strapped in the buggy; safe. My underbelly world feels so far removed; how must it feel to be normal? I pull out again for home as my mobile rings out; *Lemon Street Clinic* caller ID flashes up on the mobile screen. I clutch it between my face and shoulder.

'Hello?'

'Evie, hi, it's me.'

'Bea, you okay?'

'Hmm, but… just to give you a heads up, we've had a delivery for you.' Bea's voice becomes distant as she addresses Ruan. 'It was recently, wasn't it, Ru? As in, within the last fifteen minutes or so?'

'Yeah, yeah,' Ruan confirms.

'Eve, it's just, there's been some flowers delivered for you, here.'

'Oh?' There's obviously more to it; it wouldn't be the first time a client sent flowers.

'Yeah, the thing is, these aren't what you'd call nice flowers.'

'What do you mean, not nice? Carnations?' I hate carnations, so artificial, too perfect.

'No, I mean, it's a huge bouquet of lilies and, well, they look like they've been splattered with dark red paint. I mean, actually, it looks like blood but obviously it's not. Or, at least, I hope it's not.'

'What?'

'There's something else too, lovely. There's a card in it. It's an "in loving memory" card, you know, attached to the cellophane stuff.'

'Right, and what does it say, Bea?'

'It says, "till death do us part", Eve. Then weirdly, on the reverse, in capitals, it says – "SORRY".'

Is this you, or is it too obvious?

'Eve? You there still, Eve?'

'Yes, yes, I'm here. Who delivered them? A florist?'

'We don't know. Ru was in my room, helping me move the therapy bed. They were on the front desk when he went back to Reception. We didn't see anyone. I said to Ru, though, strange they didn't call out for us. Strange, we didn't hear them either.'

I can hear Ruan muffled in the background. 'Oh, yeah,' Bea continues, 'Ru's just reminded me, they were left on the desk, but also, the front door was being pulled to, as he walked back into Reception. He saw the flowers, so looked out of the window.'

'And?'

'He wasn't sure. There was a woman walking down the street, but also a man, loitering outside, and another woman with her children, and—'

'Okay, thanks, Bea. Basically, he doesn't know who left them, then. Bin them, out the back. Please.'

'You sure?'

'Well, why would I want to keep them?'

'No, of course, just didn't know if you wanted to see them for yourself?'

'No, I'm good, thanks. Bin them, please. Can you ask Ruan to call the local florists for me, please? See if he can find out where they came from. Also, I'm supposed to be at the hospital this afternoon, doing an awareness talk to some of the staff – can you ask him to call, give my sincere apologies? I'm not going to be able to make it.'

'Sure. You okay? I've a spare couple of hours if you want to meet up?'

'No, I'm fine, a few things to sort out, that's all. Thanks, though. Catch up with you tomorrow.'

I hang up. Lilies were your favourite flowers; we had them for our wedding. You know I've always associated them with death. But sorry? Why would you write 'sorry'? Was it the florist, apologising for delivering a deathly arrangement? Come to think of it, would they really deliver such vulgar flowers? Surely not.

I pull up against the wall; even my home has begun to feel slightly tainted. Knowing someone's been inside. I can see Gloria in her garden; she waves to me. I smile, then wave back. This is as much as I can offer; with no inclination for a neighbourly chat, I remain where I am. I let my head fall back against the headrest. So many unresolved issues remain. The note from Sam, on the back of the newspaper articles

– was it a warning? Why so abstract, why now? How does she even know about your shenanigans, given I've only just found out some of it? Then, who put the envelope in my briefcase, the only people with the means being – me, Jack, Ruan or Bea? Or does Billy have something to do with this? Who has been in my house? Again, any of the above or is this more likely to be you? Why is Jack being so secretive with his mobile at the moment? Or is this because he's a teenager? Now the flowers.

A flashback of Toby, tumbling down steps, being hurled into the boot of the car, comes pounding back. Would I have been able to intervene? I should at least have tried, but Jack was in the car; I was torn. I should have looked properly at the flash-drive too. What other evidence sits in the remainder of the recording?

I attempt to regather myself. I've been on standby for years but, despite the overwhelming urge for flight, I'm nearly ready to deal with this. You. As ready as I will ever be. I flick through my mobile to locate the text I prepared for you late last night.

I know what you want;

I have it. You'll need to come for it.

Waiting for you. I'll text you details.

I pressed send. No going back.

My mobile bleeps in my hand; I jump, as two texts jump on board together. The first, from Billy Adams.

This PM, 15.30 St Agnes pub, centre of town?

Then a text from Ruan.

Not a lot of info. But florist said it was deffo female who ordered them. She took them with her, said she wanted to hand-deliver.

Female? Female?

I'm completely shattered. I was so sure they were from you. Do you have someone working for you, who's responsible? No, not your style; not when it comes to me – you do your own dirty work. It doesn't make sense. Unless, of course, Ruan doesn't want me to know the truth? I can't keep thinking like this. I'm sure I'm edging towards paranoia.

I look across to our cottage. I can't go in. So, I take myself down towards the beach instead. Sitting in the car park, I look out across the Atlantic, for answers, anything to help clarify my thoughts. Desperately trying to keep hold of perspective. It's a struggle; I'm feeling wired for most of the time. I need to talk to Jack tonight. After the revelations of Billy, I think I'll try to get him to go and stay with Bea for a while. Just until this is over. I know she'll be happy to have him.

Why was Jack so late last night? Was he really at football? It hurts me to have to consider he may not be telling me the truth; what if you've managed to manipulate him? How can I be certain he'll confide in me, when I've been so secretive? Told so many lies, myself? I did it to protect him – is this going to end up being a perverted irony haunting me?

I watch the bluey green waters pull back, lathering whitewash breaking on the honeycombed shoreline. The tide is drawing in closer and closer. These very waters have already taken so many lives; were they all innocent beings? Or did some harbour dark secrets? Don't we all? Just some, darker than others.

An hour later, I'm joined in the window seat looking out at the world by Billy. I've been here already for some time.

I watch him tread purposeful steps in my direction, inconspicuous to the eyes of others. A trained killer, but so gentle under the guise, he smiles as he reaches me. 'Thanks for coming,' I offer.

He pulls out his chair. 'No problem; I'm pleased you took my advice.' His eyes crinkling with laughter lines. I'm not sure how.

'I didn't,' I say. 'Unfortunately, I'm not very good at taking advice. I just have questions; I need answers.'

He nods, lowering himself down opposite me, checking out his surroundings. 'Got it,' he says.

'I saw you drive past and so ordered us some coffee, unless you'd prefer something stronger?' I gesture to the bar.

He shakes his head. 'Coffee's good, thanks.' He folds his jacket and places it over the back of the chair. Ensuring the inside does not come into contact with the foreign body. 'So what is it you want to know? Or should I say, what d'you want to know first?'

'The truth, Billy; have you been in my house?'

He blows out through his mouth. 'Straight to the point, aren't you?' I don't answer; I watch for his response. I don't think he'll lie to me. 'Straight up, then – yes, I have. Guilty as charged, but only because I was looking for the flash-drive.' He holds out his hand. 'Nothing more.'

'Oh, well, that's okay, then, isn't it? It's perfectly acceptable to break into someone's house, rummage through their belongings, so long as they have something you want!' How can he be so matter of fact?

He chuckles. 'First of all, I didn't break in. You left your kitchen door open.'

'No, I did not! I thought I may have but I checked – it was locked!'

'No, it wasn't, you really shouldn't have been so bloody careless given the circumstances. You're lucky it was only me. It was, in fact, unlocked. I locked it for you, then left via the front door. In retrospect, I did you a favour.'

I sit speechless. How can he be so self-righteous about illegally entering my house?

'Secondly, I didn't rummage through your things. Remember, I'm an expert in these activities. I did, yes, admittedly, look through your house, but I carefully moved and repositioned each and every item. Exactly.'

'Don't tell me, you photographed my house, didn't you? That's what people like you do in your world. I've read about it. Better still, you've a trained photographic memory. An expert burglar.'

'Expert? Yes, I believe I am, thank you.'

'You're so—.'

'Anyway, yes, spot on. So, you'll also appreciate, nothing was disturbed. Technically.'

'Technically? Maybe not in your warped eyes.'

He's smiling at me; clearly amused that I'm indignant. Almost enjoying himself.

'Why did you do it? I mean, I know why, to find the flash-drive, but why not just ask me for it?'

'Would you have given it to me, if I had?'

'No, of course not.'

He chortles to himself as our coffees are placed on the table. 'Thank you,' we say, in unison.

'So, you are admitting, you do have it, then.'

I fell for this one, but there's no point in denying it any longer. 'Hmm,' is all I manage.

'Look, believe this or not, I was only trying to protect you.' He moves his finger to his mouth to hush my attempt to retaliate. 'Yes, I've the other… issues to deal with, including my own desire for revenge. But, I also genuinely wanted to remove you from the picture at the same time. Eve, you are in danger, you and your son, Jack. I couldn't stand by, watch him take more lives.' He sips at his coffee. 'I'm guessing, you've already suffered sufficiently at his hands.'

So if he entered my house, he had the means to place the envelope in my briefcase, but what about the note from Sam? Does he know Sam too? There must be something else he hasn't come clean about yet. I press on. 'Okay, but why put the envelope in my briefcase? Why not email me the articles instead, pop the envelope through the letterbox, if you wanted to warn me?'

'Envelope?'

'Oh, come on! What envelope? Please don't mistake me for stupid.'

'Seriously, what envelope? I've no idea what you're talking about?'

'Are you, in all earnestness, expecting me to believe you didn't look in my briefcase, when you were hunting for a flash-drive?'

'No. I did look in your briefcase, but, I've already told you, I put everything back with precision. I certainly didn't add anything. What was in the envelope?'

I stare at him; I thought I'd resolved this mystery. He's telling me the truth. 'Articles, photocopied, about the scam and stuff. I assumed it was… you visited my home, more than once, didn't you? You went back again this week. Didn't you?'

'Nope. Just the once. I only do the job once. It was last week, not this week.'

A shiver passes over me, sitting down between us. 'Someone else has been in my home, then. I knew, I could smell it. Has to be him.'

He swigs at his coffee, without moving his eyes from mine. 'You think it was him?'

'Well, who else? I arrived home, I don't know, I could just feel someone had been inside the house. Something hanging in the air. In fact, not so much in the air, on Humphrey's fur. Kind of woody but sweet, not belonging to us.' I look at his confused expression. 'Humphrey is our cat.' He nods. 'Then, Jack found the utility window open. It's quite rickety so it wouldn't have taken much to ease it open, off the latch. It was closed when we left in the morning, and Humphrey was outside. Someone must have let him in.'

'Was anything disturbed, taken?'

'No, not that I could find.'

'But whoever it was could have put the envelope in your briefcase?'

'No. It was the week before – I'd already found it in my briefcase by then. So, if it wasn't you. Who was it?'

'Has there been anyone, you know, new in your life recently?'

'Other than clients, no.'

'Gregg?' Billy asks.

'I don't know, it's not really his style. Enter my house, snoop around, to let me know he can, yes. But, to put something in my briefcase?' I shake my head. 'I can't see it. He'd rather see the reaction with his own eyes.' And then, there's the note on the back too; it can't be you, this time. 'Also, the other night, he dropped something through the door.' Billy raises his eyebrows, interested. 'It was predictable really, our marriage and Jack's birth certificate. He was there, outside. I know he was watching. A sick satisfaction, looking on.'

'Hmm.' He drains the dregs of his coffee.

'Then, today – flowers, delivered to the clinic. Splattered with red dye, to look like blood. I did think it was him. I mean, who else? But Ruan, the assistant you met, has since spoken to the florist. She said they were definitely ordered and collected by a female.' Billy's face is deadpan; he's probably the only person I could tell who wouldn't be perturbed. It's a relief to be sharing my thoughts, with a complete stranger, yet someone with a full grasp of my predicament. 'It gets worse. They were hand-delivered, with a card, "Till Death Do Us Part". On the reverse, it said "SORRY". Sorry? Sorry does not exist in Gregg's vocabulary. The lilies, spot on, definitely his choice, even the message, but not sorry. Not a chance.'

'He has an accomplice, maybe?'

'I've thought about this, but…'

'You are aware, he's been involved with someone else for some time?' Billy interrupted

'Gregg? No. I doubt it.' Billy is nodding slowly. 'Who?'

'There isn't a lot I don't know about him.' He looks out of the window, whilst turning his heavy watch over and over his wrist.

'Please understand, nothing you may tell me can possibly surprise me or hurt me. Trust me on this. What is it you know?'

'He's been seeing someone for quite a while.'

420

'What, as in, another woman?'

Billy nods.

'Since when?'

'Long enough.'

'I'm assuming by that look on you face, you mean, while we were married?' I spit the last word out, a bone in my throat; it mocks the concept beyond recognition.

He nods at me. 'Yeah, I believe so, certainly before Jack was born.'

'You're serious?'

'For most of the time you were together.'

'Wow, you've surprised me. Really? Jesus, that does surprise me.'

'Sorry to be the bearer of—'

'Don't be, really, I couldn't care less. It's just, I can't see it, didn't see it.' If only I'd known, maybe I could have left earlier. This premise brings bile to my throat. 'On reflection, I didn't see many things. Despite my scrutiny. So? Who was it, someone from work?'

He shakes his head. 'Not to my knowledge. I'm pretty sure she didn't work in the same arena as him. But she did go on to work for him, in Spain. Some kind of administrator, I suppose he'd call it.'

'I see, well, I wouldn't have known her, then.'

'Samantha Holloway, her name was – or is, I should say. As far as I know, they're still together. In fact, they've a daughter too.'

My head floats to the ceiling, before falling with a thump to the floor. I'm struggling to accept this information. I'd thought you couldn't surprise me again. I was so wrong. How could she? Even with the note on the back of the article, never would I have believed this possible. 'Are you sure? Definitely, the correct name?'

'Yep. Positive. Why, do you know her?'

'So, you don't know everything?'

How could she? She hated you, tried to talk me out of marrying you. Refused to have any further contact with me pretty much, if I was with you. Now, I know why. The truth. You hated her. I didn't see through it. All these years, feeling so incredibly guilty, believing I'd betrayed her. Let her down. Forced to choose you, over her, yet it was her who chose you over me. I've despised myself for lying to her, when the truth was she was lying to me. I'm aware of my cheeks colouring, in line with my blood pressure.

'Eve, you okay?'

'Sorry.' I sip tepid coffee. 'It's shocked me somewhat. I knew her. We were best friends from school. I let our relationship go, mostly because I hated having to lie to her, in the way I felt I had to, to

422

everyone. Didn't want her entangled in our disgusting marriage. All of my relationships, back then, were built on layers of deception. Sam asked too many questions, used to make me squirm. I never wanted to deceive her. I'm such an idiot.'

He shakes his head, sighing. 'Bloody hell, I'm sorry, I'd no idea.' He leans forward. 'But can you see – maybe he does have an accomplice after all?'

'Yes, maybe, shit, I really can't believe it.' I contemplate the bar, craving something stronger to swallow. 'You're right, maybe the flowers were her doing. God, how could she?' I let the thought drift – how did I not notice? Perception, always perception, never the truth. I believed in her because I needed to. Based on what I thought I knew. 'The flowers, the note, he made her send them, prove her allegiance, she felt guilty, hence – sorry?'

'Sounds plausible.'

'But it still doesn't explain the envelope, does it? In part it does.' I pull the folded photocopied sheet of A4 from my pocket, and begin to unravel it. 'Here, on the back,' I read aloud,

Eve,

I didn't want to have to send this, being so ashamed. And you must hate me, I understand completely. But I wanted you to know, something is going on, something to do with these articles I found. I'm worried you're in danger. If it is any consolation at all, I too am very scared, terrified. It's too late for me, I've made my bed, so to speak. But, I wanted to warn you, without making matters worse. I hope one day you will understand, be able to forgive me.

DO NOT ATTEMPT TO MAKE CONTACT. PLEASE.

Sam x

I place the note, for Billy to see. 'Without context, when I read this, I didn't see it. I assumed she was apologising, feeling guilty for her part in our friendship falling apart. Although I couldn't quite understand how she knew about him, his actions. Thought, maybe, he'd contacted her, to find me, threatened her? Now I can see gaping holes in my interpretation, but without context nothing makes sense, does it?'

'It doesn't, no. And you wanted to think the best of her too.'

'She's taken my place, hasn't she? She's trapped, terrified. Yet it's still me he seeks. She was probably only ever another one of his tools, a side prop. How much has he relished forcing her to send me sick flowers, amongst other things, spying on me?'

A reel of information parked in my subconscious plays through my mind: the woman with the sunglasses I bumped into in Truro? Some vague recollection of Ruan, talking about someone watching the clinic, receiving a parking ticket. The cancelled appointment, again, a woman, some excuse about her partner insisting, oh, Jesus, insisting on her accompanying him – to meet with his son. Jack? Dear God, Jack? Why didn't I listen to Ruan? She was attempting to warn me. 'But still, how did this—' I stab at the dirty scrap of paper '—get into my briefcase?'

'Does anyone else have access? Think, any access at all, to your home or your briefcase, other than your work colleagues and Jack?'

I shake my head. 'No.'

'Sure?'

'To my home, no. Well, there's Gloria next door – she has a key. But it can't have anything to do with her.' But then, why not? So far, it appears, I've only seen what I needed to see, but even so. Not lovely Gloria.

'Can you be 100 per cent sure, Eve? Even now, with this latest revelation? Samantha Holloway is in the UK, by the way.' He twists his watch clockwise once, twice. 'I have the photos to prove it.'

'I've seen her too. I just, didn't see her.'

'Did you know she's been to St Agnes… near your home?'

I flash back to seeing Gloria in conversation with a glamorous-looking woman last week. Only glimpsing the woman from behind. Purposely lowering my head, avoiding conversation. Then, Gloria's comment from a couple of days ago patters through my jumbled mind – *'A nice surprise, was it, love?'* I assumed she was referring to the cake she'd left for us. Thinking about it now, she often leaves us treats; she's never remarked upon it before, being such a giving person.

Billy and I walk in silence to my car. His parting words ricochet around the cortical regions. 'Eve, I want him for myself. I intend, or should I say need, to have my time with him. I've waited a long enough.' I want to say maybe it is too late, that we don't always get what we wish for. Until I think better of it. He looks on as I close my car door.

I need to have my moment in time too, if I find you first. This time, I need to see for my own eyes that it's over.

Chapter Thirty-Five

Before

I had no choice that night, with you holding Jack, a piece of meat dangling in your arms. You punched me to the side of my head; I crumbled to inflexible concrete. By the time I looked up, you were strapping Jack into your car. Then I was yanked to my feet, walked forwards, my arm bent behind my back, as you opened the passenger door. 'Would you care to join us after all?' A beaming smile, displaying near perfect teeth. My blood cooled to icy temperatures. It wasn't an option; I had to accept.

I had reason to be terrified. A voice whispered in my ear – this was to be different, unlike all those other lessons. We were divorced, for one. I'd finally said NO to you. No one said NO to you. Had you finally lost control? Were they emotions I saw carved through your expression? Felt, not used? A malfunctioning, out-of-control robot, with no off switch.

In silence, we drove further into the depths of the sparsely populated Cotswolds. No one to disturb us; you'd thought this through. Unremitting rain, perilous lanes. Dark and antagonistic. Abandoned by light. My clammy hands gripping the cold leather seat, pure fear pinning me back. None of us uttering a word.

Finally, you swung the car into the side of the bramble. Only the ticking of hot engine between us. You released your seat belt, swivelling to face me. Jack silenced, squashed behind. My panicked form caused a smile on your face as you ran a manicured finger over the curves of my cheekbone. First on the left, then, without a word, on the right. I clasped my hands together, to hide the shaking; conscious of showing – I wasn't composed but also not flustered. Either could have been costly.

You spoke to me. 'This needn't take long, need it? Needn't be too painful.' You paused to tuck an escaped tress gently behind my ear. 'You know what I need from you. Give it to me, then we can move on. I'm prepared to allow you this one last chance, Eve. One chance is all you have. My flash-drive – I know you stole it,' you said. 'You've surprised me. A thief, you – even I didn't appreciate the depths you'd sink to. Even I thought you were better than that. You never do really know anyone, do you? A thief?'

My heart hammered. 'Are you scared, Eve? Come on, you're with me now.' Your breath, misting the surface of my skin. 'Didn't I always tell you – I'd take care of everything?' You traced your finger from my chin bone to my throat. 'Remember, those good old days?'

Your lips slightly on the upturn, how your face lied. 'You know, Eve, I am asking you out of politeness more than anything; however, you really have no choice here. Perhaps give a thought to Jack. Possibly, he's seen enough, don't you think?' You angled your head to smile at Jack, as I sensed him squashing his angelic form further back into his seat.

You snorted, moving your finger from my throat, pressing a fist into my seat. I resisted the pull of leaning closer to you. 'Considering those many lessons you made me teach you.' You shook your head. 'Really sad. Could all have been avoided.'

You sick, sick bastard.

'Or does your twisted little mind believe I wanted to punish you?'

I dared not speak. I didn't trust myself. I tensed the muscles in my legs in an attempt to conceal their trembling.

'Eve? Time is running out. Make your decision.' You smiled. 'Please.'

I rummaged through a fogged mind. My trump card was the flash-drive. I needed to think, and quickly, but the intelligent parts of my brain had deserted me. How to get Jack and me safely out of the car without handing over the trump card? Once away from you, it could be our only security against you. My secret weapon. I could feel my mobile digging into me, in the back pocket of my jeans. My number was already linked to the police Quick Response database. Their idea of reassurance when the detailed notes of your repetitive battering was eventually forced to light

You clicked your fingers in front of my nose. 'Eve?'

'The flash-drive, yes, I've got it at home,' I said.

'I know,' you said. 'So, how are you going to do this? Are you going to behave yourself? Let me have back what's mine? I'm prepared to let the matter pass this time. If you behave.'

I knew this would never be the case. You would never leave us alone, especially if I no longer held what you wanted. Your dark, opaque eyes looked through me. You had no lucent windows to your soul, did you? Only void panels, obscuring the cogs.

You tapped my leg. I flinched. 'After all this, shall we say…' you waved your hand '… misunderstanding? Perhaps you should consider seeking some help. Psychological help?'

I knew your game, trying to rile me. I locked my tongue to the roof of my mouth. I'd never thought of myself as a killer, but given the chance…

'I, amongst others,' you said, 'can see you're sick, Eve, mentally unstable.' You guffawed. 'How paradoxical. An insane psychologist.'

430

Rebound your repulsive words, I told myself. Play the game.

I nodded. 'You may have a point,' I said. 'Perhaps I would benefit from some help.'

'At last, she speaks words of sense.' You spun to Jack. 'Did you hear that, Jack? Your mother has admitted she's deranged. Should have recorded those priceless words. Damn.' You slapped your thigh, laughing. 'Could have used it, couldn't we, Jack?'

Again, I fantasised beating my ex-husband to a pulp. 'I shouldn't have taken the flash-drive,' I said.

'My flash-drive.'

'Your flash-drive. It was wrong. I see this now.'

So accomplished at reading your eyes, I saw the transition from ridicule to one of self-pity. Betrayed, you were accepting my spurious words. I couldn't allow you to indulge; it could backfire. Submissions, apologies might strengthen my case but pleas and begging would destroy it. Conductor of a psychopathic orchestra, listening and watching, each and every change in tone. A game of chess, but, like the pawn, one step forward in the wrong direction, I'd be taken.

Could you smell my fear? I could.

'I'll take you home,' you said. 'Stay by your side, all the time, until I have the flash-drive in my hand. Jack will remain in the car. You see; I simply cannot trust you, Eve. Far too many lies. Such a waste. Really. We could have been something together.'

'Yes.' I nod.

'You've learned your lesson, I hope.'

We waited in cold silence for the windscreen to demist, before retreating. My mind racing with the dark jagged shrubbery hurtling past. My heart pumping against the tightness of the seat belt.

'How is your friend Sam?' you asked.

'I don't see her anymore.'

'No. Of course, you don't. I forgot. Another lesson learned, I suppose. Shame, I always liked her. Different, from you.'

No, you didn't, I thought, you hated her. You couldn't have made it more obvious. My heart ached. Why didn't I try harder? I'd missed her so much.

I subtly rolled in my seat, straining to get a glimpse of Jack. Somehow, he'd fallen asleep. Exhausted by heightened emotions. I regarded his pale innocent skin, pocket-sized pudgy hands. My poor, beautiful Jack. He didn't deserve this. We travelled on, a family in serene silence. Son, peaceful in sleep, Dad, humming the tune of rightfulness, Mum, deep in her imagination. From the outside in we were the perfect little unit, fitting the expectations of society seamlessly. Passing by undetected.

Time was trickling away. I needed help, to send a text before it was too late; once we were back at the house, it would be too late. With no choice, my only hope, I'd to ask permission to send a message to alert the police. The acerbic taste of bile. In silence, I practised a calm, subservient voice. *I need to text...* No, I mustn't state my needs. *I'm just going to...* No, I'd be dictating to you. One, two and three...

'Gregg. I'm sorry to have to bring this up, but...' You changed gear, without acknowledgment. 'I've a friend popping by later.' I felt you tense. 'I was thinking, I should put her off? We didn't arrange a fixed time. I mean, she could arrive, unannounced, any time soon.'

You sighed through your nose, your diagnostic brain ticking over.

'You have your mobile with you?'

'I do.'

'Send her a text, cancel. Now.'

With my heart in my throat, I reached for my mobile. And began typing my message with timorous fingers, the screen angled slightly away from you, but not enough to make you suspicious. Holding my breath, I hit send, then hurriedly returned my phone to my back pocket.

Your eyes were transfixed on the road.

The first trickle of sweat escaped through my hairline as an evocative atmosphere pinched the air. Pure terror. Your fingers began to tap, tap on the steering wheel. Over and over.

You held out your left hand. 'Show me. The text, Eve.'

I inhaled sharply as my body became weightless.

'Eve. Your mobile.' Your finger jabbed at my ribs. 'Now.'

As of old, I did as I was told. Panicked hands fumbling for my back pocket.

I knew it had been too easy. I placed the mobile into your resolute hand.

Your eyes wandered over the screen. You shook your head; the beginnings of a leer caught your lips.

Was this our end?

You thrusted down a gear, accelerating deeper into the darkness. Trees looming, closer and closer. Seconds spiteful in the pretext as hours. The stench of burning rubber. The acrid bouquet of hot engine. The screeching of tyres. The shrieking of my child. The din of crimpling metal. The clatter of shattering glass. The cry of my child.

All became black.

Nothing but black.

Chapter Thirty-Six

Cornwall 2016

My heartbeat disturbs me. I open my eyes; blackness is everywhere. I hold my hands up in front of me. I see nothing. I pinch my thumb and index fingers together; I have feeling though. I lie still and listen to my heart beating in my ears. Droplets of sweat, between me and the sheets.

I feel you just the other side of the glass. We can feel each other, though you can no longer see me. You are wondering if you should now leave. Just one last sniff of the air, you decide, the air we share, nothing but glass between us. Both of us together, counting each breath. Did you think I was dead, that night? You didn't know, did you? You just wished I were dead, we were dead. You lost control.

I feel for my legs, slightly numb, almost bruised to the touch. A psychosomatic delusion. I drag them one by one, cautiously placing disoriented feet on the floor. One at a time. I stand, and move towards the glass. On the last step forward, I see the stars. Tiny spotlights looking down on us in judgment. A moment of confusion on the outskirts of sleep hounds me; my feet search for familiar grounding as

I touch the pane of my bedroom window. I'm not in the car; I'm in the safety of my bedroom. Just another flashback. I peer out at the starlit darkness. Still, I see you. A dark vanquished shadow retreating. You would have come back that night, wouldn't you, if you'd known we didn't die? Have you come back this time for the flash-drive, or, as I now suspect, for me?

Because I am still breathing. Scarred, but breathing.

I'm not so afraid any more. Even the dreams cannot harm me, however real they first seem. I didn't wake for the dream; I woke, sensing you, outside my window. Calm, resolute, betrayed. Have you shrunk in size? Your shoulders less broad, your back less upright? Though your subdued shadow does not fool me.

Evil doesn't die, if it still lives.

I creep in darkness to Jack's room; old habits take a long time to perish. He's deep in sleep. I hope his dreams are somewhere safe, normal. His mobile sits goading me across the room, winking at me, daring me to take a peek. No, I will not give in to paranoia. I shiver as a chill darts across my shoulders. We are nearly there, Jack, nearly there.

Returning to my bed, I pray for sleep.

*

'Mum,' whispers the familiar voice. 'Mum?' I feel the bed give way near my legs. 'It's time to get up. We'll be late again.' I prise reluctant eyes open to see Jack grinning down at me. 'You really should get yourself to bed earlier. No wonder you can't get up in the mornings. Don't you realise how important sleep is?' he mimics me.

'Cheeky little monkey.' I prod him.

'Hey, not so much of the little – have you checked these biceps out?' He flexes his muscles. 'And, you may have noticed—' he straightens his back, getting broader by the week '—I'm quite a bit taller than you, now.'

'Hmm. Now, get yourself down those stairs, and make me some coffee? Please?'

He stands up and wanders out, seemingly without a care in the world. 'What's it worth?' he says.

'Being fed and watered,' I call after him.

I must only have dropped back off to sleep an hour or so ago. I feel like death warmed up. Each and every muscle aches, beneath the surface, bruised and battered. Moments later, Jack barges back through the door, spilling the coffee from the overflowing mug, wiping it away with his foot. 'Oops, think I've overfilled it.'

'Thanks, Jack.' I reach for the mug, and slurp. 'You're definitely my favourite. I can drop you in this morning – I've early clinic – or would you rather go on the bus?'

'Cool. No, I'll come with you. The bus takes forever.' He turns away.

'Are you home on time tonight?' I need to know how much time I have later.

'Yeah, think so. Should be. Why?'

'Just wondered,' I say. 'Quick with the shower, please. I'll jump in after you.'

I flick my mobile into action, scanning down the contact numbers. It's still there. I was paranoid I'd accidentally delete it. I study it. I still can't decide if you slipped up with one of your silent calls. Or, if you intended for me to have it? I called it anonymously, before sending that first text, just to make sure; you didn't answer. But you were studying the screen, searching for a non-existent caller ID, weren't you? You knew it was me.

Do you also know I've decided today will be the day? The end of the end.

Jack will be home on time, I'll return as normal, then, once I know he's safe, go back out, not for long. It won't take long. I release my breath. Do I really know what I'm doing? Do I know who I can trust? Have I considered all the possible outcomes? I flick back through my mobile to the last message from Billy. It arrived late last night.

Sorry so late. Listen. Keep your head down. On the move 2mor night. In touch soon. This number will cease. TU.

I read it a couple of times, to make sense of it. I texted back, asking him to explain; he just answered, TTYS. I looked it up, with no idea of its meaning; he would talk to me soon. It didn't take much to decipher the code, what his intentions were. I can't let him do it. He's suffered enough, his life already cursed from such a young age. He'd be taking my place in my metaphorical cell; we both deserve freedom. I need to act quicker than him.

Forty-five minutes later, Jack and I leave the house, ready for another not so normal, but usual day. Just as we're about to drive off, I notice Gloria pottering in her front gated area.

'One minute, Jack, wait here.' I leap from my seat.

'What? Mum, come on, you're going to make us late. I play footy before registration.'

'Wait there, I'll be one minute.'

I leave him huffing and puffing, to scamper back up the pathway.

'Gloria?' She doesn't hear me, and makes her way to her front porch. 'Hi, Gloria?'

She turns, her wizened face lights up. 'Oh, Eve, love, how are you? I've not had chance to see you for a little while.'

Kind eyes study me; I instantly know she hasn't done anything wrong. How could I have thought otherwise? 'I know, I'm sorry, I've been so busy. We'll catch up soon, promise.' She smiles warmly at me, reaching for my hand. 'I haven't got much time to stop, Gloria, need to get Jack to school, me to clinic, but can I ask you something?'

'Yes, love, of course. Anything. What is it?'

'You may not remember, but the other day you asked me if I'd enjoyed the surprise? Or something to that effect.'

'Yes, love, I did, I remember. I was very excited for you.'

'But you were not referring to the cake you made, were you? It's just, that's what I thought you meant at first.'

'Oh, no, love, no. I was talking about your friend, from overseas. Such a lovely girl, isn't she?' Gloria covers her mouth with her hand. 'Oh, have I just ruined the surprise? I thought you knew, thought you'd found her letter.'

'No, of course not, it's fine. You mean the letter you put in my briefcase?'

'Yes, love. Well, she asked me to keep it secret. She was only here for a little while, wanted to surprise you, could I put the envelope somewhere you'd definitely find it, she said. Then afterwards, I thought, why on earth did I put it in your briefcase?

440

Of all the places, it could get lost in your files, and with them being so private too, I shouldn't have. Then, when you didn't mention it, I thought I better had. Hope I haven't done wrong.'

I squeeze her hand. 'Of course you haven't, it's absolutely fine. But, can I just ask, not that it really matters, but, why didn't you just leave it in the house? I'm only curious.'

'Well, love, that's what I asked her too, why not just put it through the letterbox? But she said she wanted you to get the surprise personally. She was worried Jack might open it first otherwise.'

'I see, now it makes sense,' I say. 'Right, I must be off, hopefully see you over the weekend. Pop by for a cup of tea, won't you?' I say.

'I'll look forward to it, love.' A slight frown appears as I release her hand. 'I'm assuming she didn't catch up with you, then, your friend?' she asks.

'No, not as yet,' I say. 'Not really had the chance.'

'Because, she came back, you know, hoping to catch you in. We had a natter. I did say before, you're rarely here in the daytime, but she was passing by, so tried her luck. Shame.'

'Right,' is all I manage. 'Was she here long?'

'No, love, a few minutes. She seemed as if she was in a hurry. A little on edge. Humphrey liked her though. Made a proper fuss of her.'

The smell on Humphrey. 'Did he, now? She made a fuss of him too, I suppose?'

'Oh, yes, picked him up, loved him,' she says. 'After she'd gone, I let him at yours – meowing, he was, on the window sill.'

'You gave him some food, too?' I ask, everything beginning to make sense.

'I did. Bless him. Then I was worried he'd be trapped in the house. It was a lovely day, so I opened that small window in the utility, thought he might find his own way out if he needed to.'

*

Thirty minutes later, weighty feet carry me up Lemon Street; headstrong gusts push against me as autumn leaves loop my shoes. I still can't believe I've misjudged Sam so badly. How did it escape me, all those years ago, she was my chief bridesmaid, at the same time as having a torrid affair with the groom? I thought I knew her. Who else did I underestimate along the way? I climb the few steps, shoving at the door into clinic. I should have stayed off work today, but I have to keep my routine as normal as possible. Ruan raises his hand to me, engrossed in a telephone conversation. I continue through to my room. Minutes later, he delivers me hot coffee, still glued to the handset. Life does go on, it seems, even if you don't feel part of it.

My day is chock-a-block. I somehow manage to operate under the clinician's hat. At times, almost forgetting the magnitude of what lies ahead. A long-standing eating disorder, a consequence of early-school-years bullying. A complicated marital breakdown, with child protection issues, and someone who has developed a chronic phobia of seagulls. A telephone conversation with Milly's mum, as we're reducing our appointments, and Milly is doing well. My mind buzzing from copious amounts of caffeine, and trepidation, I write up my notes, then sit back into the depth of my chair. Close my eyes, and attempt to clear my mind. Seconds later, I jump up and pad over to the bookshelf. I pick out my grandfather's book. 'Forgive me,' a voice inside says. 'I've no choice. I have to do it; I know you'll understand.' I glance at the clock; my stomach rolls. It's time to send the text.

A familiar numbness creeps over me. Reaching for my briefcase, I locate my mobile. In my mind, I see you, sauntering somewhere, clutching your mobile, anticipating my next move. Enjoying the moment. A shiver dancing down each vertebra. In the early hours of this morning, I was more okay with this stage; things feel less real, somehow, when everyone sleeps. I can't lose my nerve, not now. Not if I want Jack to be free. Feeling unsteady on my feet, I lower myself back into the chair. Body and mind high on cortisol, mingling with adrenaline.

I stare at the screen of my mobile just as two bodies appear from behind the door: Bea and Ruan. 'We thought you might fancy a drink later?' incongruent smiles ask me.

'Umm, no, I can't. Thanks, but—' Wait, this might just work. 'What time you thinking?'

'Sixish, or whatever suits you, makes no difference to us,' offers Bea.

'I'll be there all night, so any time,' says Ruan. 'Come on, you look like you could do with a drink. No offence or anything.'

'None taken.' I do some speedy calculations. 'Actually, I might take you both up on that. I've something on, straight from here, but I should be there sometime around six. All being well.'

'Bring Jack too, if you're worried about leaving him,' Bea says.

I think about this. 'Thanks, but I think he'll be fine.'

They exchange a knowing glance. 'You sure? It's really not a problem for us,' says Bea.

'No, really. I'm sure, he'll be fine. Thanks, though.' I indicate my mobile. 'I'm just about to call a client.'

I watch them leave, closing the door behind them. I type my instructions and click send. It's the 'first foot off the cliff' moment again, I close my eyes. Seconds later, I'm informed, it's been delivered. Placing my head in my hands, elbows on the desk, I try and remind myself who I am or who I used to be. Before you swaggered into my life, I was carefree, trusting, contented. Do you have any idea how much I've needed to change, to survive? To protect our son. Would I have become the person I am now, if it hadn't been for you? But then, would I have needed to isolate myself, scratch off anyone who was important to me, if it hadn't been for all the misplaced perceptions of others? The lies, so many lies, not to protect you, but to protect my self-worth, Jack. I mean, who remains in a marriage with someone like you? Who becomes the wife of a man like you? The mind thief. I've always wondered myself.

But by the time I wondered it was too late.

You'd already walked me along the fateful path, opened the cell door, showed me in. The figurative room had many one-way windows. I could see out but nobody could be allowed to look in. You gave me the key to this room; you placed it in my naive hands, watched me lock myself in. Made no attempt to take the key from me, did you? Allowed me to believe I could escape any time. Except, this wasn't true, was it?

Lies and deceit bolted the door from the other side.

As time went on, your weakness became my strength. Our son. You viewed him as a threat, didn't you? He changed my perception, my context, built my resolve. Your plan backfired as much as mine did. Because of Jack, tonight, I will force myself to walk back through the creepy corridors of what is our past. The only way me and Jack can truly be free is for us both to revisit, face to face. It's not even about what I do tonight – more what I don't do. I can live with this. Having learned the hard way about perception and context, I wonder if you've remembered – no one knows you are here, other than those who despise you; you have no context. You do not exist. You will not be missed. I will have no guilt.

You've nothing to lose; I have it all to lose. Rumour has it, the greater of the emotions at war will always succeed.

Yours is hate, mine is love.

Chapter Thirty-Seven

Cornwall 2016

I'm taking each twist and turn one at a time, driving home to St Agnes.

I'm wondering, do we always have a say in who we are, who we become? I'd argue a say, but not always authority. I never saw myself as a killer. I was wrong. I clearly would kill if the stakes demand it. I skim the clock. Jack will already be home by now. His homework completed against a stopwatch, snacking on cereal bars, negotiating with his Xbox. I'm taking him to St Ives, to his favourite burger joint on the seafront, after I've shown my face at The Wheal. We need to begin living all over again.

My premeditated plan circling all the time, above me, like a halo. A cold-blooded killer?

I wrap my hands tightly around the steering wheel, to help ease the feeling of detachment. Reflecting on my clinic appointment earlier. Words falling from the trained therapist's mouth. I, and her, now two separate entities. Dissociated, this is what I need to be. She says, 'Your imagination is such a powerful tool. If you visualise something, your brain responds as though it's truly happening. It cannot always differentiate between the imagined and reality. Under extreme stress, we call this psychosis. Under normal states of mind, we call it positive reality generating.' She continues, 'Consider the power of seeing things that frighten us. Even our most irrational fears are then terrifying. Alternatively, your imagination is a free rehearsal platform, for practising and perfecting anticipated experiences. It is particularly effective, if you imagine how exactly you wish for it to happen. Engage all your senses, to the finest of details,' she says.

I pass the last sign for my home village, only ten minutes remaining to visualise the reunion, of me and you.

Pulling up alongside the wall, elbowing through the gate. Through the front door. I feel an increase in my heart rate, a shortness to my breath. I reach for the light switch, observing, Jack's rucksack thrown haphazardly on the sofa. Everything normal. I hear him chatting upstairs, presumably into the microphone on his Xbox headset. A taste of sour bile plugs my throat. I force it away, swallow.

Humphrey is posturing up and down the kitchen window sill.

'Jack?'

I hear him mumble, 'Just a sec.'

'Yep?' he calls down.

'I need to pop back out. Shouldn't be too long, an hour or so. Can you come down, feed Humphrey, please?'

'Yeah, be there in ten.'

I dart out into the garden to gather my tools. It's been raining; the ground is soggy and wet. I inhale the scent as I kneel in the earth and dig. Feeling muddy knees, seeing spoiled trousers, I eventually stand, clutching. Scared.

'Jack?' I call up the stairs again. 'I'm off now, see you in a while. Don't forget Humphrey!'

'Yeah,' trails down the stairs.

I leave to make my way to the beach car park, sliding into a space furthest from the entrance. Wet, cold, and sweating. With ham-fisted fingers, I check my mobile. You've replied; you'll see me at Trevellas Porth. What am I doing? I visually slap my hesitant face. Focus. The meeting point is the perfect place, out of sight, remote, yet accessible. A ten-minute climb along the footpath. Quite a fall, treacherous. The slam of my car door echoes somewhere in the distance as I begin my journey. Pulling my coat tightly around my shivering form, with the rush of anticipation. A determined calmness taking my hand. I feel my feet roaming over rocky terrain as I scramble the last steps to the cliff top.

Then, I stop in my tracks. I see you. Frozen.

Cold robotic eyes survey me, defined lips, mimicking a smile. Years haven't been kind to you; a broken android stands before me. I sense your game. Your eyes acknowledge my fingerprints on the gun I hold in my hand. Your gun, I took with the flash-drive from the house. You knew I had your gun, didn't you? I have anticipated your plan too. All that watching, learning and logging. You suppose, your own suicide would ensure my fate. You're not here for the flash-drive, are you? This is to be your last gift to me: a life sentence. You reason, if you take your own life, I will carry the sentence. Jack will then appreciate his mother in true colours. His father's killer. Genius, Gregg, I take the blame. But you will still be dead. Also, I am wearing gloves; you cannot see this, from where you loiter. See-through clinical gloves. I feel the silky texture between my fingers.

Furthermore, you don't know these waters as I do, do you? You'll be washed away, forgotten. Who knows you are here? Sam, she may well. But she won't tell; she's a prisoner too. It's just me and you. I'm willing to take the chance. Especially as, technically, I'm not truly going to kill you, depending on your perspective. You are going to kill you. Your last act of power.

Arrogance, hate and ego will kill you, not me.

I see you, free-falling from the cliff top. Arms and legs at angles. I stand over, witnessing your final gasps. Neglecting to breathe myself. Until a feeling of peacefulness washes over me.

With quickened, shallow breathing, I arrive home. My knuckles white, from clamping the steering wheel. My jaw aching, from biting down on gritted teeth. I wobble my way to the front door. Odd, the front room is in darkness. Once inside, I reach for the light switch, dropping my briefcase to the floor. Strange, no rucksack? Not like Jack. Trying to ignore the upsurge in my heart rate, I call out – nothing.

This wasn't supposed to happen. I didn't foresee this. 'Jack?' I cry out. I scamper up the stairs as fast as my legs allow, bouncing off the walls. Throwing open the door to Jack's bedroom. Nothing but darkness?

This wasn't supposed to happen.

Jack should be at home.

Chapter Thirty-Eight

One week after my story…

I'm still in Jack's room, alone.

Slowly, I push myself up, peeling back the very duvet I used to try and smother my asphyxiated mind. Still carrying his vulnerable scent. Plumping up his pillow, I gently remake his bed. It wasn't meant to be this way; I intended we'd be free by now. But at the very last minute you stole that too, didn't you? Now, I fear it's all too late; for me it is, anyway. Three years ago, I thought I could finally change things. I was wrong.

There was something crucial I missed.

Someone other than you, and other than me, had already decided your fate. And, with that decision, all of our fates. How did I not see? Because I didn't want to? So focused on how this story was to end, I missed what was happening beneath my nose. But to those who will invariably ask the questions as life stumbles on, the so judiciously rehearsed version of events, in my mind, will always be my truth. Truth will only ever be a perception, in a twinkling of time. You are dead. It happened a week ago.

Jack's mobile still sits on his chest of drawers winking at me, goading me. I think back; Jack never would be parted from his mobile. Now, me and it are alone. Wishing I'd insisted on him showing me, my mind bursting with 'if only's. With the torturous knowledge I could have saved you, Jack, back then. I could have changed this outcome. I hate hindsight, the way it draws on punishing memory boxes. Judging and goading, each breath you take.

You took a bite, didn't you? Couldn't possibly just let go. Now, a lasting part of you eats at my flesh. My heart remains restricted by a clenched fist. Disquiet bounds and suffocates, as if I'm back in that car, peering into the dark obscurity. Except this time, we are on the cliff, for the last few breaths of your sick life. The widest self-satisfied smirk scrawled across your disgusting face, yet still a perfect picture of calm and control. Inwardly flying high. Reality thumping at my consciousness. There was nothing I could do. With the crushing weight of acceptance, I realised.

Someone was going to die.

As the fist tightens on my chest, I snatch up Jack's phone. Why did I push away my concerns? My instincts warned me. I didn't listen. I desperately wish I had. I grasp at the mobile and flick through the deathly texts, already aware of the content, but I need to see with my own eyes. I keep scrolling until I locate your stored number, saved under the name of

HATE. I brace myself as I prepare to re-enter this last week of Jack's world. If I had the energy, I'd be sick. The screen illuminates, as I read.

Leave us alone. I hate U.

Is that you, Jack?

Kill yourself!

Jack, it's Jack isn't it? I knew you'd make contact. You're different from her. After all, I'm your father. I've lost everything. I need your help. Your mother has lied to you about me. I want to see you.

Jack?

I need to see you. Please.???

Why? I hate U.

I need your help. Your mother has stolen something of mine. If you only do this one thing for me, I will leave again. Promise, I will leave you be.

What is it?

She has my flash-drive. It has all my contacts and files on. I need to rebuild, start afresh. Please Jack. Then, I'll leave. Promise.

??? Please Jack, I am your father.

Answer me Jack. I will not leave you alone, until I have it.

You owe me. Jack?

I will not leave without it!

Answer me, Jack. Come to me, or I'll come to you both???

I'll meet U.

I knew I could count on you! When? Where? Do you know where the flash-drive is?

Yeah. Trevellas Porth. No one will see us.

Good boy. Just let me know when. Then, I will leave you alone, I promise.

Yeah. U will.

I delete the evidence and shut down the mobile, every muscle in my tired body tingling with regret. In trying to protect Jack from you, I left him exposed. What was I thinking? Why didn't I tell the truth in the beginning? Whatever truth is: yours, mine, his, hers, theirs? All pointless. Subjective poppycock. Holding so much power.

I stare emptily out of Jack's closed window as I allow myself to fall back to the night I assumed we would gain closure. One last time before I set it away in a box at the back of my mind. I place myself back to a week ago, in my mind's eye. I had it all planned, was so sure of how I would rid us of you. It all fell apart with the missing rucksack. Why were you not at home, Jack?

I ran back down the stairs, frantically trying to locate my mobile. Jack was missing. As soon as I entered the kitchen, I saw the handwritten note on the table.

Mum

Have gone rock jumping, Trevellas P. Don't worry, I'll be careful, promise! Yep, I have wetsuit, dry towel, drink, food. No signal there, see you when get home.

Jack x

Trevellas Porth? He hadn't mentioned it that morning? Please, God. Putting aside the dangerous conditions of night-time rock jumping. I'd already sent the text to you. Jack, what had you done? What had I done? A revolting thought hurtled through my mind as shivers crept one by one over my soul. I'd sent the text for you to meet me at Trevellas Porth. I'd flung Jack straight into your open arms.

I frantically called Jack's mobile; each time it diverted immediately to voicemail. I tried Billy's mobile and waited for what felt an eternity for it to connect, remembering his text to me, advising me his number would cease working that day. It was probably too late in the day to hope for it to connect. But a transient moment of relief rolled over me at the sound of his voice.

'Eve? You okay?' I heard.

'Billy, where are you? Jack's gone to Trevellas Porth and...' Did I want to tell him this? I had to. Jack was in danger. 'He's there too. Gregg. They're both heading for Trevellas Porth.'

'What the...?'

'Where are you?' I asked.

'The old bomb factory, Perranporth head.' Billy's intentions dawned on me at the sheepish tone of his voice. Nobody went to the bomb factory at that time of the day. Derelict and deserted. 'Gregg's supposed to be here, now. Meeting me. He's late.'

'Jack left me a note, said he's gone rock jumping at Trevellas. Oh, Jesus, Billy, he's on his own with Gregg!'

'Eve, calm yourself a minute. Gregg's supposed to be meeting me here. He thinks I have the flash-drive. Maybe you're jumping to conclusions. Jack's probably with one of his mates. Gregg's coming here, I've made sure – he'd be scared not to…'

'You don't understand. I sent Gregg a text. He was supposed to be meeting me tonight with the flash-drive. At Trevellas, where Jack is. I've got to go; I need to find him.'

'Eve. Wait. I'm on my way. Wait for me. Eve? Wait at yours.'

I didn't wait. I didn't answer. I chucked the phone down, before charging out into the back garden. When we moved in, Jack and I had planted a holly shrub together, to celebrate our new life; new beginnings. A mark of where we'd come from; but most importantly where we'd wanted to be. It had also been a personal marker for me. I hadn't thought that Jack had seen. For underneath the woody shrub, a foot to the left, was a small metal trunk in which I had buried my weapons. The flash-drive and the gun.

I fell to my knees, and began to pull frenziedly at sodden craggy soil. It was only seconds before my worst fears were realized: the trunk had gone. Jack, oh, dear God, Jack! Where were you? What were you doing? What had you done? Slipping and sliding, scrambling back through the back door, as best I could on jellied legs; I grabbed my car keys and mobile. Storming through the house and out through the front door, hurtling down the cobbled path to my car.

I sped down to the seafront car park and leapt out. The winding path was just about visible but was fading away with the natural light. I dashed for it. The sea beneath me lashed rhythmically at the rocks as the tide drew in. My feet, feeling disconnected from my legs, urgent but unsteady as smaller rocks moved under my pressure. Pure dread surged me forward. The shadowy light was against me and I hit a rutted rock, obscured in shingle and plunged forward. Pain daggered my left wrist, shooting up to my elbow as it hit the ground to break my descent. My ankle twisted jammed behind the rock, to the sound of a rubbery crack. I needed to get to Jack. I could just about make out the cliff top. I was nearly there. I pushed myself up to my feet, brushing my bleeding gritted palms on my pale grey trousers.

I pressed on aware yet oblivious of the ascending coastal wind, eerie looming shadows cast by dense shrub high like heathers, following me. My heart pounded through my ears as I forgot to breathe. Still, surging forward, wrapping my pointless cotton jacket around me tightly as it attempted to escape. I was nearly there. I strained my eyes to the top and allowed them to follow the fall of the cliff. Nothing. Just a murky unnerving ocean, scattered with sinister daggered rocks. A total divergence from its exquisite daytime form. My legs burning with numbness as I made what I thought was my final perilous climb.

As I reached the plateau of the top, I mechanically ground to a halt to hold my breath. In front of me, just a few steps to the edge of the cliff top, stood a dark shadow. Jack. Facing away from me. Before him was another obscure shadow; merely a sigh from the edge. Facing down to murky waters. It was Billy. Thank God, it was Billy. I released my breath, allowing my hands to fall to my knees, and bent over. But wait – how did Billy get here so quickly? And what are they both staring at? Why is Billy standing so dangerously close to the edge?

'Jack? Billy?' I desperately called.

At the sound of my voice, the obscure shadow turned away from the ocean. Time slowed down, my breathing fast-tracked, my legs creeping without instruction closer to the shadows. In the muted light of the moon, you smiled. I was no longer in control; my head floated as my legs gave way. My body collided with the ground in slow motion. Struggling for air. Images whizzing through a hollow mind on a loaded carousel.

No! Screamed through my inner voice as I resisted the pressure to vomit. I gazed up, the former shadow of Billy evaporating. You. You stood, confidence powering your smile. Arrogance beaming from your eyes. The years rewound in front of me.

I screamed. 'Leave my son alone, you sick bastard.'

You laughed.

Then, I saw it. What stood between you and Jack, the unmistakable solid silhouette. Held in perfect position. I scrambled. Grappling to stand on two quaking props. Any words jarring in my throat. Panic.

The echo of your laugh passed through me.

As the words, 'Why did you have to be my dad?' hit me.

You laughed, louder than ever.

Jack, my innocent boy, pulled the trigger.

Bang.

'Jack. No!' I bawled. 'No, Jack. Please, no.'

Wasted, hopeless words bounced off the cliff and circled us.

It was too late.

I clambered across unsteady ground to reach and pull my son into my arms as he sobbed. The full weight of his body leaning on me. We gave way to the floor, holding tight. Years of undiluted pain passing between us. We remained immobile for some time, I wasn't sure how long, but enough for the cold to creep over us, until we began to shiver. Over Jack's head, I pondered as the moonlight glimmered on the surface of the water. It was over. But the relief I'd imagined had been replaced with something even more cumbersome. I'd observed my son morph into a killer. Slowly I stood, gently pulling Jack to his feet. I removed the gun still gripped in childlike hands and hurled it, breaking the speckled surface. I stretched up to kiss his tear-damp cheek, with the vision of the small boy trapped in the back of the car, that night. Frozen, and stunned as now. I hadn't been able to free him then and now, I could never free him.

I squeezed his hands. 'I had to do it, Mum. Couldn't take any more. Couldn't go back to how it was.' I wiped a rolling tear from his face. 'Didn't want him to hurt you, again.'

'It's over, Jack,' I soothed.

'I brought him this.' He held the flash-drive up to show me. 'Thought it was what he wanted. Thought he'd leave us alone then. Leave you alone. But it wasn't what he wanted, was it?'

I shook my head. 'No. He wanted us. But not in the normal way; but to ruin our lives. Couldn't abide the fact we'd moved on without him. Built new lives. You're right, he would never have let us go.'

'I didn't mean to do it. Shoot him. I don't think I did. But, when he laughed, I wanted him dead. More than anything, I wanted to kill him.'

I grasped the spark of hatred running through his gentle eyes. 'Jack, listen to me. You're not the bad one, he is. But no one will ever understand this. You must promise me; you will never, ever, tell anyone about this. Not anyone. Your friends. No one. This, like everything else, always has to be our secret. Do you hear me? Our secret. Forever.'

He nodded as a blub was released, a four-year-old child, looking to me for guidance.

'But… what if someone finds him?'

'No one will report him missing. He's been off the radar for so long. People get lost to these seas, are never found again, even when they're looked for. But, one last thing, for me. Call it my living and dying bequest.'

'What?' He sniffed.

'If his body is ever found – it won't be, but if it is – I want you to remember, I shot your father. Not you, Jack. I shot him. I killed him.'

'But…'

'No buts. I mean it, I pulled the trigger. I took the gun from your father's drawer. I buried it in the garden. It was my weapon. I pulled the trigger.' Ultimately, I did. I married you, I brought Jack into your world. I knew one day you would find us, hunt

463

us down. I always understood, someone was going to die.

Together, we stumbled back along the broken path. Battered and bruised; shocked and frightened. As we turned the final twist towards the beach, I could just make out the dark shadow running towards us. Billy. The irony wasn't missed – a life for a life; as I remembered, it was the exact spot where Gregg murdered Billy's friend, Tom, all those years ago. Silently, I prayed. Take the revolting body, please, Tom; hide it well in the obscure depths of the ocean. Take the truth and guard it. Because sometimes the truth is dishonest.

Billy placed a supporting arm to join mine around Jack, looking to me for explanation. I simply shook my head.

Now, I gently place Jack's deadly mobile back on his chest of drawers, peel back the undisturbed duvet protecting his bed, lie down and wrap it around me, inhaling his vulnerable scent, with my cotton-wool-stifled mind. Perhaps it's better this way, numbness, guarding the doors to dark memory templates. If I'm honest, if it weren't for Jack, I could let go now, slide away to a supposedly better place.

He'll be home soon from football, life labouring on as it has to. Miffed that he left his mobile behind. He'll smile his boyish beam, hair pushed back from slightly sweaty hands, and kiss my cheek with the smell of fresh new air. But behind his eyes, I will meet the pain, and in those out-of-context moments when perspective implodes I will, alone, see what you have done to him. Those blameless, innocent blue eyes, his informers to his soul, do not tell the truth.

They never have and, now, never can.

The unheard voice of a child.

Epilogue

Six Months Later...

Ghostly cirrus clouds pale the azure sky as I wander away from the centre of Truro. A steady uphill climb, sandwiched between rows of terraced houses that guide me towards the train station. I've thought long and hard about this reunion. Early-hour awakenings with the warmer summer nights, wondering how I should feel, how I need to feel, how I truly feel. It took many months for me to appreciate... this was necessary for a form of closure. Since then, I've wondered, over and over, what I will say, how I will greet her, how I will feel, face to face, after all these years. We've communicated many times by email, since the day she walked free. A freedom Jack and I will never touch. I had to fight with this, but in the end, I could clearly see this wasn't the fault of anyone but you.

Hopping from foot to foot, I watch as the train from Cheltenham arrives. Every conceivable emotion having already chipped away at my soul. Today, despite the fluttery feeling, I am ready. Six months of blurred emotional rehabilitation. Billy has been an unconditional rock, unselfishly spending time with me, but mostly with Jack. Proper boy time. They've become good friends. I've looked on from a distance, listened to the shared words of wisdom, which eventually led to banter, then laughter. It still hasn't quite obscured the pain behind Jack's eyes. I'm hoping in time this subterranean sadness will fade.

Steely doors sling open. A gaggle of festival-attired youths cackle by, laden with overflowing carrier bags of mostly food and alcohol. I smile to myself, bursting to tell them to hang onto autonomy, exuberance. An immaculate elderly couple tread carefully past, hand in hand, wrapped up for winter despite the rising temperatures; she wears a woven hat. Laughter lines etched around prudent eyes, oozing warmth. A deep sense of mutual understanding seals the small space between them.

On the floor in front of me, I spot a penny. I stoop down to pick it up.

'So, you still believe in all that stuff, then, Eve,' she says.

Gently, I right myself. 'I have to,' I say.

Six months ago, I had so much pent-up hate for this person before me. The betrayal ran like hot lava, as blood, through my veins. We've since travelled over these grounds: how she was sucked into his charms, without the strength to escape. Entangled, further and further by lies. Until she could bear to face me no longer. You threatened to tell me, either way, and by this time her entire life was consumed by you. Her job, her home, and her unborn child – I now know to be Iris. In time, my hate morphed to hurt, then to a level of appreciative understanding. Now, I only see someone who was taken in by you. In the same way each and every one of us was.

'My luck has to change some time. Doesn't it?' My eyes plug with tears, mimicking the ones rolling down her cheeks, as I reach out to pull her into my arms.

She hugs me tight. 'I'm so sorry,' she whispers.

Eventually, I pull back, holding her at arm's length. 'Sam, we agreed, didn't we? No, more "sorry' "s, no more looking back. It's the only way.'

She sniffs loudly, whilst pulling a tissue from her bag, as I discreetly wipe my own tears. 'We did. I just can't believe… I'm here, with you. Together. It's so bloody brilliant.'

I link my arm through hers as we begin to walk. 'Lunch is most definitely on you,' I say. 'You do realise, you still owe me for the Chinese takeaway.'

A couple of hours fly by, as we plunge back to a fraction of who we once were before you. Giggling about all the antics and scenarios we've shared. I talk to her about Billy, who's also now moved on to pastures new. Returning to his old love, sailing, and living on his new boat in Dartmouth harbour. But, mostly, I talk about my Jack. Then I learn about Iris.

I look up from my glass of Merlot towards 39b Lemon Street, and notice Ruan ambling towards it. I nod in his direction. 'Over there,' I say. 'Look. It's Ruan.'

'That's Ruan!' she says. 'Just as you described. Couldn't look more like a surfer, could he?'

'He'll be opening up for me,' I say, still watching him.

'But I thought you said you'd closed the clinic down, couldn't cope with it?'

'I did, I couldn't. But it's been six months, Sam. Time to move on, don't you think?'

She takes my hand, squeezing tightly. 'This is the most wonderful news!'

A couple of weeks ago, I opened my eyes. Sharp sun rays piercing the windows. The cotton wool a little more transparent. Jack exhausting his vocals to some latest song. I wouldn't allow you to do this. To take any more of me, us, than you already had. I hotfooted myself to the beach to find Ruan. To ask for his help, to re-establish my business, our life. He was thrilled. The next day, Ruan, Jack and I arrived at 39b Lemon Street. We scrubbed off the old, splashed on the new. Only stopping for sustenance and sleep.

It occurred to me from somewhere, in the early hours of that morning.

You may always be there, skulking in the depths, amongst the swirling lies. But ultimately, it came down to a truth to finally unlock my door…

…evil can live on, even when it's dead, but only if I allow it to.

We hope you enjoyed this book.

Sarah Simpson's next book is coming in 2019

More addictive fiction from Aria:

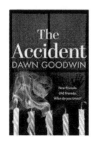  

Find out more
http://headofzeus.com/books/isbn/978178669963
3

Find out more
http://headofzeus.com/books/isbn/978178669965
7

Find out more
http://headofzeus.com/books/isbn/978178669901
5

Acknowledgments

Writing the book was almost the easy stage, what came next was probably the most daunting of all. Hoping for hope and wondering how on earth I was to go about seeing my work published. I was completely and utterly, walking in the dark, my hands tied behind my back and with no idea of the environment I was treading. Until I was united with the best literary agent I could ever wish for. Who is my rock in the world of books and story-telling. With her natural empathic, wise and supportive words and precious guidance. Broo Doherty, I can never thank you enough for taking the leap of faith to believe in me. I really wouldn't be here today without you. I am so very thankful to know you are by my side on this journey. I have complete trust in you. And, thank you to all the lovely people at DHH Literary Agency, I owe you all so much. What an all-embracing and dedicated team you make.

For my wonderfully, talented editor, Lucy Gilmour. I am eternally indebted for your reassuring enthusiasm and belief in my story. For helping me to take my story to another level but most of all for helping me to believe in my work. To the lovely, Melanie Price who has been on the receipt of so many questions and queries and for all her jovial, generous responses. And for all the wonderful team and authors at Aria Fiction for including me in your family – thank you. Also, a special thank you for the brilliance of the fine-combing copy and proof editors for the clever polishing and incredible attention to detail, Sue Smith, David Boxell and Sue Lamprell.

To all the authors out there, until now I never did appreciate just how dedicated you have needed to be and continue to be. I salute you all. Your commitment to see something you love through, in early, late and extended hours, often juggling other obligations, with no promises of anything at the end. The whole community of writers has gifted me a wealth of understandings and invaluable support. I have nothing but admiration for those who embark on and ride the waves of the writing passage. My special thanks to Sam Carrington for her frequent, support and encouragement.

Thank you to the devoted handful of friends and family who have read my work, sometimes over and over in its earlier stages of development. For all of your thoughtful and cheering words and for never allowing me to give up. Katie, Anth, Mom, Sam, Sheila, thank you.

About Sarah Simpson

Sarah Simpson has a first-class honours degree in Psychology and has worked in a neuro-psychology department at a Brain Rehabilitation Hospital. When she first graduated she formed a mental health consultancy and worked as a psychologist within the family court system of Warwickshire and Oxfordshire. Three years ago she moved to Cornwall with her husband and three children, and runs her own practice at the Duchy Hospital in Truro.

Find me on Twitter
https://twitter.com/sarahrsimpson

Become an Aria Addict

Aria is the new digital-first fiction imprint from
Head of Zeus.

It's Aria's ambition to discover and publish
tomorrow's superstars, targeting fiction addicts and
readers keen to discover new and exciting authors.

Aria will publish a variety of genres under the
commercial fiction umbrella such as women's
fiction, crime, thrillers, historical fiction, saga and
erotica.

So, whether you're a budding writer looking for a
publisher or an avid reader looking for something to
escape with – Aria will have something for you.

Get in touch: aria@headofzeus.com

Become an Aria Addict
http://ariafiction.com/newsletter/subscribe
Find us on Twitter
https://twitter.com/Aria_Fiction
Find us on Facebook
http://www.facebook.com/ariafiction
Find us on BookGrail

http://www.bookgrail.com/store/aria/

Addictive Fiction

First published in the United Kingdom in 2018 by
Aria, an imprint of Head of Zeus Ltd

Copyright © Sarah Simpson, 2018

The moral right of Sarah Simpson to be identified as
the author of this work has been asserted in
accordance with the Copyright, Designs and Patents
Act of 1988.

9 7 5 3 1 2 4 6 8

A CIP catalogue record for this book is available
from the British Library.

ISBN (E) 9781788544825

Aria
c/o Head of Zeus
First Floor East
5–8 Hardwick Street
London EC1R 4RG

www.ariafiction.com

27465211R00273

Printed in Poland
by Amazon Fulfillment
Poland Sp. z o.o., Wrocław